> "Wit, passion, and adventure,
> Elizabeth Boyle has it all."
>
> **Julia Quinn**

Oh, how I wish . . .

When a promised inheritance turns out to be a fraud, shy spinster Charlotte Wilmont makes an impetuous wish that despite her lack of charm and fortune, she could capture the heart of the one man whom she's forever adored—Sebastian, Viscount Trent.

Be careful what you wish for . . .

With that utterance, Charlotte awakens shocked to find herself entwined with her beloved Sebastian. But the respectable man she knew is now a most rakish devil and she is . . . well, by some inexplicable magic, London's most infamous mistress.

Even passion comes at a price . . .

Being the scandalous Lottie Townsend affords Charlotte unimaginable freedom—passionate nights with Sebastian, endless days of shopping, and adoring fans. But all too soon, Charlotte finds that being one man's mistress isn't the same as being his wife. Yet if she returns to her old, respectable life, can Charlotte trust there will be enough magic left to recapture Sebastian's heart . . . *and reawaken his rakish desires?*

Avon Romantic Treasures by
Elizabeth Boyle

ELIZABETH BOYLE

HIS MISTRESS BY MORNING

An Avon Romantic Treasure

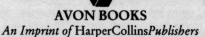

AVON BOOKS
An Imprint of HarperCollinsPublishers

This is a work of fiction. Names, characters, places, and incidents are products of the author's imagination or are used fictitiously and are not to be construed as real. Any resemblance to actual events, locales, organizations, or persons, living or dead, is entirely coincidental.

AVON BOOKS
An Imprint of HarperCollins*Publishers*
10 East 53rd Street
New York, New York 10022-5299

Copyright © 2006 by Elizabeth Boyle
ISBN-13: 978-0-06-078402-7
ISBN-10: 0-06-078402-4
www.avonromance.com

First Avon Books paperback printing: September 2006

Avon Trademark Reg. U.S. Pat. Off. and in Other Countries, Marca Registrada, Hecho en U.S.A.
HarperCollins® is a registered trademark of HarperCollins Publishers Inc.

Printed in the U.S.A.

10 9 8 7 6 5 4 3 2 1

To Nicholas,
for his boundless imagination
and unending curiosity.
And for saying one night,
"Mommy, what would you wish for
if you had a magic ring?"
and thereby inspiring this book.
To you, Peanut,
this story is lovingly dedicated.

Thomas Marlowe, Earl of Walbro
(b. 1760)

The Honorable
Griffin Marlowe
(b. 1781)

Lady C
Marl
(b. 17

Sebastian Marlowe,
Viscount Trent
(b. 1779)

His Mistress by Morning

featuring
Miss Charlotte Wilmont
(b. 1784)

(m. 1779) Lady Clarice Pembly
(b. 1761)

|elia
ve

Lady Hermione
Marlowe
(b. 1787)

Lady Viola
Marlowe
(b. 1799)

Elizabeth Boyle's

Marlowe
Family Tree

For more book information,
please visit www.elizabethboyle.com

Chapter 1

London
May 9, 1810
An Ordinary Wednesday, or at Least One Presumes So

If one were going to define what gave a family that air of prestige amongst their peers, set them apart in the bustling *ton,* first and foremost you would list those admirable qualities of respectability, social standing, and, most importantly, wealth.

Of course none of those things described the Earl of Walbrook or any of his five children—with the possible exception of the earl's eldest son and heir, Sebastian Marlowe, Viscount Trent.

But we'll get to him in a moment.

Luckily for the Marlowes, they rarely noticed their pariah status in Society. Snippy mentions in gossip columns were of no interest to them. And if they had a host of detractors, they had one very enthusiastic admirer.

Miss Charlotte Wilmont. She thought them the most glorious family in London.

Why, their cluttered house on Berkeley Square, which housed the odd objects that the earl sent home from his travels, the leftover stage sets and costumes from the countess's numerous private theatrical productions, Griffin's scientific experiments, Cordelia's Roman treasures, and Hermione and Viola's collections of neatly clipped fashion plates from *The Ladies Fashionable Cabinet,* was more odd museum than house, but it felt like home to Charlotte.

Even now, standing in the middle of the foyer, awaiting her best friend, Lady Hermione, and dreading the terrible news she had to tell her, Charlotte couldn't help but feel a sense that she, plain and ordinary Miss Wilmont, belonged *here.*

She could just imagine what her mother, Lady Wilmont, or Cousin Finella, with whom they lived, would say about that. Especially when faced with the ornately carved chest that stood front and center in the entryway, decorated as it was with a rather large male fertility statue standing tall and erect atop it.

The ebony phallus would have been banished to the dustbin at Cousin Finella's. Feeling a little bit guilty for even casting a curious glance in its direction, Charlotte forced her gaze over to the silver salver beside it, piled up as it was with mail and notes and calling cards for the family.

Envy tugged at her heart over the sight of such a friendly pile—for no one invited her to soirées and parties, called upon her cantankerous mother (for good reason), or sent lovingly penned letters expressing whatever it was one put into such tidings.

Surely Charlotte didn't know. No one had ever sent her a letter.

And atop it all sat the most coveted missive of all—an invitation to Lady Routledge's soirée.

Though Hermione had spent the last month expressing dread over having to attend the upcoming event, Charlotte knew her dear friend would have been positively distraught not to be invited. For Lady Routledge's annual evening had launched any number of young ladies from veritable obscurity onto that very coveted pedestal, the most sought after title a girl could attain: that of *Original*.

But to do that took a lady of some talent—able to sing, perhaps a dab hand on a pianoforte, or possess the composure to give a stirring and dramatic reading. Not that such a lack of proficiency didn't stop any number of hopefuls from getting up (or more to the point, being prodded up by their anxious mothers) and giving a rather, *ahem*, memorable performance.

Having had only lessons from Cousin Finella on the pianoforte, and neither an elocution or singing lesson, Charlotte would rather die than get up before the assembled ladies and lords, gossips and dandies, and make a cake of herself. So perhaps it was a good thing that society had forgotten Sir Nestor Wilmont's spinster daughter.

She was about to turn away from the overladen salver when a note peeking out from beneath the stack caught her attention, a tiding written in a neat feminine hand and addressed to *The Right Hon. the Viscount Trent*.

Sebastian, Charlotte sighed. Hermione's older brother and the heir to the Walbrook earldom.

Even as Charlotte rose up on her tiptoes and tried to spy some sort of indication who this missive was from (not that she couldn't make a very educated guess), the door from the back of the house swung open.

She straightened immediately, and to her horror, none other than Lord Trent himself strolled into the foyer. He was lost in thought and didn't even notice her as she shrank into the nearby curtains.

With *his* arrival, Charlotte went into a deep blush and that tongue-tied inability to sputter out any word that could be deemed intelligible.

Oh, bother, Charlotte, she chided herself, *say something, anything.*

What was it Hermione always said?

Truly, Charlotte, if you would but talk to him you would discover he is as dull as they come. Mother swears her real son was snatched away at birth and Sebastian left in his stead, for no child of hers could possess such a sensible nature!

A sensible nature? How could Hermione pronounce such a virtue as if it were a sin? Charlotte wondered as she peered out from the shadows of the curtains.

Certainly Sebastian's sensibility was one of his most endearing characteristics in her estimation. He'd taken over the family accounts and properties at an early age— just after his father had departed for his South Seas adventures ten years earlier. While the viscount's peers and friends had spent the last decade gadding about, Sebastian had kept the Marlowes afloat with careful management and a tight purse over his mother's and sisters' propensity for shopping.

Why, just look at what had happened to Charlotte and her mother when her own father had died! There had been no one to manage things, and as a result they lived with Cousin Finella.

And when Hermione exceeded her pin money, or one

of Griffin's scientific experiments went awry and left half of Mayfair shaken from yet another explosion, or Viola brought home yet another stray dog, did Sebastian ever complain? Did he harangue them with lectures? Did his ire overflow into a great rage? Never. What Charlotte observed was a man who loved his family, patiently listening to their various complaints and observations and kept their scandal-prone and eccentric antics from leaving them completely beyond the pale of the *ton*.

Say something, she told herself again. Why was it in the quiet of the night, in her narrow little bed, she could think of a thousand witty things to say to him, but when she stood before him, opportunity as golden as a shiny new guinea, those fine words scattered like ha'pennies tossed to the crowds?

Of course in the shadows of the night, her perfect Sebastian was a bit more rakish, with a pirate's queue and a wicked gleam in his eye. And she was . . . well, she was dressed in blue velvet.

"Oh, Sebastian, you found me," she'd whisper. *"I've been waiting for you."*

(Perhaps that might not sound perfectly witty to anyone else, but to Charlotte just the notion of being able to put a sentence together in the presence of her pirate viscount sent her heart racing.)

Then he'd take her hand and draw it to his lips. "Charlotte, my dearest, loveliest Charlotte, will you, dare I? . . ."

She'd never considered what might happen next, but it certainly wasn't dull or prudent.

And right now, with him just a step away, her imagination raced and she was quickly turning into a quivering bundle of nerves.

Never mind that all he was doing was standing before the salver, sorting through the notes, tossing aside those for his mother and giving scant regard to the cards and other missives directed to him.

It was a good thing he hadn't noticed her, for it was all Charlotte could do to breathe as she looked at him, standing there in all his dashing glory. Dressed to the nines, he wore a dark green jacket, buff trousers, and shining black boots. His cravat, of the whitest white and perfectly tied, marked him as a flawless gentleman.

But in that same second, a cold dash of reason hit her as she realized where he must be going—for how could she have not noticed the bouquet of orange blossoms he'd deposited beside the salver?

That could mean only one thing: He was on his way to visit Miss Lavinia Burke.

Charlotte cringed. Lavinia Burke. It could only be pronounced with the same disdainful tone and inflection with which one said "bubonic plague" or "Napoleon Bonaparte."

Not that the rest of London found her so. Miss Burke was this Season's perfect debutante, and every mention of her (at least to Charlotte) held a particular sting.

For the girl was everything Charlotte was not.

Rich. Fashionable. Witty. Youthful. And most loathsome of all, extremely pretty.

Since being proclaimed an Original by no less than three reliable sources (the *Morning Post,* Lady Routledge, and, of course, the impeccable and fastidious Brummell), the popular heiress was now the most sought after young lady in London.

Charlotte couldn't think of Miss Burke without some highly uncharitable notion springing to mind, but today, of all days, she saw not only the gaping chasm between herself and the other girl, but the impossibility of her own most closely held dream.

"Oh, gracious heavens, Charlotte," Lady Hermione Marlowe called out as she flew down the stairs, "I thought you would never arrive! Is it a huge fortune? A tremendous one? For if it is, I saw the most perfect gown yesterday at Madame Claudius's shop that you must buy at once. She made it up for another woman, but now the lady has disappeared and I do think it will fit you perfectly. But first we must go to the park, for it is nearly three, and you know who will be riding by and I have a new pose that I am sure will catch his attention." She struck it at once and it was vastly ridiculous, but Charlotte was still struggling to find the words to speak to Sebastian, let alone answer Hermione. Not that her friend noticed, for she continued on in her own distracted way. "Why, I daresay between your new dress and my fine stance we will make that odious Miss B—" At that moment, Hermione noticed her brother and faltered to a stop.

Sebastian gaped at her as if she had gone mad. "Whoever are you talking to, Hermione?"

"Charlotte," she said, pointing just beside the cabinet.

Sebastian turned around, his eyes widening with surprise at the sight of her so close by. "Miss Wilson, I didn't see you there."

Oh, the humiliation of it. He hadn't been able to discern her from the draperies *and* he couldn't even get her name correct.

Charlotte stepped forward out of the shadows, a little bit too hastily and not quite as gracefully as a lady might hope for, and she bumped into the chest.

The earl's prized phallus teetered and tipped, then

toppled over. Charlotte caught it just in time, relieved that she hadn't broken the smooth and solid statue, but in the next moment realizing that now she stood before Lord Trent holding a huge male . . . male . . . oh, bother, piece of anatomy.

The heat of a searing blush rose to her cheeks. "I, um, yes, well, um," she stammered.

Hermione, nearly always poised and confident, came to her rescue, descending the stairs in record time and scooping the statue out of her hands and setting it firmly back up on the chest as if it were merely a proper Wedgwood vase.

"Sebastian, you are the most trying brother alive," she was saying. "Her name is Wilmont. Not Wilson. Not Wilton, but Miss Charlotte Wilmont. My dear friend for these past five years, and the fact that you cannot remember her name marks you as the worst sort of ninny who ever lived."

"My apologies, *Miss Wilmont*," Sebastian said, bowing ever-so-slightly toward her.

Charlotte nodded, not trusting her tongue to do anything more than flap insipidly.

Hermione wasn't done. "You should be more considerate of Charlotte. She has just come into a great fortune and will, in no time, be the toast of the town."

Charlotte's gaze wrenched from Sebastian to her friend, her head shaking furiously. "Oh, no, it isn't like that."

"Silly girl!" Hermione wound her hand around Charlotte's arm and tugged her up to Sebastian with a great flourish of her other hand, as if she were presenting royalty to him. "Miss Wilmont's great-aunt died and left her an immense—"

"Hermione!" Charlotte protested. "Don't!" Oh, this was turning into a terrible nightmare. First the phallus, and now this!

The girl's hand fluttered again, waving aside the objection, as if it were nothing more than unnecessary modesty. "Charlotte, it isn't like everyone isn't going to know when you turn up in society in the finest gowns, at all the best parties. Being exceedingly wealthy won't turn you into a vulgar little chit, like some people we know." Hermione tipped her nose and shot an accusing glance at the bouquet. "You aren't going to call on *her* again, are you?"

Sebastian's brow arched. "And whatever business is it of yours?"

Hermione groaned. "It is every bit my business. Miss Burke is a terrible snob and I can't believe you would even contemplate pursuing her. If I thought for a moment you loved her, that might be a consideration, but I don't think even you could be that dull."

The viscount tossed the letters back atop the salver and retrieved his orange blossoms. "I am not going to have this conversation with you."

His tone spoke of finality, one that would not brook any further interference, but Charlotte knew better than to think that Hermione would respect her brother's authority. The Marlowes were infamously informal, and that Hermione would ignore her brother's position as de facto head of the household was no surprise.

Luckily, Fenwick, the family's butler, made a timely arrival with Sebastian's hat, gloves, and coat, saving the brother and sister from a complete row. Sebastian handed the sprays of orange blossoms to Hermione as he shrugged on his coat and pulled on his gloves.

The sweet and spicy scent of oranges curled around Charlotte's senses, and her earlier feelings of envy returned, as if carried on a zephyr.

Flowers. And callers. And balls.

How she had dreamed of those things in the past few weeks, ever since she and her mother had received the letter from the solicitor announcing Great-aunt Ursula's death and Charlotte's inclusion in her will.

Sebastian reached for his bouquet, and Hermione held the blossoms back. "I think you are making a terrible mistake," she told him, her nose wrinkled, as if the sweet flowers held all the appeal of a pile of horse droppings.

"Then it is mine to make," he replied, taking his flowers and frowning at her interference.

"Whyever would you want that prosy Miss Burke when there are plenty of other ladies who would make a better choice?" At this, she nudged Charlotte forward. Again. Oh, there was nothing subtle about Hermione. "Miss Wilmont's fortune will make Miss Burke's ten thousand a year look paltry."

The heat in Charlotte's cheeks was nothing compared to the black pit knotted in her stomach.

"Hermione, please," she whispered. "Don't do this."

The girl was not going to listen, not when she had a chance to cast anything up at her sensible and dull elder brother. "I declare by tomorrow Charlotte will be the most sought after young lady in London, especially now that she's inherited—"

"A ring," Charlotte sputtered. "All I received was a ring."

That brought Hermione's crowing to an abrupt end. "But your mother said you stood to inherit . . ."

Charlotte shook her head, the sting of tears bringing an even greater threat of humiliation.

First the disastrous news from the solicitor that Aunt Ursula's storied fortune was nothing but a fiction, then her mother's rage at being so deceived, so cheated, and now having to face it all yet again and in front of Sebastian, no less.

"But all our plans," Hermione whispered, shooting a glance at her brother, then back at her friend. For a moment she wavered, but this was Hermione Marlowe, and she was always a veritable fountain of hope. "Is it a big ring? A large diamond perhaps, or a ruby or emerald? Just enough to buy the gown at Madame Claudius's?"

Charlotte tugged reluctantly at her glove until it came off. She turned her face away as she held out her hand.

"'Tis lovely," Hermione said, trying to sound cheerful as she inspected the odd little ring. She glanced up. "Are you sure there wasn't more to your aunt's bequest? Some property perhaps? An annuity the solicitor overlooked? Annuities are often overlooked, I've heard."

Charlotte shook her head. "Nothing. Nothing but this ring."

Her friend's eyes grew moist with tears, the spring running over. "Oh, Charlotte, this is a tragedy. A horrible, wretched tragedy." As a Marlowe, Hermione resorted to dramatics, pulling out her handkerchief and sobbing as if the lost fortune had been destined for her pockets.

Charlotte gulped, holding back her own tears. She'd done admirably well at the solicitor's office, but now in front of Hermione, and in front of those wretched orange blossoms, it was terribly hard not to give over to a well-deserved spate of tears.

"Yes, well, if you will forgive me," Sebastian said at all this overwhelming feminine display of emotion. He nodded to Charlotte, and then said to Fenwick, who until now had been standing near the stairs, ever at the ready to serve, "Tell my mother I will be dining with the Burkes, so do not expect me home."

"You're dining with them?" Hermione sputtered, this alarming news shocking her out of her distress over Charlotte's loss. "Whatever for?"

"Because I was invited," he told her. "And I like the company."

Hermione made a sputtering noise, then collected herself enough to follow him. "Am I to suppose you are also going to their Venetian breakfast tomorrow as well?"

"Of course," Sebastian told her. "You and Mother had better be there, and on time." With that, he turned and opened the door.

"There you are!" said the woman standing on the front steps, her hand upraised as if she had been about to pull the bell.

Charlotte cringed. *Cousin Finella.*

Because of their impoverished state, Charlotte and her mother, Lady Wilmont, lived with her mother's cousin, Finella Uppington-Higgins. Finella had inherited the house years ago, and combined with the small amount Lady Wilmont received as Sir Nestor's widow, it was just enough for three frugal women to scratch by on.

"When I couldn't find you in the park, I suspected you might come *here.*" Finella sniffed and took a discerning and critical glance around the Marlowe foyer. When her gaze fell on the fertility statue near the salver, what little color she did possess drained from her pale features, and she looked instantly away. A stickler for propriety, she thrust out her hand and said in a tight voice, "Come along, Charlotte. Your mother needs you at home. Now."

Oh, Charlotte knew what that meant. Her mother was in high dudgeons and wanted an audience for her laments and agonies over Aunt Ursula's broken promises.

Hermione leaned close and whispered softly, "I understand. Come back as soon as you can. We'll find a way for you to have your heart's desire."

At this, Charlotte's gaze flew not to her friend but over to Sebastian.

Her heart's desire. Holding orange blossoms for another woman. A woman, if gossip was correct, he would most likely marry.

Charlotte wondered what Cousin Finella—or, worse, her mother—would say if she let loose with her own loud and strident lament.

Probably have the same shocked reaction as the one Finella was exhibiting, for the lady's gaze remained locked on Lord Walbrook's prize cock sitting atop the chest of drawers.

A museum piece, he had written when he had sent it home from a South Seas island. As such, Lady Walbrook had dutifully and proudly displayed it without batting a lash at the impropriety of such a treasure.

From the narrow glint in Finella's eyes, Charlotte had no doubt of her cousin's opinion as to the earl's treasure, and just exactly where it belonged.

"Charlotte, now!" the lady managed to choke out.

After shooting an apologetic glance at her friend, Charlotte allowed herself to be led down the steps.

"Good afternoon, Miss Wilmont," Sebastian said as he strode past them, sidestepping an elderly street vendor tottering down the street with a basket clutched in her wrinkled hands.

"Flowers, milord?" she asked him. "For the young lady?"

"Um, no thank you, madam," he said, holding up his own offering. "These should be quite adequate."

"If you think so," she said saucily, pushing her way past Finella and Charlotte and muttering under her breath. "Orange blossoms, bah!"

"Farewell, Lord Trent," Charlotte whispered after him, feeling as if this was the last time she would ever see him. That wasn't true; she'd probably see him again tomorrow, for she was forever coming over to see Hermione, but from now on she would have no more hope, no more dreams, no more wishes left when it came to Sebastian Marlowe, Viscount Trent.

"Good riddance," Cousin Finella muttered. "What you see in that family I will never understand."

Charlotte didn't bother to reply. There was no use arguing with Cousin Finella—the lady had a very hard and narrow line of what was proper and what was correct, and any deviation, even the slightest hint of impropriety, was enough to propel even the loftiest of families from Cousin Finella's good graces.

Not that anyone in the *ton* gave a whit as to what Finella Uppington-Higgins thought of them, but Finella continued to believe that she was the lone voice of decorum in London, and she went about her duties with the diligence of a Tower guard.

By this time in the afternoon, Berkeley Square was filled with carriages—happy couples, dashing rakes, and carefree Corinthians making their way to the park for the afternoon promenade.

When an opening in traffic appeared, Finella was about to tug Charlotte across the street, that is until a devilishly fast curricle came racing through the throng.

Finella hauled Charlotte back, and when she spied the driver, she said, "Avert your eyes, child. It's that *Fornett* woman."

Charlotte did as she was bid, only because it afforded her another glance at Sebastian, who was nearly to the corner.

Some of the drivers shouted at Mrs. Fornett, decrying her madcap pace, but there were also whistles and cat-calls from the more dashing men nearby.

For Mrs. Corinna Fornett was one of London's most notorious courtesans, and her arrival, whether on the streets in her smart carriage and its infamous matched set of blacks or at her private box at the Opera House, always caused a stir.

And so it seemed, she also stirred Lord Trent. Charlotte watched in shock as the very proper and straitlaced viscount, the only Marlowe who never gave Society a moment of gossip, actually tipped his hat at this scandalous woman.

Admonition or no, Charlotte turned and looked back at Mrs. Fornett, if only to see what it was that had caught the viscount's attention with such an uncharacteristic display.

The lady wore a red dress—a gown one certainly didn't expect to see on the afternoon parade, but there she was like a vibrant peony set amongst a field of forget-me-nots. Atop her head sat a smart hat with jaunty plumes and a wide black ribbon that fluttered down her back.

While it would be easy to say that any woman who dressed in such an outlandish fashion in the middle of the afternoon would stop traffic, Charlotte spied right there and then why it was that Corinna Fornett held London's men in her thrall.

She sat in the driver's perch with her nose tipped up and her eyes alight at the mischief she was causing. The reins sat in her hands with an easy grace, belying the fact that her horses looked ready to bolt at the slightest provocation.

It wasn't that Mrs. Fornett was a beautiful woman, for in truth she wasn't that unlike Charlotte in coloring, with her brown hair and fair brow; rather it was the confidence with which she carried herself that set her apart from every other female on the street.

With the traffic parting before her, like Cleopatra making her entrance into Rome, Mrs. Fornett took her due as if it was her birthright, no matter that popular gossip held that she was the bastard daughter of a smuggler and a serving wench. Cousin Finella's opinion or the petty gossip of matrons held no sway over the lady. She wasn't cowed by propriety—rather quite the opposite. She let her notoriety and very improper reputation spread out before her like a wave.

Charlotte raised herself up a little bit straighter and took one last peek at Sebastian before he turned the corner.

He too was taking another appreciative look at Mrs. Fornett, until he glanced down at the flowers in his hand. The slight smile on his lips faded, and he turned to continue on toward Miss Burke's.

If only, Charlotte thought . . . If only, she wished . . .

I could be the woman he loved.

For a moment, all the hubbub and clatter of the street faded away, leaving Charlotte in a swirling void. The ring on her finger grew oddly warm, and a wave of dizziness swept over her.

She swayed and teetered on the uneven cobbles. *Dear heavens, whatever is wrong?* For the first time in her life, she thought she was going to faint.

"There now," Finella said with a bit of uncharacteristic concern in her voice. She took Charlotte's arm and steadied her. "You've had a trying day as well, I imagine. Poor child. Come home, and once your mother is done with her wailing, we'll make the best of all this. There is nothing else that can be done."

The finality of her words snapped Charlotte out of her odd reverie. And then just as quickly as the odd sensations had overcome her, they were gone and once again, London came alive around her, and there was nothing left to do but fall in step beside Finella and hurry home.

To her dull life, and to a future with no hope of love.

Meanwhile, the old woman selling flowers paused. "I wouldn't be so sure of that," she whispered after Charlotte. "I wouldn't be so sure."

Chapter 2

May 10, 1810
A Thursday of Some Note

When Charlotte awoke the next morning, she could feel the warmth of the sun on her face, but she kept her eyes closed, if only to avoid facing the day for a few moments more.

Her mother had spent the entire evening decrying Aunt Ursula's cruelty, lamenting how the ancient lady had led them on for years about Charlotte's supposedly priceless inheritance, and then leaving her just a small, worthless ring.

Lady Wilmont had even gone so far as to demand the object of her distress from her daughter, with every intention of consigning the mocking bit of gold to the fire. But oddly enough, Charlotte had been unable to pull it from her finger. The little ring, despite a good bit of soap and lard, had remained on her hand as if only to vex Lady Wilmont further. So Charlotte, at Cousin Finella's quiet urging, had sought out her bed and taken refuge in a night of dreamless sleep.

She stretched a little, wishing she could spend the entire day in the drowsy warmth of her bed, that is until she stretched a little further under the covers and her toes bumped into something warm and solid.

And alive, for it moved and stretched right along beside her.

"O-o-o-oh!" she gasped, her eyes springing open.

Then, just as suddenly, her shock over finding something, or rather, someone, in her bed gave way to a newfound horror—she wasn't in her own bed.

And this certainly wasn't her room.

She blinked and gaped at her opulent surroundings, perhaps more stunned by the unfettered wealth around her—red brocade curtains, gold fringed swags, red and white chinoiserie paper on the walls—than by the fact that there was someone sharing her bed.

Her bewildered gaze fell on an enormous, gilt-framed painting of a naked woman who looked vaguely familiar. Why, if she didn't know better, it was a portrait of—

"Lottie?" murmured a deep, sleepy voice beside her. "Lottie, my love, where are you?" A thick masculine arm wound around her waist and tugged her under the coverlet and into his warm embrace.

Suddenly she was surrounded by the scent of bay rum and an air of something else, a deeply masculine essence that tugged at her senses, enticed her to inhale deeply, and beckoned her closer.

"Mmmm, there you are," he said as he nuzzled at her neck, while one of his hands found her breast, his fingertips brushing over her nipple.

"Good heavens!" she cried, struggling to escape his

grasp, to wiggle free of this wretched tangle even as he pulled her further under the covers and rolled atop her, covering her with his, dare she say it, *naked* body.

And he wasn't the only one who had no clothes on. Her nightrail was missing. Which meant . . .

The heat of a devastating blush rose from her bare toes to the rosy tips of her . . . Charlotte shuddered, panic setting in as this blackguard continued to stroke her with no regard for propriety.

At least she could be thankful for the coverlet over them, so she couldn't see this shameless man. And she did her best to ignore a tiny errant and very suggestive thought that "just one peep" wouldn't hurt.

No! she chastened herself, clinging to every lesson in self-control she'd ever learned from Cousin Finella. What she needed to do was muster enough courage to cry out, set up an alarm, but even as she drew in the necessary breath, his lips captured hers in a kiss.

Not a kiss like she'd imagined—soft and gentle, full of loving tenderness and honorable intentions—but one that claimed her as if it was his right, his due.

Hungry and avid, seeking and taking.

So much so that when his tongue swept over her lips, teased her and taunted her to open up to him, a delicious thrill ran down her spine.

Like a memory of something she had no right to claim, and every bit as dark and dangerous and persistent as Mother and Cousin Finella had once whispered about—but without all the rest of their dire admonitions about "painful" and "dreadful" and "turgid deviltry."

No, her body reveled in a hazy warmth that made her languid and restless all at once.

Oh, heavens, what was wrong with her? She needed

to escape this man immediately. Balling up her fists, she pummeled at his wide shoulders, tried twisting out from beneath him, but her efforts only garnered rough laughter.

"Lottie," he growled into her ear, in a voice both familiar and sensual, "are you in one of *those* moods this morning? Hmmm. Whatever the lady wants."

Lottie? Why did he keep calling her that? And whatever did he mean by "one of those moods"?

She all too quickly found out.

Suddenly her arms were trapped over her head and his hips pinned her to the mattress. Then his mouth crashed over hers and he kissed her again. This time with a savage hunger that frightened her.

"There you are, my little wildcat," he said between kisses. "I know how to tame you. Wait and see that I don't."

She wasn't about to wait and see anything this ruffian had in mind. Charlotte pulled her wits together enough to find the air to scream for help. But even as she drew in a deep breath, his lips took possession of one of her nipples, sucking the tip into his mouth and letting his tongue whirl over the surface until it was pebbled and tight.

His kiss, his touch had bewildered her innocent senses, but this, this feeling he drew from her as easily as one might pluck a daisy, sent a shock wave of desire through her that rocked her virtue right off its foundation.

And her desperate cry turned into a gasp of surprise.

"Ah, yes, little Lottie, I know what you like," he told her as he moved from one breast to the other and began working his hypnotic magic over again. Then he shifted again until something hard and insistent thrust against her thighs, between her legs.

And here all these months she'd thought the Earl of Walbrook's South Seas prize had just been a grand exaggeration of male endowment.

No, having now been presented with solid evidence, she realized there was some truth in her mother's dire warning of "turgid deviltry."

If that wasn't bad enough, he'd caught her hip with another hand—gads, how many limbs did this fellow possess—and tugged her closer to him.

Closer? He wanted to get closer?

Indeed he did, for he shifted yet again, pushing the tip of his manhood so it dove deeper toward . . . her very ruination (as if waking up naked with a man wasn't enough).

Yet in his efforts to completely ravage her, she realized he'd let go of her arms, released her hands as he'd caught hold of her hips, and was even now steering a course she had no intention of undertaking—no matter that her body seemed quite willing as her hips arched upward, seeking out his offering with a mind of their own.

She caught the top of the coverlet and yanked it down, only to find herself blinded by the sunlight streaking through the gauzy window covering.

Charlotte blinked and shook her head until the red curtains came into focus, then the oddly familiar painting across the room. Then, and only then, was she able to look up at the face of her assailant.

A man she knew only too well.

"Lord Trent?!" she cried out.

His face split into a wide grin. "You're further along than I thought, if you're calling my name already," he said, as if it were a grand joke. "But you needn't be so formal, Lottie, my love. A rousing 'Sebastian! Oh, now, Sebastian!' will suffice."

He swept down to kiss her again, his hips moving perilously toward her ruination as they thrust down to meet hers.

Lord Trent. Naked. Atop her. Calling her Lottie?

'Tis all a dream, she told herself, and for a split second that logic gave her some reassurance. Yet, honestly, whenever in her dreams had Lord Trent suckled at her breasts, as he was doing now, or ever in her imagination had his fingers raked through the curls . . . *down there* . . . her thighs parting willingly before him, allowing him to stroke her expertly with an intimacy that sent mesmerizing bolts of pleasure racing through her?

When in any dream had his fingertip rolled over the nub hidden there? How could a dream lover know about that place when she barely knew of its existence?

Oh, heavens, this was no dream.

She struggled out of his grasp, towing a bit of sheet with her.

"What do you think you are doing, my lord?"

"I thought I was doing you a favor." He grinned, wickedly, rakishly. "Doing us both a favor, if you know what I mean." He started to crawl toward her, crossing the expanse she had hoped would deter him.

"Stop right there," she ordered with as much force as she could muster pointing at an imaginary boundary in the sheets. "My lord, I don't know how it is that you are here, or how I am here, but I will not—"

She was cut off when his hand snaked under the linens, caught her by the ankle, and tugged her back into his embrace.

"You had too much wine last night," he teased. "It's made you cantankerous this morning." He nuzzled her neck again and said in a thick voice, "Let me wake you up properly."

His fingers went back to work teasing a path toward her cleft, and that delicious tempting warmth started to cloud her reason. . . .

Oh, Sebastian! Now, Sebastian . . .

Whatever was she thinking? Charlotte's reason clamored back to the forefront and she found the wherewithal to scramble out of his grasp once again. "What do you think you are doing?"

"I told you, I'm waking you up."

"Like this?" She tugged the sheet higher.

He shrugged, that wicked grin tilting his lips yet again. Her boundary line wavered in the face of such temptation.

So Charlotte chose a new line of defense. She closed her eyes.

"Demmit!" he sputtered.

The mattress tipped beneath her, and her eyes flew open, only to find that all the nakedness she'd *felt* was now outside the bed and on display.

Sebastian Marlowe. Naked. Why, it was scandalous!

Gloriously so, she found herself thinking until her sense of propriety snapped her eyes shut again and she shuttered her vision with both hands.

Not that he seemed to care about propriety in the least. "Demmit! Demmit! Demmit!" he was muttering. "I'm going to be late to the Burkes' Venetian breakfast. And you know that old codger, he's a stickler for punctuality."

She stole a peek between her fingers, only to find him bent over and sorting clothes, tossing a pair of breeches, white shirt, and a rumpled cravat on the bed. Her hands dropped away from her eyes and her mouth fell open.

He strode across the room, utterly and completely naked, as if such an arrangement between them was commonplace.

Had a man ever been crafted so flawlessly? She'd spent enough time at his Berkeley Square house, stolen enough glances at the earl's notorious art collection to know that this Marlowe was a magnificent example of manly perfection.

A lean, solid torso sat atop long, muscled legs. His arms and shoulders, the ones she'd so impotently tried to fight, seemed an impervious expanse. Her fingers curled up and then stretched, and the memory of his steely flesh against her left her quivering anew.

"Where the devil are my . . ." he said, looking left and right. "Ah, there they are." He plucked a pair of boots out from beneath a chair, then reached for his breeches. With them tugged on, and his shirt tossed over his head, he then examined his cravat, frowning at its wrinkled state. Holding it out for her inspection, he asked, "Do you think Finella would press this?"

Finella? Why, if her Cousin Finella were to see her thusly, see him—well, ironing would be the least of their concerns. The poor woman would fall over with a fatal case of vapors.

"What do you think?" he asked again, shaking the poor limp cloth. "Wager she's up? Most likely not. She looked rather foxed when I arrived last night."

Charlotte could only shake her head. Foxed? Cousin Finella drunk? Had the entire world gone mad?

He shook it out again and examined it. "Eh, you're most likely right. It's probably not worth risking her tart tongue to get her to do it, especially if she's still jug-bitten."

He finished getting dressed and threw himself back onto the bed, gathering Charlotte into his arms and kissing her soundly. "Have a splendid day, my love." He paused and looked into her eyes, a moment of concern crossing his features. "Are you well this morning?"

"I don't feel like myself," she managed to whisper.

His hand cupped her chin. "Not having second thoughts about me, are you?"

More like a thousand and one thoughts, none of which made sense. Still, she managed to shake her head.

He grinned and got up. "Tonight we'll make sure of that. After the opera. You'll be there, won't you?" He tugged on his jacket. "The sight of you in your box will make a predictably dull evening bearable. I'll be devising the perfect seduction for later. Think of that as the second act drones on." He plopped a kiss on her brow and ruffled her hair. "Wear blue, and don't you dare arrive with Rockhurst, you contemptible little vixen. You know what the sight of you with him does to me." He strode to the door. "Then again, maybe that's why you like to flaunt him before me." He winked and was gone.

Charlotte didn't know how long she sat there staring at the closed door through which he'd departed.

Lord Trent. Kissing her. Naked.

She went over the events slowly, trying to make sense of them.

Lottie, my love.

Wake you up properly.

Oh, now Sebastian!

Wear blue.

She heaved a large sigh and looked around the rich room trying to find some clue as to where she was and how she'd arrived in this puzzle.

For some reason, her gaze fell on the large painting she'd spied earlier, the one of the naked woman reclining on a sofa.

The familiar-looking lady.

Charlotte tentatively got down out of the high bed, catching up a blue silk wrapper that lay negligently tossed on the floor. She pulled it on as quickly as possible and did her best to ignore the fact that it fit as if it had been made for her. Then she padded softly and cautiously across the room.

She stopped before the painting, her eyes lighting on the signature at the bottom.

E. Arbuckle.

Ephram Arbuckle? Her eyes swung up to the painting with a newfound awe. Arbuckle was *the* portrait painter of the *ton*. It was said that to have Arbuckle paint you was to live immortal, for he captured the very soul of his subjects.

She looked up at the lady and blushed at the sight of her, so natural and relaxed, her breasts thrust upwards as she reclined, the look on her face so smugly content, as if she'd just been . . .

Charlotte turned away, embarrassed to even think such a thing, let alone have a sense of jealousy that this scandalous creature probably wouldn't have wasted the morning ducking out of Lord Trent's eager embrace.

Now, Sebastian. Oh, please now . . .

She opened her eyes and found herself staring at a long mirror standing in the corner.

"No," she whispered, her eyes widening at the image

of a woman with ruffled hair and sultry eyes staring back at her. "No, it can't be—"

She turned around and glanced at the Cyprian in the portrait.

Then she turned back to the mirror and considered what she had to do. Biting her bottom lip, she took hold of either side of the wrapper she wore and flung it open.

"Oh, dear heavens." She glanced over her shoulder and then back at the mirror. The same breasts, same tousled locks, same long limbs.

She was the woman in the Arbuckle painting.

Her knees wobbled beneath her and she thought she was going to topple over, that is, until the sound of footfalls in the hallway jolted her out of her shock. Snapping the wrapper closed again, she turned toward the door.

Her body tensed, not in a frightened way but in a manner she had to imagine her twin in the painting would understand.

Sebastian . . . he's come back.

The door handle turned and Charlotte held her breath.

To her disappointment, an older woman bustled in. A wee bit of a thing, she barely came to Charlotte's shoulder.

A plain apron covered a dove gray gown, while her white hair seemed to glow above her dull clothes.

Yet it was her eyes that startled Charlotte—as green as moss and sparkling with a lively light that belied the deep wrinkles in her face or the stoop to her shoulders.

"Oh, good, you're up," she said, as she went about the room picking up discarded clothes and unmentionables, clucking at the general disorder of the place.

Instead of the usual odors of a charring woman—those

of hard work and coals and bedpans—this woman smelled of something fresh and clean. As if she'd brought the first flowers of spring into the room with her.

"Who are you?"

"Quince," the maid told her, having picked up a pair of smallclothes that were decidedly masculine.

Charlotte blushed, for she could well imagine who they belonged to.

This Quince didn't seem nonplussed in the least by the sight of them, for she simply tossed them onto the growing pile of laundry.

"What are you doing here?" Charlotte asked, dodging out of the woman's path as she bustled around the room, now putting the pots and paints on the dressing table in order.

Quince turned around and stuck her fists on her hips. "Straightening things out, what else would I be doing this morning?"

There was a challenge in her eyes that suggested to Charlotte that her answer was twofold.

"Where am I?" she asked cautiously.

"Your room, of course." Quince gathered up the pile of clothes and headed toward a door Charlotte hadn't noticed as yet. She flung it open and disappeared inside.

Curiosity assailed Charlotte—as to how this room could be hers, and where this Quince was going—so she followed, only to find herself in the most glorious closet she'd ever seen. Suddenly the hundred other questions she wanted to ask vanished.

Sunshine streamed in from the narrow windows high above them. Two walls were lined with racks of gowns— and not just ordinary gowns, simple muslin things that respectable girls wore, but gowns of brocade, of velvet, of rich, iridescent sarcenet that enticed one to come closer, if only to touch them.

To touch the wearer.

Quince seemed singularly unimpressed by this lavish collection and instead was methodically putting everything in its place.

She pulled open a drawer and tossed inside a pair of silk stockings. For an instant Charlotte could see other intimate items—in vibrant colors and rich with fancy lace. Whatever sort of lady spent so much money on her undergarments?

Quince snapped the drawer shut with a thump, and the noise was enough to wake Charlotte out of her distracted reverie. "You'd best be quick about it," Quince told her as she left the dressing room, Charlotte trailing along after. "I've other tasks to attend to this morning and can't spend it dawdling about your room."

Charlotte shook her head. "This isn't my room."

Quince snorted. Loudly. The sort of noise a fishwife would make if you offended her by offering too little for her wares. "Of course it is your room."

"But Finella would never allow—"

"What has she got to say about it when this is your house."

My house? "I haven't a house."

Quince was already over at the mantel rearranging the flowers in a vase. "You do now."

"A house? This is nonsense. How can I have a house?"

"It was a gift."

"From whom?"

Pausing in her labors, Quince bit her lip and considered the question for a moment. "That's always been a matter of debate. Some say it was the Duke of Chesterton, while most think it was the old Earl Boxley, trying to steal you away. Since they are both dead now, I suppose you're the only one who can settle that debate."

The Duke of Chesterton? Earl Boxley? "How could I receive a house from men I've never met?" Ridiculous notions both. That is until that odd whirring noise started to buzz in her head again, as it had the day before, and the room started to spin.

Quince must have seen her distress, for she took her by the arm and led her to a chair by the window. "Easy there, my dear girl. 'Tis a lot to take in on the first day. But you need to understand that some aspects of your life have changed."

"This isn't my house," Charlotte insisted, feeling childish for continuing the point.

"Now, there, don't fret over it. Of course it is your house," Quince told her, patting her hand with a practiced air. "And this is your room, and this is your life. Exactly what you wished for."

Wished for.

The buzzing returned, and a jumble of images competed across her thoughts like the tangled jumble of traffic that had clogged the street the day before in front of the Marlowes' town house.

Flowers for the lady, milord?

Sebastian striding down the street.

The saucy Mrs. Fornett in her smart carriage.

Quince sat down beside her, catching up her hand and patting it reassuringly. It wasn't the lady's kindly gesture that struck Charlotte as odd, but the way she smelled. Like a bouquet of posies.

"You!" Charlotte whispered, as she made the connection. "You were selling flowers yesterday in Berkeley Square."

Quince nodded, smiling at her, encouraging her to think harder.

Aunt Ursula's ring grew warm, tightening around her finger, while the buzzing in her ears became nearly piercing.

"Yes, that's it," Quince encouraged.

Charlotte found herself in front of the Marlowe house anew, gazing at Sebastian and giving voice to the one thing she desired above all else.

I wish I could be the woman he loved.

"I wished," she whispered.

"That you did," Quince said, letting go of her hand and wiping her palms across her apron. "And here it is."

"Here is what?"

"Your wish!" The lady sat back and grinned, as if she expected Charlotte to start lauding her with high praise.

"But how?"

Quince nodded at her hand. "The ring. The one your dear aunt left for you. Gave careful thought to whom she was going to leave it, and I'm so glad Ursula found someone so bonny. Someone who knows how to wish so grandly." She waved her hand about the splendid room.

Charlotte wanted to get more to the point. "You knew Aunt Ursula?"

"Of course," Quince said matter-of-factly. "Since the day she received the ring." The lady bit her lip again. "Oh, dear me, when was that? Fifty, no, sixty years ago. She knew how to wish, your aunt did." The lady sighed. "But she understood the dangerous nature of an imprudent wish and kept the ring locked up all these years. Don't think I didn't pester her to pass it along, but she was too fearful of what might happen if—" The lady snapped her lips together and forced them up into a smile. "Oh, what do you care about all that? What is important is that you've made your wish and here we are."

Charlotte looked down at her inheritance with no small bit of wonder. "And this ring—"

"Grants the bearer one wish," Quince said, getting up from the bed and pulling a rag from her pocket. She glanced around the room, then took a few swipes at a chest of drawers. "But only one wish, and I must say, yours is the most romantic wish I've heard in . . . well, let's just say, a long time." Her eyes sparkled mischievously. " 'To be the woman he loves.' Oh, such a fine wish. And here you are," she said, gesturing about the room. "The woman Sebastian Marlowe loves."

Charlotte tried to breathe. It couldn't be true. Lord Trent loved her? Just like that. In one simple wish, she was the woman he loved.

Her heart filled with a sense of wonder and joy. Sebastian loved her.

Lottie, my love.

Her hands went to her lips as she remembered his kiss, so possessive, so enticing. So full of . . . passion and desire.

All because he loved her.

It explained so much. That was why she was in his bed. He'd fallen in love with her and now they were . . .

She rose to her feet. "Married." The declaration gave her an enormous sense of relief. "I'm his wife." For heaven's sake, that was the only explanation for why she'd woken up beside him. *Naked.*

However, the bubbling bit of laughter spilling from Quince was anything but reassuring.

"I'm his wife," Charlotte insisted. "Lady Trent."

"Lady Trent!" Quince waved a hand at her before she clutched her stomach with it, which did very little to hold back the gale of laughter that rose within her. "His wife? Oh, that is a fine one."

"But I have to be his wife if I am the woman he loves."

Quince hiccupped through a few more guffaws and then went to the door. She pulled it open and laughed once more. " 'His wife,' she says." Then she wiped at the tears in her eyes and leveled a deep, serious glance across the room. "You're not his wife, Charlotte. You're Lord Trent's mistress."

Chapter 3

H is *mistress?*

Before Charlotte could even utter the scandalous words, make sense of what Quince had just told her so matter-of-factly, like it was perfectly normal that she, Miss Charlotte Wilmont, would be some man's mistress, before she gathered her wits about her enough to demand an explanation (and a retraction), the woman was gone.

"Quince," she called, scrambling up from the chair she'd collapsed into when the lady had revealed the truth of her situation. "Come back here!"

She yanked the door open, not caring what she was going to find beyond it or that she was wearing nothing beneath her wrapper.

But instead of seeing Quince, she found herself nose-to-nose with Cousin Finella.

The sight of her mother's strict relation took a measure of haste out of her steps.

Gracious heavens! Of all the people to see her thusly, why did it have to be Cousin Finella?

Charlotte braced herself for the hysterics. Which would be second only to her mother's wrath.

Yet none were forthcoming. At least not the ones she expected.

"You aren't dressed!" Finella complained, the familiar disapproval in her voice, though that was the only thing familiar about the lady before her. "Then again neither am I." She flounced, actually flounced, into Charlotte's room, with not one bit of her usual ramrod-straight posture.

"Where is she?" Charlotte said, looking down the empty and unfamiliar hallway.

"Where is who?" Finella said, on her way to the closet.

"Quince."

Finella stopped at the door. "Quince? Who's Quince?"

"The maid," Charlotte insisted. "The one who was just in here."

Her cousin snorted. "If you mean the new maid, her name is Prudence. And I don't think that lazy chit has even made it above stairs yet. Probably too afraid she might see Trent in his altogether again. Gads, she nearly quit the other morning when he came down early looking for a pot of chocolate." Finella shrugged. "I thought she might be too young for this house, but you and your soft-hearted ways. Afraid she'd be picked up by some abbess or worse, and made to work the streets."

"No, not a young girl. An old woman. About this high," Charlotte said, putting her hand at her shoulder.

Finella laughed. "Heavens, Lottie, and here I thought I was the one who'd had too much to drink last night. Quince, indeed! When you start seeing little fae maids, then you need to give due consideration to how much you are drinking—or give up brandy and switch to claret."

She winked at Charlotte and flung open the door to the closet, disappearing inside.

No Quince? Charlotte pressed her fingertips to her brow. Finella had never heard of her, and now she'd disappeared as quickly as she'd materialized.

Oh, this couldn't be happening.

From inside she heard Finella sorting through the gowns and continuing on as if nothing was amiss. "You promised him you'd be over by two and here it is half past one already."

Charlotte moved toward the dressing room and peeked inside.

Finella held a green day gown in one hand and a blue sprigged muslin in the other. The blue one went back on the rack while she held the apple green silk up to light for a closer inspection. Yet when the sunshine caught her eyes, she closed them quickly and rubbed her temple. "Gracious, I feel dreadful today. And here I am giving you a wigging about your drinking when I was corned, pickled, and salted last night." She laughed and shook her head as if it had been a grand lark all the same.

Charlotte stepped back. Certainly she hadn't heard that correctly. *Cousin Finella? Admitting to being drunk?*

"Was it obvious?" she asked, looking up from where she was poking through one of the drawers. "I fear it showed when Trent came in last night. I think I even flirted with him a bit. But who can remember or care when you've spent a better part of the evening tossing back a good portion of old Kimpton's cellars."

Charlotte caught hold of the doorjamb to keep her knees from buckling.

Lord Kimpton? The most pious man in all the *ton*? Drinking with Cousin Finella?

She certainly didn't recall wishing for that, but it appeared that her simple wish had turned everything about her life, her world, upside down.

You need to remember, Quince had said, *that some aspects of your life have changed.*

Some? That had been an understatement. Just look what she'd done to Finella!

And not just the admissions to drunkenness and the flighty nature: Cousin Finella *looked* different. Her hair, usually pulled back into the most painful of tight knots at the base of her head and dutifully covered in a starched white cap, fell in a long braid past her shoulder, untidy and . . . lush.

Why, Charlotte couldn't imagine that she'd ever seen Cousin Finella's hair released from its practical pins, and here it was, beautiful.

And without it pulling her face back, she looked softer, younger, more relaxed. In place of the modest gray wool gown that she wore from dawn to dusk, she was wearing a wrapper just as rich and expensive as the one Charlotte wore. The red fabric wrapped around her figure to reveal a curvy silhouette that the old Finella had never possessed.

Why, she must weigh a good stone more, perhaps two, Charlotte wagered. And the added pounds were all well placed, for suddenly the always stick straight Finella, who disavowed sweets and any indulgences lest they give way to licentiousness, had a full bosom and hips.

And saucy manners to match.

"Now why don't you put on these," she was saying, pressing a feather-light green corset and lacy garters to match into Charlotte's hands.

She gaped at the unmentionables in her hands. A green corset?

Finella was plucking about in a drawer for stockings and came up with an expensive lacy pair of the same hue. "Arbuckle loves you in green, and it will inspire him when you arrive—not that you'll need any of it for long, but it will get the man in the mood."

"Arbuckle?" Charlotte said absently, looking back over her shoulder at the lush painting on the wall. She still couldn't imagine how any man could have painted her thusly, known such details about her.

That is unless she'd been . . .

"You haven't forgot about your appointment with Arbuckle, have you?" Finella said, hands going to her now ample hips. "You promised him most sincerely that you would go over to his studio so he could put the finishing touches on the new portrait. None of us will get paid until it is done."

Paid? She was being paid to model for Arbuckle?

Finella pulled off Charlotte's wrapper and began dressing her as if she were nothing but a recalcitrant child. "When you finish at Arbuckle's, I daresay you should go down to Madame Claudius's for a fitting. She sent a note around yesterday that your new evening gown is ready. And then you'll need to be home by seven if you are to have enough time to dress before you go on to the Opera with Lord Rockhurst." She pulled the green silk over Charlotte's head and pinned and tugged it into place, then pressed her into a chair before the dressing table, where she began to arrange her hair.

Rockhurst? Charlotte stared at her reflection, the shock in her eyes matching the trembling fear running down her spine. She was to eat dinner with the Earl of Rockhurst? One of the *ton*'s most notorious rakes?

She didn't know how to dine with such a man. Why, hadn't Hermione once told a group of curious friends that she had overheard her brother Griffin saying that the earl could entertain several ladies.

At once.

And what sort of lady was she that she consorted openly with such a disreputable man—especially when she had the love and protection of a man like Lord Trent?

Yet something niggled in the back of her mind that said there was more to all this than met the eye . . . and that she couldn't merely judge her current situation by her old frame of reference.

For hadn't everything changed in one night? With just one wish? Everything but her sensibilities, she told herself. She was still the same.

"There you are!" Finella said, patting the last curl into place.

Charlotte looked up and barely recognized the woman staring back at her. This was her hair?

She'd never done her hair any other way than the same unyielding chignon her mother and cousin wore, yet what Finella had composed was like something from one of Hermione's French fashion plates.

"Oh, gracious, it is so beautiful," she whispered, bringing her fingers up to her curled and pinned tresses with an almost reverent adoration.

Finella, already fixing her own hair, smiled approvingly. "You do look pretty as a picture. Seems a shame that Arbuckle will want you to take it all down when we get there, but at least you will look good for your admirers." She tipped her head and gazed at her work, then began making a few minor adjustments to the arrangement. "Not that any of those loungers will care what your hair looks like." She sighed. "But this style does become you, if I do say so myself, and it will ensure you'll get your mention in the *Post* tomorrow."

Admirers? Loungers? Mentions in a gossip column?

Charlotte looked again at the lady in the mirror. What sort of woman was she? Unwittingly, her gaze fell on Arbuckle's painting yet again.

Dear heavens, how could *she* ever be such a creature?

Another wave of anxiety washed through her, twisted her stomach into a tight knot, for what had Lord Trent said, promised really?

I'll be devising the perfect seduction for later.

Later? As in tonight? He'd return here and want to . . . With her. Naked.

Her hand went to her belly, and Finella, noticing her, said, "Go on downstairs, and see if Prudence has at least gotten your tray right this morning. I told her to serve it to you in the front room." She prodded Charlotte out of her chair and pushed her toward the door. "I'll go get dressed, and by the time I get down, the carriage should be here. Eat something, dearling. You look rather peaked this morning." Finella shook her head. "And Lottie?"

"Yes?" Charlotte said, almost afraid of what her cousin would say next.

"Have a care with the brandy, child. You'll lose your looks drinking too much, and then where will we be?"

Thus warned and prodded yet again, this time toward a stairwell, Charlotte made her way downstairs, where she found what she suspected was the front room, since a pretty tray sat on a small table by the wide bow window. Flowers were tucked in vases throughout the room, and there was a tremendous pile of notes and letters on the salver beside the tray.

Charlotte glanced at the missives, but didn't know what she should do with them. Rather, she ate a roll and some strawberries—done up nicely with cream—and wandered about the room, unable to settle down in this unfamiliar setting, so unlike Finella's house on Queen Street.

Cozy and warm, the room was filled with whimsical bric-a-brac. A long settee sat in one corner, and two over-stuffed chairs were placed in front of the window. On the mantelpiece sat a blue-and-white Chinese vase filled with tulips. Beside it sat a miniature that, when Charlotte got closer, she realized was a decent rendering of Lord Trent.

Her fingers traced over the frame, her mind still trying to grasp how this all could be.

She was his mistress. And Cousin Finella seemed quite content with that arrangement.

Shaking her head, and casting one last glance at the rakish fellow in the portrait, she made another loop around the room, discovering another Arbuckle hung in the corner, this one of a small girl with a basket of puppies, along with several small landscapes and one of a gorgeously gowned woman who Charlotte thought resembled a younger Finella.

In a matter of steps she found herself back in front of the overflowing salver and unable to resist, she picked up the first letter, turning it over in her hand.

Mrs. Townsend, No. 4, Little Titchfield Street

Mrs. Townsend? Charlotte set it down. It must have been misdirected, for any lady who lived on Little Titchfield Street could only be . . .

Hastily, she picked up another. *Mrs. Lottie Townsend.*

Lottie. No longer Charlotte Wilmont, Quince's magic had not only gained her Sebastian's love, this house, but also a new name. She bit her lip and looked again at the letter. *Mrs. Townsend.* As in married?

Her knees quaked, and she sought the refuge of a chair, her hand shaking as she glanced again at the seemingly innocent looking correspondence in her hand. Even worse, there was something vaguely familiar about the handwriting.

The click of heels echoed down the stairs, announcing Finella's return, and with it, Charlotte's gaze jerked upward to find her mother's cousin parading into the room, gloriously gowned in burnished gold, an outrageously large hat perched atop her head, aflutter in plumes and silk flowers.

"Come along," she ordered, starting to shoo Charlotte out of her seat. "You can read those idiotic verses from your would-be poets when we—" Her words came to a breathless halt as she too spied the handwriting. "Harrumph," Finella sputtered, snatching the note up and tossing it into the fireplace. "Aurora! I suppose that prosy bitch wants more money." She swiped her hands over her skirts and made another disgruntled noise. "You haven't been paying her debts again, have you?"

Charlotte shook her head, shocked not only at her cousin's reaction to a note but also the animosity she displayed.

"Well, make sure you don't!" Finella made the most unladylike snort as she bustled her from the room, catching up a wondrous hat from a young maid, the aforementioned Prudence, Charlotte guessed. The pretty confection was deposited atop Charlotte's curls with a great huff.

A pelisse and gloves came next, and Charlotte found herself rushed out the door, down the steps, and into a waiting open carriage. A liveried driver and tiger snapped to attention at the sight of them, and soon they were being whisked away.

Her fingers went up to touch the glorious creation atop her head. Why, she'd never worn such a hat in her life, and she felt almost queenly beneath such fashionable perfection.

All the while, Finella kept up her tirade. "And where was Aurora when we had thin cupboards and were freezing our arses off every winter, I ask? Where was she? Up in that fancy Mayfair palace of hers, warm and snug, drinking pekoe and happily ignoring us."

Charlotte scrambled to catalogue all this information. But one point stood out.

Her mother lived in a palace?

"I don't understand," she said, then corrected herself in hopes of gaining more information. "I mean to say, I've never understood why she should ignore us."

Other than the fact that Charlotte was now apparently something of a scandal.

Finella snorted again. "The high and mighty Countess Pilsley calling on us? On Little Titchfield Street? Now that would be a lark. Oh, she'll help herself to your fortune but deign to acknowledge you?" The lady's brows rose in a significant arch. "No, it's better that she left us to our fate and married Pilsley after Wilmont died. At least *we* aren't up to our ears in debt."

Charlotte did her best to take this all in and not appear completely shocked. Her mother had left her to Cousin Finella and remarried?

Not just remarried, but having landed an earl? That was quite a step up from Charlotte's father, who had been naught but a poor knight with barely a noteworthy estate.

"I thought Pilsley had money," she said aloud without thinking.

"Harrumph! Not enough to cover her gambling debts," Finella shot back, her dour looks replaced quickly with a wide smile as she rose up in her seat to wave gaily at a lady in the street.

Looking over at the fancily dressed recipient of her cousin's enthusiastic greeting, Charlotte nearly toppled out of the open carriage—for it was none other than Corrina Fornett, fluttering her elegantly gloved hand back at them as if they were old and dear friends.

Mrs. Fornett? The same woman Finella had regarded just yesterday with such animosity it was surprising she hadn't fired off a letter to the *Times* in complaint of the notorious lady being allowed to drive in Mayfair?

"Oh, yes, doesn't Corinna look well today. I daresay if she wasn't such a lovely girl, I'd despise her utterly." Finella flounced back down in her seat, pulling at her gloves. "Now, where was I?"

"Lady Pilsley," Charlotte said absently, her gaze still fixed on the departing Incognita. She was so overcome with shock that she barely listened to Finella's continued rail against the former Lady Wilmont.

"Oh, yes! If Aurora weren't so affable, why I daresay they'd both be ruined, but that cousin of mine has always had charm enough for ten women. Still, I shudder to think what Pilsley would do if he ever discovered just how much his beloved wife owes from her whist and dicing."

"Dicing? Unbelievable," Charlotte muttered. First, it

was nearly impossible to imagine her mother being described as "affable," but gambling?

"You're a fine one to chastise someone about a few games of chance!" Finella crossed her arms over her chest. "Especially after last night."

Whatever had she done last night? Given the set of her cousin's jaw she had to imagine she wouldn't have to wait long to find out.

"Lottie, you drink too much and you play too deep." Finella's finger wagged up and down with the precision of one of those newfangled metronomes. "You are going to gain a terrible reputation."

A terrible reputation? As far as Charlotte could see, given the liberties Lord Trent had taken this morning, her reputation was the least of her worries. Still, she needed to make some amends with her cousin. "I'll sincerely do my best to improve."

The lady looked anything but impressed. "Bah! Play the contrite Mayfair miss on someone who doesn't know you better." Finella tugged at her poor gloves again. "Really, Lottie, you can't let yourself go. Not now. Not when just a few more annuities would allow you to retire. And to get those, you cannot let yourself overindulge—"

That admonition, Charlotte mused, at least sounded like the Finella she knew.

"—especially since Mr. Ludlow was quite clear on the point last month. But why do I think you will listen to your solicitor when you won't even listen to your own dear Finny? A house, Lottie. You need to find someone capable of bringing another house into the arrangement. If not a decent property, then shipping stocks, perhaps. I recall a Mrs. Wallace who did quite well with shares in a ship. But first of all, you need to find the protection of a man with the means to provide those accommodations." Finella's lips drew into a thin, firm line of disapproval. "Not that you'll see any such carte blanche from *him*." This, apparently, wasn't a new lecture. "That impoverished, impertinent, wretched bounder will—"

"You mean Lord Trent?"

"Of course I mean him," Finella said, all but exasperated. "That man will be your ruin!"

"I think he already has been," Charlotte muttered under her breath, recalling the rebellious way her hips had thrust upward as he'd covered her with his naked body, the way her thighs had parted eagerly at his touch.

"Now Rockhurst, there is the sort a woman can depend on." Finella sighed dreamily. "Why, if I'd had a few like him, I certainly wouldn't be here."

Charlotte's gaze flew up. Cousin Finella had . . . with . . . If Charlotte hadn't been seated, she would have collapsed for certain. Not only was Cousin Finella saying she'd . . . well, had been . . . but she was saying all this as if it were normal that she, Miss Finella Uppington-Higgins, respectable spinster and upholder of propriety, was a former Cyprian.

But some things hadn't changed, and Finella returned to form, all business and straightforward as ever. "Send Trent packing, my girl. You cannot afford to keep him much longer."

"But he loves me," Charlotte said, thinking of her wish.

"Loves you! As if that pays the grocer's bill." Finella moved across the carriage and settled down next to her. "You aren't getting any younger, and the Rockhursts of the world will start looking elsewhere before you know it. Why, I hear he was most generous with Mrs. Vache when they parted company last winter." The bright flame of avarice illuminating Finella's gaze could have lit every lamp in Mayfair.

The carriage wheeled around a corner and Finella straightened, her face rising to look ahead. "Dear heavens! We're almost there." She turned around and examined her companion like one might a prize racehorse. Putting her hands on Charlotte's cheeks, she pinched them a few times, then smiled. "You look perfectly lovely this morning, and there is a fine crowd gathered to give you an excellent mention in the *Morning Post*. Now smile like I taught you and make every single one of those fools wish they had diamonds enough to make you theirs."

Crowds? *The Morning Post*? Whatever was Finella nattering on about?

Just then the carriage came to a stop before an average-looking house, but that was the only thing normal about the place—for gathered there before the plain brick residence was a large group of men.

Why, it was as if they'd emptied the entire membership of White's and Brooks' and Boodle's and dumped them on this very spot.

A throng of dandies and Corinthians and dashers jostled each other to be front and center to the door of her carriage.

Finella nudged her from behind. "Smile, Lottie. For gad's sakes, smile at them."

Doing her best to turn her lips up and not turn and order the driver to hurry away with all due haste from this mayhem, she got up on shaky legs.

Immediately the door to the carriage was flung open and a volley of "huzzahs" arose from the crowd.

Charlotte thought she was going to faint, but with Finella pressing her from behind and a gentleman's hand now holding hers and pulling her forward, there was nothing she could do but go along with this farce.

The handsome man who'd claimed her hand was none other than the Earl of Rockhurst—the man Finella had been urging her to consider for her next . . .

"Green, gentlemen! Just as I wagered. The lady is wearing green," he announced. "Pay up!"

They were betting on the color of her gown?

Another stepped forward. Boxley, she thought his name was. The new Earl Boxley. "Rockhurst, how the devil do you always know what she is going to be wearing? What are you doing? Slipping in behind Trent?" He stepped forward and took Finella's hand, kissing it and giving the saucy lady a broad wink.

Male laughter, rough and hearty, filled the street. Charlotte didn't know whether to be shocked that the entire *ton,* at least the male half, seemed to know about . . . well, were aware that . . . well, of the fact that she and Lord Trent were . . .

Oh, she couldn't even think it without blushing furiously.

Lovers.

But now to add to that, here was this fellow insinuating that Lord Trent wasn't the only man who took such liberties with her!

"Demmit," one of them cursed as he paid off his companion. "I thought she'd be wearing yellow this morning."

"Perhaps her garters are yellow," came the suggestion of someone in the back of the crowd.

This brought out a hearty laugh, and Charlotte felt the heat of a blush fall from her cheeks right down to her very *green* garters.

"I'll take that wager," said Lord Boxley. "Fifty pounds says her garters are yellow."

"You've got a bet, Boxley," countered Lord Fitzhugh, who had jockeyed his way to the front of the crowd. The man grinned at her. "Come on, Lottie, be a dear girl, and let us see your garters."

"M-m-m-y-y garters?" Charlotte managed to sputter, now bent on reversing her course and heading back to the questionable safety of her carriage. The color of her gown was one thing, but her garters? Heavens above, what sort of lady did they think she was?

Given the lively betting and expectant looks on their faces, obviously the sort who would accommodate them by lifting her hemline.

She didn't imagine they would take her word for the matter.

"The garters, Lottie!" came the shouts. "Show us your garters!"

Finella nudged her in the back with her elbow. "Oh, dear heavens, gel, show them your garters."

"I say not!" Charlotte protested. Quince could make all the changes she wanted to her life, but her wish had never included lifting her skirt on a public street.

She shot them all a haughty glare and huffed her way up toward the steps.

It didn't help when she heard Finella explaining behind her, "She had too much to drink last night," in a whisper that could have been heard in Brighton. Charlotte turned around to protest this as well, only to find the saucy woman winking at the lot of them. "Any wagers on the color of my garters, gentlemen?" She swished her skirts back and forth, giving them a good view of her ankles.

The crowd roared with laughter, and to Charlotte's horror wagers started flying. She doubled back, caught Finella by the elbow, and towed her up the steps, the laughter, wagers, and jests following like a pack of hungry, baying hounds at their heels.

"Now that was a fine way to treat the lot of them," Finella scolded as she tugged her arm free and cast a look of flirtatious longing back at the crowd on the street. She even had the audacity to blow a kiss at Boxley.

Gads, the cheeky earl must be twenty years Finella's junior!

But before anything more could be said, the door opened to reveal a short, thin man. A pair of spectacles sat perched on his nose and his bald head glistened in the sunlight streaming through the transom above the door.

Arbuckle. It had to be, given his rough-hewn hands and the blotches of paint on his rumpled shirt.

"Mrs. Townsend," he enthused. "You did come! I feared you wouldn't make it today. Such rumors about you of late."

Charlotte flinched. Seeing the name on an envelope was one thing, but being addressed so . . . well, it was a bit disconcerting. She really needed to discover what had happened to Mr. Townsend, and as quickly as possible.

That, and the answers to a thousand and one other questions about how it was that no one seemed to realize that she wasn't this infamous creature. Not even Arbuckle seemed to notice, for he'd taken her arm and pulled her into his house like a protective uncle. He handed her pelisse to the housekeeper and then led her to the stairs.

"Radiant! You are radiant this morning. Green is the perfect color for you. Delightful! Wonderful!" He waved his hand as if it held a brush, taking broad strokes and filling her ears with a monologue of praise. "The next time I paint you, I intend to do you in green. Not that you aren't perfect the way you are in the other portraits, but the possibilities, my dear girl."

"Diana at her morning adulations," Finella offered.

"An excellent suggestion, Mrs. Birley!" the man said, his eyes sparkling with delight. "From Helen of Troy to Diana. It will be the centerpiece of my exhibition next fall."

Charlotte's head spun. Mrs. Birley? When had Finella gained a new name as well?

Meanwhile, as Finella and Arbuckle began to haggle over her services as the model for this next composition, Charlotte did her best not to gape at the art dotting the walls.

Engravings, drawings, sketches, and watercolors.

Of people, of horses, of vistas lush and green.

She stopped before one of them, a small painting of a meandering stream, with a soft green meadow spreading out from its verdant banks. There, beneath a tree, sat a woman, her skirt ruffled by an unseen breeze, which also pulled at her bonnet strings. The painting wasn't finished, but that hadn't stopped Arbuckle from hanging it.

There was something so wistful, so sad about the scene that Charlotte sighed.

"Don't even try," Arbuckle told her.

"Pardon me?"

"Don't even offer for that again," he told her. "I tell you

every time that it isn't for sale, and every time you come here you try to induce me to sell it. No matter how you toss those lashes or force tears from those priceless eyes of yours, I'll stop painting before I let you hang my Emma inside that scandalous boudoir of yours." He waggled a finger at her. "I'm not like that gaggle of fools outside. I'm immune to your charms, Lottie Townsend. Have been since the first time I painted you fifteen years ago."

He pointed at a frame hanging a little higher up the stairs.

"Precious," Finella said, walking past the portrait of the young girl, a basket overflowing with flowers cradled in her lap.

That's me, Charlotte thought as she passed it.

Yet how could this be? She'd just made her wish yesterday, but it was as if her entire life, the one that she remembered, had never existed, while this life had played out on some other stage without her having a single memory of it.

They had climbed up to the top of the house and were standing at the threshold of Arbuckle's studio when from down below came a ruckus.

"I have every right to be inside here. I've a ticket."

Charlotte looked from Arbuckle's furrowed brows to Finella's gaze, which had rolled innocently upward, as if the ceiling offered more interest than the brouhaha from below.

"Mrs. Birley, I warned you—"

"Arbuckle, my dear man," Finella said, "you must realize that gossip will only increase the value of this painting. A percentage of which belongs to my dear girl." She crossed her arms over her chest, looking like the Finella of old when the milkmaid sent over less than a full measure of butter. "Speculation and rumor will only do so much, but a full report by an eyewitness will bring crowds when you auction it."

"I do not paint before an audience. I am not some Grimaldi to be gawked at by a gaggle of geese and baboons."

Finella snorted at such artistic temperament. "An audience is essential to making this sale a success, and Lottie concurs with me."

They both looked at her, Finella nodding at her to affirm her statement, Arbuckle looking positively furious at this intrusion.

Charlotte swallowed. "I think, that is to say . . ." She glanced again from Finella to Arbuckle. "What I suppose would be best, at least for today," she added for Finella's benefit, "is that an audience might be a little distracting."

Arbuckle snorted in Finella's direction—not that the lady appeared to notice, for her nose was already pointed upward in obvious displeasure. "I suppose now I must be the bearer of bad news," she sniffed before heading down the stairs toward the soon-to-be disappointed ticket holders.

"Come along, my girl," Arbuckle said, taking Charlotte by the arm and leading her into his studio. "Mrs. Birley would sell your laundry in the *Times* if she thought she could make a profit."

"She means well," she replied, though she rather suspected Arbuckle had the truth of it; she'd seen the wink pass between Finella and Rockhurst, and she remembered how Finella had deliberately chosen the green gown this morning.

And urged Charlotte to take the earl as her new lover.

Whatever did she need a new lover for when she hadn't

the slightest notion what to do with the current one?

"Come along, come along," Arbuckle said, pulling her into his studio far from the echoes below, where Finella was refusing to refund the tickets she'd sold.

But all that was forgotten as her foot crossed into the artist's inner sanctum, and she found herself awed by a world she'd never imagined. Sunshine streamed in from the windows, as well as from skylights above. The entire studio was awash in illumination.

Tripods with paintings stood patiently waiting attention at varied places in the room. The portraits were covered with Holland covers, so their contents were as mysterious as this life she'd tumbled into.

As she continued slowly into the studio, her nose wrinkled ever so slightly at the thick scent of paint, the oils and chemicals competing in acrid and sharp contest. The odors had another effect: Suddenly she was struck by an overwhelming familiar feeling.

I've been here.

Arbuckle had left her side, crossing the wide space to take his place before an easel on the other side of the room. Beside it was a stool and a small table covered in pots and brushes—all awaiting the artist. Ever so carefully he removed the cover over the canvas and for a moment contemplated his work. A slow, satisfied smile plied his lips. "Helen! You are my Helen of Troy, Lottie. My masterpiece, and I have you to thank."

Weaving her way through the painter's works in progress, she drew closer to his masterpiece—his words, not hers—wondering how she could be the face that launched a thousand ships.

Arbuckle thinks I am his Helen? Charlotte was still mystified by how this all could happen. Granted the wardrobe and hair helped, but she was still just Miss Charlotte Wilmont of Queen Street, and hardly worthy of all this adulation, this lavish praise.

But before she could come around the easel, he waved his hand toward the space behind her. "Go on with you. Get changed so we can begin. Besides, I suppose you've fittings and appointments enough later and will be all atwitter in an hour or so to be gone." He glanced over his shoulder. "Besides, the light is perfect right now."

Recalling Finella's recitation about the rest of her day, Charlotte saw no point in disagreeing with the man, so she made her way toward the screen he'd pointed at. She got behind it only to find a simple gilt crown and a long gauzy strip of fabric that she hadn't the least idea what she was supposed to do with.

For one thing, it wouldn't cover her and for another, the silk was nearly transparent. *Well, I might as well go naked.*

That one thought stopped her in her tracks, the image of the scandalous portrait in her bedroom coming to mind like a thunderclap. The one of her sprawled out on a divan without anything on.

Yet how could Arbuckle have painted it unless she'd been . . . naked.

Oh heavens, no! Whatever was she going to do?

"Perhaps he just forgot to set out the costume," she told herself softly, forcing the words to sound reassuring. After all, he'd been painting her since she was a child, and most of his paintings were filled with a fatherly devotion.

And what were his intentions when he painted you in that Cyprian pose with that look on your face?

"Where is she?" she heard Finella call out.

There was a noise, a grunt really, from Arbuckle, and Charlotte could swear she could see the man impatiently waving a brush in the direction of the screen.

Irrationally, she looked around the cluttered corner for a place to hide.

"Dearest, whatever is keeping you?" Finella made that clucking noise in the back of her throat again. "Well, foolish me, of course you need help getting out of that gown. I'll be right there."

Charlotte didn't know which was more disconcerting, having Finella call her "dearest" or offering to help her undress so she could pose in her altogether.

As the lady came bustling behind the screen, Charlotte whispered quickly, "There isn't a costume."

"Of course there is," Finella said, confirming Charlotte's worst fear by sending a quick nod toward the silk.

"But there isn't enough to cover me," she protested, while backing out of Finella's reach. She took a deep breath, forcing the words from her lips. "I'll be naked."

She waited for the Finella of before to react, to swoon at the very mention of uncovered body parts, or at the very least, declare such a notion highly improper.

But as with everything she'd once taken for granted, this Finella didn't even bat an eye.

"Lottie," she said, hands fisting onto her hips, "it was your idea to pose naked again. Heavens, whatever is the matter with you today?"

Lottie's idea, mayhap, she wanted to tell her cousin, but certainly not a notion Miss Charlotte Wilmont was going to cozen.

"Now off with those clothes," Finella said, "or as much as it pains me to say this, I'll tell Kimpton to stop stocking our cellars."

Charlotte didn't care what Finella told the baron.

She had no intention of remaining in this life, wish or not. She pushed past Finella and fled Arbuckle's house as if the entire Greek army was hot on her heels.

Chapter 4

"This is not my life, this is not my life," Charlotte muttered under her breath all the way from Arbuckle's studio to Mayfair. She ignored the haughty stares of those she passed, ignored the whistles and masculine taunts from passing carriages. She was making a cake of herself, and she didn't care.

This is not my life, she wanted to tell one and all.

She hadn't even realized where she was going until she stood in Berkeley Square before the Marlowe town house. *At least,* she thought, sighing in relief at the sight of No. 15, *some things are still the same.*

There it was, in all its Palladian glory—with the rounded fanlight over the door, the soft cream stone, the arched windows, and the long triangular pediment across the top of the house that set it off from every other residence on that side of the square. Of course, the Marlowe house had to be different, and that carved, classical pediment gave the house its distinct flair.

Of course now that she was here, whatever was she

going to do? The idea of seeing Lord Trent again hadn't even crossed her mind as she'd made her mad dash from Arbuckle's.

Well, perhaps it had a little, she had to admit. But what would she say to him? Tell him everything? How she'd made a wish and woken up his mistress? Oh, yes, she had to imagine that would work out quite well.

Lord Trent, I am not who you think I am. And I am certainly not Lottie Townsend. I received this ring from my great-aunt, but it's not a regular ring, you see. And then I made a wish, and I became this . . . this person, who everyone thinks is . . . oh, dear . . . I mean to say I'm certainly not your . . . your . . .

And most likely by the time she managed to stammer that out, he'd have her in his arms and be kissing her. Probably wouldn't have heard a word she'd said, so intent on trying to get her out of "one of those moods."

Taking a deep breath, she blew it out. She was Miss Charlotte Wilmont, she reminded herself. A gentlewoman. The daughter of a nobleman. Everything fitting and decent a young lady was supposed to be.

Her mother and Cousin Finella had certainly seen to that.

And most importantly, she was an innocent. Her virtue firmly intact.

Yet Sebastian's words from earlier suggested something else.

I'll be devising the perfect seduction for later. Think of that as the second act drones on.

Tonight. This very night. Whatever would she do when he arrived and wanted to . . . to . . . seduce her?

"Dear heavens," she muttered. "I can't allow him in my bed."

"Scandalous!" came an outraged protest.

In her state of shock, Charlotte hadn't even considered that her distracted pacing before the Marlowe household might draw an audience. Blinking the dust from her eyes, she looked up at the trio poised before her on the steps.

One very shocked matron and two wide-eyed young ladies gaped at her, obviously having just heard her panicked babble. In their plain, yet proper, straw bonnets and elegant, but modest, sprigged muslin gowns, they looked the epitome of respectable Mayfair ladies out for an afternoon stroll now that they had made their call at the Marlowe household.

Perfect! she thought. Now who else had witnessed her humiliation? Taking another glance at the ladies before her, her heart stopped at the sight of a stark black tendril of hair poking out from beneath that oh-so-plain bonnet, out from which stared a pair of wide green eyes.

"Hermione," Charlotte whispered, barely recognizing her best friend. Gone were the bright colors and fancy feathers. And beside Lord Trent's sister stood his mother, Lady Walbrook, minus her penchant for bold and (some may say gaudy) silks and sarcenet; and on the other, Lady Cordelia Marlowe, Hermione's older sister, dressed in much the same dull fashion. Lady Cordelia? What was she doing in London?

"Oh, Hermione, how glad I am to find you," Charlotte said without even thinking, reaching out to take her friend's hand.

At the utterance of her name, Hermione colored in embarrassment and drew back in horror.

Charlotte looked from her dearest, most bosom friend to Lady Cordelia and then to Lady Walbrook and realized that these women, whom she knew so well and loved like family, were not the same.

Just as she wasn't the same Miss Wilmont.

The countess's face turned a livid red. "Be off with you, baggage," she screeched, waving her parasol at Charlotte as she might at a stray dog. "How dare you come lurking about here as if you belong!" Then she caught each daughter by the arm and pulled them away, towing them down the street and around the corner.

"But I do . . ." she whispered after them. *Belong.*

She looked up the steps at the house that was like her second home to find Fenwick glowering down at her. Before she could say anything (as if she would know what to say in such circumstances) the butler closed the door with a definitive thud.

He hadn't quite slammed it, but the meaning was all too clear.

You, madame, are not welcome in this house.

Charlotte backed away from the steps, stumbling across the curb and down into the street. Hot tears stung her eyes, ran down her cheeks as she made her way across the square and into the garden in the middle. She sank onto a bench, her hands knotting into a tangle of worry in her lap.

Between quiet sobs and hiccups, she tried to catch her breath, make sense of this utterly impossible morning. "Whatever has happened to me?"

"You made a wish, that's what happened," said a familiar voice.

Charlotte's head swung in the direction, and to her shock, there seated beside her sat the charwoman from this morning. "Quince!"

"Oh, aye, that's good you remember my name." The woman's wrinkled cheeks dimpled even further.

"How could I forget it?" Charlotte said, an uncharacteristic temper rising inside her. She poked a finger at the woman, now back in her flower seller's guise, a large basket of posies perched in her lap. "What have you done to me?"

"Done to you?" The woman had the nerve to look affronted. "I gave you your wish." She fussed over her bouquets, rearranging the already tidy flowers and ribbons.

"This is *not* what I wished," Charlotte told her. "To be shunned by my friends, to be accosted on the streets." She glanced over at the Marlowe house, and tears threatened to spill from her eyes. "To be thought a common . . . a soiled . . ."

"Dove?" Quince asked, handing her a worn handkerchief. "Point in fact, your wish was rather vague. You asked for love, and you got it."

"I am not this woman," she said, her hands fluttering from the top of her flirtatious hat, over the low cut of her bodice, and ending at her embroidered and trimmed skirt.

"Of course you are!" Quince told her, tipping her head as she surveyed her handiwork.

Charlotte leaned forward. "I haven't the wherewithal for this life. Why, Arbuckle wants to paint me . . . well, I was supposed to wear . . . what I mean is, not supposed to . . ."

"Nude." Quince looked heavenward. "My dear, if you can't even say it, you are going to be in quite a quandary."

Charlotte sputtered. "Exactly my point! I cannot

pose . . . I mean, stand about . . ." She still couldn't say the word.

"Like *that*," she finally managed. Naked. Bare to the world. It reminded her too much of how she'd found herself this morning.

Of seeing Lord Trent striding across the room without a care or a stitch . . .

"I think you've made a mistake," Charlotte told her. "I am not this sort of woman."

Quince clucked her tongue. "Well, you're certainly not the Charlotte you were, but Lottie Townsend doesn't find these situations objectionable."

Charlotte spoke slowly and deliberately. "I am not Lottie Townsend. I have nothing in common with this creature."

"But you are wrong," the lady told her, still sorting her flowers. She pulled out a pansy and a rosebud. "People are such complicated creatures, my dear. Faceted, flawed, their characters ever up for interpretation. We all have varied potentials, aspects of our personalities that for whatever reasons we never explore. Society, choices, and, dare I say it, outright cowardice keep us from living out our lives completely. Charlotte Wilmont and Lottie Townsend are just different aspects of you. You aren't doing or saying anything that isn't true to your self."

"But I don't remember any of this," Charlotte replied, waving her hands at the scenery before her. "I've never been married." She paused for a moment, then lowered her voice. "I haven't, have I?"

Quince shook her head. "No. Finella made up a story about a shipboard romance with an officer under Nelson while you two were in Italy. The tale goes that he died at Cairo and you've mourned him deeply. Such a tragic history and his heroic name lends an air of respectability to your situation."

"I was in Italy?"

The old woman grinned and nodded. "Oh, aye. Finella took you to Paris during the Peace, and then on to Italy. To give you some polish before you started your career. 'Twas a brilliant move on her part. And just look at you, so very splendid!"

Charlotte took a deep breath and shook her head. "But it's not just me—everyone is different. Why, Cousin Finella is—"

"Quite a corker, don't you think?"

Pressing her fingertips to her forehead, Charlotte didn't know what to say. Cousin Finella a corker? There were so many things wrong with that statement that she didn't know where to begin.

Quince didn't seem to notice her distress and just kept nattering on. "Certainly, there were some small adjustments that had to be made to accommodate your wish. Most things are the same, the important ones," she assured her. "But time is like a garden, touched by winter one year, kissed by a gentle spring the next. You never know what will take root and bloom. So you must see how you can't adjust someone's life without some ripples. Finella was one of the things that had to change a bit."

"A bit? What utter nonsense! You've turned her upside down. Turned me into a-a-a—"

"A woman beloved by a man. That was your wish, wasn't it? To be the woman he loves." Quince pulled out a bundle of posies and pressed them into Charlotte's hands. "And desired not just by Lord Trent, I'd point out. You've a bevy of admirers. That's just a little extra I tossed in." She sighed, a dreamy look on her face. "Really, truly, no need to thank me."

"Thank you?!" Charlotte exploded, rising to her feet, ready to throttle this well-meaning, quite possibly mad, busybody. "I'm a disgrace. Ruined." With her heart thumping wildly and her chest heaving as she tried to catch her breath, she suddenly realized that she was making a scene. In public.

Taking a deep breath, Charlotte settled back down on the bench, willing herself to find a measure of composure. *I am a lady. I am not Lottie Townsend.* Having gained the wherewithal to continue she said, "You don't seem to understand. Tonight, Lord Trent plans on visiting me. He thinks that we will be . . . he seemed to be of the opinion that we would be . . ."

Intimate. Lovers. In bed. Naked. Entangled. Everything that she'd only barely managed to avoid this morning.

Heavens, wasn't the fact that she couldn't even manage to say any of this without blushing herself crimson and sputtering about proof enough that she wasn't this Townsend creature?

Quince seemed unfazed. "Oh, listen to you go on as if your life is over when in fact you have everything you've ever desired. Charlotte, you're no fool. This is your chance to have everything you wished for."

"But—"

"No buts. Certainly your sensibilities are a bit shaken—"

Shaken? She was a soiled dove. A lady of ill repute.

Beloved by Sebastian Marlowe, Viscount Trent.

She pressed her lips together. There was that. *Lord Trent.*

An oh-so-changed Lord Trent. Rakish. Naked. Hardly the sensible man for whom she'd carried her quiet torch about for years.

"And what about him? What did you do to Lord Trent?" she asked.

Quince shook her head adamantly. "I didn't change a thing about the viscount. That's all your doing!"

"My doing? How could I have done anything? I merely went to bed last night and woke up with a—" Even as she was about to finish her sentence, a nanny with two small children strolled by, and Charlotte waited for the frowning lady and her charges to pass before she finished, lowering her voice when she did. "He's a rake. The Lord Trent I knew"—loved, she would have said, but she certainly didn't trust such a confession in front of this creature— "would never have been so . . . so . . ." She tried to find a word that best described him.

"Lustful?" Quince said with a sigh. "Devilish? Glorious?"

"No!" Charlotte colored. "You're wrong. He's all wrong. Lord Trent is a proper, respectful, honorable man."

Quince waved a hand at her. "And he still is, but as I was saying before, you've changed him."

"I've changed him?" Her hand went back up to her brow and she closed her eyes. This was all madness.

"Yes, you," the lady asserted. "And quite admirably, I must point out. He was a bit of a stick before he fell into your illustrious company. Caused quite a scandal, for he dotes on you quite shamelessly."

Charlotte put her hands over her ears. "I will not listen

to this. I do not believe it. I would never . . . he wouldn't . . ."

"But you did, and he does," Quince told her. "Imagine, Charlotte, what his life would have been like if he hadn't found you. Fallen in love with you."

"He's in love with *her,* not me," she argued back. "Why, up until this morning he barely knew I existed."

"I'd say he knows now," the lady chuckled.

"A little too much, if you ask me," Charlotte said, feeling a bit annoyed at all this. It was one thing to wish for a man's love, but quite another to have it—especially when he thought she was someone else.

"So would you have it back the way it was?" Quince said, an ominous note to her words. "Have him calling you by the wrong name and picking flowers for another?"

Charlotte didn't even ask how the woman knew those things, for the image of Miss Burke rose up in her imagination more frightening than a banshee.

"You freed his spirit, Charlotte," she added softly. "And discovered your heart as well."

"I just can't believe it," Charlotte said, glancing up and into the lady's clear eyes. "I don't believe any of this."

"Believe what you will," Quince said, rising to her feet, basket settled on her hip. "But this is your wish, so you'd best make the most of it." With that, she turned to leave, and Charlotte sprang to her feet, catching her by her arm.

"You can't leave me like this," she told her. "I don't remember any of this. And I most decidedly don't know what to do."

"Let him love you, and the rest, well . . ." Quince's wrinkled face softened, her odd green eyes sparkled. "And in the meantime, don't fret so much. Soon the memories of your old life will fade and you'll have nothing but the love you desired above everything else. I'm rarely wrong about these things."

Rarely wrong? That was supposed to reassure her?

"Of course there is always a price, some necessary changes, but look now," Quince was saying, nodding toward the Marlowe house. "Isn't he worth every one of them?"

Charlotte turned to see the viscount coming down the steps of his father's town house.

He had changed from the clothes he'd been wearing earlier and was now a sharply and fashionably dressed Corinthian. His hat tipped at a rakish angle, his breeches taut and snug, and his rich wine-colored coat and bright waistcoat were all out of character with the somber man she'd known.

She turned to tell Quince to put him back the way he'd been, but the woman was gone, having disappeared as easily as she'd arrived.

Charlotte stared at the empty space for another moment or two until her gaze fell upon the posy of simple violets on the bench, tied with a blue ribbon. She picked them up and held them to her nose, inhaling their deep, sweet scent. When she looked up, she found that the driver had brought around Sebastian's carriage and he was about to climb into it.

Without a second thought, the violets still clutched in her hand, she made her way toward him, drawn by that inexplicable attraction.

She started to step off the curb, but a carriage rolled into her path, the driver yanking his horses to a stop just in time. Startled, she glanced up at the man clutching the reins and in an instant forgot the fact that she'd just been nearly run down.

"If it isn't the enchanting Mrs. Townsend," he sneered. "A bit lost, aren't you?" He tossed the reins to the tiger clinging to the back and jumped down from his seat. As he came striding around the front of the horses, she realized who he was.

Lord Lyman. One of the most eligible and notable men about town. Why, just last week, her mother had declared him perfect as he'd ridden past them in the park.

But perfect wasn't the feeling running down her spine as he stalked toward her.

"So what say you, *madame*? Shall we ride off for an afternoon of delights?" His brows waggled up and down, while his gaze never strayed from the top of her bodice. Before she realized what he was about to do, his hand snaked out and caught her by the elbow, yanking her close.

Charlotte gasped, not just from the shock of being mauled like this but also at the memories, images that had no place in her thoughts, that came tumbling forward like a bad dream.

A dark corner at the theater. His hand on her elbow, tight and unyielding, just as he was holding her now.

"You'll be mine, you little bitch. You'll be mine before the Season is out."

She tried to shake him loose, to free herself from his cruel clutches, but he held her fast, proof of his power over her.

"Never, milord. You'll never gain my favor."

"I don't want your favor, just the pleasure *of your company." He pulled her closer until his hot breath stung her earlobe. "I'll take you hard and fast. Teach you some manners, you overpriced bitch. Some respect."*

A chill of fear filled her heart.

His other hand reached out and curled under her breast, squeezing hard. "Trent won't last another month with all his debts, and then you'll come looking for protection. Begging for my help. See that you don't."

Charlotte shook the dreadful recollection from her mind. How could these thoughts be hers? She'd never met, let alone spoken to, this man before, and yet here he was holding her and she knew he was the very devil. Knew it from the bottom of her heart.

"Let me go," she said, issuing forth every bit of the old, staunch, and haughty Finella she could muster.

He only laughed and pushed his face closer.

"You'll have me because I have the gold to buy you. And have you I will," Lyman said, a cruel sneer turning his otherwise perfect countenance ugly. His gaze continued sweeping over her breasts, his desire a dark, frightening light in his otherwise pale blue eyes.

There was one thing Charlotte knew for certain: Neither she nor Lottie would ever have anything to do with this man. And like Quince had said, she felt a power within herself that she'd never suspected she possessed, but here it was, rising up inside her like a torch blazing to life in the darkness.

Words, thoughts, deeds that no Mayfair miss, no shy spinster would ever consider, let alone utter, came to her lips, along with the nerve and daring to match them.

"Over my dead body, you bastard," she said, spitting at him and trying to wrench herself free.

But while Lottie might have been able to handle the likes of Lyman with the nerve of a fishwife, Charlotte was no match for this bounder.

He reeled back from her, his face contorted with rage. "A whore in the bedroom and a whore on the street, as I see it." And then he struck her.

She felt, more than saw, the blow. It sent her reeling backward, and she toppled over, her head clipping the curb, an explosion of sparks lighting her vision as she struggled to stay conscious.

For a moment Lyman leered over her and she thought he meant to boot her completely into the gutter. But just as suddenly, the man flew up and backward.

"How dare you," came the black words from her rescuer.

Charlotte's lashes fluttered open. *Lord Trent.*

Strong and tall, he held the smaller man in the air, his feet swinging.

"How dare you!" Lyman seethed. "You're no better than that strumpet."

Trent replied by smashing his fist into the man's face. "If you ever dare to speak to Mrs. Townsend again, if you even whisper her name, I will thrash every last bit of life out of you, you miserable little cur."

She didn't know what was more shocking—the cold, deadly intent in Lord Trent's voice or the fact that he looked ready to kill the other man in front of half the *ton* on her account.

"Leave him be," she said. "'T'isn't worth the gossip." She nodded in both directions, where all the traffic had come to a halt and nearly every curtain on the square was parted with a pair of eyes watching the row.

So instead of giving the man the accounting he deserved, the viscount hoisted Lord Lyman up and heaved him into his carriage, where he landed with his head down, his legs pedaling helplessly in the air.

"I'll kill you for this," Lyman choked out as he struggled to right himself.

"You'll try," Sebastian scoffed.

"My seconds will call tomorrow," Lyman sputtered as he climbed shakily into the driver's seat of his expensive phaeton.

"If you can find anyone who considers your honor worth standing up for." Sebastian tipped his head and clucked at the restless pair, sending them dancing out into the traffic at a fast clip.

Lyman barely remained in his seat, and his hapless tiger could do nothing more than cling precariously to the back.

Lord Trent turned immediately to Charlotte, closing the distance between them in an instant and catching her up in his arms. "Good God, Lottie! Are you hurt? That bastard didn't harm you, did he?"

Charlotte found herself folded up against Sebastian's chest, warm in his embrace, surrounded by his solid strength.

She inhaled deeply, caught by the fresh scent of bay rum and that masculine air that had bedeviled her senses earlier. His hands roamed over her, not as they had before, but carefully and gently. "That bastard," Sebastian repeated, holding her out at arm's length and giving her a worried once-over. "If he ruffled one hair on your head, I swear I will—"

Charlotte gazed into his eyes, awe unfolding in her heart at the depth of his concern for her. The ringing in her head, the pain on her forehead was nothing compared to this.

He loved her.

She knew it without even hearing the words from his

lips. She'd always wondered what it would be like to have a man look at her, to see in his eyes the admiration and affection that sprang freely from his heart.

And here it was. Staring back at her. Lord Trent loved her. Just as she'd wished, just as she'd always dreamed, just as she'd desired. Not only that, he loved her enough to pitch a fight over her! Who would ever have thought such a thing of sensible, practical Sebastian Marlowe?

"Dear God! You're bleeding!" He turned his furious continence toward Lyman's carriage where it was just disappearing into traffic. "I'm going to kill that bastard."

Charlotte didn't care that she was injured, didn't care about the impropriety of being held in his arms in the middle of the square, didn't care that he was willing to commit murder for her.

Lord Trent loved her. Oh, the very wonder of it.

"You need to be seen by a surgeon," he said as his hand dove inside his jacket and yanked out a handkerchief. Then ever so gently he put it up to her forehead. "Does that hurt?"

She shook her head slightly. "No." Charlotte had to imagine that she could bear any pain with him holding her thusly.

But he wasn't satisfied with her answer, and after another glance around at the curious stares being leveled in their direction, he said, "I must get you off this street."

He caught up her hand and put it over the handkerchief at her temple. "Hold this in place—unless you want to explain to Finny how you got blood all over your gown." Then without any further warning, he swept her up and started toward his house with her in his arms.

"Lord Trent!" she protested. "This isn't necessary."

"It is absolutely necessary," he shot back, boldly crossing the street with great heroic strides. It was as if he relished the chance to be her knight-errant, her protector.

She glanced back toward the spot where she'd fallen. "Oh, dear, you mustn't do this!" she protested. "Put me down at once."

"I will not."

She glanced back again. Her head throbbed, and the encounter with Lyman had toppled her sensibilities completely. Well, nearly. "You must stop. You forgot my hat!"

He laughed. "Delirious over that monstrosity? You *have* been hit in the head."

"My hat," she repeated. She had to imagine it had cost a fortune, and she certainly wasn't going to leave it in the street.

"Only you," he muttered as he turned and went back. Balancing her in his arms, he managed to lean over and snatch it up. "Now I insist you see the surgeon." His thick, stern tone brooked no protest. Back across the street they went, causing a wave of whispers and gaping.

When they were halfway up the steps, the front door swung open and Fenwick hurried out. "My lord! One of the maids said there was a ruckus in the street and that you—" His words tumbled to a halt, and he gaped at the sight before him. "Heavens!" he finally managed. "Whatever are you doing?"

"Mrs. Townsend was hurt, she needs a surgeon." Even as Sebastian's foot started to cross into the Marlowe house, Fenwick let out an anxious protest. "My lord!"

Sebastian turned around. "What is it, my good man?"

Fenwick took a deep breath, as if considering his words

carefully. Instead he just nodded at Charlotte. "Do you think it is advisable?"

The viscount looked down at her and cringed.

At first Charlotte couldn't figure out what the two of them were about, until she realized just exactly what Fenwick's protest had to do with.

Her.

Certainly before it had made no difference if Miss Charlotte Wilmont had come and gone, but bringing a lady of Mrs. Townsend's ilk into the Earl of Walbrook's noble house, and in broad daylight no less, was another matter.

"Perhaps you can call me a hackney," she offered. "I can wait out here."

"An excellent suggestion," Fenwick agreed.

The viscount's brow furrowed. "Nonsense! And have Lyman or one of his ilk come along? Or worse, have Lady Parwich across the square see you?"

Even Fenwick couldn't argue with that. Notoriously high in the instep, Lady Parwich would have a field day with such an *on dit*.

Whatever is Mayfair coming to? You'll never guess who I saw loitering about the steps of the Marlowe house like a common—

"Agreed," Fenwick finally said, though his assent held only a modicum of accord. Sighing deeply, he waved the pair in, looking heavenward, as if he sought redemption for this most unholy visit.

Sebastian started across the threshold, when the most wicked of smiles tipped his lips, his serious expression taking a moment's holiday as he looked down at her. "You owe me a pony, madame."

"A pony?"

"Yes, and I want the entire twenty-five pounds," he asserted. There was a glittering light of amusement in his eyes, as if he was suddenly and immensely proud of himself.

She struggled a little bit in his arms, and he hoisted her closer in response. "Whatever for?"

"Don't you recall?"

Believe me, she would have liked to tell him, *there is very little I recall today.* Instead, she shook her head.

"I bet you twenty-five pounds that one day I would carry you across that threshold. And now I have." He winked at her. "Not quite how I imagined, but a wager is a wager."

Her hand fell away from her temple, the handkerchief clutched in her fingers. "I don't think—"

"Lottie Townsend!" he said, giving her a warning jostle. "You are many things, but I've never known you to disavow a wager. Now put that handkerchief back up where it belongs and admit that I've won fair and square." His emerald eyes glittered again. "If you haven't the money, the usual fashion will suffice."

The usual fashion? Heavens, what did that mean? Charlotte's imagination barely had time to consider the implications of his words when she realized the house they'd entered in no way, shape, or form resembled the Marlowe house she loved. She gaped at her surroundings as if she'd just tumbled into a foreign court.

"Where is everything?" she said aloud without even thinking.

Sebastian paused at the door to the salon. "Whatever do you mean?"

Charlotte faltered, for she didn't know where to begin. "Your father's collections?"

"My father?" He snorted. "The only thing he's ever collected are gambling debts."

Fenwick colored. Whether it was in agreement or censure for having something untoward being said about the master of the house, she couldn't tell.

"You mean to say he's here? In London?" Charlotte had never met the infamous Lord Walbrook, for he'd been gone long before she'd become friends with Hermione and her family.

"No, thank God," Sebastian said. "Off shooting or some cross-country hunt, something of that nature."

"Fishing," Fenwick supplied.

"Yes, that's it," Sebastian said. "Trout fishing he claims, but he'll come home dirty and with a monthlong hangover most likely."

"But what about his studies?" she persisted, looking to where the Oriental cabinet and the earl's infamous statue should be; instead there stood a rather ordinary sideboard with a plain salver atop it.

"His wha-a-at?" Sebastian stammered.

"His studies. His theories on early cultures and aboriginal—" She paused and glanced around, searching for the wonderful oddities the earl had sent home: the South Seas war mask, the pair of grand Indian vases, the silken painting with the intriguing Chinese characters.

In fact, all the things that had made the Marlowe house such an interesting place were gone. Instead her surroundings were just as ostentatious (and ordinary) as every other house in Mayfair. And it seemed the Earl of Walbrook was just as changed.

"What have I done?" she whispered under her breath. Suddenly she was plagued with questions, and she would have asked them if she hadn't found Fenwick and

Sebastian staring at her, the very weight of their aston-
ishment weighing down at her. Why, she could almost
hear the questions that lay in their eyes.

Whatever are you talking about?

Oh, heavens, far more had changed in the Marlowe
house than just Hermione's plain dress and Sebastian's
rakish new spirit.

"I meant to say, I thought with your father's travels
there would be—" She stopped midsentence, realizing
by the puzzled looks they shared that they hadn't the
vaguest notion what she was talking about. Panicked, she
glanced back to where the fertility statue had made this
entryway the scandal of the *ton*.

"My father's travels?" Sebastian shook his head. "I
hardly consider his shooting trips to Scotland worthy of
note." He gazed at the cabinet and salver, then looked
back at her. "Whatever are you looking for, Lottie?"

Charlotte took a quick, deep breath, shaking off the
alarm welling up in her chest. It was all gone.

"Nothing," she whispered. "I thought I . . . that is, well,
'tis nothing, my lord."

"I daresay a surgeon needs to be summoned. You look
positively pale." Sebastian turned to the butler. "Send for
Mr. Campbell immediately. And keep that handkerchief
on your head, Lottie. Unless you want to ruin that gown
with blood."

"A surgeon? Are you positive, my lord?" Fenwick
made a low noise in the back of his throat. "I don't know
if that is advisable."

"It's just a bump," Charlotte added. "If you would put
me down and let me find my feet again—"

Fenwick dove to add his hasty agreement. "Madame is
probably correct. A little rest, a quick restorative, and

then she can be—" The man's lips pressed together, and she had to imagine how he would have liked to end that protest with—*on her way before I am sacked.*

Sebastian looked quite put out with both of them. "Then have a footman bring a basin of hot water, some cloths, and a brush, as well as a decanter of brandy, up here. The good stuff, mind you."

"Yes, milord," Fenwick replied, his brows furrowed. "I think it would be best if you both retired to the breakfast room."

In other words, Charlotte surmised as Sebastian carried her down the hall, as far out of sight as possible.

The breakfast room, like the rest of the house, had also undergone a transformation. Sensible paintings hung on the walls, chintz draperies and subtle colors were now the order of the day.

Charlotte never thought she'd miss Lady Walbrook's Greek statue of Artemis and Actaeon, wolves and all.

Sebastian settled her down on a large chair in the corner and strode around the table to fetch a glass from the sideboard.

"Hey, ho, Sebastian," called out a male voice. The door on the opposite side swung open and the viscount's younger brother, Griffin, came barreling in. "Loan me a monkey, will you? And before you say no, I promise this time—" His words fell to a stop as he let out a low whistle, his gaze fixed upon Charlotte. "Lawks!" was all he could manage, before he glanced at his brother. "Tell me which it is: Mother is either out for the afternoon or she's gone aloft."

"Grif—" the viscount said in a low growl. "Have a care with what you say."

This slighter version of the Marlowe heir caught his older brother's arm and pulled him aside. "What the devil are you thinking? Mother will have your hide—and now that I think about it, mine as well—if she finds out about your . . . your . . . guest." He spared another glance at Charlotte and smiled almost apologetically.

Well, at least here was something that was familiar. For Griffin hasn't changed a whit in this upside down world, Charlotte thought. He was as cheeky as ever.

"Mrs. Townsend had a mishap," Sebastian told him. "I simply brought her here to recover."

"Trampled by your admiring hordes," Griffin jested in her direction.

"No," Sebastian said, filling two glasses from a decanter he'd purloined from the back of the sideboard. "Lyman."

His brother's wry grin turned to a thin line immediately. "What did that bastard do?" Griffin paused to glance at Charlotte and take in her rumpled state. "Someone ought to thrash him."

"Lord Trent did," Charlotte told him. "In the middle of the square."

Griffin's mouth dropped open. "You thrashed Lyman? Out there? In front of . . . everyone?"

Sebastian tossed back a drink and nodded.

His brother groaned. "That settles it. I'm staying at Sir Joshua's for the next few days. Won't be a quiet moment around here once the old girl hears this." Griffin started from the room as quickly as he entered. "I'd suggest telling her you were top-heavy and didn't know better." He shook his head. "Never mind that one. Didn't work last week when I had that little accident. Oh, about that money, can you spare it?"

"What is it for this time?" Sebastian asked. "The alchemy experiments or the elixir of life?"

Griffin snorted. "Old hands, those. No, I've discovered something new. Sir Joshua and I think we've found a way to trick time."

Sebastian closed his eyes and groaned. "Dare I ask?"

Charlotte put her fingers to her lips. Griffin hadn't changed a bit. He was still the same irrepressible fellow, chasing one crazy dream after another. Recently he'd begun to share work and theories with Sir Joshua Smith, an amateur scientist who lived next door.

"Oh bother, you'd never understand," Griffin told him. "Can you spot me the monkey or not?"

"Not," Sebastian told him.

Griffin's face fell. "Didn't think so. Hadn't any better luck with the old girl. Told me I was around the bend if I thought I could build a machine to travel through time."

"A what?" Charlotte sputtered.

Griffin turned to her, eager for an appreciative, or at least trapped, audience. "A time machine. Like a carriage, but instead of driving from London to Bath, instead you travel to, say another century or so, like 2010." He waggled his brows at her. "What about you, Mrs. Townsend? You wouldn't want to spot me a few quid for a new book over at Hatchards on the possibilities of electricity, would you? Contribute to the betterment of mankind?"

She laughed, then shook her head. "I don't believe I have anything to spare at the moment." Why, she'd never possessed that amount of money in her life, and here was Griffin acting like it was pocket change.

He paused for a second, smiling hopefully, as if he thought one of them would have a change of heart. When it appeared he wasn't going to get his boon, he bowed slightly, then started out the door, muttering to himself.

"Make us all rich once I determine how to use the relative speed of—"

Sebastian shook his head, then refilled his glass. Crossing the room, he handed one of the glasses to her and set the other down on the table behind him. Ever so slowly, he began to pull some of the pins free from her hair, looking over her carefully. "My apologies for my brother. He's rather—"

"Delightful," Charlotte said.

"Delightful? That's debatable. He's mad, is what he is. Like to put Mother in Bedlam with all his theories and experiments. Why, he blew up the garden wall night before last, taking Sir Joshua's prized climbing rose with it." Sebastian shook his head.

"He doesn't mean any harm," she said.

"You don't know him," Sebastian pointed out. "But he puts me in mind of something that I nearly forgot." He turned from her, then glanced over his shoulder and grinned. "Don't move."

Then he was gone, out of the breakfast room in a flash. She could hear his boots pounding up the stairs and tromping around on the next floor. Before she knew it, he'd returned, with one hand behind his back and a foolish-looking grin fixed on his lips.

"Close your eyes," he told her. She opened her mouth to say something, but he shook his head. "Close your eyes, Mrs. Townsend. That is an order."

Not knowing what else to do, she did as he bid her and closed her eyes. She heard him come closer, smelled the subtle air of bay rum come closer.

"Open your eyes," he whispered.

She did and found him holding out a small book for her.

"I hope you like it," he was saying. "I had it commissioned for you. All the verses and poems you love in one volume."

Charlotte took the offering, her mouth falling open. The first poem she came to, she stared at in wonder. "Coleridge? How did you know?" She loved Coleridge—though in secret and behind closed doors, for the man's verses were quite, ahem, scandalous.

"How did I know?" he laughed. "I suppose all those nights of reading him to you might have been a slight hint. And there is some Blake, and a bit of Donne and Milton as well. Oh, and a few limericks in there in case Finny happens upon it."

She turned the book over in her hands, staring at the red leather binding in wonder. He'd done this for her? Yet before she could say anything more, Fenwick came bustling inside, carrying a basin and supplies. Instinctively she tucked the slim volume into a pocket in her gown, hiding it from sight.

"Excellent!" Sebastian was saying to the man. He wrung out the cloth and began cleaning the side of her head, taking his task quite seriously. "This isn't as grievous as I thought it was, so perhaps I was a bit hasty about the surgeon. Just a bit of a scrape and there will be a little bump. I should be able to patch you up myself," he said to Charlotte. Once he had the area sponged, he opened up a pot of a pungent salve and dipped his fingers into it.

Her nose wrinkled. "That smells terrible," she protested, stopping his hand.

"I'll have you know this is Cook's prized balm." He freed his hand from her grasp and applied it to her head.

"When did you become so accomplished?" she asked, flinching slightly as his fingers touched a tender spot.

Sebastian pulled his hand back. "Does it hurt?"

"Not with you here," she said.

Fenwick let out a disapproving snort.

Charlotte had forgotten he was still in the room, and Sebastian winked at her, a sort of "ignore him" gesture.

"When did you become such a fine surgeon?" she persisted, telling herself not to look at the Marlowes' exasperated butler.

"Boxing at Eton. Had to have Cook express a crock of this down one semester because I kept getting floored by Rockhurst."

"You box?"

He sat back on his heels. "Oh, that's a fine one. I think that facer I landed on Lyman was quite admirable." He dipped his fingers back into the jar.

"I didn't know," she said, biting her lip.

"Didn't know!" He shook his head and continued applying the wretched balm. "Maybe you do need the surgeon. You've won more than your fair share of bets on my boxing and now you have the temerity to tease me. Ought to toss you into the streets for that one, Lottie Townsend." Then he grinned at her. "But you can add that to my accounts for later."

He boxed? And she wagered on the outcome? Quince was completely and utterly wrong. She'd never manage this farce.

"Ahem," the butler said, coughing slightly to remind the pair of his purposeful presence.

Sebastian wiped his fingers on a cloth. "Finished, and, thankfully, I don't think you'll have much of a mark. Like I said, 'tis only a scrape, and your hair will hide most of it. If anything, Cook's salve will keep your hordes of admirers away for a good week or so."

Charlotte closed her mouth and considered pinching her nose shut as well. "That might make it worthwhile if there are any more like Lord Lyman," she told him as she rose, a little shaky on her feet. With his help, she managed to get over to the mirror.

Other than the smelly unguent, she looked no worse for the experience. "I think I am quite restored," she told him. "I have you to thank, my lord. How ever will I repay you?"

"Oh, we'll get to that part later," he said in that same smoky and scandalous voice he'd used this morning.

Charlotte blushed, for she'd meant it quite innocently. In the reflection, she spied Fenwick glancing heavenward, obviously viewing such a statement as only one more burden for him to bear for this household.

Just then a footman came bustling in the room. "Fenwick, where is his nibs? I've got a message from 'er ladyship that the old girl wants 'em to—" The man came to a fumbling halt before the startling tableau of the family butler, Lord Trent, and his lordship's mistress standing together as if such a sight were perfectly normal. The man muttered something in Gaelic, then snapped his mouth shut.

Fenwick straightened. "What is it, Patrick? Be quick about it, lad."

The butler's authoritative voice snapped the poor servant out of his shock. "Her ladyship sent me to see what is taking Lord Trent so long. She's in an awful state over his absence. Ready to ring a peel over someone's head about it, she is." He bobbed his head toward the viscount. "'Iffin you don't mind me saying."

"Not in the least. My mother can be, well, shall we say, a rather formidable pain."

"Her ladyship is correct," Fenwick said. "You should be at the Burkes'. They are probably waiting to make the *announcement*."

His emphasis on the last word startled Charlotte probably more than Lyman's foul treatment had.

Announcement? But that could mean only one thing. . . .

Sebastian heaved a sigh and wiped his hand on one of the leftover cloths. "There now, Paddy, you've delivered your edict, and I am off to my . . . breakfast," he said, correcting Fenwick. "Come along, my dear, I doubt I can trust you to Fenwick's tender care—I hear tell he was a lascivious devil in his younger days and may still have a bit of the masher left in him."

Fenwick colored, while Paddy smirked—that is until the butler shot the younger servant a quelling look that warned both against laughing at his lordship's jest or repeating it.

Sebastian led Charlotte along, not that she really noticed herself being towed out of the house, for she was lost in thought.

It wasn't just a mere Venetian breakfast the Burkes were throwing this morning, but a betrothal party. For Lord Trent and Miss Burke.

Outside the house, his smart and dashing curricle awaited him, and they stopped before it.

"I suppose you must go," she said, once again feeling all too lost and alone.

"What? Are you leaving me to the wolves so soon?" he said, taking her hand and drawing it to his lips. The entire scene would have been delightfully romantic if she hadn't known where he was going. "There now, Lottie, my love. You don't think I'm going to leave you here on

the street, do you? Actually running into you was fate—
you've saved me from myself."

"But your mother . . . and . . . and . . ."

"Miss Burke," he said, finishing it for her. "You know
how I feel about all that."

No, no, she didn't.

"My parents are putting pressure on me to marry the
chit, her family is delighted, but . . . I . . ." He took a deep
breath, then looked down at her. "She's not you."

Charlotte took a step back. *Not me?*

"Don't look like that," he rushed to say. "I know you
think I should marry her."

Marry Miss Burke? She'd rather see him marry
some . . . Cyprian. Charlotte winced.

Sebastian continued to explain. "Certainly would
plump up the pockets, marrying Lavinia and all, but de-
mit, Lottie, how can I? Not until I know for certain
that . . ."

He gazed into her eyes, a pleading look that pierced
her heart.

Know what? she wanted to demand.

"Oh, you are a wretched girl," he laughed. "I swear I
could drown in those eyes of yours. Now do what you do
best and lead me astray today." He grinned, once again
the rakish devil she didn't recognize but found utterly ir-
resistible. "Or at the very least let me take you home—
unless you want to walk?"

It was on the tip of her tongue to say that she didn't
mind walking since it was only just around the corner,
but then she remembered she didn't live around the corner anymore.

For that matter, she didn't have any idea how to get to

Little Titchfield Street, as she hadn't been paying attention earlier.

"Oh, yes," she said. "I would be in your debt."

He laughed at her prim speech. "You are in an odd mood today. 'In my debt,' indeed!" He bowed formally, deep and low, and when he arose, there was that mischievous light in his eyes. "Come along, Lottie, my love. I have a better idea. Let us see how this day fares. Forget the Burkes, forget my mother, forgo your fittings and interminable admirers, forget everything but us. Will you? Will you spend the day with me?"

Her heart quaked, for wasn't this what she had always dreamed? Wanted more than anything? Wished for all these years?

So what else could she do but take his hand. . . .

Chapter 5

The horses set out smartly and quickly, and Charlotte caught hold of the first thing she could find to hang onto, which happened to be Lord Trent's solid arm. She'd never ridden in anything so high, and now she found herself almost dizzy, what with the way it swayed and the speed with which Sebastian drove.

"Must you go so fast?" she asked as he wheeled daringly around a corner.

"How else can I get you to hold me so?" he teased, glancing down to where she had a tight grip on his sleeve. "Of course, father's valet will be in a pique over the creases." He winked at her and tore around another corner.

The ribbons of her bonnet flapped wildly, and her heart beat with the same incoherent flutter.

Whatever am I doing here? she thought. *This is utter madness.* Proper ladies certainly didn't ride about unescorted and in such a madcap fashion.

But never in her wildest dreams (which, given her

current circumstances, had been rather tame) would she have imagined what it was like to be the object of Lord Trent's affections.

His very heart.

She slanted a glance up at him, and right then he turned and grinned at her, the kind of bonny, shared bon vivant sort of look that tugged at her heart. As if he knew just how to please her and delighted in doing so.

"Why aren't you at Arbuckle's?" he asked. "Studio too cold for you?"

Charlotte colored. The temperature had been the least of her concerns.

"I wasn't inclined to pose today," she said quite honestly. She didn't care what Quince said; she and this Lottie creature were about as far apart as King George and the poor man's sanity.

Standing about in her altogether? Charlotte shuddered.

He laughed and shifted the reins from one hand to the other. "No wonder you turned up in Mayfair—you've put that old fusspot Arbuckle in knots, and I gather you've left Finny in a snit." He turned and smiled at her. "To be honest, I don't like the idea of you posing for him."

"You don't?" she said, feeling thrilled to have someone on her side.

"Certainly not," he told her, buoying her convictions for a moment until he continued, "can't afford to buy the demmed thing myself, and it will cause a regular riot when Arbuckle exhibits it. Not that you care—you'll be purring over the added attention. Buried in flowers and offerings."

"Exhibit it?" Charlotte barely heard the rest of his lament, still stuck on the notion that this painting would be hanging for all to see. Her stomach sank with dread.

"It will be last year all over," Sebastian said, shaking his head. "You'll be the talk of the town for weeks." He turned and looked at her almost wistfully. "Sometimes I wish you were plain and proper, a regular miss like one of my sisters."

"But I am," she protested.

Sebastian burst out laughing, as if he'd never heard anything so funny. "You? Ordinary?" His gaze swept over her artful gown and fancy bonnet. "Lottie, there isn't an ordinary bone in your body."

She crossed her arms over her chest and sighed. She didn't feel anything but ordinary. Certainly the clothes and hair were different, but she was the same Charlotte Wilmont he'd overlooked so easily yesterday.

Oh, what a tangle.

"What say we attend the races out at Lord Saunderton's?" he was asking. "He and the earl intend to settle their bet this afternoon over the earl's new Arabian and Saunderton's roan, but I hear tell they've opened up the afternoon for all sorts of contests."

"Horse races?" she managed. He wanted to take her to something as scandalous as a private horse race?

Hadn't she heard her mother aver that those sort of events attracted the worst sort of triflers and rakes, pickpockets and sharpsters and all sorts of ladies of negligible reputations like Corinna Fornett . . .

Or Lottie Townsend.

His brows waggled. "They're going to be running your favorite, Rathburn."

"My—" Charlotte pressed her lips together. She had a favorite racehorse?

"And if that isn't enough, they've got O'Brien and McConnell slated to box—but this time bet on McConnell. I know you fancy that O'Brien's more handsome, but I hear tell McConnell's in rare form of late, and I do say, O'Brien is due to lose."

"O'Brien?" she repeated, a bit dazed. First a favorite racehorse, now a pugilist?

"Oh, then have your O'Brien," he said, not even noticing her shock and confusion. "But don't you remember the last time Saunderton had one of these races and you insisted on betting on that Scottish fellow, oh, what was his name—" He looked at her as if she was going to have it on the tip of her tongue.

She shook her head wanly.

"No matter, we were both rather foxed that afternoon," he said, settling back in his seat. "You insisted that Scottish bloke was going to win and you bet all your money on him, only to see him take a facer two minutes in and land at your feet." He laughed uproariously, then paused and looked at her as if he expected her to be just as gay about it. "Oh, you can't still be vexed, 'tis a funny story. I don't know who you were more in a temper at—me for letting you bet all your money or the poor delirious Scot for bleeding all over your new gown."

Blood? She'd have to see blood? Oh, she didn't care what Quince averred about this life being hers—she couldn't imagine ever choosing to watch two men pummel each other, let alone get close enough to find herself in the midst of it.

"I'm sure there will be dice and quinze enough to delight even you," he told her. "What do you say, Lottie? Shall we spend the day doing what we love?"

As scandalous as it all was, never mind the fact that she hadn't the least notion how to play quinze, dice or bet on a horse, Sebastian had said the one thing that would have convinced her to dare the very gates of hell—which surely a race at Lord Saunderton's was as close as one could get.

"We."

Never mind Miss Burke's Venetian breakfast. Forget his pending betrothal. His family's expectations. Society's scorn.

"We."

The connotations of those two letters pressed together tangled up her common sense and let the wild beat of her heart be her answer.

"Yes. That sounds utterly delightful," she told him, primly folding her hands in her lap, as if she'd just accepted a dance at Almack's.

Sebastian laughed uproariously. "Delightful? That's yet to be seen. We'll see how delightful the day is if we come home with empty purses like we did the last time." He continued chuckling. "Hope you've learned your lesson since then."

"I assure you," she told him, "I am quite a changed woman."

He took her hand and kissed it. "Don't change too much, Lottie. I love you just the way you are, just the same as you were the day we met."

The day we met. Those words brought Charlotte's gaze up. How had they met? Since it was obvious she was no longer bosom bows with Hermione, they would have had to have met some other way.

"Lord Trent—"

"Gads, Lottie, you are formal today. Is this your way of sending me packing?"

"No! Never!" she gasped. She couldn't imagine herself ever sending him away.

"Sebastian, then," he told her.

"Sebastian," she repeated, liking the intimacy of it. "How did we meet?"

He looked over at her, his brow furrowed. "You are an odd one today."

"Humor me," she said, smiling as winsomely as she could. "Tell me how we met."

He shook his head. "Whatever for?"

"I just like the way you tell it. Indulge me, *Sebastian*." She let his name purr over her tongue, and it seemed to do the trick.

"Well, enough. I won you in a bet," he said as they wheeled past a grinning old woman selling posies of violets from the wide basket in her arms.

"Quince!" called out a deep, sultry voice.

The lady flinched and tried to duck into the crowd, but a strong hand clapped down on her shoulder and held her fast.

She glanced around at the tall, stunningly handsome man who held her. Stylish to the point of perfection, he wore his burnished hair a la Brutus, while his azure coat only made his sky blue eyes look all that much more piercing. He hadn't shirked on a perfectly tied cravat—a waterfall, she believed it was called—and finally, his long, muscular legs were encased in black Hessians that shone like a new moon.

His beauty and perfection would have turned heads—female and male alike—if he'd been able to be seen, but Milton barely tolerated this realm, considered it beneath himself to be gaped at by mere humans.

"Milton, you bothersome devil!" She tried to twist free, but his hand went to her elbow and he started to steer her toward an empty alley. "Whatever are you doing here?"

He snorted in reply.

So he knew about the wish. That couldn't be good news.

Quince decided another tack was needed. "Posies, my lord," she said, taking one of her bundles and shoving it up under his nose.

He brushed aside her offering and frowned at her. "I'll have none of your tricks, Quince. I can only imagine what sort of deviltry you've doused those blossoms in. Tell me, will they turn my affections to thoughts of love? Make me more amenable to this disaster you've concocted? I hope not, since you've been warned time and time again not to play such games with these poor defenseless mortals."

She buried the violets back in her basket, hastily and with no small measure of guilt.

"Now where is the ring?" he demanded, only letting her go once they'd reached a large pile of refuse. The stench burned her delicate nose, and she turned and gazed longingly toward the bright sunshine filling the street from which they'd come.

But Milton stood between her and freedom, and he looked in no mood to let her pass.

Not until he'd concluded his business.

"Where is the ring?" he repeated.

Quince shifted the basket in front of her. Poor protection, but it was all she had. "I fear that's a long story—"

He crossed his arms over his vast chest. "I have as long as it takes."

Of course he did. This was Milton.

"I truly meant to retrieve it—"

"You always do—"

"This time was different," she insisted. "I had every intention of arriving in time to gain it, but when I got there it was already gone."

Milton shot her one of his infamous arched glances, the kind that sent the rest of her kin into a panic, but she clung to her resolve.

And her story.

"The solicitor arrived before I—"

"A solicitor?"

"A fellow who assists in the law, a lawyer."

Milton snorted again, showing his disdain for the profession. Time had never given lawyers and their ilk a favorable impression. "And so what does this . . . this . . ."

"Solicitor," she supplied.

"Lawyer," he said, "have to do with the ring? Slipping past this fellow should have been no problem for someone with your proclivity for, shall we say, avoidance."

Quince smiled, despite the fact that she knew he wasn't offering praise for her "talents." "He already had the ring and had passed it on. With it on her finger, what could I do?"

"It took you that long to find it?"

"I, um, well, you know dear Ursula died rather abruptly, and there was that other matter, which, I might remind you, you insisted I finish first—"

"Quince, if I didn't know better, I'd guess you deliberately dawdled and let my ring pass on to Ursula's niece."

"My ring"? Of all the high-handed, arrogant . . .

"Well, did you or didn't you?" he demanded.

She pressed her lips shut and decided it was the better

part of valor to say nothing. No use telling an outright lie. Milton would see right through that, and then there would be hell to pay.

Literally.

"What's done is done," she finally declared. "And now Charlotte has the ring."

"Yes, she does. You should never have let her keep it."

"What was I to do? Like I said, it was on her finger by the time I arrived."

"Then you should have stolen it back," he pointed out. "It isn't like you haven't done *that* before."

Quince glanced away. Milton and his impeccable memory.

"And now see what has happened!" he declared. "She's gone and made a wish. Another wish, Quince." He shook his head.

"Hers was such a tiny one—"

Milton's gaze darkened like a thundercloud, and this time Quince's bravado started to crack.

"A tiny one?" He pressed his lips together. "You've turned the entire world upside down. You've made a mess of things." His jaw set with the same impassible fortitude of a Scottish mountain. *"Again."*

"Again?" Quince ruffled at this. "When have I ever—"

"The Hundred Years War?"

"I hardly think you can still hold me responsible for that," she huffed.

"It was only supposed to last for fifty, Quince!"

She stared at the toes of her boots and didn't dare look up into his most likely furious gaze.

"End this wish, Quince."

Her head swung up. "I can't! She's wished, and you for

one know I certainly can't just end it like that," she said, snapping her fingers at him.

"Yes, you can. From what I heard her saying, protesting more like it, she was none too pleased with your handiwork. Find this girl and tell her the truth—that all she has to do is disavow her wish and all will return to normal."

How like Milton to eavesdrop. Hadn't the man any pride?

Anyway, a little protest was normal in these circumstances. Charlotte would come around eventually.

"But Milton, with a little time—"

"How long?" he asked. "Ten years? Twenty. *A hundred?*" His brow quirked upward.

Gracious, couldn't he forgive her for that one?

"Quince," he said, his words thick with warning. "None of your protests, none of your chicanery. Tell this girl at once that she can go back, and when she does, get my ring."

"You won me?" Charlotte said, not knowing whether to be insulted or outraged.

Rather a bit of both, she had to imagine.

"Perhaps I cheated a bit," Sebastian admitted, looking well pleased with himself.

"Cheated? For me?" Why, she'd never heard anything so unromantic in her life. Not only was she his mistress but he'd also gambled to have her!

"It was that or see Rockhurst win your favors," Sebastian said so matter-of-factly that it made her believe that such wagers were commonplace. "So I cheated. Stole you right out from beneath his easy grasp. I don't think he's quite forgiven me. I know I wouldn't have."

Perhaps to the fallen women of London that might sound delightful, but not to a proper miss from Mayfair, Charlotte wanted to tell him. She turned a bit in her seat, away from him.

"Oh, Lottie, now what have I said?"

"I thought you loved me." She heaved an aggrieved sigh. "Not that I was akin to a pile of coins to be won."

"Of course I love you, you silly chit!" he exclaimed. He wheeled the carriage around the corner so fast that she had no choice but to catch hold of his arm again or tumble out. "I might not have loved you then—wanted you devilishly bad, I'll admit, not that every man in London doesn't desire Mrs. Townsend—but loved you?" He shook his head. "You know that came later." His features softened and he winked at her, driving the truism of his words deep into her heart. "And you know why."

Oh, heavens, she wished she did. This seemed an important enough thing that she should remember.

They slowed to stop at an intersection and waited for a mail coach to pass through. "Whatever has gotten into you today?" he asked, turning to face her. "You've turned as missish as one of those Bath ninnies my sisters run about with. All this 'Lord Trent' nonsense and fishing for compliments. I thought we were well past all that." He gave the reins a toss, and the horses jumped back into the traffic.

"I suppose I just needed to be sure."

"Sure of what?" He heaved a sigh. "Is this because of Miss Burke?"

"I don't see her charm, is all," she said quite honestly.

The rich little heiress had been the bane of her existence in her other life, and now it seemed Quince's changes hadn't rippled far enough. Why couldn't Lavinia

Burke have ended up a poxy tavern wench in this world? Or some fishmonger's wife?

"She has her charms," he teased back, the sparkling light in his eyes a devilish lure.

"Yes, ten thousand a year of them," she shot back.

He whistled at the sum. "Has a way of making the most unlikely of ladies popular."

"Harrumph!" Charlotte sputtered, crossing her arms over her chest.

"But she hasn't your fine eyes or sweet temperament," he told her, gauging her aggrieved stance with a gaze that twinkled with mirth.

"Oh, now you are teasing," she said back. She ignored his laughter and looked out at the unfolding countryside before them. They'd finally left London behind, and now nothing but green meadows and soft breezes lay before them.

The spring had been wet one day, sunny the next, and the result was that the grass had grown in lush and rich, the wildflowers thick with blossoms.

Having lived her entire life in London, with only the rarest of trips into the countryside when she'd been a child, Charlotte had forgotten how fresh and clean the world could be. She inhaled deeply, the air filling her lungs with its rich bounty.

Even Sebastian seemed to appreciate their surroundings. He sat back in his seat, the reins held lazily in one hand, while his other arm was thrown scandalously around her shoulders. His tall beaver hat, tipped at a rakish angle, only added to his mischievous, devil-may-care appearance.

"What a lovely day," Charlotte said, changing the subject and going to the only safe one she could think of.

"Very lovely," Sebastian told her, his deep gaze suggesting that he wasn't discussing the fine spring day.

"Stop teasing me," Charlotte said, swatting at him, amazed at her own daring.

"Now, now, madame—first I come to blows with Lyman and now you strike me down—"

Charlotte had forgotten about the other man. Lord Lyman had challenged Sebastian to a duel. How could she have forgotten such a thing?

"He wouldn't dare if only you'd—" Sebastian bit off his declaration and looked away. "Well, I suppose there is no use going over that again. You've made yourself clear on that subject."

If she'd what? What subject?

"Thought I must admit, it was a fine sight to see him with his arse in the air," he told her. "I've wanted to smash that smug fellow's face since Eton, but I've never had the chance. I suppose I should thank you for that, even if it's made him as mad as a hornet."

"He's going to send seconds!" she sputtered. "He's going to kill you. Oh, Sebastian, you cannot fight a duel. Not for me."

"What? You're afraid for me?"

"Yes!"

"You needn't worry," he told her with a laugh.

"But he'll shoot you!"

That wicked brow quirked again. "Think so little of my skills with a pistol, do you, madame?"

"Well, I—" She had no idea if he was skilled with a pistol. She'd never given it any consideration. Men didn't usually come to blows over her, nor end up facing each other at dawn over her honor. "I just don't want you harmed."

His eyes widened. "You needn't fear for my poor life.

Lyman makes plenty of threats, but he never has the courage to make good his complaints. He's a cur and a coward."

Oh, thank heavens. Charlotte let out the breath she hadn't realized she'd been holding.

"Besides, even if he does call me out, I can't think of a better reason to have grass for breakfast—your pretty face would be my last thought." He grinned at her.

Charlotte didn't even want to think of him lying face-down in a field, that is until she looked up and spied that mischievous light dancing in his dark eyes. "Oh, you bothersome man! You're teasing me."

"You're right," he admitted. "It wouldn't be your face I'd be recalling in my last agonies, but your bonny pair of—" His gaze fell longingly to the low line of her bodice.

"Oh, you are dreadful," she told him, pulling her pelisse around her shoulders. "If you aren't going to take this seriously, then I am not going to waste another moment worrying about you."

"I was being very serious," he said, feigning mock horror. "I'd think how a man chooses to spend his last moments on earth reflecting on his life would be a very important matter. And I consider your bosom a pair of the most perfect boons this side of heaven."

Charlotte's face flamed. "You are shameless!"

"I hope so. Never would have caught your fancy if I wasn't. But here I'm beginning to think I shouldn't have left your bed this morning." He leaned over and stole a kiss from her lips. When her mouth turned into a moue of surprise, he whispered into her ear, "We'd be there still if I'd had any say in the matter. And you would be in a better mood."

Charlotte's neck tingled at the warmth of his breath.

Or was it the viscount's scandalous proposition that made her quiver? Whatever could he mean, that they would be there still?

Why, it had been ages since she'd awakened in his arms. . . . Was he suggesting that he might have spent all that time kissing her, touching her, pulling her beneath him and . . .

She closed her eyes and drew in a deep breath, trying to ignore the way her breasts seemed to grow heavier, her thighs tightened.

"What, Mrs. Townsend? No tart opinion regarding my lament? That will teach you to drink too much—makes you positively cat-faced the next day." He grinned smugly and after a few minutes gave her a nudge. "You're quiet over there. Plotting out what to wager on Rathburn? Because I think you are going to lose today."

"Wager?" She shook her head. "I don't have any money to—"

Sebastian snorted. "Any money? Lottie, I've never known you not to have at least fifty pounds in that reticule of yours. Never know when you are going to run into your favorite bookmaker or a good game of dice."

Fifty pounds? Such a sum? She tugged the strings open and cautiously poked her hand inside. Deep down, inside a pocket sewn into the lining, she could feel a wad of bank notes tied together with a ribbon.

She pulled them out and stared down at the small fortune in £2 notes in her hands.

The viscount let out a low whistle. "Good thing Griffin doesn't know you like I do, or we'd never have been rid of him. He'd be pestering you still to loan him enough to build his time carriage—"

"Time machine," she corrected.

"Waste of money, more like it." He nodded at her purse. "Will you have a care, and stow that fortune? I'm not of a mind to go another round for you today."

She nodded and carefully stuffed the notes deep inside her reticule. Like he'd said, there must be at least fifty pounds. What was she doing wandering about with such a sum in her purse as if it were pence?

"Tie those strings tight," Sebastian said as they crested a small rise. There beneath them a wide, green field came into view.

Charlotte gaped, for she'd never seen such a sight. Why, it seemed all of London had come out to Lord Saunderton's, the lure of racing and a fine day too much to resist. A vast array of carriages, curricles, and phaetons stood alongside an impromptu track that ran in a great oval over nearly the entire heath.

Horses of all sizes and colors were being paraded along, while hordes of people milled about, shouting wagers and challenges and words of encouragement for their favorites. The thick stomp of hooves punctuated their cries, while there was the ever-present din of neighs and whinnies as the animals seemed to be doing their best to show their fleet spirits and eagerness to run.

At the far end of the field, tents had been set up, fluttering ribbons tied to their lofty poles. Around them vendors with smoking grills and barrels of ale and casks of wine were doing brisk business to keep all the patrons well fed and jovially inclined to wager heavily.

"Well, I never," was all she could say. Of course she knew these sorts of races existed, but the way her mother and Finella had clucked their tongues over the events that often unfolded (fortunes lost, gentlemen ruined), she had thought them dark and dangerous affairs.

To her eyes it looked like a glorious fair, something magical and scandalously tempting, all at once.

Sebastian pulled the horses to a stop. "Now some ground rules before we venture into that madness."

Charlotte turned to him. "Rules?"

"Yes, rules, minx. I won't see you ruined down there. Try not to wager more than you can afford."

"Me?" she asked, truly askance. But even as she made her protest, she felt her gaze being pulled back to the field, her sights settling on a large black Arabian that was giving its trainer a wretched time as the poor man tried to lead it. The unruly beast stood out with its powerful, thick chest and long, strong legs.

That one, Lottie, my girl. He'll make you rich, a winsome voice whispered in her ear. And even more annoying, it sounded like her own.

"Lottie! Are you listening?" Sebastian was saying, giving her a nudge in the ribs. "Demmit, woman, you've got that look in your eyes already."

"Whatever do you mean?" she said, sitting up straight and trying her best to keep her gaze focused on Sebastian.

The other unruly beast in her life.

He heaved a sigh and glanced down in the direction where she'd been staring.

"Now I know you have the devil's own luck when it comes to horses, but Saunderton's got a few surprises today. Wants to see Rockhurst humbled. You'd best not play too deep—lest you find yourself in dire straits." He reached out and with one finger tipped her chin up. "Lottie, I can't pay my own debts, let alone yours if you do yourself in down there. Have a care so we don't have to—" His brow furrowed. "Well, you know what I mean."

She could guess. Besides, what did she know about betting and horses and racing . . . other than the way that unmanageable black kept catching her eye.

He turned her face toward his again. "Lottie—"

"Sebastian, I swear I will—"

"Well, bless my soul, it's Mrs. Townsend!" came a cheerful cry in the crowd.

And suddenly a new kind of temptation began.

Chapter 6

Charlotte glanced up to find a short, stubby man in a patched coat and a tattered gray cap waving enthusiastically at her. As he came closer, she could see stubs of pencils and paper tickets sticking out of the various pockets covering his coat.

"I knew you couldn't resist, I knew it," he declared. "Says to meself just this morning, 'Self,' I says, 'tis too fine a day not to have Mrs. Townsend about.' And here you are, pretty as a strawberry roan."

The man held out his hand to help her down, and Charlotte didn't know what else to do other than let him assist her.

Sebastian tossed the ribbons to a lad who'd come running forward and gave the boy hasty instructions about seeing the horses walked and watered. He then came striding around the carriage and took her hand out of this interloper's grasp.

"Away with you, Merrick," he said. "Mrs. Townsend isn't betting today."

This brought the industrious and agitated Merrick to a sudden and complete halt. "Not betting? Not betting? How can this be?" He posed these questions to Charlotte, ignoring Sebastian entirely. He leaned closer to her. "We'll send his nibs here off to see the boxing and you can come along with me. I've got a fine one to show you, mum. A great beast of an animal. When I saw 'im arrive, I says to meself, 'Self, that's the sort of horse Mrs. Townsend likes.' "

"The black Arabian?" Charlotte asked before she could stop herself.

Merrick slapped his hand on his thigh. "Spotted him already, have you? Should have known you would. Unruly wretch of a beast. Never won a race 'afore. But he's got the blood of Eclipse in 'im."

"A likely claim," Sebastian muttered.

Again, Mr. Merrick ignored her companion and continued his enticing banter. "Mrs. Townsend, if you'd only take a closer look at 'im. He's your sort—obstinate and arrogant." With that, he shot a significant glance at Sebastian.

Charlotte covered her mouth to keep from revealing the smile there. Dear heavens, what a brash, outspoken fellow this Merrick was. And he smelled something terrible, like horses and onions and sour ale, but there was also something about him that she liked immediately.

The bookmaker continued abashedly. "Now if you'd come over and give this beastie your fine blessing, I just know you'll tame 'im into running 'is heart out for your fair favors."

There was something so delightfully impish about Merrick that Charlotte found herself enthralled. She turned to Sebastian. "May we?"

He took a step back and stared at her. "Now here's a day to mark in your book, Merrick," he declared. "Mrs. Townsend is asking my permission!"

Both men laughed.

Charlotte didn't see what was funny about that, but she forced a smile to her lips anyway. "I was just being polite."

This pushed both men into gales of laughter.

"Mrs. Townsend!" Merrick said, slapping his knee yet again. "You are in a fine mood today. Sly as ever."

Whatever was wrong with being polite? Though from their astonished looks, apparently Cyprians were allowed to avoid good manners. So instead of deferring to the men around her, apparently being Lottie meant she could order them around, hold them at her beck and call.

An oddly unsettling sense of power ran down her spine. Charlotte looked up from beneath the brim of her hat to find Sebastian winking at her.

"'Tis your money, Lottie, my love," he said with a laugh. "But remember the last time Merrick had one of his 'great beasties' for your blessing, the devil came up lame before the race even started. You had to cut back your millinery visits for a month."

Emboldened by the light in his eyes, she teased him back. "I believe I have hats enough for this month."

He laughed again, grinning at her with a joy that melted her heart. "You have hats enough to last you two Seasons, but that won't stop you. Win or lose, you'll be sporting some new confection by the end of the week." His fingers playfully ruffled the ridiculous plumes atop her hat, then curled to cup her chin, stroking her cheek. "Do as you wish, madame. You know that as long as you hold my heart, I am powerless to your whims."

Charlotte's breath caught in her throat as he claimed her with this simple but oh-so-very-intimate gesture.

He was powerless? The man must be joking. For his touch sent a thrill racing through her limbs, all the way down to the tips of her shoes. Her knees quaked, and, by their own volition (for surely she would never have thought of such a thing), her lips pursed, actually pressed together as if ready for another kiss. Something heady and thorough, not like that stolen peck in the carriage.

"Ahem," Mr. Merrick coughed. "Yer horse, Mrs. Townsend? I'd hate to have you not get your wager in on time."

She broke her gaze reluctantly away from Sebastian's, still all too mesmerized by his revelation.

"Of course, sir," she told the man. "The horse. How could I forget?"

How could she remember anything when Sebastian looked at her thusly?

Merrick beamed. "Mrs. Townsend, you are the finest woman alive." He tipped his hat off and bowed to her. "I says it every night when I says my prayers. 'God,' I says, 'take extra care of Mrs. Townsend. She's a most excellent lady despite what they says about her.' "

After this amazing speech, she glanced over at Sebastian, only to find him strolling over to the man's side and throwing a companionable arm over his shoulders. "It wouldn't be that percentage you get, Merrick, every time she wagers with you that has any influence on your great affection for the lady, would it?"

Merrick shrugged him off and turned his full attention to Charlotte, launching back into his list of seemingly impossible virtues that this sterling horse possessed.

Charlotte listened closely, nodding when it seemed

appropriate though she barely understood a word he said.

"The pair of you are incorrigible," Sebastian said. "And Merrick, you're the very devil to keep tempting this woman with racehorses."

"Milord, how can you say such a thing?" Merrick turned and shook his head at Charlotte. "He doesn't understand because he hasn't your eye for cattle, mum."

She leaned over toward Sebastian. "I have an eye for cattle?"

"Oh, that and a good many other things," he said wryly. "Now, lead on, my good man. Let's take a look at this paragon on four legs that has caught my lady's eye and has you convinced will make her the richest woman in London."

Even as they started through the crowd, heads turned and watched them approach. Like a brisk breeze, news of their arrival—more to the point, Mrs. Townsend's presence—spread through the crowd like a two-year-old let out to pasture.

The greetings and whistles were disarming enough, but Charlotte found herself dazzled by the vice and revelry surrounding them.

In the distance, an elevated boxing ring had been constructed. Inside, a pair of men pummeled each other, O'Brien and McConnell, she imagined, while the spectators shouted bloodthirsty cries of encouragement.

They wove their way through a maze of tables offering amusements of all sorts: dice, roulette, and cards.

"Mrs. Townsend!" came a merry cry from a man in a bedazzling suit of mulberry with an emerald waistcoat. "A game of quinze?" His companions wore an equally glittery array of bright coats and gold-trimmed waistcoats, while large jeweled stick pins and blooming cravats only added to their ostentatious display.

"Don't even think about playing with those sharpsters," Sebastian told her, at the same time tugging her in the opposite direction. "Or you'll walk back to town."

Charlotte shot one last look back at the trio, relieved not to have to join their party. She hadn't the least idea how to play quinze.

Let alone assess a racehorse.

Oh, heavens, what had she wished for? How could this Lottie be the sort of woman that Sebastian Marlowe would love? As well as, suffice it to say, most of the men of London? A woman of loose morals, a penchant for all sorts of vice, and, apparently, no manners.

Charlotte brushed the plumes out of her eyes and took a deep breath. Her mother and Cousin Finella's years of lectures on propriety were about as useful to her now as the lessons in Latin and comportment they'd also insisted upon.

"Have a care with your reticule," Sebastian was saying. "Seems a rather unruly lot today."

That, Charlotte decided, *is an understatement.*

Tulips and mashers strolled through the crowd, while a collection of rather scurvy-looking fellows lurked about the fringes.

She tightened her strings and tucked her purse close.

There was cock fighting, a wrestling match, and, alongside the track, an impromptu footrace between the grooms.

"You're extra quiet," Sebastian commented as they strolled along. "Plotting your return to the tables with Trowbridge and his lot? Or are you trying to reconcile your accounts in your head so you know just how much you can afford to lose on this nag?"

"Neither," she said quickly.

"Oh, you can't fool me," he said. "You have that look in your eye—like you can't quite decide which direction to go—a little boxing, some roulette, or see if that fine fence you love is here with some new bauble you might fancy but I haven't the blunt to purchase but you'll wheedle me into buying anyway."

"I wouldn't—," she began and then realized that this Lottie would. This woman he thought her to be was capable of all sorts of things she hadn't the least idea how to manage.

A lady could tempt a man to buy her jewels? However was that done?

The horse, an agitated bundle of Arabian nerves, paced and pranced at the end of the trainer's lead, while the jockey, a slight lad all of fifteen, tried to gain his seat.

"I don't see it, Lottie," Sebastian said. "I doubt he'll make the first corner before tossing that boy into Sussex."

Sussex? Charlotte had to imagine the poor jockey would end up halfway across the Channel. Besides, what did she know of these matters? Horse racing, indeed! But she couldn't shake the vague memories plaguing her thoughts.

Long legs. Fine chest. Narrow head.

Despite the way the animal pranced and tossed, Charlotte could see it running through a pack of competitors like a champion, passing them all, hell-bent for the finishing line.

She shook her head. Whatever was she thinking?

"He'll be at Tatt's in a fortnight 'iffin he doesn't win this week," the trainer was saying to another fellow. "Blood or not, his nibs won't be wasting more money on 'im if he don't win."

"Who's his owner?" Sebastian asked.

"I am," came a deep, rich voice behind them.

"Rockhurst!" Sebastian exclaimed. "I should have known this ill-mannered beast belonged to you."

"Ill-mannered?" The earl crossed his arms over his wide chest. "Rather reminded me of you, Trent."

Charlotte turned around to find the infamous Earl of Rockhurst standing behind them. How was it that the man kept turning up wherever she might be? Worse yet, he cast the same deeply assessing, thoroughly scandalous look of longing at her as he had in front of Arbuckle's.

Charlotte gulped. While Hermione thought Rockhurst the most "dashing" man who'd ever lived, Charlotte found his restlessness disconcerting.

Of course, she found the changes in Sebastian rather unsettling as well, but that was a different matter.

In the meantime, Sebastian greeted the earl like a long-lost brother, the two men slapping each other on the back and trading a few playful jabs.

Sebastian and Rockhurst friends? Now *that* was disconcerting.

And then into this masculine world came tumbling the earl's infamous wolfhound, Rowan. Infamous because he went nearly everywhere with his owner—and kept at bay more persistent matchmakers and footpads alike.

Charlotte had always eyed the massive dog with some trepidation, and today was no exception. Especially when the animal came to a loping halt beside his owner and, after a moment's pause, turned his great head and stared at her. Then he growled, low and menacing.

"Rowan!" The earl caught the dog by his collar and gave him a shake. "That is our good friend, Mrs. Townsend. Whatever is the matter with you?"

But the dog would not stop, growling and barking at Charlotte as if she were a threat to King and country.

Rockhurst finally caught him by the lead and tugged him into a sitting position. "Enough, you witless beast!"

The dog gave one last bark, then settled down, lying at the earl's feet, his eyes still fixed on Charlotte.

Shaking his head, the earl turned to Charlotte. "My apologies, madame. I haven't the least notion what is wrong with him."

"No matter," Charlotte said, casting one more glance down at the wary dog. Her spine tingled, and she could have sworn the hound knew the truth. Knew she wasn't Lottie.

"Merrick, have you convinced Mrs. Townsend to bet on my fine horse?" Rockhurst was saying to the bookie.

"I was just letting her have a gander, milord," Merrick replied. "Fine animal, this."

As if on cue, the horse gave another disgruntled snort and toss of his head and left the poor jockey clinging to his seat.

"Yes, fine beastie," Merrick said, flinching even as he made his sales pitch. "He'll run like no one has ever seen."

"Straight for the nearest mare, if he's anything like his owner," Sebastian commented.

Rockhurst snorted and cut between the viscount and Charlotte, smoothly taking her hand from Sebastian's sleeve and placing it on his, escorting her around his horse, separating her from Sebastian's steady presence. "Such a beast needs only the civilizing influence of a rare beauty."

She wondered if he was talking about the horse, his dog, or himself.

Now the horse, Charlotte found mesmerizing—the Arabian's scent, the solid, commanding way his hooves pounded against the ground, and the way her heart raced as in her mind's eye she saw this animal running, its mane fluttering wildly, its tail undulating with every fleet and pounding step. She'd never been so close to such a magnificent creature. "Does he have a name?"

"No, not yet," Rockhurst said. "Hasn't really earned one yet. But if you will, would you name him, Mrs. Townsend?"

"Me?" Charlotte couldn't imagine why he would want her to name his horse. "Seems a rather important task to just ask anyone to do it."

"You, madame," he said softly, "are not just anyone."

Then she looked up at the light in his eyes and understood. He was seducing her. Not with jewels, or poetry, or flowers, but with this beast of a horse of his, with a magnetic power that she had to imagine would eventually overcome any woman.

"What would you call him?" he prompted, his other hand coming to close down over her fingers.

A shiver ran down her spine as she looked at the horse, felt Rockhurst's caress, one meant to tempt and tame. She pulled her hand free, her gaze going to Sebastian's.

He stood across from them, watching her intently. She couldn't imagine what he was thinking, but all she wanted was for him to be at her side. To fly across this sudden chasm between them and claim her.

Lottie would know what to do, she thought. And then so did she. She smiled at him. Just simply smiled her invitation. *Fly to me, Sebastian.*

And then she looked again at the unruly, unpredictable horse between them and knew the perfect name.

"Boreas," she said, turning her gaze up at Rockhurst, setting her features so there wasn't anything there that would give the man the slightest suggestion of her favor. "I think you should call this horse Boreas."

"After the North wind," Sebastian said, striding around to reclaim her.

It was all she could do not to sigh in relief to have him back beside her.

"Boreas," Rockhurst repeated. "'Tis a perfect name for him."

Charlotte stepped closer to the newly christened horse and stretched out her hand to stroke the animal's dark neck, caressing his thick mane, the silken coat beneath it.

"I wouldn't do that, mum," the trainer called out in his lilting voice from where he was busy consulting with Merrick. "He's as likely to take your fingers off as he is to lose today."

"No one has any faith in you, do they, Boreas?" she whispered, ignoring the Irishman and moving closer. "Forget them. I think you are a fine beastie. I haven't the least idea why, but I think you are going to win. And quite handily."

She stepped back and smiled.

"What say you, Mrs. Townsend?" Merrick asked, sidling up alongside her. "A beauty, isn't he? Just gives you that feeling."

Charlotte met the man's earnest gaze and nodded, for she knew exactly what he meant.

This horse was going to win.

"So what say you, mum? Your usual bet?"

Her usual bet? Who would have thought that being Sebastian's mistress would be so complicated?

"You are giving Merrick just the edge he wants," Sebastian whispered into her ear.

"What do you mean?"

"You know exactly what I mean. He wants your endorsement on this animal so as to deceive all those devotees of yours who are convinced you have the gift when it comes to picking horses."

"Do you think I have a gift?" Charlotte asked, doing her best to ignore her pounding heart, the enticing sound of cheers rising as Boreas streaked across the finish line.

"You have something," he admitted. "But this horse, Lottie, he's as likely to throw his rider as he is to run in the wrong direction."

"I suppose so," she whispered back. "But I see him winning."

Sebastian laughed. "You always do and are quite vexed when they don't."

"But I do," she insisted. "I know Boreas will win today."

He took a step back from her and studied her. "You really think he will win."

She nodded.

Looking back over at the horse, Sebastian's face was a mask of concentration. And then it was as if a candle ignited in his features. "By gads, I think you're right."

Charlotte's spine tingled again. "Yes, Merrick, my usual bet."

"And add the same sum under my name," Sebastian told him.

This took everyone around them aback.

Rockhurst stepped forward and said quietly, "I say, Trent, can you afford that? I won't have you go into dun territory for my sake."

Instead of being embarrassed about having his financial woes being aired so publicly, Sebastian shrugged off his friend's concerns. "If Mrs. Townsend says this horse is going to win, that's enough for me."

Merrick didn't seem to care either, for he was busy filling out tickets. "A fine day, it is," he said, after hastily finishing and dashing off to gather more bets before the race.

"He'll drive the odds down, now that he has your endorsement on the race," Rockhurst said.

"We'll just need to fix that," Sebastian said to his friend.

"How's that?"

"We tell everyone that Mrs. Townsend was excessively drunk last night and isn't in her right mind this morning."

Rockhurst bellowed with laughter, while Charlotte tried to close her gaping mouth.

"Lord Trent!" she protested. "That is terrible. I wasn't—" Oh, heavens, it was hard to protest such a statement when she hadn't the least notion what Lottie had been doing the night before. Instead, she tried a different tack. "What will people think of me?"

"That you are as utterly delightful as always, my dear," he said, kissing her forehead. Then he nodded at Rockhurst, "You take that half of the crowd, and we'll take the other."

"If you think I am going to be any part of this deception—" Charlotte started to say.

"Demmit!" Rockhurst's curse cut off her protest. "Here comes that prosy Battersby. We've no choice now but to be quick about it."

Charlotte glanced down the meadow at the fellow fast approaching them.

"I do say, is that you, Trent? Rockhurst?" called out the tall, angular dandy.

Rockhurst didn't even bother to make a decent bow or take his leave but rather cut into the crowds and disappeared in the blink of an eye, Rowan loping happily at his heels.

As for Sebastian, he barely wasted another second, catching her by the hand and tugging her in the opposite direction. Her hat went akimbo and she clung to it as she found her feet flying beneath her skirts to keep up with the viscount.

"That was close," he said as they wheeled around the corner of a tent at a fast clip. He tugged her into his arms and held her close, peering around the corner to gauge their success.

"Why ever are we fleeing poor Battersby as if he were a French brigand?" she asked, still trying to right her bonnet.

"Rather face a raft of Frogs than run into Battersby right now." Sebastian glanced around and noticed the vendor behind them selling baskets of food. "Hungry?"

Charlotte nodded. It had been hours since her breakfast of strawberries.

"A basket," he told the man, pulling out the coins and laying them down on the counter before he turned back to her. "Now all we need to do is steer clear of Battersby."

"You still haven't told me what he has done," she

reminded him, her gaze wandering over toward the man filling the basket.

As Sebastian scanned the crowd around them, he explained, "Battersby won the last remaining shares in the *Agatha Skye,* the ones that have been floating about Town for months." As he spoke, his fingers reached out to twine around a stray strand of her hair.

She found it unsettling that he continued to touch her so intimately. As if such circumstances were normal between them.

But they are, a voice whispered in her ear. *That and more.*

Shivering, she did her best to listen to what he was saying and ignore the way her lips quivered slightly as if awaiting another stolen kiss, her body tensed in delicious anticipation, in places she'd never realized could be so . . . opinionated.

Sebastian didn't seem to notice her awkwardness. His hand came to rest at her waist.

"Are they worth anything?" she managed to ask, despite the way her breasts grew heavy, her nipples puckered scandalously, as they had this morning when he'd been . . .

Naked. Atop her. His hands roaming . . .

Steady, Charlotte, she told herself. *Don't think of such things!*

Oh, but it was so terribly hard not to now that she knew . . . knew what it was like to wake up with a man.

So she did her best to focus on the conversation at hand. "These shares must be worth something."

Sebastian snorted. "No more than the paper on which they're written, I'd say. Battersby won them last week— hadn't been in town long enough to hear they're worthless, thought he was gaining a stake in a fortune." His hips pressed forward, pinning her to the tent pole, and Charlotte swore she could feel every inch of him.

Even *those* inches.

"Where is the ship, this *Agatha Skye*?" she stammered, trying to forget what he'd looked like so gloriously naked striding about her bedroom. So strong and lean. Muscled and moving with such magnetic grace.

She hadn't been able not to look then, any more than she was able to forget now.

He shrugged. "It's months overdue. The poor blighters are most likely at the bottom of the sea." Sebastian gazed down at her, and for a moment he just looked at her, as if he couldn't get enough of her, as if he were imagining her without her clothes, just as she had been thinking the same of him.

Charlotte tried to breathe, tried to blot out such thoughts, but goodness, how could she when he held her so, when he looked at her as if he could devour her right here and now?

A pair of fellows came up to the booth and began ordering from the man behind the table. When one of them sent a leering glance in Charlotte's direction, Sebastian rose up to his full height and sent them both a menacing glare, using his body to block their lascivious gazes.

"Yer basket, milord," the vendor called out, hurrying to avoid a conflict in front of his stall.

"Thank you, my good man," Sebastian told him, reaching for the laden basket with one hand and catching hers with the other, pulling her away from the pair.

Charlotte tugged her pelisse on tighter with her free hand and wished yet again that her gown was a little more modest. Sebastian led her along with a determined stride, past numerous booths and tables where games of chance were drawing as many participants as the races beyond.

"Too bad those shares aren't worth something," he continued saying as they passed a large roulette wheel. The man running it called out in greeting to her, but Sebastian didn't give her a chance to stop. "Would have filled some lucky bastard's coffers if she'd managed to make it to port—her sister ship, the *Mary Iona*, made Loxley a tidy sum. But I doubt anyone is going to see a farthing out of the *Agatha*—she was last seen floundering around the Cape, and there hasn't been word of her since."

"How terrible," she said, glancing back at the spinning wheel, wondering what it would be like to bet on such a contraption.

"Terrible for all of us," he quipped. "Now we have to spend the next few weeks avoiding Battersby, overly persistent fellow that he is, until he finds some unlikely dolt to dupe into buying them." He stopped for a moment and glanced around them.

From another roulette wheel came a small cheer. "Look, mates. 'Tis Mrs. Townsend! Come on over, love, and bring us some good luck, will you?"

Charlotte turned in their direction even before she could stop herself. The admiration in their voices and the "click, click, click," of the wheel drew her in their direction.

"Lottie!" came Sebastian's warning.

"But I—" Why, she'd never felt anything like it in her life.

"You promised," he said. "Besides, I think I can offer you something a little more diverting."

Right now the urge to try her luck at roulette seemed quite diverting.

"What would you say to a little bit of privacy?"

"I suppose—" she said without even thinking, her gaze locked on the bouncing ball.

When he started pulling her along so that she had no choice but to trot behind him, she thought again about her answer.

Privacy?

He didn't mean . . .

Charlotte cursed her imprudent lips . . . for responding so quickly to his request . . . and for ever so slightly, oh-so-hopefully, wishing that privacy meant another kiss.

"You look as tempting as Eve with that apple in your hand," Sebastian teased.

Charlotte paused, suddenly feeling every bit as seductive as the Lottie-in-the-portrait. Though she'd been about to take a bite from the fruit, instead she stretched out her hand, offering him a bite.

His fingers, warm and strong, curled around hers, and when his teeth bit into the fruit, the sweet juice ran down into her palm.

Pulling the apple from her grasp, he brought her hand to his mouth and slowly and seductively kissed her fingers, her palm, taking up every bit of the apple. And then some.

Charlotte tried to breathe as his lips ignited her flesh, sent shivers of delight down her limbs.

"So very tempting," he murmured as he kissed the back of her hand and then gave her back her apple.

Let him take another bite, whispered a wicked little voice.

She shivered and didn't dare. Why, they were seated in plain view of what seemed like half the *ton,* for Lord Saunderton's great meadow had continued to fill through the afternoon with spectators as the time for the infamous race drew closer.

Given the very daring light in his eyes, she suspected that Sebastian was quite willing to suggest something untoward right out here . . . with the cool grass beneath her, the sunshine warming their bare flesh . . .

Despite the way her body thrummed to life, alive and trembling from his kiss, she pulled back, taking a nervous bite from the apple. "I do so love the country," she said, as a way to change the subject.

Sebastian laughed. "'Tis a fair distance from your milliner," he teased, nodding toward her bonnet.

"I daresay I could survive the deprivation," she shot back.

"I don't know about that," he said. Then glancing over at her, he asked, "Do you really like it out here?"

"Yes," she enthused. What wasn't there to love? "The air is so clean, and I do so love the grass." She wiggled her toes to prove her point.

"You mean the turf and the horses—" He was teasing again, and she realized that she loved the way he liked to tweak her. Rile her a bit. It brought out a daring in her she hadn't known she possessed.

"No, the grass and the flowers," she countered, raising her nose in the air. "And the carriage ride, but the company I am starting to rethink."

"You aren't mad at me, are you?" he asked, tugging the cork from a bottle and taking a drink from it. Just like that. No glasses, not even a tumbler. Charlotte found it deliciously wicked.

"Mad? Whatever for?" For giving her this perfect picnic? This delightful afternoon?

Charlotte lay back on the carriage blanket Sebastian had purloined from the Earl of Rockhurst's curricle and gazed up at the blue sky, wondering what heaven could offer that she hadn't found in the last hour or so.

They'd feasted on roasted fowl, thick bread with a large pat of butter, two kinds of cheese, and a pair of apples from the basket Sebastian had purchased, along with a bottle of French wine (also purloined from Rockhurst's carriage).

"For taking you away from your pleasures."

Her gaze jerked up to meet his. "Pleasures?"

He offered her the bottle, and she politely shook her head. After a shrug, he took another drink and shoved the cork back in. "Your usual pleasures—dice, the races, the cards . . . the boxing." He waggled his brows.

Charlotte sat up. "Oh, heavens, no."

" 'Heavens no'?" he repeated. "You sound like one of my spinster sisters. Where's my salty gel, my plain-spoken Lottie?" He feigned an exaggerated pose, his hand thrown back on his forehead and his voice rising in a falsetto, "Demmit to hell, Trent, if I want to dice my garters away 'tis none of your bloody concern."

Charlotte laughed despite herself. "I would never say such a thing."

"Yes, I suppose not," he conceded. "It was missing at least one more profanity and at least two obscenities."

This was perfect! She knew as much about cursing as she did . . . about other matters. Yet there was something else about his performance that stopped her. "You don't find this procliv—I mean—my proclivity for such language rather shocking?" She sat up on her heels. "Scandalous, really?"

He laughed. "Lottie, nothing you could ever say would shock me—I love everything about you."

His confession took her aback. He loved this Lottie despite her penchant for gambling, for her unladylike vocabulary? Loved her despite the fact that nearly every man in London knew what she looked like in her altogether?

Loved her utterly and completely?

"In fact, I wager there is nothing you could say that would shock me." His brows waggled at her, his challenge thrown down like a gauntlet between them.

Charlotte knew a proper lady would never respond to such a wager. Try to scandalize a gentleman of one's acquaintance? Why, the notion was ruinous.

Yet his smugness turned out to be too tempting.

What have I to lose? As far as Lord Trent—oh, bother, all of London—is concerned, I am ruined.

So whyever shouldn't she try?

Propped up on one elbow, he was in the process of plucking the petals from a hapless daisy, pretending to ignore her. "What? The indomitable Mrs. Townsend speechless? Shall I send a notice to the *Morning Post*?"

"Oh, let me think."

"You have to think about it?" Sebastian stole the apple from her hand and took a bite from it before he gave it back. He crunched happily on his stolen fruit, making it all that much harder for Charlotte to think of something truly scandalous.

After a lifetime spent avoiding anything even remotely untoward, it wasn't easy to just dive into such unknown waters. Why, before this morning, she'd never been kissed. Never seen a man in his . . . well, without his . . .

The image of Sebastian's naked body striding about her room teased her imagination. Ruinous. And suddenly the most scandalous thing she could think of was quite obvious.

"I want to go to the museum," she declared. "I want to see Lord Townley's collection of Grecian statues."

Sebastian's mouth opened. Gaped, actually. He just stared at her. "You want to see what?"

"Townley's Grecian marbles."

And suddenly she realized she'd done it, quite shocked him.

But not for the reasons she supposed.

"You minx," he said, starting to laugh. Rolling on his back, he let out a roar. "You nearly had me there, Lottie. Townley's statues, indeed!"

She poked him in the ribs. "I'm serious," she told him. "I want to see them. I've heard tell they are breathtaking."

"From one breathtaking nude to another?"

She crossed her arms over her chest, not amused in the least. "I think the experience would be edifying. I've read the guidebook and all the accounts in the papers . . ." What she couldn't say was that his sister and mother had regaled her with descriptions of the statues since they'd gone to see them, and she'd been dying of jealousy to view what most of proper London deemed indecent.

He stopped laughing and turned his head toward her. His eyes narrowed as he studied her. "You're serious! You want to go see those demmed things."

She nodded.

"And here I thought you couldn't shock me. Lottie Townsend, millinery aficionado, whist wastrel, denizen of the dice, a secret bluestocking?" He let out a low whistle. "Who would believe such a thing? Not even the *Post* would print such a revelation." He shook his head. "You don't really have the guidebook, do you?"

She nodded.

His eyes widened, then he threw up his hands in defeat.

"So I won?" she asked. "I shocked you?"

"Yes, you won," he conceded. "But don't think of collecting anytime soon. I've already put up everything I've got to cover that bet with Merrick."

His glib words nearly tripped right past her, for she was still in alt over her victory. Yet there had been a small trembling note when he'd said "put up everything I've got" that rattled her attention.

"You did what?" she whispered.

"Bet everything on that horse you fancied." He grinned recklessly, with no apology. "If it loses, I'll be in dun territory for sure. Won't be anything left for me to do but—"

Charlotte's heart stilled as his whimsical grin faded. *Marry Miss Burke.*

Those unsaid words hung between them like a hangman's noose.

Marry Miss Burke? Why, it would be the end of everything.

Of them.

"How could you do such a thing?"

"You funny girl," he said, reaching out to ruffle her hair. "What is money when I've lost my heart? That's always been enough for us. And we've always known that it was only a matter of time before . . . well, at least as long as you remain dead set against—"

From the field below, a horn bellowed, stopping his

speech. Whatever he'd been about to reveal might have been important, but as the horn blared again, they sat up in unison and looked down at the track.

"The race!" Sebastian said, jumping to his feet. "Come along, Lottie, my love. Let's go see what the Fates have in store for us. Let's see if this Boreas is as fast as the wind, or at the very least, faster than Lord Saunderton's storied nag."

Chapter 7

*O**h, how can this be?** Charlotte worried as they ran hand in hand down the hillside. How could Sebastian have bet all his ready cash on the outcome of a horse race?

Bet their future on her hunch?

They dashed past the now empty booths, forgotten hands of whist, and the quiet roulette wheels. Everyone, it seemed, had left their vice of choice to watch the much anticipated and heavily wagered race.

"Demmit!" Sebastian cursed. "They've already started."

"What does it matter but the finish?" she shot back.

"True enough," he admitted as he pulled her through the crowd.

Instead of sharing the excitement of everyone around her, Charlotte's heart clenched with a sense of dread. "I wish you hadn't bet your money on this. What if I'm wrong?"

He turned and stared at her. "Whatever has come over

you today? Worried about me losing? I'd think you'd be more concerned about going home and telling Finny that you've lost the greengrocer's money for the month—or worse, the blunt to cover her half of Madame Claudius's latest bill. You know how she is about your gambling." He chucked her lightly under the chin, then kissed her forehead. "Never mind her—if she starts to ring a peel over your head, tell her you heard about her offering her stockings to Lord Reynolds the other night to pay her *vingt-et-un* losses." He laughed again. "That Finny!"

"Oh, yes," Charlotte agreed, "she's quite something." She closed her eyes and tried to blot out the image of her proper and spinsterly cousin offering her stockings to anyone. No, she needed to think, and think quickly.

What if Boreas didn't win? What if Sebastian lost all his money?

Then where would her wish be? She might still be the woman he loved, but he'd be married in short order to Lavinia Burke and her ten thousand a year.

Charlotte looked up at this man she'd thought she'd known, this man she'd wished to know, with his tall beaver hat askew, his cravat ruffled and open, his eyes sparkling with excitement, and his arm tossed over her shoulders without a care in the world. He looked down at her and winked, as if there was nothing more than this very moment.

"Never you fret, Lottie," he whispered, "nothing will part us but time."

And then Charlotte understood what it was she'd wished for. For a moment like this, when they were pressed from all sides, surrounded by the cheering crowd, hardly alone, and yet in their own world.

Because he loved her.

And she him.

But there was no denying that his financial state would bring them both to a choice she had no desire to make. Not yet. Not now.

Not when she'd just gotten her wish. And discovered the true joy of love.

A shout rose even as the ground began to tremble with the thunder of hooves.

"They're coming," Charlotte said, rising up on her tiptoes and straining to spy the finish line. "Oh, bother, I can't see!"

"Neither can I." Sebastian looked around, then caught her by the waist and tossed her up atop a large keg. "How's that?" he shouted at her above the cheers and cries filling the air.

Teetering on her perch, she clung to his hand to steady herself. Over the sea of beaver hats and the occasional plumes, Charlotte's gaze swung first in the direction of the horses.

Boreas looked like his namesake, streaking across the meadow in a blinding dash, his jockey clinging to his back while the great horse thundered toward his destiny. But to her horror, he was just behind Lord Saunderton's roan.

Behind?

Charlotte's panic hurtled her well outside the constraints of her ingrained Mayfair manners.

Oh, the devil take the beast, this would never do! "Demmit, run!" she screamed. "Run, Boreas, run!"

The horses moved neck and neck, and Charlotte clung to Sebastian's hand, even as she found herself precariously hopping up and down, shouting every bit of encouragement she could to the horse.

And then the race was over as quickly as it had started,

and Charlotte froze, lost in a daze, as if she couldn't quite believe what she'd just seen. Around her, a portion of the crowd went wild with glee, while a good part of the company groaned as they realized they had lost whatever gold they had bet.

"Who won?" Sebastian demanded, spinning her to face him. "Demmit, which one was it?"

Her gaze slid down toward his, and for a moment all she could do was stare at him in wonder.

Then she gave over to the wild grin that sprang from her heart.

"Huzzah!" Sebastian shouted.

Toppled by a boisterous pair of men well into their cups, Charlotte fell happily into Sebastian's embrace, let him catch her in his arms and pull her into a heady kiss.

His lips plundered hers, covering her mouth, his tongue sweeping over hers, tasting and tempting her. One hand tucked beneath her bottom, he tugged her closer yet, until they were nearly as intimate as they had been this morning in her bed.

Her heart, still beating wildly from the excitement of the race, now went into a tempestuous tattoo. His lips went from her mouth to her neck, and the heat of his kiss was enough to make her knees sag beneath her.

"Gads, Lottie, I love you," he whispered in a ragged sigh. "I love you like no other. Always will, my girl."

With his hands cupping her face, he kissed her again, this time slowly and with a note of tenderness that left Charlotte thinking just one thing.

If only I had one more wish. . . .

"And don't get any ideas about me coming in," Sebastian told her a few hours later. "As much as I'd love to spend the rest of the evening in your bed, you know very well I can't." He paused for a moment, then grinned. "At least not until later."

After Boreas's win, they had kissed and danced a wild jig together round and round the barrel. Never mind that the crowd had laughed with them or just outright stared at their outlandish antics, Charlotte hadn't cared. She'd never felt so unencumbered, so very free in her entire life.

And rich! When Merrick had come ambling up to tell her the sum of her winnings (given the fact Rockhurst's unpredictable horse had been a long shot), she hadn't been able to fathom what she would do with such a windfall.

Then, when the sun had dipped low in the horizon, they'd driven the hour back to town, crossing under the gates into London, and venturing through the streets of Bloomsbury.

When Sebastian had turned down a street—Little Titchfield—and pulled to a stop before a house in the middle of the block, she'd been about to protest that this wasn't where she lived.

Yet it was. She reminded herself that she no longer resided in Cousin Finella's old, narrow house off Berkeley Square. She glanced up at *her* house and gazed in wonder at the cheery window boxes filled with flowers, the gauzy curtains and the bright blue door.

"Here you are," he announced.

Charlotte took another glance at the door. Suddenly an uneasy air of shyness settled over her. Lottie's infamous house. Her new life.

Whatever did she do now? She resorted to the only thing she did know. Mayfair manners.

"Thank you for bringing me home, Lord Trent," she said, still eyeing the house before her with a measure of trepidation. If she invited him inside, then he'd want to . . .

Charlotte sucked in a deep breath. Kissing Sebastian was one thing, but finding herself with him like she had this morning, naked and entwined, that was another altogether.

However could she do that?

Meanwhile, he'd laughed at her prim offering and bounded down from the carriage, coming around to her side to help her down. "I'm glad I could be of assistance, Mrs. Townsend." His mock formality held little pretense, for he winked saucily at her when he said it.

His flirtatious, covetous gaze slanted right through her sensibilities. She tried to breathe, tried to think of what she should do next. Thank him politely at the curb and offer a sincere handshake before sending him off to . . . to *her*?

No, no, a handshake would never do! She couldn't send him off to the Burkes with his last thought of her being the embroidery pattern on the back of her glove.

It irked Charlotte, much as it had before, that Lavinia Burke held a part of Sebastian's life that she couldn't enter.

Charlotte screwed up her courage as he tugged her down from her seat, his hands catching her by her hips and swinging her down to the cobbles. She let herself fall into his chest, and her hands went straight to his shoulders, finding a steady hold. Without even realizing what she was doing, she stepped closer to him and tipped her head back to look up into his dark eyes.

Perhaps this wasn't as difficult as she'd thought.

"Now don't you even dare," he warned.

"Dare what?"

"Your tricks."

She had tricks? "Whyever not?" she ventured, feeling positively daring. It was hard not to feel thusly with him holding her so.

"You know exactly why. First it will be, 'Sebastian, see me to the door—'"

"And what is wrong with that?"

"Because once we're at the door, you'll turn to me, just as you are now, and demand a kiss."

Oh, this Mrs. Townsend was a cheeky chit. "Me?" Charlotte tried not to grin, impressed with Lottie's prowess in these matters.

"Yes, you."

"Would it work?" she asked, trying not to sound too hopeful.

Lottie Townsend was cheeky; Charlotte Wilmont still had a respectable foot in Mayfair. Yet something pushed her to forget about that previous existence. Whatever had being a proper spinster gained her? And there was something all too tempting about being Sebastian's mistress, the woman he loved, that lent her a brazen sense of adventure.

"Do tell, my lord," she said again. "Would it work?"

"Not today it won't," he declared, setting her out of his arms and standing his ground.

But Charlotte wasn't so convinced and moved back into the warmth of his shadow. "And say you did see me to the door—"

He crossed his arms over his chest, his brow arched. "Which I will not—"

"Yes, so you say," she agreed readily, reaching up and placing her hand on his sleeve. "But say you did. And at the door, I was bold enough to ask you for a kiss and you, being the gentleman that we know you are, gave in to my forward request? What harm is there in that?"

An odd, wary look crossed his features. "Why do you do this, Lottie?"

"Do what?"

"Spend all day convincing me that you are utterly and completely in love with me—"

"But I—"

He waved off her protest. "And then in two days' time you'll be pelting me with your pretty little shoes, calling me all sorts of vulgar names, and tossing me out your door."

Charlotte shivered. She did that? Suddenly her admiration for Lottie went down several notches. "Perhaps I've had a change of heart," she rushed to say.

And life . . . and outlook . . . and well, everything.

He snorted and kept his wary stance.

With both hands on his sleeves, she pulled herself closer. "Believe me, the last thing I would ever do is cast you from my life, from my heart."

He stared down at her, and she sensed the struggle within him, wary, yet full of longing to believe her. With a strangled sort of cry, his hands snaked out and caught hold of her, tugging her close. Without any prelude, let alone a request, his lips covered hers.

As it did each time, his kiss took her by surprise. For a moment, she felt (despite all her bravado) nothing but panic—for after all she was being kissed quite shamelessly by Lord Trent in the middle of the street—but that fleeting bit of alarm had little time to find roots before it was cleared away by that same delicious warmth of pleasure that he brought to life within her.

Her body melted into his, her breasts pressed against the sharp crisp wool of his jacket, her hips coming home against his.

She didn't even realize she was sighing as she made out the hardness beneath his breeches.

And since she'd had a rather startling introduction earlier to just exactly what the viscount had concealed in his breeches, Charlotte felt a guilty desire to see it freed from its prison of buff leather.

Then just as suddenly as he'd started this kiss, he ended it, abruptly setting her aside and standing there staring at her with a turbulent fury ablaze in his eyes.

"You are a dangerously tempting woman, Lottie Townsend." And with that he got into his carriage and began to drive away, but not before he said one last thing that sent a shiver of anticipation down her still trembling limbs.

"We will finish this tonight, madame."

"Get inside with you," Finella said, towing Charlotte up the last few steps by her elbow.

She heaved a dewy sigh. Really, her cousin needn't tug so hard; she felt as if she could float along like a balloon.

Finella shot an aggrieved look at the departing viscount, then turned her critical gaze on her errant charge. Her hands fisted at her hips, her elbows jutted out like a pair of sails. "Look at you! Putting on another show in the street for Mrs. Spratling to see. Why you love to vex that old gossipy cat, I know not."

Since Charlotte had no idea who this Mrs. Spratling was, she couldn't really answer Finella's lament.

She was still lost in Sebastian's kiss, the dizzy, heady power of his touch.

"Lord Trent thinks I'm tempting," she said in a dreamy voice.

Finella shook her head. "Heavens above, what has come over you? You're acting as if you've never been kissed before." She steered her up the stairs toward her room. "Come along with you. You've barely enough time to get ready for this evening. Good God, what did you do to your dress? It's covered in mud and grass." She heaved an aggrieved sigh and made her way into the closet.

Charlotte barely heard a word she said.

We will finish this tonight, madame.

Finish this? Charlotte bit her lip and looked into the mirror over the dressing table, searching for answers in her reflection. What did that mean?

Her thighs tightened and her nipples grew taut. Well, yes, she had a vague idea what it meant, but however would she manage to . . . well, finish him?

And despite Quince's promise that she would eventually gain Lottie's memories, she needed them sooner rather than later. Or at least before Sebastian arrived.

"Lottie, I don't like to nag," Finella was saying from the depths of the closet.

Charlotte sighed and glanced in that direction. Quince had one thing right: There were some things that just couldn't be shifted.

Finella poked her head out the door. "I want you to pay special attention to the earl tonight."

"The earl?" Charlotte replied.

"Yes, the earl. Rockhurst." Finella eyed the dirty hem of Charlotte's gown again and shook her head. "You invited him to your box tonight, and it won't do if you spend the night flirting with him just to get Trent into some jealous rage."

She turned back inside the closet, so Charlotte called after her, "That works?"

Apparently her innocent question didn't set well with the lady, for there was a desperate groan from inside. "Lottie, you are incorrigible. You know as well as I, there isn't anything wrong with getting a man worked up a bit afore he comes to call." Finella returned carrying a large bundle wrapped in brown paper and tied up with string. "There were times when I fancied it a bit rough like that," she said with her own little dreamy smile. Then she sighed and went to a drawer, fetched a pair of scissors, and clipped the strings. She turned to Charlotte, wagging the scissors at her. "But it won't do to treat Rockhurst so shabbily. Not when he's been so attentive of late. You are going to have to send Trent packing sooner or later— sooner, I pray—and it is better to have your next favorite ready and happily willing, rather than leave yourself out there with no protection." She stowed the scissors back in the drawer and started to unwrap the mysterious bundle.

Protection. That word tolled in Charlotte's ears like a funeral bell. "Lyman," she whispered.

"Lyman!" Finella gasped, the paper and tangle of strings forgotten. "Don't tell me that sanctimonious prig has been bothering you again?"

Charlotte turned toward the mirror, tucking a stray strand of her hair over the scrape. She could imagine the scene Finella would raise if she knew the entire story. She certainly couldn't tell her cousin that she'd gone home to Mayfair, since it really wasn't her home anymore. Besides, she had a feeling that such a tale would give the lady another lament to lie at her feet, like an eager bricklayer. "He drove past me when I was—"

"You stay away from him," Finella said, with nothing

left to shake but her finger. "Stay well out of his path. Besides, you'll never have to take the likes of him to your bed, not as long as you have your looks and this . . ." She held up a gown for Charlotte's examination.

"Oh, my," she whispered, her gaze feasting on the gorgeous blue velvet evening dress. With cut work in the front of the low bodice, and slashing in the short sleeves, it was the most elegant creation she'd ever beheld . . . let alone worn.

Finella smiled, her pique over Charlotte's disappearance and reluctance as to Rockhurst's attentions completely forgotten. "I think Madame Claudius outdid herself on this one. I picked it up for you this afternoon, as well as the hat." She handed the dress to Charlotte, then went back into the closet to return with a narrow blue silk hat, trimmed around the edges and finished with three great plumes that fell saucily from one side.

"I won't lose you to the likes of Lyman," Finella continued. "But Rockhurst—" She made a purring noise that sounded as satisfied as the Lottie-on-the-wall looked. "Now he would treat you well. And be a very good lover. Can last all night. And he's not about to get up and take his leave when he's spent his share, if you know what I mean. Likes to do it in the French fashion as well. At least that is what Mrs. Vache told Madame Claudius."

Thankfully, Finella pulled the blue gown over Charlotte's head at that moment, for she thought her cheeks were now as red as her cousin's dress.

French lovemaking? Oh, dear heavens! She hadn't the vaguest notion of English relations, let alone exploring Continental inclinations.

"And Monsieur Detchant told Madame Claudius, oh, you know him, that tailor down across from Madame

Claudius's, well, monsieur tells her that Lord Rockhurst does not need a bit of padding in his breeches. That he's like a stallion." Finella made that hungry, purring noise again.

"Please!" Charlotte protested, covering her ears lest Finella go into further details. "Enough about the earl." Gads, how was she ever going to look at the man, let alone sit next to him through an entire opera knowing that he was . . . well, um, sufficiently male.

Having seen Lord Trent in his natural state had been enough. If Rockhurst was more generously endowed, she had to think the earl had more in common with his unpredictable Boreas than just temperament.

"Oh, don't be so missish," Finella cackled. "I know you think Lord Trent is the finest lover in all of creation, and Lord knows, you look well satisfied most days, but he's up the River Tick."

"Not quite," Charlotte told her. "He won a tidy sum at the races today." Even as she said it, she realized she'd stepped into another quagmire with her cousin.

The lady's hands went back to her hips. "The races? That certainly explains your hemline! But Lottie, you promised! No more gambling. Do you know how many ladies in our delicate situation have been ruined by dice and horses?"

"Or one too many hands of *vingt-et-un*?" Charlotte replied, thinking of the little *on dit* Sebastian had shared earlier.

Finella's jaw worked back and forth, and she eyed Charlotte as if trying to determine just how much she knew . . . and it seemed that the lady didn't want to risk a comparison of recent losses. After a few minutes of fussing with Charlotte's hair, she asked ever-so-nonchalantly, "Did you win?"

Charlotte nodded. "Eight hundred pounds."

This brought a wide grin to her cousin's face. "Well, I suppose that makes up for what we haven't been getting from Trent." And while Charlotte's bounty seemed to take some of the wind from Finella's determined sails, the lady soon returned to her favorite subject.

"My dear girl, it's well enough to take a lover for the pure entertainment of it, but you've been with Trent for nearly a year and your income is dwindling. You need another Chesam, a man who'll leave you a tidy annuity and another house." Finella plopped the hat on her head, the plumes undulating with seductive charm. "Preferably one in the country."

Charlotte discovered that Mrs. Lottie Townsend did little in moderation. The finest gowns, the fanciest carriage, and a splendid box at the opera.

A subscription, she had learned from Finella, left to her by old Chesam.

Charlotte wasn't too sure she wanted to remember *every* aspect of Lottie's life—recalling nights spent with Sebastian were one thing, but two years with an aging duke hardly sounded entertaining or worth reminiscing over.

She settled into her seat and started looking through her reticule for the glasses she'd seen Finella drop inside.

"Mrs. Townsend, how nice to see you this evening," came the greeting over the low wall that separated her from the next box.

Charlotte glanced up and was stunned to find herself being greeted by Lord Pilsley.

Her mother's husband.

"Lord Pilsley," she managed, craning her neck to see who else was with the viscount.

"A lovely gown you have on tonight," the old man was saying. "But then you always are a fair sight to behold." The man lurched forward, as if prodded from behind, and indeed he had been. It wasn't until he sat down in his seat, smiling apologetically at her, that Charlotte saw the woman beside him.

Her mother.

She opened her mouth to greet her, looking for recognition, but all she received from Lady Pilsley was the arched and furious look that Charlotte knew from experience was a harbinger of an angry outburst. Nose in the air, and with another poke into her husband's ribs with her fan, Aurora made a very obvious point of shifting herself away from Charlotte's box.

Shunned! By her own mother! Charlotte sat back and tried to blink away the growing moisture in her eyes. However had this come about? Certainly her mother had never been a fine example of maternal affection, but Charlotte had always supposed that her own shortcomings had been the cause of the lady's coldness toward her only child.

There was no time to puzzle this mystery further, for a deep male chuckle from the curtain behind her interrupted her thoughts.

She turned to find Rockhurst standing there, looking ever the dashing Corinthian.

Her gaze swept for an alarming second down past his waistcoat to his taut black pantaloons. *Like a stallion.*

Leave it to Finella to uncover the truth of the matter, as it were.

However, the evidence of Rockhurst's endowment only alarmed Charlotte rather than enticed her, contrary to Finella's assurances that such a thing was desirable.

She yanked her gaze up at the man himself and tried to smile as if she hadn't the vaguest notion of what he possessed beneath his stylish and too-snug breeches.

From the cocksure look on his face, he'd obviously witnessed her curious glance, and he strode into the box with an air of smug confidence. Throwing himself down in the seat beside her, he stuck his legs out in front of him and turned a dazzling grin at her. "Provoking Lady Pilsley again? You have a devilish sense of humor, Mrs. Townsend." He tipped his head closer. "'Tis why I like you."

Charlotte pulled back, alarmed at his proximity. "You like me?"

He laughed. "Obviously I'm not tipping Finny enough, or the depth of my affections wouldn't be such a surprise. Then again, you know well enough that everyone in Town admires you." He glanced over at the next box. "With the distinct exception of Lady Pilsley." He looked around Charlotte's empty box and smiled again. "I see we are alone tonight. No hungry hordes of your admirers to crowd me? Perhaps that case of brandy I sent 'round to Finny wasn't wasted after all."

That explained Rockhurst's knowledge of her gown this morning and Finella's enthusiastic and unending stream of praise for the man.

The earl continued, "Or is our intimate evening planned so our mutual friend has a clear vantage from which to see you flirt so outrageously with me?" He nodded his head across the floor of the opera house to the boxes opposite hers.

She looked up to find Sebastian staring at her. A smile rose on her lips immediately, and she was about to wave at him until she realized he wasn't alone.

Beside him sat a glowering Miss Burke.

For a moment, Charlotte forgot that she was wearing the most elegant gown she'd ever seen. Forgot that she was Lottie Townsend, celebrated beauty and most desired woman in London.

Looking at Lavinia Burke, who was still the same pretty, polished, and perfect miss that she had been before, it was hard to think of herself as anything other than Miss Charlotte Wilmont, poor overlooked spinster.

Charlotte sank in her seat, her heart trembling. How could she compete with the likes of Miss Burke?

Oh, it was hardly fair! Why had so much changed but not *her*? When Quince had turned the world upside down, why hadn't she tipped Miss Burke on her pert nose and given her a good shake?

"She's quite pretty, don't you think?" Rockhurst asked, leaning close again. "If I were in Trent's thin shoes I'd probably chase after her as well. When you must marry an heiress, might as well marry a pretty one, I say."

Only one thought saved Charlotte from a bout of frustrated tears. "He doesn't love her."

Rockhurst laughed, loudly and thoroughly, drawing a censorious glance from Lady Pilsley. "Love? When did you, my cynical, mercenary little light-skirt, have anything to do with such a foolish notion as love?"

"I-I-," she stammered and hemmed as she tried to explain herself.

Meanwhile, Rockhurst leaned back in his seat and was

taking in the crowd filling the house. "If I didn't know better, I'd say you were in love with him." He made an indelicate snort. "Now wouldn't that be a lark?"

"I-I-" *Of course I am in love with him. I've been in love with him for years and I intend to stay that way until the day I die.* But instead of making her very Charlotte protest, she turned away, remembering Finella's tirade on the same subject.

Whatever is wrong with being in love? she wanted to ask them all. *Whatever is wrong with Sebastian being in love with me?*

She snuck another glance over at Sebastian, who sat there, smiling down at Miss Burke, hanging on her every word, every flutter of her yellow silk fan. *Please, Sebastian,* she wished, *look at me.*

And by some miracle of fate, he did. His gaze rose immediately and met hers without hesitation. His eyes narrowed for a second, but then she saw it.

A flash. That connection. And moreover, she felt it. Right down to her silken-clad toes. As if his gaze had raked over the bare skin of her neck with the same heat that his kiss had evoked earlier.

And that wasn't the only place she felt it, but she still wasn't Lottie enough to admit such a thing.

Not that Sebastian stopped there. His hand rose and raked through his dark hair.

And she could feel it. *Remember it.*

"Lottie, how I love your hair." His fingers combed through the strands, greedily pulling the pins free to gather it all into his eager grasp.

The sensation was so real, the memory so vivid, her fingers rose to check to make sure her carefully arranged coiffure was still in place.

Even so, her scalp tingled, her body coming alive, clamoring greedily for its fair share of his touch.

And across the opera house, Sebastian smiled ever so slightly. *As if he knew.*

Charlotte shifted in her seat as a devilish heat spread through her veins.

Sebastian's hand moved from his head down over his coat, slowly and carefully brushing at an imaginary hair or bit of lint on his breast.

Her nipples tightened as if his fingers were giving the same lazy attention to her. Charlotte's breath froze in her throat. How was he doing this?

A deep, tempting voice whispered up from the recesses of her memories. *Do you want more, Lottie? Do you like it when I do this?*

As his fingers picked at his coat, slowly and tantalizing, she swore her nipple was going to burst with need.

Oh, enough, she wanted to tell him. Better that than give into the wanton desire to tug down her bodice, free her tortured breasts and plead with him to help himself. To kiss her. To kiss her aching nipples until she . . .

Now, Sebastian. Please, Sebastian.

Memories crashed down on her like waves of something she didn't understand but craved with a need that couldn't be quenched.

His naked body tangled with hers. The glimmer of sweat on his back, the salty taste of him. The smooth plain of his chest, the thick corded muscles of his thighs. The way he grinned as he rolled her beneath him and covered her.

Filled her, thrusting inside her.

Her hips rising to meet him. Her needs and his so very

intertwined, until she knew not how to distinguish the two, didn't care.

Charlotte writhed in her seat. She hadn't the vaguest notion how this was happening, but one thing was for certain, now she knew. Knew so very much.

Images, memories filled her dizzy thoughts.

Sebastian's kiss spreading a fire through her limbs, and his lips blazing a tortured path across her body. She spread herself open to his touch, to his exploration, only too willing to be his India, his distant shore.

His breath, hot and thick, blew over her very core, sending a trembling wave of desire through her.

He wasn't going to kiss her *there* . . . he couldn't . . . why, it was . . .

Heaven.

Suddenly her fears over Finella's lectures on French relations seemed silly, for if this was Paris, she was going to find a tricorn hat, stick a cockade in it, and let out an impatient and heady cry of "*Vive la France.*"

And when his tongue touched her, washed over her in hurried laps, she writhed again, her hips rising to meet this memory with a ragged need.

Charlotte could see where this writhing could become quite contagious. She closed her eyes, tried to blot out the memories, tried to stop the flow, but she couldn't any more than she could stop the trembling need inside her.

. . . his hands pressed her thighs further apart, while his tongue delved deeper, swiping over her hungrily, sending stabbing waves of desire through her.

She looked up wildly at him, her gaze meeting his darkly dancing eyes.

Now, Sebastian, please, Sebastian, her imagination cried out.

A slow smile spread over his lips, as if he knew her thoughts, held her need in the palm of his hand. Had the power to grant her this release, this completion that she'd never known.

Until now. Until she'd wished for his love and discovered that it held so much more than his kind regard, than just a handful of orange blossoms.

How could she have been so naive? Charlotte glanced up at him again and understood what love meant, not the starry-eyed version of poets and lovelorn fools but the deep, abiding passion that rose between a man and a woman when they shared each other's thoughts, choices, their very desires.

Please, Sebastian. Oh, demmit, please.

He nodded to her, ever so slowly, while his tongue slid over his lips.

"Oh my," she gasped, as the rest of the memories burst free inside her. Brought with them that same sweet joy that Lottie-on-the-wall held in her secretive smile.

Oh, this isn't possible, Charlotte thought as she tried to catch her breath, as her body continued to unravel in pleasure. Waves of it.

Then the lights came up and a thunderous applause filled the house. The first act was over and she hadn't noticed a single note of it.

She raised her gaze to Sebastian and smiled at him, sighing with completion.

In turn, he grinned at her.

And then their moment was broken as Miss Burke, looking from one to the other, realized that her almost-betrothed wasn't giving her the due attention she deserved.

She said something to Sebastian, and when he didn't reply, she fluttered her fan clumsily and sent it flying into his lap.

It landed like a thunderbolt and ripped the two lovers apart.

Sebastian retrieved the ivory and silk and with great gallantry handed it over to the pretty little heiress. After a few more exchanges, the preening debutante shot a hot glance across the way, lobbing it like a cannonball in Charlotte's direction.

He will be mine, her cold eyes seemed to say. *Completely.*

Something hot and green stabbed through Charlotte's veins. *Never. Never. Never.*

She doubted the other girl would find much joy in a purloined picnic or a wild carriage ride, or dancing a jig over gambling winnings, let alone nights spent reading Coleridge. But most importantly, she would never know his passion.

Oh, yes, his passion.

What was it Quince had told her when she'd protested about all these changes?

Let him love you, and the rest, well . . .

Let him love you . . .

Charlotte smiled, for now she understood exactly what Quince had meant. And what she needed to do.

She'd love him back, with her heart, her soul, and, most decidedly, with her body.

Chapter 8

Sitting in the Opera House and giving into fantasies spun from Lottie's memories was one thing; it was another entirely to be standing in her drawing room waiting for Sebastian to arrive.

So much for Quince's assurances that all she had to do was remember. . . .

Charlotte hugged herself and closed her eyes. It was the remembering that had her quaking from the top of her plumes to the bottom of her tasseled shoes.

Oh, it was easy to pretend to be Lottie Townsend, she realized, having spent the rest of the evening enthusiastically greeting her rush of admirers in the hallway with a wide smile, and then flirting outrageously with Rockhurst through the second act while watching Sebastian glower from across the way.

But when Rockhurst had dropped her off, and the chill of the cobblestones had come creeping through her slippers, Charlotte had stopped at the bottom of the steps and looked up at her house.

Her house. A boon she'd gained by being the mistress of a duke. By letting him into her bed and allowing him to . . .

She'd shuttered her eyes and told herself that hadn't been her. That had been Lottie's scandalous doings. But she was Lottie now, and that meant that Sebastian would be coming up these same steps sometime during this very night, with expectations that had nothing to do with daydreams and everything to do with satin sheets and a decided lack of clothing . . .

"Mrs. Townsend, mum?"

Lottie turned and found the maid in the doorway of the salon. Oh, heavens! Was he here already?

"Um, uh," she stammered, trying to think of how she should respond. It might help if she could remember the maid's name. Botheration, what was it?

The girl shifted from one foot to another. "I took the tray over to that Herr Tromler fellow, and if you don't need anything more, I'll be going down to my room for the night. Mrs. Finella said she wouldn't be home until late and wouldn't need me."

"Herr Tromler?"

"The German fellow."

Charlotte bit her lip and shrugged.

The maid sighed. "The one next door. You said I was supposed to feed him at least once a day so he'll play his violin for you."

As if on cue, sweet strains of music exquisitely wrought could be heard, the notes winding their way through the open windows.

Charlotte stood spellbound. "That's him?"

"Oh, aye, ma'am. Nice of you to feed 'im, if you don't mind me saying. His landlady made him sell his coat last week to pay 'is rent." She paused and tipped her head to listen, a puzzled look on her face. "Fancy music that, but don't see that it's worth a beefsteak."

Not worth a beefsteak? Charlotte closed her eyes and listened. Why, it was worth the entire cow. She stood there for another moment, wondering why this Herr Tromler wasn't playing for the *ton* every night, giving command performances for the King himself, the music so seductive, so sensual it eased her fears, made her forget her usual worries of being cautious and prudent.

Prudence! Her name was Prudence.

"Yes, Prudence!" she declared.

"Aye, mum. Is that all, mum?" the girl prodded.

"Oh, yes. So sorry. Yes, I don't see that I'll need anything else."

" 'Cept the door, I suppose."

"The door?"

"Aye, ma'am. That's the bell ringing. Should I see who it is?" She had a sly look on her face, as if it were no surprise that someone would be calling at this hour.

Charlotte's frantic gaze flew up. He was here? *Now?*

Oh, heavens, how would she ever manage to survive this night?

From the window, the enticing notes from Herr Tromler's violin stole around her fears, enticed them to flee into the night and let the hour be given over to another kind of pleasure.

"Mum? The door?"

Charlotte's head snapped up as the bell jangled yet again. What if he was, as Cousin Finella had suggested earlier, "worked up a bit"?

Well, it seemed she was about to find out. Taking a deep breath, she nodded to Prudence. "Yes, please see to it."

The girl bobbed her head and left Charlotte alone, surrounded by the softly sensual and all too romantic strains of Herr Tromler's violin.

She stood transfixed listening to Prudence open the door and, in turn, Sebastian's deep voice inquiring if Mrs. Townsend was at home.

All so formal and proper. Charlotte would have laughed if it hadn't been for the panic welling up inside her. Better that, she reasoned, than him storming in, tossing her roughly over his shoulder, and carting her upstairs for a night of French debauchery.

Oui, oh, oui, cried out that scandalous part of Lottie's memories. *Très bon!*

"Oh, yes, very easy for you to say," Charlotte muttered back. "But whatever will I say to him?"

She turned and paced about the room as she listened to Prudence taking his coat and hat, and Sebastian making a few flirtatious comments about Prudence's red hair.

That was it! Small talk. About the weather. She could see the entire scene scripted like one of Lady Walbrook's wretched adaptations of Shakespeare.

SEBASTIAN: 'Tis a fine night.
CHARLOTTE: Verily, my lord. Quite mild for this time of year.
SEBASTIAN: Shall we to bed, anon?
CHARLOTTE: Thou art a knavish, impatient fellow.

Oh, heavens. She swallowed down another wave of panic. Would he ask or did she have to invite him to come upstairs to . . . to . . .

Charlotte closed her eyes and hoped that he was the one who was supposed to suggest they retire anon, for she hadn't the vaguest notion how she would ever get the words out.

"Do I hear correctly? You're still feeding Herr Tromler?"

She whirled around to find him standing in the doorway, resplendent in his evening clothes.

A dark blue jacket, lacy white cravat spilling over his embroidered waistcoat, the silver threads twinkling in the candlelight. His buff trousers cut just so—just so it was obvious that Lord Rockhurst wasn't the only man in the *ton* who didn't need padding.

But it was more than the clothes, for while they gave him polish and flair, his chiseled jawline, his black hair, his deep green eyes, the commanding taut set of his shoulders would have made him a standout anywhere.

Sebastian Marlowe had to be, in her humble estimation, the most handsome man in all of London.

For one wild moment, Charlotte's panic took another turn. He would need to remove those clothes to . . . well, to get on with this business, and she certainly didn't know how to undress a man.

She wasn't even going to consider how hers came off, though she suspected, given the dangerous light in Sebastian's eyes, that he'd manage.

He tipped his head, still listening. "Whatever are you feeding him, Lottie? He's in rare form tonight."

"Beefsteaks," she whispered, almost afraid to say anything.

Sebastian grinned, crossing the room and pulling her into his arms. "You have a heart of gold, Mrs. Townsend." With that, he began nuzzling her neck, sending frissons of desire down her spine.

So much for the small talk.

"You are exquisite," he said. Then, just as quickly as he started, Sebastian pulled back. "Hold up there. I'm furious with you."

"With me?"

He strode over to the settee and settled down on it, not even waiting for her to sit. There was room next to him, but she chose the chair near the window.

Some courtesan you make, she could almost hear Lottie saying in her ear.

"Yes, with you. Don't think I didn't see you tonight. *With him*."

"Rockhurst?"

He laughed. "You sound as innocent as some Bath miss. Yes, with Rockhurst. If he wasn't my best friend, I'd probably call him out for his cheek. Courting you when he knows I can do naught about it but watch."

"You're jealous?" Charlotte tried to quell the joy that sprang up within her heart. Sebastian jealous over her! Why it was as unbelievable as all this wish nonsense.

"Of course I am. I was stuck listening to accounts of the weather, and whether it is proper to give a stirring recitation of a moral lesson or a sweetly recounted ballad for Lady Routledge's soirée." He shuddered at either notion. "And then what do I have to look at? You. Looking like a dream. I swore for a moment there I could smell your perfume from across the room. Feel the silk of your breasts beneath my fingers. Recall how we spent last night . . ." His words trailed off. "Devilishly embarrassing to be sitting there, hard as a rock and hoping like hell Lady Burke doesn't notice and think I am in this state over her preciously dull daughter." He snorted.

He wasn't even fond of Miss Burke?

No, wait . . . he'd felt it as well?

"I never meant to . . . I mean, if I had known—"

Sebastian came up from the couch and crossed the room in two easy strides. He caught her by the hand. "All I could think about was coming here, taking you in my arms, letting Herr Tromler's music seduce you into dancing with me in that German fashion everyone finds so scandalous." With that he swung her about the room, his hand on her waist and holding her right up against him.

"This is where you belong. Where I belong," he whispered in her ear.

For a time they danced, Sebastian whirling her about the room to the strains of the sensual music. "Do you remember the night we danced liked this until Finny came downstairs and told us to go upstairs and get on with our business so she could get some sleep?" Sebastian chuckled.

Charlotte didn't remember, so she just smiled in return. As the music swelled, Sebastian pulled her closer, and she felt as if she were floating about the room. Before, dances and balls had been torture, for she'd been sure she would miss a step or move out of turn, but this German dancing wasn't complicated in the least— especially with him holding her so . . . so . . . tightly. "I love this," she whispered.

"Yes, I know," he said, grinning down at her. "Perhaps it is a good thing you can't get vouchers—you'd set all the matrons teeth on edge because every man in Almack's would be lined up to dance with you."

"I doubt it would be like that."

"Undoubtedly. And there I would be, as footsore as I was last winter when you and Corinna threw that crush you called a ball and you wanted me with you at every dance. How very scandalous and unfashionable of you, Mrs. Townsend."

Charlotte sighed and wished again she could remember. She'd thrown a ball? With Mrs. Fornett? Better yet, she'd danced the entire night with Sebastian.

"I don't think I should worry about Rockhurst, it is that fellow next door I should be worried about," he was saying.

"How so?" she asked as he swirled her around again.

"Listen to his music," he said, jerking his head toward the window. "That is a man in love."

"With beefsteaks," Charlotte corrected.

"Not if he saw you in this dress . . . or better yet, out of it," he said, his lips coming down atop hers, softly, slowly, surely.

Like he had earlier, he left her trembling with his kiss.

"I know exactly what you were about this evening," Sebastian said as he turned her around the room one more time.

"You do?" Gads, she was glad he did, for she hadn't the vaguest notion why she would want to spend the evening with the earl when she could be kissing Sebastian.

"Oh, yes, you little minx. You spent the evening flirting—"

"I was not!"

He snorted. "You, madame, were flirting. And you did so because you wanted me to come storming over here afterward, angry and hot, and ready to lay claim to you." He caught her by the hand and tugged her quickly into his hard chest, his strong arms binding her to him with not the least bit of his earlier gentleness. His lips nibbled at that spot right behind her ear, his teeth nipping at her skin, while his hand clapped down on her bottom and pulled her right up against him.

Up against *that*.

Charlotte tried to breathe as her body reacted with needs that Lottie might love but she feared for the unknown fire they seemed to be kindling.

"Oh, yes, I know what you were about," he whispered, his voice rough and ragged. "You wanted me to come in here hot and hard and in a mood to ravish you thoroughly."

"I did?" Charlotte trembled, but not for the reasons he might think.

"Oh, yes, you did, you devilish little tease," he said, his knee nudging her legs apart, his hand running up her thigh, roaming right toward the very heat of desire.

"Oh, no," she whispered. Not as much from this forceful, towering Sebastian as from the dangerous course his hand was taking.

"But I'm not going to do that," he said, releasing her just as quickly as he'd snatched her into his grasp, just as she thought his fingers were going to reach their reward.

Her reward.

Charlotte staggered back, teetering on her high heels, teetering on the brink of need. She was panting—panting with a desire for this man—and her body trembled again, this time not from fear but from need. Bone jolting, down deep need.

"No, Lottie, I have no desire to ravish you, for I've devised a much better punishment."

Worse than this state she was in now? Charlotte didn't know if she could take much more.

"No, you little mistress of my heart, I've decided not to throw you down on that settee and claim you in that hot and fast way you crave."

Hot and fast? Right now if it would relieve her of this tormenting, trembling desire, she'd take the risk.

He circled behind her and she leaned back, letting her body meld into his, so she could feel that heat of his again. So they could sway again to the music.

But he didn't touch her, didn't attempt to drag her closer, and Charlotte was at a loss as to what she needed to do to get him . . . in a more ravishing state of mind.

She needn't have worried, for he leaned over and whispered in her ear, "I plan on seducing you tonight, madame. Slowly. Perfectly. Until you beg me to finish you."

Charlotte tried to breathe.

"Just breathe," she muttered under her breath as he circled around her, his hawkish gaze fixed on her with a predator's smug self-assurance.

Oh, heavens, what would Lottie do?

She closed her eyes. What Lottie would do wasn't going to help her right now. The woman was a veritable scandal. And Charlotte was . . . too innocent for this game of cat and mouse.

And her innocence was about to be devoured, she realized, as Sebastian reached out and trailed his fingers over her bare shoulder, making her nearly jump out of her heels.

"You're trembling," he whispered. "Are you worried, my love?"

You have no idea, she would have told him if she thought her lips could form the words.

"It isn't that I won't give you your reward," he was saying as his fingers trailed over the edge of her bodice. "But it will come at a price."

Her shoulders rolled with his touch, her skin tingling.

His lips nibbled at her neck, the back of her shoulders, her earlobe.

There was a price to all this? Whatever it was, she'd happily pay.

Tromler's music still filled the room, moody and taunting, much like Sebastian. He spun her around so she faced him, and immediately caught her lips in a staggering, hungry kiss.

Before when he'd kissed her it had left her unsteady and off balance, shocked by the intimacy of it. Beneath his kiss there was a sense of possession, of marking, his unspoken declaration of his desire, his love.

This tantalizing torture made her thighs clench together, as if trying to stop the fire kindling there with each swipe of his tongue.

Images from Lottie's memory assailed her as he kissed her.

His mouth on her breasts, sucking her nipple until it peaked, tight and hard. On her belly, blowing his hot breath over her skin. Going lower still and parting her nether lips, taking these same slow, dangerous swipes over her tight, throbbing nub.

"Oh," she moaned softly, both at the memory and because his hands had moved to cup her breasts, to roll his thumbs over her nipples.

"This dress is gorgeous," he said, casting barely a glance at it. "But I prefer you naked."

Before she could say anything, even try to lodge a protest, he pulled the short sleeves down. Somehow he'd managed to loosen the laces in back already—how, she wasn't quite sure, but it only proved her early realization that removing her clothes wasn't going to be any problem for him.

All too quickly, her gown plummeted to the ground in an expensive puddle of blue velvet, leaving her standing before him in nothing but her corset and garters.

Charlotte tried to breathe.

She wasn't the only one.

Sebastian gaped at her. "Lottie, you are perfect. Divine." His eyes continued to devour her. "You were created to tempt me into this hell."

Perfect? Divine?

Those two words went a long way toward sending her fears scurrying.

And the third one, *tempt,* gave them a boot over the hill.

She, Charlotte Wilmont, tempted him?

Unable to resist, she straightened, letting her breasts rise up and forward.

A dark, strangled look crossed his features. He groaned and pulled her to him again; this time his kiss plundered, ravished, left her breathless.

And then it happened. Without so much as a "by your leave," or an "anon."

He swept her into his arms and carried her up the stairs to her room, traveling through the shadowy and dark house without any need for light.

She had to imagine he knew the way.

And now she was about to as well.

Sebastian dropped her on the bed, then left the room.

Charlotte scrambled to sit up, worried that part of her punishment was to be left in this terrible state.

Needy and tantalized, she wanted more. Everything.

And just as she was about to call out to him, beg him if she must, he returned with a taper from one of the downstairs sconces. He kicked the door shut behind him and proceeded to light candles here and there throughout the room. Enough light to see, just enough to leave the far corners in shadows.

"So many?" she asked, wondering how she wouldn't die of shame over all this.

"If I'm to torture you as you tortured me tonight, I want to see your face. See all of you."

Her hands went to her hot cheeks. He wanted to see her? She glanced over at the shadowy portrait of Lottie and sought some self-assurance in the lady's smug expression. When she peeked back at Sebastian, she found, much to her dismay, he was undressing hastily—most likely as he had the night before—his cravat flying across the way, his waistcoat going another, the orderly room quickly turning into a litter of discarded clothing.

"Flirting with Rockhurst, you wretched girl," he said, as he tugged his shirt up and over his head.

She knew she shouldn't, but she stared at his smooth, bare chest, her fingers fisting in the sheets with a desire to touch him.

"Won't stand for it, Lottie. Not any longer. You're a wicked, wretched tease and it's about time some man brought you to heel."

The dangerous promise behind his words left her shivering.

Oh, if only she were a wicked tease. Then she'd have the nerve and skill to give into this unholy desire to run her palms over the muscles of his chest.

To kiss him, as he'd kissed her, everywhere and anywhere. To taste him.

Taste him? She chewed at her lower lip and wondered if that notion was Lottie's or hers.

Does it really matter? she thought as his boots came off, and then his pants.

"But now it is time for us to get one thing straight—" He stretched his arms out, his manhood thrusting into view.

Too many times to count during the day, she'd thought perhaps she'd imagined what she'd seen when she'd awoken in his arms. But no, there he was, as magnificently endowed and masculine as she'd recalled.

"—I won't be toyed with, Mrs. Townsend. You are mine."

Mine. The very word sent shivers down her spine.

He stalked toward the bed and instinctively she backed away from him, unwittingly tangling in the sheets and falling on her back, exposing herself to him.

He caught her by an ankle and retrieved her, tugging her within easy reach. Sebastian towered over her, devouring her with his gaze, as if he was planning his own manifest destiny, how best to conquer her.

Oh, whatever was she to do?

Charlotte needn't have worried; her body responded before her Mayfair sensibilities had a chance to interfere, her hips rolling upward, her thighs opening ever so slightly in an unspoken invitation.

Touch me, Sebastian. Touch me here.

He slowly raised one of her ankles up and began to kiss her calf, his tongue plying a slow, easy trail toward her knee.

She didn't know much about waging war, but Charlotte now considered herself an expert on the terms of surrender. *Just give him anything he wants.*

Again, he pulled her closer yet, then knelt before the bed, catching her by her hips and bringing her toward him.

Warm, hot breath assailed her thighs, sent tremulous waves through her.

Kiss me, Sebastian, she would have begged if she could have said a word.

And he did, his thumbs slowly parting her flesh, his fingers brushing over the curls there.

Charlotte shivered again, but this time it was from something very different.

Desire.

"You don't deserve this," he said, a wicked grin on his lips even as he bent his head down to taste her.

And the moment his mouth touched her, his tongue dipped to swirl over her very core, a sense of delicious wonder spread through her. She shuddered and her hips rose up to meet him.

Not deserve this? Oh, she did. She'd be as wicked as he wanted her, over and over, if just to gain this boon.

She'd flirt with Rockhurst, she'd wear a bodice that defied decency, she'd let Arbuckle paint her stark naked in the middle of Hyde Park.

Just to drive Sebastian wild, to spark his ire. To bring him to her bed in this dangerous, passionate state.

His mouth covered her, his tongue darted over her, left her breathless and gasping for air.

"Aaah," she moaned, her hands letting go of the sheets and twining in his hair, holding him in place. Her greatest fear no longer was that she was undressed but that he would stop.

Over and over, his tongue continued to dance across her, lapping at her and driving her onward, upward in a spiral of desire. Her head swung back and forth, the shadows and candlelight flitting in the distance. She stretched down toward him, seeking more, wanting more.

Oh, heavens, what was he doing to her?

Her body began to tighten, to thrum with a wild music, her hips rising up, her back arching, her every nerve reaching out for something, something so ethereal, so elusive.

And then just as she thought she was about to find the answers she sought, she needed, he stopped. Tugged his head back and eyed her.

Charlotte knew she must look a state. She'd tossed all the pins from her hair, and the once-perfect curls now lay in a damp wild halo about her. Her body glistened with sweat, while her breasts rose and fell. She couldn't stop trembling, couldn't help but reach out to him.

"Please, Sebastian, please don't stop," she whispered. *No, she begged.* "Please."

He rose up, still watching her, that wicked, terrible grin on his lips. His erection, so thick and rampant, standing so proud out in front of him, no longer left her scared.

Trembling, yes. Trembling with need.

"Please, Sebastian," she whispered again.

And then he was atop her, covering her. He reached beneath her and tugged her corset strings loose, then whisked it over her head and sent it flying across the room.

"Tell me you were wrong," he said, dipping his head down to suckle one of her nipples.

It went tight and taut immediately, her thighs clenched against this renewed passion.

"I was wrong," she gasped. "So very wrong."

His hand ran up her thighs and her legs fell open, only too willing to acknowledge defeat before the battle began. "Tell me I'm the only man for you."

"You are," she ceded, breathlessly. If only he knew how much so.

You've always been the only man for me.

His fingers teased and toyed with her, bringing her right back to that endless brink that his tongue had driven her toward.

She moaned again, this time without any hesitation.

"Tell me you want me," Sebastian whispered into her ear, even as his fingers slid inside her, spreading the wet, slick evidence of her desire.

"I do," she gasped, her body starting to quake.

Sebastian's green eyes glittered, and in one quick, hard motion, he caught her by the hips and thrust himself inside her. And then just as quickly, thrust again.

"Ohhh," she gasped, her hands catching hold of his shoulders and hanging on for dear life. He was so thick, so hard, she felt every bit of him as he stroked her, stretched her, made himself as much a part of her as a man could.

Charlotte looked up to find him watching her, even as he stroked her again, her hips rising up to meet him. His head tipped slightly as if he wasn't too sure as to what he was seeing—as if he knew—that she wasn't the Lottie he loved.

Her breath caught in her throat and they lay there for a moment, joined together, their bodies thrumming with desire, clamoring for completion, and yet he paused and looked at her, into her eyes, searching for something.

"Lottie?" he whispered.

"Yes?" She reached up and touched his face, wondering at the intimacy of it. Her fingers grazed over the hint of stubble there, marveled at the warmth of his skin, the solid strength of his jawline, her finger tracing the cleft in his chin.

Her other hand clung to his shoulders, unwilling to let go . . . at least just yet.

He knows. He knows I'm not her. Charlotte closed her eyes and buried her face in his chest. Oh, whatever was she to do?

Let him love you, came a whispery bit of reassurance. *Let him love you.*

"Oh, please, Sebastian," she whispered. "I'm begging you." And he moved again, quickly falling back into that gloriously sensual rhythm. Her fingers, still clinging to his shoulders, as if unwilling to let go, to fall free into the passion he brought out in her, finally uncurled.

And she fell. Tumbled really, adrift and afloat into a sea of ecstasy. Her hands grasped and reached for something to hold onto and came to rest on his hips, pulling him closer to her, urging him to continue.

As she arched her back, rose up to meet him, his head dipped down and he caught her mouth in a kiss.

Instead of the hungry, jealously fueled kisses from a few moments ago, this time his lips caught hers with a tenderness, a desire that spoke of something else.

A soulful chorus, like the violin's sweet chords, his kiss held all those things and something else.

Love.

If Charlotte thought she'd fallen before, now she toppled, pushed by her own awareness.

He loved her, thoroughly, tenderly, from the depth of his heart, and as he continued to make love to her, the length of his manhood stroking a blaze of desire within her, Charlotte rose with him, kissed him back, hungrily, full of desire.

Her body growing tenser yet, her need narrowing her thoughts, her vision, until everything was centered in one place, in their joining.

Over her, Sebastian's breathing became more ragged, his body tightening, his movements more frantic, pushing her along, driving her upward.

At first she didn't know what was happening, her mind going blank as an entirely new world of passion exploded within her, her body trembling in a wild surf of release.

Charlotte gasped and clung to Sebastian even as he gave out a mighty groan—a roar filled with triumph—and he drove himself into her, hard and fast, thrusting over and over until he too lay trembling atop her, his body shuddering with the last throes of his release.

"Lottie, oh, my darling girl," he whispered, as he pulled her close and held her so they were still joined, still connected so very intimately. "I love you, Lottie."

"And I you, Sebastian," she whispered back. "I you."

The candles glowed low in their holders the next time Charlotte looked around. Sebastian had made love to her again, holding her gently and bringing her to her release slowly and skillfully.

Now as he slept beside her, she smiled softly.

So this is why one never sees a rake before two in the afternoon, she mused. Their real labors kept them up very late indeed.

Yet she felt anything but tired. Given the past day, she should be exhausted, having found herself in this shocking life, but Charlotte had to imagine she'd never felt more alive.

Here in Sebastian's arms, the trifling matters of the world, of manners and invitations, of new gowns and proper connections, gave way to a world that belonged only to lovers. A world of passion and exploration. Of the faraway shores that could be a lover's body, a lifetime of discovery and desire.

She glanced over at him and found him studying her.

"I've always loved this house," he told her, reaching over and trailing his finger along the edge of her face. "Loved being here with you. Just us, like tonight. Dancing, playing cards—well, perhaps not cards because you always win—even reading those horrible French novels you love, and I thought I knew all your moods, all your secrets, until tonight . . ."

His voice trailed off, and Charlotte found herself biting her lip. Oh, dear, what had she done?

He gazed at her intently.

"For a moment there, when we were . . ." He shrugged. "You know—"

"Yes, I know." Oh, how she did.

"As odd as it sounds, for a moment there, I didn't recognize you."

"How so?" she breathed, almost afraid to ask.

"This sounds funny," he said, reaching out to pull a strand of her hair. "You looked so innocent, so . . . so surprised."

I was . . . "I did?"

He reached out and tousled her hair. "What has come over you? You funny girl, you seem so different suddenly, you even sound different."

"I-I-I . . . ," she faltered. Oh, heavens, how could she explain? He'd think her mad. Not that it wasn't a possibility. Hadn't Mrs. Kingston at No. 15 on Queen Street woken up one morning and thought herself the Duchess of Kent?

"Of course your little flirtation last night with Rockhurst

contradicts all that," he teased, but she could hear the testing in his voice.

"I wasn't flirting with Rockhurst," she protested.

He snorted and rolled on his back.

She clambered atop him, her hands splaying over his bare chest.

"I was not flirting with the earl."

One aristocratic brow arched.

"I was not," she continued to protest. "Whatever would I want with him?"

"He's rich," Sebastian offered. "Don't think I haven't heard Finny extolling his virtues and his pocketbook."

Now it was Charlotte's turn to snort. "She has no right to interfere."

"She has your best interests at heart."

"But that's just it," she told him. "'Tis *my* heart. And I want you. Only you. And I wish—"

She came to a stop. She wished so many things, but how could she say them? She'd used her one wish, and there was nothing else she'd ever want more than Sebastian's love.

"What, Lottie?" he asked, sitting up and gathering her into his arms. "What do you wish?"

"I already have it," she told him, cupping his face in her hands. "I have you and that is all I could ever want."

He sat back a bit and stared at her. "You truly mean that."

She nodded, unable to get another word past the lump in her throat.

"But what about the last few weeks—I thought you were—"

She pressed her finger to his lips and stopped him. "Forget what you thought . . . what you knew of me. If I haven't told you how much you mean to me, then I've been a fool. There is no other man for me but you."

He studied her again, searching her features. This time she didn't look away—she let him survey her to his heart's content, until a slow smile spread across his lips.

"So we'll make a go of this?"

She nodded. "Oh, yes. Please. I would be ever so grateful."

He laughed and tousled her hair. "Wherever did you find these Mayfair manners? If I didn't know better, I'd say you hit your head harder yesterday than we thought."

"Something like that," she whispered as his mouth swooped down to cover hers and his hands began seeking out her body in a quest she knew now would end in rapture.

Chapter 9

If she had ever wondered why women like Corinna Fornett and the other infamous fallen women of Society always looked so well pleased with themselves, Charlotte now knew why.

After a night, and a good part of the next morning, spent in Sebastian's arms, Charlotte counted herself as one of them. It was easy to see why the Lottie-in-the-painting smiled so smugly.

Now as Sebastian strode about her room indecently naked, instead of averting her gaze and sneaking peeks, she watched him openly, admiring his form and shape and wishing she knew a few more of Lottie's tricks to keep him with her thusly, always.

"Oh, Lottie, my girl," he said, tossing on his clothes, a rakish glint in his eyes. "I'll be back tonight . . . if you'll let me in."

Charlotte scrambled up from the sheets, gathering up her wrapper as she went. While she didn't mind his nakedness, she still wasn't all that comfortable with her own in front of him. "Tonight? So long?"

And here she'd been spinning fancies about a day of idleness, of picnics and cool breezes and horse races and all kinds of things that spinsters from Mayfair never did.

"'Fraid I must. Got business to attend to," he said, a dark shadow passing over his features. He turned and tugged on his trousers.

He needn't have avoided her gaze. She knew exactly what his business might be.

Miss Burke.

Drat that wretched heiress! Charlotte glanced down at the ring on her hand. If only she had one more wish!

For a few moments, she gave into gleeful fantasy of Quince arranging a spectacular display of warts about Lavinia's fashionable and much lauded face.

"But I will be back tonight, so don't make any plans," he said over his shoulder as he bent to retrieve his boots from under a chair. "I have a surprise for you."

Charlotte looked up. She'd been adding to her wish for Lavinia the additional boon of a severe case of head lice and a dreadful, seeping rash. "A surprise?"

"Yes, but get that look off your face." He wagged his finger at her. "You won't wheedle it out of me, so don't even think of trying."

Charlotte nodded. No one had ever given her a surprise before, and from the teasing glint in Sebastian's eyes she had to imagine it was going to be delightful.

Dressed, though more rumpled than sharply clad Corinthian, Sebastian strolled back to the bed and gathered her up into his arms. His green eyes turned serious and his brow drew into a hard line. "You stay out of trouble today. No gambling, no drinking, no forays out with that questionable friend of mine. Just be dressed and ready for me. I'll call for you after eleven."

"Yes, my lord," she replied, ever the dutiful miss.

He leaned back and looked at her. "That was terribly easy. What's come over you, Lottie?"

"You," she said quite honestly. "You, Sebastian."

He grinned and leaned down to kiss her. From the moment his lips covered hers, she sighed and opened herself to him, didn't mind that her wrapper slipped from her shoulders and left her bare and quivering in his arms.

Much to her chagrin, he pulled back and laughed. "I should have known you'd use that innocent act to try to lure me back into your bed."

"I did not—"

He snorted and strode from the room. "Lottie, you are a good liar, but not that good." Then he blew her a kiss from the doorway and was tromping down the stairs. "Be ready at eleven," he called up to her. "I think you will find my plans quite . . . edifying." There was more laughter and then the slam of the front door.

She flopped back down on the bed and crossed her arms over her chest. "Now whatever am I to do until then?"

And as if on cue, there was Finella bustling into the room, tossing the draperies open to let in the afternoon sunshine. "I feel like a bit of shopping." She turned to Charlotte with her hands on her hips. "What say you?"

Shopping when one had money to part with, Charlotte discovered, was quite fun.

She and Finella had marched up one side of Bond Street and down the other, filling their carriage with hatboxes and packages until there was barely room for them.

And now, all these hours later, Charlotte stood dressed in a blue satin evening gown. White ribbons crossed over the front of the bodice and over the tops of the sleeves, giving it a Grecian air. To add to the theme, she begged Finella to do her hair up like it was in the portrait—though Finella saw no reason to go to such trouble when Sebastian's heart was secure and his pocketbook empty.

But Charlotte's pleas finally prevailed, and Finella worked her magic, adding a gold headband studded with sapphires to her creation and pulling from a locked chest an elegant pair of hoop earrings and a tiered necklace that matched the headband.

Finally, when the lady tucked a white plume and gold-tinged feather into the side of Charlotte's hair, even Finella had to smile, pronouncing Lottie "utter perfection," as well as "an utter waste of time."

Then she sighed, complained a bit more, and with Charlotte too entranced with the notion of Sebastian's surprise to care, departed: It seemed a night of gaming with the young Earl Boxley was more tempting to Finella than continuing her laments about her charge's favorite.

But eleven came and went, and at half past one, Charlotte paced about the small front salon in her house, pausing every time she heard a carriage. She'd race to the window and wonder aloud, "Wherever could he be?"

Two and a half hours late! She knew she should be furious with him, but at the same time, well, this was Sebastian, and she'd waited so long to have his affections that she supposed she could forgive him a bit of tardiness.

Meanwhile, her feet throbbed from the new shoes, a pair of high-heeled, embroidered satin creations, that Charlotte had thought divine when she'd purchased them. Now with her toes pinched and the makings of a terrible blister on her heel from the gold thread, she teetered over to the settee and kicked them off, wiggling her stockinged feet.

She blew the enormous plume out of her eyes and glanced at her reflection in the mirror. Her curls appeared to be drooping, and the kohl Finella had insisted on lining her eyes with was making a determined march down her cheeks like a pair of black caterpillars.

Some courtesan she was turning out to be.

"That's because you are a fool," she told herself as she went to the mirror and began to wipe away the layer of cosmetics.

"A fool?" came a quiet, but very masculine, question from the doorway.

"Sebastian!" she said, spinning around. "I didn't hear the bell—"

"I didn't ring it." He dangled a key on a ribbon. "I let myself in."

Charlotte nodded. Of course he'd have a key. He owned the one to her heart, why not her front door? "You must think me a fool, standing about nattering on to myself."

"Never." Pocketing the key, he strode into the room, confident and handsome and dressed tonight in plain dark jacket and dark breeches. When he paused before her, instead of hauling her into his arms and carting her upstairs for a night of ruin (as she half-expected, half-hoped), he studied her, as if caught by the sight before him.

Then he took the handkerchief from her hand and finished wiping up the errant liner. Tipping his head to one side, he studied her. "Now, there is the lady I adore. Absolutely perfect."

Charlotte didn't know what to say, mesmerized as she was by his smoldering gaze, his softly spoken praise.

"I fear I *was* being foolish, with all this finery, with all this," she said, waving at the plumes and the jewelry.

"You, a fool, Lottie?" He smiled again, his hand coming out to touch one of the ornate curls Finella had tortured her hair into. "Some might say so." He affected a funny pose, like a crotchety old matron, or ancient Corinthian. "Mrs. Townsend? A fool? Look at her madcap, spendthrift, ruinous antics. Why I hear tell she bet two hundred pounds on that crazy nag of Rockhurst's. She's a foolish, wicked lady." He grinned, then with a single finger tipped her chin upward so she looked directly at him. "But I know better. And I intend to prove it this very night."

Charlotte gulped. *This very night.* Those words sounded so ominous. "How so?" she managed to whisper, almost afraid to ask.

Almost. For his dark green eyes glittered in a dangerous invitation that she found spellbinding.

"I intend to give into your most secret desires," he told her as he stroked her cheek.

"M-y-y desires?" Oh dear, she hoped this didn't venture into those shady regions of Continental habits that Finella had intimated at. Lord only knew what a woman like Lottie Townsend would hold locked away in her devious heart.

"Yes, yours. I intend to indulge you utterly tonight." He drew her into his arms and started to nuzzle her neck. "Will you come along with me, Lottie, my love?"

She nodded, for she couldn't get a reply past her trembling lips, past her beating heart. As he swept her from the room, a breathless sort of anticipation and panic spread through her. But when they got to the hall, instead of turning right and up the stairs to her room, he towed her to the left and toward the front door.

Not going upstairs? Now wait just a bloody moment, a very Lottie-esque part of her clamored.

She dug in her heels and plowed to a stop. "Sebastian?" Charlotte tipped her head in the other direction. Toward the stairs . . . her room . . . her bed.

He threw up his hands. "Of course. You need a wrap."

A wrap? He truly wanted to go out? At half past one? The time wasn't so much the concern, rather his intent. He wasn't dressed for a ball, or even a card party. Why, he looked like he was out to set up shop as a highwayman.

"Where are we going?" she asked, trying to keep the chill of disappointment out of her words. She still held out some hope that if he was going to give her Lottie's heart's desire, they'd need to go upstairs to accomplish the feat.

Before she could prod him again with another question or even gain answer, he found the shawl she'd dropped on a chair earlier and threw it over her shoulders. Then with a contagious enthusiasm, Sebastian pulled her once again toward the door.

"Sebastian?"

"Yes?"

"I haven't any shoes." She held up the hem of her skirt so he could see her stocking-clad feet.

He raced back in and retrieved her new pair, the ridiculously decorated ones, the gilt embroidery and feathers now looking all too foolish. Holding them, like one might something picked out of a horse's hoof, he studied them. "Shopping again?"

"I couldn't resist," she said as she retrieved them and bent to pull them back on.

"You should have," he told her. "Resisted, that is. They look dreadfully uncomfortable."

"They are," she confessed.

"Then they will never do." He bent down, and before she knew it, he'd reached under her skirt and plucked off first one, then the other.

Charlotte teetered this way and that before she caught her balance by catching hold of his shoulders. Meanwhile Sebastian started digging under the bench and fetched out a sensible pair of boots. He held them up with a triumphant gleam in his eyes. "These will do," he told her.

She studied them with nothing but disdain. They were something a Miss Wilmont might wear, but never Lottie Townsend. "They belong to Prudence." Staring down at the plain brown leather, she tucked her feet back under her skirt. "And they don't go with my dress."

Instead of arguing with her, he shoved them into her hands, and before she could sputter another protest, he swept her up into his arms, so he held her face-to-face. "They'll do. You can put them on in the carriage," he said, grinning wickedly.

And with that, he carried her outside and into the night.

They rode through Bedford Square and then down along Great Russell Street into Bloomsbury. At first, Charlotte hadn't a care where they were going, for it was like magic being out like this. London was nearly silent, clothed in shadows and oddly comforting in its state of slumber. So oddly out of character with the bustling, sharp-edged city she'd known all her life.

Then again she'd never been out like this, in the middle of the night, alone with a man.

But as they drove along, her curiosity started to outweigh her sense of wonder.

"I know I don't shower you with jewels, or stock your

cellars or pay your modiste bills, like your other admirers have," Sebastian was saying. "However, this is something I can do for you." He pulled the horses over toward the curb and nodded toward the building before them.

"I give you the British Museum," he said, waving his hand grandly at the stately building that had once been Montagu House, the London home of the Duke of Bedford. Sebastian's eyes crinkled at the corners, his amusement, nay, glee, turning his strong sensual lips into a devilish smile.

Charlotte shook her head. And here she had thought, well, hoped, that they had been headed toward some gambling hell, or other disreputable party that Miss Charlotte Wilmont should never see, let alone know about. Mayhap some Cyprian's ball, filled with incognitos and their beaux.

Something scandalous, something unholy.

Instead, he was teasing her with the very secret she'd revealed to him yesterday. She might have been hurt if it hadn't been for this niggling suspicion this wasn't the end of his surprise.

"You don't look properly pleased," he said, stowing the reins and turning to face her. "I'll have you know, I went to great pains to manage this. What with my immeasurable charm and a bit of my winnings from Merrick, I find myself able to give you the British Museum, my unlikely bluestocking." He waggled his brows at her.

"You are giving me the museum?" She laughed. "Now that is a gift." She held out her hand, only too happy to play along with him. "My keys, if you will."

He made a great show of fishing about in his pockets, and then when the light of discovery sparked in his eyes, he pulled out of his waistcoat a dull-looking key, which he dropped into her hand. "Shall we go explore your new palace?"

She looked down at his gift, ever-so-warm from his body, and it sent a little thrill down her spine.

How was it that even the barest hint of his masculine heat left her breathless?

"Well, do you want to see your treasure trove, or not?" he asked.

She shook her head, the key in her hand like a tempting whisper. "Are you telling me this will get us into there?"

He nodded.

She tried to hand it back to him. "I think you've gone mad."

"Not at all." He bounded down from the carriage and tied the horses up at a hitching post. "Shall we have a go of it?" he asked as he reached up to help her down from her perch.

She leaned back in her seat, now convinced he had gone mad. "Sebastian Marlowe, you've gone round the bend. This key won't open that door," she said, pointing at the enormous and formidable front doors.

"I never said it would open those doors. I fear, my dear Queen, you must deign yourself to enter from the rear."

And before she could protest further, he hauled her down, then reached beneath the seat and caught up a box, tucking it beneath his arm.

Frantically, she retrieved Prudence's boots from the seat, for she still had as yet to put them on. But before she could slip into them, Sebastian was already towing her around the corner of the museum, through a small gate in the fence and into the shadows.

The onetime ducal residence rose up above them, as

lofty and self-important as its former owner, the Duke of Montagu.

A dreamy sense of wonder filled Charlotte's heart as she padded along in her stocking-clad feet. Certainly Sebastian had gone as mad as Dick's hatband, but his lunacy was now becoming hers.

"Where are we going?" she asked, as they rounded another corner.

"To the back."

Yes, well, she'd noticed that much. "Should I point out that it is the middle of the night?" A very Charlotte part of her continued to rebel against this folly. "I suppose it is also beside the point that we haven't the necessary tickets or permission."

The gravel path they'd been following stopped before a narrow wooden door tucked in between the shrubbery that lined the museum's walls.

"Yes, well, it turns out that at night tickets are not required," he told her, taking her hand and guiding it and the key she held toward the lock. Together they pushed it into the hole, and he turned her hand so the tumblers rattled into place.

She shook her head as the door opened before them. "Heavens, Sebastian! You can't mean to go in like this? Why, if we are caught, we'll be in ever so much trouble."

"Yes, I suppose," he said, pulling her inside. "But as I said, tonight this is your palace."

Charlotte still didn't quite believe it and nearly fainted when a voice from within called out, "Who goes there?"

Sebastian showed no signs of fear but continued into the darkened recesses. Down what appeared to be a hallway sat a single candle, offering a meager hint of light, and hardly all that welcoming.

"I said, who goes there?" the voice called out again, this time as fierce as a bulldog.

Charlotte clung to Sebastian's sleeve.

"Deetch?" he called out.

"Oh, aye, my lord. Is that you?" the man answered. Suddenly his rough voice sounded a bit more friendly.

Charlotte's gaze narrowed as she looked from the man beside her to the sturdy-looking fellow in the dark coat. He held a thick cudgel and, while not great of stature, looked capable of using the devilish club with some familiarity.

"Is it as we discussed?" Sebastian said in a low voice.

The man nodded, his beetle brows blending into one thick line. "Oh, aye. Those bottles did the trick. The whole lot of them are half-seas over." He nodded toward another door. "Don't even realize they're locked in."

"Thank you, Mr. Deetch. I remain in your debt."

"Never mind that, milord. Let us say you have repaid me quite handily," the man said, rubbing his breast pocket, a glint of avarice sparking in his eyes. He handed over a small brace of candles and pointed down the hall. "'Tis yours for the night, milord."

"Whatever have you done?" Charlotte whispered to Sebastian as he pulled her past a grinning Mr. Deetch.

"Nothing so alarming," he said, holding the candle aloft and leading her further into the darkened museum. "I donated a case of French brandy to these poorly paid and oft-neglected fellows who spend their nights guarding these hallowed halls." He grinned. "An act of charity, a moment of indulgence on behalf of the arts, as it were."

"You got the guards drunk?" Incredulous at such a notion, she took another look back down the hall at a smug-looking Deetch.

"Yes. But never fear, I stole the case from Rockhurst's

cellars. And happily for us, their palate isn't too discerning."

"What about this Mr. Deetch?"

"Seems the fellow isn't as inclined to drink as his compatriots. Prefers a small donation in a more solid form."

Gold. Visions of a grinning Sebastian as he'd collected his winnings from Merrick filled her mind. "You bribed him?"

"Exactly!" he declared. "I told you this evening was going to be edifying, and so it is."

They made their way up a narrow staircase. Without missing a step, Sebastian pushed the door open and led her into the grand Townley Gallery, which had been added to the back of Montagu House two years earlier.

There were candles alight here and there, just enough to give a bit of light, but not so much to call attention from outside as to this clandestine viewing.

Charlotte drew in a deep breath. Prudence's sensible boots fell from her hands, and her mouth opened in a most unladylike fashion. "Oh, my!" she finally managed to gasp.

Down either side of the room stood ancient statue after ancient statue. Gods and goddesses captured for all eternity in these prisons of perfectly wrought marble. It was as if Sebastian had given her the key not to the museum but to Mount Olympus.

He came up behind her, his hands resting easily on her shoulders. "Your heart's desire, Lottie," he whispered into her ear before he nudged her forward. "Indulge that secret bluestocking of yours."

With eyes shining with tears she couldn't explain, Charlotte ventured into the museum. Her steps, at first hesitant and tentative, traced a wary path down the middle of the long hall.

"In that dress, you look like you've just escaped from one of these pedestals," he said from where he lounged against a wall.

She glanced over her shoulder. "I hardly think so—"

"I do."

Charlotte might have argued the fact further if a simple, yet elegant, sculpture hadn't caught her eye. "The greyhounds!" she called. "Oh, look, they are as dear and quaint as—" She'd been about to say "as Hermione told me," but she stopped herself. "As I read in the guidebook."

"I still don't believe you have the guidebook," he said.

"Well, I do," she declared, hoping she didn't have to prove the point—for the book was inscribed "From Hermione to my dearest friend, Charlotte," and more to the point, she'd kept it under her mattress at Queen Street lest her mother find the scandalous book.

Sebastian came alongside her. He'd set his mysterious box down behind him. "Friendly-looking fellows," he agreed, looking down at the pair of dogs, one licking the other's ear in companionable friendship. "And more manageable, I'd suppose, than that brindled elephant Rockhurst calls a hound." He shook his head. "Wonder what had Rowan so out of sorts at you yesterday. Usually can't keep him from falling at your feet and acting like a besotted puppy."

"Strange, yes," she agreed, her fingers twining around the ring on her hand. She moved down a few more steps while he went across the room.

"Now here's a horse for you, Lottie," he called out.

She joined him at a marble relief depicting a nude

young man trying to restrain a rearing horse. "Yes, I think I would have wagered on that one!"

He leaned back. "The horse or the young man?"

"You are wicked," she said, nudging him. "That is art."

"So says Arbuckle when he's leering at you with a brush in hand," Sebastian shot back.

This wasn't the first time she'd heard that tone from him. "You don't like Mr. Arbuckle all that much, do you?"

He shrugged. "He's fine enough. But when he starts painting you—"

"What?"

Sebastian's jaw worked back and forth before he said, "It's as if he's trying to steal a part of your heart for himself."

"No one can do that," she said, catching hold of his hand and squeezing it tight. "My heart belongs only to you."

He nodded and leaned over to kiss her forehead. Then they continued through the gallery, admiring Sir Charles Townley's infamous collection.

"Now here's a pretty bit," he said, holding up a lantern to illuminate the bust of a woman. "She looks like you."

Charlotte blushed. "This must be Clytie." She walked around the pedestal. "Townley called her 'his wife.' During the riots, when he had to flee his house, he took her over any other piece in his collection."

"Probably because she didn't nag him overmuch."

"Do stop teasing," Charlotte chided him. "I think she looks sad. Such a wistful expression."

"Perhaps she had your kind heart," he murmured in her ear.

They moved further down the hall, hand in hand, until they got to the prize of the collection.

"The Venus! Oh, look Sebastian, here is Townley's Venus," she whispered, looking up at the elegant lady. Charlotte couldn't help but think she'd never seen anything so lovely.

The amazing statue stopped even Sebastian's glib tongue.

So much so that when she turned to ask him what he thought of it, he'd retreated down the hall to fetch his mysterious box.

He returned with not only it, but an extra brace of candles. "Stand right where you are."

"Whatever for?"

He knelt down before the box and started to unpack it. "I intend to sketch you both. Townley's Venus and my Aphrodite."

"Sketch me?" Charlotte said, glancing from the graceful goddess behind her to the man before her. "You draw?"

"Yes," he said, as he sorted out a sketchpad, pencils, and a rag. "Been a while, but I'm not half bad." He glanced up at her. "I'm no Arbuckle, but I think I know my subject well enough." At this he grinned, and Charlotte couldn't help herself; she blushed.

He certainly did—every inch of her. Then she looked back at the Venus again. "You don't expect me to . . ." She waved her hands at the lady's naked torso, draped only from her waist down.

Sebastian settled down on the floor with his sketchbook propped up on his knees. "Whyever not? You do it for Arbuckle."

"I-I-I—" she stammered. Oh, dear, how could she argue

with that? "What if one of the guards came along, or . . ."

To her relief, he laughed. "Don't get into such a state. I actually prefer you just as you are. That dress is perfect, as is your hair. Makes a nice contrast." Then he nodded at one of the lamps. "Put that one over there, if you would please, closer to the pedestal so it casts a shadow up on the wall."

She did as she was bid, then stood nervously to one side. "I didn't know you liked to draw."

"Seems I have a few secrets of my own." He rose and came over to her. He eyed the statue, then moved Charlotte slightly to one side of it, tipping her head to make it look as if she were gazing up at it. "Perfect!"

He rushed back to his tools and set to work.

"Why didn't you tell me?" Charlotte turned her head toward him, and he shook his pencil at her to return to her pose.

"Have you ever asked?" he said, drawing quickly and only sparing her a few short glances.

Obviously not. "But your—" Again Charlotte stopped herself. She couldn't tell him that of all the times Hermione had catalogued his virtues and sins for her, she'd never mentioned that he had an artistic bent. "Does anyone know?"

Sebastian stopped. "You mean like, Miss Burke?"

"No, not her," Charlotte said quickly, dismissing the girl altogether. She had to imagine a proper young lady like Miss Lavinia Burke wouldn't approve of an artistic husband. "I mean, like your mother or your sisters?"

He shook his head. "My family isn't overly fond of the arts."

And Charlotte realized that in their other world, Lady Walbrook would have made much of his proficiency and pestered him incessantly about it. No wonder no one knew.

But that he was sharing it with her said much.

Charlotte snuck another glance in his direction and as she spied the delight in his eyes as he drew, it struck her—she'd been in love with Sebastian Marlowe all those years and never really even known the man. Oh, she'd had a good understanding of his outward character—his loyalty to his family, his overriding sense of duty and honor, but there was so much more to the man—to anyone, she supposed—than met the eye.

In the past two days she'd discovered a Sebastian she doubted she would have ever found in her old Mayfair existence. Even if he had deigned to look in her direction and court her, they would have continued as virtual strangers until the day they'd wed. And even then, would he have taken her to the races? Danced with her so scandalously? Sketched her thusly?

Charlotte snuck another glance in his direction and smiled to herself. She'd been able to discover a Sebastian that not even Lottie knew.

"Seems I'm not the only who sought their heart's desire tonight," she said.

He chuckled. "I suppose you've caught me. I never could get much past you. Now hold still and let me finish. We haven't much time, and I don't know when we'll ever have such an opportunity again."

"Would you rather have had some bauble? Diamonds for your retirement?" Sebastian asked a few hours later as he drove her home.

She shook off the drowsy, sleepy languor surrounding her and said, "No." Leaning her head on his shoulder, she sighed. "Never diamonds. For tonight you gave me something no one else would ever have done for me."

He grinned, a foolish sort of expression that spoke of his exuberant pride in his accomplishment. It was boyish and teasing and, most importantly, full of love.

Her wish really had come true, Charlotte realized. Up until this very moment, a very bluestocking, ever-the-wallflower, spinsterly part of her heart hadn't quite believed that Sebastian Marlowe could truly love her. That is to say, the Charlotte part of her.

But he did. With his entire heart.

As she did him.

And that made everything that was so very improper, so very wrong with this mixed-up life Quince had fashioned for her, pale in comparison to the heady warmth that now sparkled within her soul.

Chapter 10

Quince tried time and time again over the next fort-night to catch a moment alone with Charlotte, but the lady was nearly impossible to corner.

Even for someone of, say, Quince's particular talents.

If it hadn't been for Milton's looming ultimatum, she might have been immensely proud of how Charlotte's wish had turned out.

Oh, yes, there were a few stray threads of time here and about that needed tucking in, but over all, one look at Charlotte's shining face and it was obvious she'd bloomed.

She and her handsome Sebastian were nearly inseparable—evidence, she told a glowering Milton, that this wish was fated—proved over and over again with lazy picnics in the countryside, late-night suppers of shared tidbits and kisses, watching the fireworks at Vauxhall Gardens, creating their own explosive passions whenever the opportunity presented itself.

Which, in the case of Charlotte and her lover, proved to be often—in the afternoon while Finella was out shopping, during the long drive home from the countryside, through the wee hours of the night and into the morning until they were both spent and exhausted.

It wasn't that Quince was spying, per se, but even she had to admit to being surprised by the explosive heat that sparked between Charlotte and Sebastian at the least bit of provocation.

And in truth, the world was none the worse for it—for when had true love ever been a bad thing?

At least for the time being . . .

A carriage rolling down the street roused Quince out of her reverie, especially when it stopped in front of No. Four, Little Titchfield Street.

The driver went up and rang the bell, then returned to the curb to await his mistress.

The door opened shortly thereafter, and as luck would have it, Charlotte came down the steps with only her maid, Prudence, in tow.

Quince glanced at Charlotte's dress—a beautifully trimmed muslin gown and a Tyrolese pelisse in green velvet that fell to her knees. Atop her head was a wonderful hat with a great ostrich plume and green satin ribbon.

Lovely, Quince mused before looking down at her own drab gown. A bit of long-forgotten vanity got the better of her, and for a moment she envied Charlotte her fancy silks and glorious gowns.

Oh, but it was no use wishing for what she'd given up. And, worst of all, there was this wretched task before her. "Now it is," Quince muttered, gathering up her basket and hustling toward her quarry.

"Lottie, my dear girl," she called out, catching Charlotte's arm and pulling her back from the carriage. "We need to talk."

"Away with you, you old crone," the driver said, shooing her back. "Get yer dirty hands off 'er!"

Charlotte stopped him. "That's enough, Mr. Gallagher. I know this woman. 'Tis my good friend, Mrs. Quince."

Quince shot a look of triumph at the cheeky fellow. "As she says, I'm her good friend." She shifted her basket and tugged at Charlotte's arm again. "Can you spare me a moment?"

Gallagher displayed his disbelief with a pair of furrowed brows and a loud snort. "Friend, my arse. Another bleeding charity, I'd say," he muttered under his breath. "Now away with you."

He eyed Quince with a narrow, assessing glance that sent a shiver down her spine.

Irish, she surmised. Troublesome lot, all of them. Still had enough fey in their blood to be wary.

No, this would never do, she realized, glancing around for some way to distract the man.

"Your horses look a bit restless," she said, waving her hand toward the pair of blacks. Even as she spoke, the horses began trotting forward.

"What the bloody hell!" Gallagher spat out. "I set that brake."

"Not as well as you thought," Quince offered as he chased after the carriage looking only too embarrassed.

"Who are you?" Charlotte asked, her gaze flying between Gallagher and Quince.

"Oh, we haven't the time for that right now, my dear." Quince pulled her a bit down the street, out of earshot of her maid and especially out of Gallagher's hearing. "I fear I neglected to tell you something the other day when we met in the park. It was terribly remiss of me, but given your state of distress, you'll understand why it slipped my mind." Quince patted her arm and looked around to make sure no one was nearby. Like Milton. "There is one thing more you need to know."

"More?" Charlotte asked. "I don't need anything more." She laid her gloved hand on Quince's sleeve and smiled. "You've given me my wish. My heart's desire. I don't know how to thank you."

Quince felt a bit of panic frisson down her spine. *Oh, this didn't bode well at all.* "It's just that you must understand—"

"Whatever it is, I'm sure it can wait," Charlotte told her. She patted the lady's forearm again and turned toward the carriage in which Gallagher was now returning.

Given the stubborn set of his jaw, Quince knew he wouldn't be so easily distracted again. Blast his Irish hide.

"But you must listen, my dear girl," Quince insisted, chasing after her, that bit of panic now blossoming into full-fledged alarm.

The maid had climbed into the carriage, and Charlotte was about to join her.

"You can go back," Quince blurted out.

This stopped Charlotte in her tracks. Ever so slowly she turned around. "Go back?"

Quince nodded. "Yes. I should have told you before, but you were in such a terrible way, and then you saw Lord Trent . . ."

She watched the play of emotions on Charlotte's fair

features, waiting breathlessly to see which one landed, like a ball in a roulette wheel.

To Quince's dismay, it wasn't the one she'd wagered on.

"Oh, you dear thing! You've been worried about me. I know I was upset at first, but . . ." A sweet pink blush stole across her pretty features. "He loves me," she gushed. "Certainly this isn't quite the life I had in mind, but as long as I have Sebastian . . ." Her sigh added volumes to what she'd already said. "I have you to thank for everything."

"Me-e-e?" Quince stammered, definitely hoping Milton wasn't anywhere near enough to hear this.

"Oh, yes, you," she enthused. "Thank you ever so much." Charlotte turned and with a spry step climbed up into her elegant carriage in a thrice.

Unable to stop her, Quince rose to the tips of her toes and stuck her nose into the window. "You need to know this. You must know now."

Charlotte tossed her head back, the plumes fluttering elegantly about her pretty face. In an instant the once demure Miss Wilmont disappeared, replaced by the indomitable Lottie Townsend. "For heaven's sake, Quince, whyever would I want to do that?"

As if on cue, Gallagher clucked his tongue at the horses and the carriage took off down the street at a smart clip.

Oh dear, that didn't go well at all, Quince thought. She glanced nervously up and down the street, half expecting to see an elegantly clad Milton stalking toward her.

But it seemed she had a bit of luck left, for there was no one in sight. Seen or unseen.

Not willing to tempt fate, she bustled down the street,

wondering where in London she could hide from him—for at least a decade or so, since there was little chance he'd stop or, saints be praised, forget about that accursed ring.

The only thing left was to hope that Charlotte discovered that even a perfect wish had unforeseen consequences and changed her mind.

Quince's revelation echoed through Charlotte's thoughts like a discordant note for the next few hours.

Give up my wish? Charlotte thought indignantly. *What utter madness!*

Then to add to her dismay, her perfect afternoon of shopping hadn't turned out anything like she'd thought it would. She'd planned on going with Corinna Fornett, for it seemed she and the lady went shopping together once a month, or as Sebastian referred to it, their monthly assault on the delighted and willing merchants of Bond Street. Much to Charlotte's disappointment, the lady had sent a note around at the last minute stating she would be unable to go. Despite this setback, Charlotte had persevered, especially since she had money to spend freely, a carriage, a driver, and a maid to see to her needs, and the freedom to choose whatever her heart desired. And she had—shopped without a care for the price, or whether she truly needed another hat—yet something was missing.

So much so that finally she'd sent Prudence off to the carriage with the packages and had been about to join her, when she'd stopped in at a ribbon shop that she and Hermione had often frequented.

How much more fun it would have been to spend the afternoon choosing silks and trimmings and hats with . . .

The bell over the door jangled and a young lady entered the shop. "Mother, I want to see if they still have that braided silk I saw the other day."

Hermione!

Charlotte opened her mouth to greet her, then clamped her lips shut and stumbled back behind a display case.

Greedily she eyed her best friend, realizing how much she missed her. Why, before there hadn't been a day go by when she and Hermione hadn't gone walking, or shared books and confidences. Besides, if it hadn't been for her friendship with Hermione, she'd never have met Sebastian.

On more than one occasion she'd had to stop herself from asking Sebastian questions about his family. How was Griffin's time machine progressing? How was it that his father had never gone to the South Seas? Why wasn't Cordelia in Bath with their Aunt Davy? What trouble had Viola caused this week? Looking across the shop at Hermione, Charlotte realized how terribly she ached to spend just one afternoon in the Marlowes' noisy, eclectic, haphazard house.

An impossible notion now, not so much because of who she was but because her wish had taken all that, and so much more, away.

Just look at Hermione! Charlotte felt no small measure of guilt as she beheld this dour, plainly clad version of her colorful friend.

It didn't seem fair that she, Charlotte, should have gained so much when so many others had lost their passion, those unique qualities that had made them stand out in her eyes.

Hermione wandered through the shop, stopping finally to pick up a roll of trim. She bit her lip as she turned it this way and that, considering the lovely, bright length of embroidered silk.

"Now I have exactly what you were looking for—" the shopkeeper was saying as she came out of the back room.

Charlotte shook her head at the woman and slunk back further into the shadows.

The good woman, used to the oddities and peculiarities of London's *ton*—and most likely its demimonde—didn't say anything else but turned her bright smile toward her new customer until she spied who it was.

"Lady Hermione," the lady said through clenched teeth.

Hermione took a deep breath and held up the silk. "How much is this?"

Charlotte almost laughed. When had Hermione ever considered a price when she'd gone shopping?

Fashion is an essential and price a secondary concern had been her friend's motto.

Then, to Charlotte's horror, the shopkeeper said something truly dreadful. "The price matters not, my lady. Unless you intend to pay cash."

Hermione blushed crimson and hurriedly dropped the ribbon back down on the table. "No, I had only hoped—"

The bell jangled again, and this time Lady Walbrook and Lady Cordelia entered. "There you are, Hermione. Did you get your ribbon?"

"I'm afraid that won't be possible, my lady," the owner said, sounding anything but sorry, her arms crossing over her chest. "I was just explaining to your daughter that I can't give you or your family any further credit until what is outstanding on your account is paid. In full."

Charlotte felt Lady Walbrook's, and moreover Hermione's, shame right down to the tips of her own outrageously expensive slippers.

Lady Walbrook's lips flapped in outrage as she obviously struggled to find the right words for such an awful scene. Then she glanced around the small shop in a moment of panic, and Charlotte ducked down to avoid being seen. She hardly wanted to embarrass the countess further by letting her know there was a witness to this humiliation.

"Do you know who I am?" Lady Walbrook said in a level, elegant voice. Behind her, Cordelia, Sebastian's eldest sister, stood with her eyes downcast, her expression unreadable.

"Yes, my lady, but—"

"How dare you stand there and—"

"Never mind, Mother," Hermione interjected, gathering together no small measure of grace and using it to separate herself from this growing scandal. "I don't think the ribbon is the right shade after all."

No one believed her, especially when a tear of mortification welled up in her green eyes.

Charlotte's heart sank that her best friend should have to suffer so.

Well, they weren't friends currently, but that mattered not to Charlotte. Hermione *was* her friend. Always would be. Really, there was nothing left to do but . . .

"No, wait," Charlotte said, the words bursting out before she could stop them. "I'll pay for it, Hermione. Whatever you want."

Every pair of eyes in the shop turned and fixed on Charlotte, who had risen from her hiding spot. In an instant she knew she should have held her tongue and stayed safely ensconced behind the counter.

For instead of gratitude, Lady Walbrook's features came into sharp relief. She sucked in a deep breath of indignation before she barked out, "Hermione! Cordelia! Await me outside!"

The sisters scurried from the shop, the bell over the door jangling in a discordant flurry.

A deep voice rose above the cacophony, paying respects to the Marlowe sisters as they fled, but Charlotte hadn't time to pay it any heed for suddenly a furious Lady Walbrook stood before her.

Even the shopkeeper possessed the good sense to retreat to the safety of her storeroom.

"How dare you!" the countess erupted.

"I only meant to—"

Lady Walbrook raised her hand, and Charlotte thought for a moment the woman meant to slap her. The dreamy and flighty woman she'd known was nowhere to be seen, replaced by this all-too-virtuous and outraged matron.

"Hear me well, you harlot," Lady Walbrook said in a menacing voice. "If you think that offers of money will smooth your way, you are most decidedly wrong. As long as I have a breath left in my body, my son will not marry you."

"Marry me?" Charlotte felt as if the woman had indeed slapped her. Why, it had never occurred to her that Sebastian would . . .

It was a lie, of course. And Lady Walbrook could see that. "Oh, aren't you the coy one. Do you think I haven't heard the gossip? Know where my son has been this past fortnight?" Her lip curled into a snarl. "Entrapped by your devious charms. But listen well: you'll not have him. He's bound to another and there is nothing you can do about it. He'll come to his senses any day now and toss you back into the gutter where you belong."

Charlotte tried to breathe, tried to think of something, anything to say to mollify the lady, assure her that she wasn't the ruinous vixen that the countess thought her to be.

"You are nothing but baggage. Foul baggage!" the lady declared. "It is blood and breeding that defines a lady—not the reticule full of silver and gold she finds on her dresser in the morning. I'll go in rags before I see a tuppence of your ill-gained fortune go toward my family."

With that said, the matron gathered up her skirts as if she stood in the middle of a stable yard and stalked from the tiny shop, nearly bowling over the man at the door-way.

He bowed and murmured, "Good day to you, my lady."

"Rockhurst," she acknowledged with a grudging sniff. She might be cross as crabs, but she was still the mother of three unmarried daughters and the man before her was an earl. An unattached one, to boot—which demanded a hasty return to some semblance of manners.

"My lady," he replied. "Good day to you."

"Harrumph!" she sputtered, shooting one last, hot, peevish glance at Charlotte.

And then she was gone, bustling out into the street, shooing her daughters along as if they were in flight from the plague.

Charlotte stood frozen in place, the countess's blister-ing attack still stinging in her ears.

Foul baggage!

How could Charlotte have forgotten, even for a second, the great divide between proper society and those outside the privileged walls. Lady Walbrook's words had gone a long way toward reminding her of the true nature of her existence—Sebastian's true love or not—she was no better than a Seven Dials whore in the eyes of Lady Walbrook.

She glanced up, tears clouding her vision. As she swiped them away, the Earl of Rockhurst came into clear focus. And from the polite yet strained look on his face, she knew he'd heard every word of the lady's tirade.

"That was unpleasant," he offered.

All Charlotte could do was burst into tears.

For a moment, Rockhurst glanced around the shop, looking for some other female to appear and take over. When no help arrived, he did the unexpected and gathered Charlotte into his arms.

"There now, Mrs. Townsend. I daresay this isn't the first time that has happened to a lady in your circumstances, and I daresay it won't be the last."

Once Charlotte regained some semblance of her composure, Rockhurst sent Gallagher and Prudence on home, taking Charlotte by the arm and walking with her down Bond Street.

A disgruntled Rowan trotted behind them, occasionally knocking Rockhurst in the back with his great gray head and growling from time to time at the lady on his master's arm.

It didn't take more than half a block for the earl to reveal the truth of the Marlowes' situation to her.

"I can't believe any of this," Charlotte said, glancing over her shoulder at the massive wolfhound. The beast left her with the uneasy feeling that he *knew* she wasn't the Lottie Townsend everyone thought her to be. "The Marlowes have never been all that plump in the pockets, but broke?"

"Up the River Tick," he told her. As they continued along the busy street, the matrons and regal ladies shot the pair scandalized looks and whisked their skirts out of Charlotte's path. Rockhurst, if he noticed, paid them no heed. "Near as I can tell, they've got a few weeks at most before their creditors leave them without a rag."

"That explains Miss Burke," she mused aloud, not really meaning to give voice to her conclusion.

"Exactly," Rockhurst said softly. "Miss Burke's dowry is more than enough to see them out of dun territory and back into the good graces of the merchants. That's how Trent and his father have been holding off the worst of them—for you see, everyone expected a betrothal announcement by now."

"But they aren't engaged," she said with a little too much force, coming to a stop before a jeweler's shop.

Rockhurst's brows rose slightly. "No, they aren't."

"It isn't as if he needs *her* money," she declared recklessly. "He could have mine."

"Ah, yes, your money. Certainly your tidy fortune would satisfy the likes of Bond Street, but after that scene back there, do you honestly see Lady Walbrook as the welcoming mother-in-law?"

Charlotte turned from him, putting her gloved hand on the window and staring absently at the wares displayed behind the glass. The expensive and beautifully wrought gems and gold held little interest to her. "She'd come around."

"Would she?" He reached over and ruffled Rowan's bristly head. The dog let out another growl of protest, then with a curt word from his owner, sat obediently at his side, though his large, dark eyes never left Charlotte.

Rockhurst continued. "Ah, yes, she'd be quite enchanted by your charms when the rest of the *ton* cut them off. When her three unmarried daughters can't gain vouchers to Almack's, let alone an invitation to some cit's wretched card party because of their sister-in-law."

"It wouldn't come to that," Charlotte declared. But even as she said it, she knew Rockhurst's predictions held the same clarity as the diamond necklace in the shop's window. Society would turn their collective backs on the Marlowes without a pitying glance if she and Sebastian were to marry.

But certainly their love could breach something even so seemingly insurmountable as the *ton*'s displeasure?

Her fingers toyed with the ring hidden beneath her glove. Perhaps Quince could help.

'T'was only one more wish. Such a small thing.

"Unfortunately for Trent," Rockhurst was saying, "he's torn by his affection for you and his duty to his family."

"He loves me," she whispered.

"Aye, he does." The earl glanced up and down the street. "Though I never thought you held his regard with the same intent. . . . I don't know what to make of you, Mrs. Townsend. I had thought . . . well, been under the impression that we had reached an agreement a few weeks ago, and then suddenly you, well, you've—"

"Changed?"

He nodded, his eyes narrowing as his gaze swept over

her. "Very much so. Not that I mind, but it makes the situation all that much more difficult—for I am not a man inclined to share a lady's favors, and I have a terrible suspicion that you share Trent's dilemma."

Charlotte looked away as the sting of tears once again filled her eyes. She had no idea why such an admission should make her cry, but after the encounter with Lady Walbrook she felt a terrible sense of shame over her feelings, her desire for Sebastian.

If she hadn't wished for his love . . .

"Egads," Rockhurst said, his voice sounding almost as scandalized as Lady Walbrook's. "You *do* love him."

Her chin tipped up. "But you just said you suspected."

"Suspected, yes. Believed it?" He shook his head.

She picked up her skirts and started to walk around him, but Rowan blocked her path, giving Rockhurst the chance to reach out and catch her by the elbow. "Don't be offended, madame. In all honesty, I envy the man." Then just as suddenly as he'd stopped her, he let go of her and took a step away, his words letting slip more than possibly even he had intended.

Yet the truth of it was there as she looked up into his eyes. The light of desire she spied revealed that Rockhurst held more than a friendly, competitive *tendre* for her.

As much as Lady Walbrook's outburst had stung, Rockhurst's confession astounded her.

The Earl of Rockhurst in love with her? Charlotte didn't know if her life could be any further complicated.

But whatever feelings the man held for her, his tone turned light once again. Too light. "Come now, Mrs. Townsend, take a look over your shoulder. If you were to set Trent free, let him marry his dour little heiress, then

I would be inclined to show you the very generous heart I possess."

Charlotte laughed, against her own better judgment. She turned around and eyed the gaudy, showy piece. The double row of diamonds twinkled and sparkled seductively.

He leaned closer. "They haven't half your flair, but I daresay you'd look dazzling in them."

"You are joking," Charlotte said. "You'd buy me those?"

"Those and more, if you wanted," Rockhurst said, his voice full of sensual promise, the kind that made Charlotte recall Finella's lusty description of the man. "If you only say the word."

"What word?" came an inquiry from behind them.

Charlotte and Rockhurst spun around to find Sebastian looking anything but pleased to see his best friend and mistress together.

He strode forward and looked at the necklace Rockhurst had pointed out. "Hmm. A bit tawdry even for you, don't you think, Lottie?"

The bitterness and suspicion in his voice cut her to the quick. "I-I-I-," she sputtered, while taking a hasty and deliberate step out of the earl's lofty shadow.

Sebastian said nothing to her; rather, he greeted his friend in a brusque manner. "Rockhurst."

The earl paid little heed to the tension. "Ah, Trent! Done with your afternoon calls so early?"

"Yes," Sebastian replied. "I thought to discover Mrs. Townsend at her shopping, and here she is, looking quite diverted." He turned to Charlotte. "I thought you said you were going with Corinna."

"I was, but——"

"So I see," Sebastian said, not letting her finish.

Rockhurst smiled. "I was just pointing out a necklace to the lady. What say you, Trent, do you think it would suit her?" The earl pointed at the diamonds in front. "I think the stones match her fire."

Sebastian took another hasty glance at the necklace, his jaw tightening at the expensive token.

A token, Charlotte now knew, that sat well beyond his strained pockets.

Hastily she spoke up. "I was about to tell Lord Rockhurst that I thought it too showy."

"When did you ever think any diamond too showy?" Sebastian asked her. He looked over at the stones again. "Rockhurst is right. They do have your fire . . . and your flaws."

That last bit held a horrible note of displeasure, of a jealousy and anger that had no place between them.

It was all Charlotte could do not to rush to explain everything to him, to make him see how it was she had come to stand here of all places with the earl.

The man whose name held the most places in White's betting book as her next protector.

He was only trying to help me, she wanted to say. *I was in this shop and I ran into your mother—*

Oh, that would never do. She couldn't tell him about that. Tell him she knew of the predicament she had placed him in.

Then an awful, niggling doubt tugged at her heart. What if it was only Quince's bit of magic that had turned Sebastian's affections in her direction? Could he have ever loved her without her wish?

Meanwhile, Rockhurst had stepped in to take up her

defense, which only served to make that vein in Sebastian's forehead bulge further. "Come now, Trent! You mustn't blame the lady. I found her quite distraught and was engaging her in a little harmless wager as to how much this—"

Oh, yes, this was perfect! Point out yet again the necklace that Rockhurst could afford and Sebastian could not.

"Lord Trent," Charlotte blurted out. "Will you be so good as to escort me home? I'm afraid I've lost Prudence and Mr. Gallagher."

Sebastian's gaze rose from where it had been fixed on the priceless bit of jewelry and met Rockhurst's.

His expression reminded her of how he had looked when he'd confronted Lord Lyman in Berkeley Square, and now she feared he was about to come to blows with the earl.

She caught his arm. "I fear I am getting a megrim from the sun."

It was overcast, but neither of the gentlemen seemed to notice. Rockhurst was too busy acting as if there was nothing unusual about his shopping for jewelry with his friend's mistress, and Sebastian, well, he appeared ready to call for seconds.

"Please," she whispered.

Then to her rescue came a very unlikely knight-errant. *Lord Battersby.* "Ho there! Trent! Rockhurst! Just the pair I've been looking for," he called out from across the busy street.

Luckily for them, the traffic prevented the man from crossing. Just yet.

Rockhurst tipped his hat at Charlotte. "Lovely day,

Mrs. Townsend. Trent," he said, before giving Rowan a sharp whistle. The pair of them set out at a fast clip down the street.

Sebastian glanced over at her, and for a moment his hard features softened. Then he took her hand and placed it deliberately on his sleeve. "Oh, come along. My curricle is just over here."

They dashed over to his carriage, and he helped her up. He bounded around the other side and they were off, just as Battersby finally found a chance to cross.

Sebastian took off at a breakneck speed and left the poor man in the dust.

Nothing was said between them for a block or so, but the silence was driving Charlotte to distraction.

"Sebastian, I was just—"

"Don't, Lottie. Don't explain to me what you were doing with him."

"I wasn't doing anything with him." Charlotte supposed she should be surprised at the amount of brass that had come out with that statement, but she doubted Lottie would be easily cowed by his dark mood. So neither should she. "Sebastian Marlowe, you are many things to me, but right now you are being a complete ass."

He stiffened in his seat, probably never having been spoken to thusly in his entire life (at least not by a woman).

Undeterred, Charlotte continued. "I love you. I love you with all my heart. I know that Rockhurst is considered by all to be my next choice of protector—" She raised a gloved hand to stave off his sputtered exclamation. "I am no more immune to gossip than you are, but if I were to leap into the boughs every time you went off to woo Miss Burke—that's where you were this morning, isn't it?"

He nodded. "Her father . . . my father, as well, are pressing me to have the banns read."

She sighed. "You have them and I have Finella badgering me at every turn, and so we are caught in the crosshairs. So what ever are we to do? Spend our time with this ridiculous bickering? I don't know why we aren't using our precious time for what matters most."

They rode in silence for a moment before he asked, "And that would be?"

Charlotte threw up her hands. "Our love! What the devil is wrong with you? Do you think me such a dolly-mop that I would be tempted away from you by the mere sight of diamonds?"

He gave her another one of those looks that spoke volumes.

"It doesn't bother you to drink my wines—which are supplied by Lord Kimpton, or stay in my house, which was a gift from—" Oh, bother, that bit of history hardly mattered at the moment. She'd gained the house because Lottie had warmed another's bed, and there was nothing she could change about that. "Well, from someone else." She let out a frustrated sigh. "Do you love me or not?"

"Yes," he ground out.

"Then why can't you believe the same of me?"

"I do," he said, so passionately that Charlotte's heart stilled. "It's just that—"

She stopped him with a single finger pressed to his lips. "Say no more. I know."

Yet something changed. Beneath her the world shifted ever so slightly. Not as it had the day she'd made her wish, but she knew she was precariously close to losing everything.

Oh, heavens, what had Quince said? She could go back? It certainly would make things easier for Sebastian. He'd marry Miss Burke and the Marlowes would be secure.

And she'd be . . . back at Queen Street, living with her mother and a staid and prudent Finella.

Charlotte let out the breath she'd been holding and watched the passing streets with eyes glassy from unshed tears. When they arrived at her house, Sebastian drew the horses to an abrupt halt.

"Lottie, I—"

She didn't let him finish. Instead she moved into his arms and pressed her lips to his, sealing her fate to his. She couldn't let him go, let go of this life.

No matter the consequences.

He returned her kiss, greedily, hungrily. Though they'd only been apart for a few hours after having spent the night making love until the wee hours, it was as if they'd been parted for a month.

She stretched closer to him, relishing the feel of his hands on her, his lips teasing her earlobes, the tingle of desire running down her limbs.

Give up this? Never.

"Is Finella at home?" he whispered into her ear.

She knew what he was asking and was only too eager to reply. "She was gone when I left. I think she planned on being out all afternoon with Kimpton."

He growled happily, lustfully into her ear, "Shall we go inside? I would like to apologize for my boorish behavior with something a little more to your liking."

"Oh, yes, please," Charlotte said, her body aching to feel him naked, atop her, inside her.

They tumbled out of the carriage, dashing shamelessly hand in hand up the steps and through the door.

And into a scene of mayhem that spelled disaster.

Chapter 11

⟨~⌒⌒⌒~⟩

"**O**h, ma'am, I'm so glad yer home," Prudence gasped. "She's like to harm herself, she is."

Charlotte gaped at the scene before her.

Finella lay sprawled on the stairs, a bottle in one hand, a glass in the other. A glass she was in the process of filling.

The hallway reeked of spilled brandy.

Her usually well-dressed cousin looked like a Seven Dials slattern, her face contorted, her gown disheveled.

"To Lord Kimpton," she called out, raising her glass. Brandy sloshed down her sleeve. "May he rot in hell. I curse the day I let him put that miserable, little, shriveled—"

"Finella!" Charlotte snapped, stopping the woman's drunken declaration before it slid completely into vulgarity.

She looked up, wild-eyed and sloppy. "Lottie! Come have a drink with me, my dearest child. Come drink to my unhappiness." She teetered forward and looked about to topple right down the stairs, given her state of intoxication.

Charlotte rushed forward and caught her before she landed in an ignoble heap. It took all her power to push the lady, who suddenly seemed to have gained another two stone, upright. "Finella, whatever is wrong?"

"Lord Kimpton, that miserable, rotten—"

"Yes, yes, I gathered all that," Charlotte said. "What has he done?" She lowered her voice. "I thought you and Kimpton had an understanding."

"An understanding!" Finella scoffed, filling her glass again. "What is an understanding when you have to make it with a man?" She started to tip the glass to her lips but stopped when she spotted Sebastian standing in the doorway. "All of them. They are all the same. Mark my words, Lottie, love matters not. They'll toss you aside when you become inconvenient." She threw back the brandy in a hasty toss. "Marry another."

Her cold prediction sent a chill down Charlotte's spine, and without even thinking, she caught hold of Finella's glass and took it from her, setting it on the table well out of the lady's reach.

"Give that back," Finella protested. "And then leave me be." Her head lolled back and forth, and for a moment she seemed to have passed out.

Charlotte turned to Prudence. "Whatever is wrong?"

"Lord Kimpton got married."

"Married?" Charlotte glanced from Prudence over to her stricken cousin, everything suddenly making sense.

Prudence continued the sad tale. "Seems Mrs. Finella went over to see him. For their usual afternoon and all, and his butler sent her packing. Said her services were no longer required. The old blighter hadn't even the decency to come down and tell 'er 'imself. He was too busy up-stairs with 'is new bride. Seventeen, she is and some cit's by-blow."

"Graddige's daughter," Sebastian supplied. "He's made a fortune in shipping. Half the *ton* owes him favors. Kimpton more than most."

"Oh, dear God," Charlotte whispered. "Poor Finella."

"Yes, yes, poor Finella," her cousin said, rousing enough to cast a wild eye about the audience before her. "Poor me. He's been promising me he would marry me for years. Oh, yes, Finella, I'll marry you. Oh, my dearest Finny, I love you with all my heart," she wailed. "Just waiting for his dear sainted mother to go aloft so he can make it all legal and then he goes and marries some child. He takes her over me because he owes that bitch's father five thousand pounds." Moving with a speed that belied her rare state, she caught hold of the brandy bottle and bypassed the glass, tipping it up to her lips and drowning her sorrows.

The rich amber liquid spilled sloppily down her cheeks, running in a thick stream down the front of her once pretty gown.

Charlotte sucked in a deep breath and knew not what to do.

"We need to put her to bed," Sebastian said, stepping forward. He caught hold of the bottle clenched in Finel-la's grasp and wrenched it free. Ignoring the woman's spiteful complaints, he handed it to Prudence. "Hide this and then lock up the cellar."

Prudence nodded and fled into the back of the house.

Sebastian leaned forward and in one swift motion, plucked Finella up into his arms.

"Leave me be, you bastard. You aren't any better than

the rest of them. Full of promises and half-truths. But I know better, I know what you are. A liar. Like the rest," she wailed, her hands beating impotently at Sebastian's strong chest.

"Where to?" he asked, ignoring Finella's cater-wauling.

Charlotte couldn't even look Sebastian in the eye as she said, "Her room would probably be best."

He nodded and with very little effort carried the lady upstairs.

Finella didn't go quietly. "I suppose you'll toss me out as well, won't you, Lottie? You don't need me either. I know it. I'm nothing but an old woman. A sad old woman with nothing left."

Her sobs cut Charlotte to the core.

"No, Finella. This is your home as well as mine. You will always be welcome here."

"So you say, but I know better. I know you want to throw me out as well. I can see it in your eyes. You don't love me any more than he did." Finella gave into her sorrows, keening loudly. All too quickly her tears left a dark stain on Sebastian's coat.

Charlotte hurried ahead, only to discover the lady's room was in no better shape. It appeared she had taken her first course of wrath out there before she'd drowned the rest of her anger in the brandy bottle.

The stench of perfume filled the air, the result of a bottle having been thrown against the mirror over her dressing table. Broken glass lay on the floor, and clothes, bottles, trinkets, and other pieces of finery lay in heaps and broken piles.

"Oh, heavens," Charlotte said, standing amidst the chaos.

Sebastian said nothing about the scene but carried the poor woman to her bed and gently set her down on the tangled sheets.

If there was anything to be thankful for, it was the fact that Finella had passed out and now lay snoring away.

"At least she has some peace," Charlotte said.

"For the time being," Sebastian agreed. "Best keep the key to the wine cellar well hidden. And have Prudence do a good search of the house to make sure Finella hasn't more of that brandy stashed about. You know how she was last winter when she and Kimpton quarreled."

Charlotte nodded but didn't dare look at him. She kept her gaze fixed on Finella, wondering if she too would share the lady's fate one day.

Broken and alone, no income and no protector.

She heard him shift from one uncomfortable foot to another.

"It's probably best that I go—"

She glanced over her shoulder and nodded.

"I'll call again soon."

The words held a pall to them that chilled Charlotte's heart. But before she could turn to him, find something to say to bridge this sudden awkwardness, he was gone.

Charlotte sighed, as much from the dark promise of Sebastian's words as from the sight before her eyes.

Oh, poor Finella. She retrieved the coverlet from the floor and lay it gently atop the older woman. "Whatever will become of you?"

Become of me . . .

Absently, she went to work setting the room to rights, not wanting the lady to awaken surrounded by the evidence of her rage and disappointment.

"Never you mind that wretched baron," she told her. Stooping to pick up a hat that lay precariously in front of the hearth, Charlotte spied a letter beneath it.

Old and yellow, it caught her eye, and moreover, it sent a chill down her spine like a warning.

Leave it be.

But she couldn't. She picked it up and turned it over, reading the directions:

Miss Finella Uppington-Higgins, No. 11, Queen Street.

The house Finella had inherited from her parents, which had later become Charlotte's home when Finella had taken her and her mother in after Sir Nestor's death.

From its well-thumbed edges, Charlotte realized that this missive had come to her cousin before she'd become . . . well, before she'd turned into this ruined version of Finella.

Before Quince's changes. Her fingers trembled.

How many times in this past fortnight had she wondered how it was that Finella had entered the trade, never mind had brought up her young cousin in the business as well. And why had Charlotte's mother abandoned her to Finella's questionable care?

Charlotte glanced around the room and realized this wasn't the only letter. There was one sticking out from beneath the bed, two perched atop the mantel, several more littering the floor and a few more encircling the chair near the dressing table. Some were folded up like the one she held, but several of them had blossomed like spent flowers, their contents open for any prying eyes to see.

Charlotte tiptoed around the room and plucked them

up like wayward petals, clutching them in her still trembling hands.

For some reason she couldn't help shake the notion that she'd seen these letters before. That Lottie knew their contents intimately, but those memories, like so many others, were still locked away in the ethers.

Yet here it was. She could wait for those recollections to reappear or . . . Taking a deep breath, she opened the first one.

My dearest little poppet,

She glanced over at Finella and laughed a little. It was hard to imagine either the staid and proper Finella or the blowsy and immoral Finny as any man's "dearest little poppet."

"Love letters, Finella? How I would love to tease you about such a sentimental secret, but I daresay it wouldn't be very fair of me." Charlotte smiled at the secret tidings. She certainly couldn't imagine the blustery Kimpton using such a phrase.

So who was Finella's secret admirer?

"No, I shouldn't be doing this," she whispered, determined to set the letters aside, when the rest of the opening lines caught her eye.

My dearest little poppet,

Imagine the way my heart leapt when I spied your note this morning. It was as if you awoke beside me and we had spent the night—

Charlotte set it down, suddenly feeling that perhaps it wasn't such a good idea to be doing this. After all, she wouldn't have even been in Finella's room if it hadn't been for the lady's grievous misfortune today.

Not to mention her own dilemma, she mused, as she glanced at the doorway through which Sebastian had fled.

"Perhaps," Charlotte reasoned as she ever-so-slowly reopened the letter, "there is a lesson to be learned from Finella's mistakes."

She certainly didn't want to live her life in such a hopeless state, so she continued to read . . . just a little past the more passionate passages.

> . . . as for the other matter in your missive, surely you must be mistaken. You are giving too much credence to the gossip regarding my situation. It has made you nervous and prone to fancies. I sincerely doubt you are breeding, for we were only together that one time—

Breeding? Charlotte's hand went to her own flat stomach. How often had she and Sebastian been together?

She blushed to think of how many times they had made love. And up until now, Charlotte, naive and sheltered as she had been, hadn't given a single thought to what might come of their unrestrained passions.

Charlotte shook her head. *No. Such a thing only happens to—*

Those sorts of girls. To ladies of low character. To girls destined to become . . .

Courtesans.

This time she read with a bit more haste, feeling the web of Finella's fate entwine with her own.

*No my love, you must give me another fortnight
here at home in the country to ensure that my father will give his blessing to our union. A child
now would be unforgivable in his eyes, not to mention the loss of your aunt and uncle's good opinion. I'll wear the old man down and then I'll be in
town for the Season. I promise you, my love, only a
fortnight more and then we will—*

Charlotte's heart skipped an odd beat as her gaze went
unwittingly up to the date at the top of the letter.

February 1784.

The same year her father had died and her mother had
found herself a young widow with a child on the way.

Had Finella been in much the same circumstances,
though without the blessing of having had a husband
first?

Charlotte searched for more answers and found one at
the bottom of the letter, in the form of a single scrawled
name.

William.

She turned the letter over and spied an address.

*Tultern Abbey
Kent*

Charlotte's brow furrowed, and she continued to read
William's assurances, which had arrived for the next few

weeks, until she came to one dated the first part of April. Apparently William had still not returned and had written to explain.

Sweet Finella,

You mustn't write so often, and do try to keep your secret concerns just that, hidden away in your heart. I cannot return to Town just yet, but when I can steal away, I will. There is plenty of time to have banns read, or if we must, I will carry you away to Gretna and see that you and I are properly married. You and the child are not ruined. Not yet. Just hold to the promise of our love, the promise that I gave to you the night you gave me so much of your heart, of your love.

A veil of tears rose up in Charlotte's eyes. An undeniable sense of foreboding permeated every line.

You don't love me any more than he did. Finella hadn't been talking about Kimpton . . . she'd been talking about this William. And she had to imagine it was this man who'd left Finny with her hard, and broken, heart.

Charlotte sorted through the letters quickly and realized she had read all of them.

But there had to be one more. At least one more. Surely William had come in time before Finella's shame had been undeniable?

Charlotte paced around the room and even went so far as to get down on her hands and knees searching for the tiding that would reveal what she had to imagine Finella would never tell.

And then to her joy—and dread—she spied another

letter, hidden beneath a discarded and trod-upon hat. The plumes were bent, much as the letter was tattered and stained. Charlotte had no shame; she snatched it up and pulled it open.

The greeting this time held none of William's warm and easy greetings.

Miss Uppington-Higgins,

Even Charlotte, two and a half decades later, could feel the chill of disaster written all over this missive.

Miss Uppington-Higgins,

I am returning your letters forthwith and request that you send no more to me at this address or any other for that matter. Despite your apparent distress and current problem, I must inform you that shortly after you receive this, there will be an announcement in the Times *of my impending betrothal to Lady Portia Salcott.*

He was marrying another? When Finella was pregnant with his child?

Charlotte made a very unladylike noise in the back of her throat and borrowed one of her cousin's more expressive phrases. "Wretched bastard." How could he? She read on to discover the truth, but there was little else to the letter but more admonitions not to contact him again with her troubles.

Charlotte's jaw worked back and forth in anger—that is, until she realized there was a small packet tucked into the letter.

A second letter added to this very cold one.

My beloved,

"Harrumph," she sputtered. " 'Miss Uppington-Higgins' one minute and 'My beloved' the next. You blighter. How dare you even try to win her affections anew."

Still, Charlotte's curiosity got the better of her and she read on.

I have every hope that this letter will arrive with the one my father has composed for me to copy so I can tell you what is in my heart. I mourn for you and for us, but I cannot escape my fate here. My father has burdened our family with an insurmountable mountain of debt and I am to wed Lady Portia for her twelve thousand a year. If I do not, my family will be ruined. My duty in this situation has been made all too clear by my father and mother. For the sake of my sisters and all that we hold dear, I must do this.

"And what of Finella, you coward?" Charlotte said. "What of your child?"

It seemed though, that William had thought of them.

I know this leaves you in a terrible fix, but an item in the Post *yesterday caught my eye and may offer you the salvation that I can no longer provide.*

Sir Nestor Wilmont, I believe, was married to your cousin, Aurora. With his death, his title and estate will revert to a distant cousin if he is without a legitimate heir. I know not the state of your cousin's health, but perhaps Sir Nestor's death can be of some good. Go to your cousin, Finella. Confide in her as to your dilemma. If she is not with child, perhaps then our child could serve a greater cause if you were to bear it in secret and make it appear to be Sir Nestor's. The child would then, to all the world, be legitimate. Your cousin could keep her home and income, and in time, you could return to Society with none the wiser.

Charlotte's heart stilled as her eyes reread the passage over and over.

Go to your cousin.
Confide in her. If she is not with child, perhaps then our child could serve a better good . . . appear to be Sir Nestor's.

Charlotte tried to breathe, tried to push aside the startling notion of William's outrageous proposal. The floor shifted beneath her and she clamored to her feet and retrieved the earlier letters, glancing at the dates and making a hasty count of months.

Seven months. The first letter was dated seven months before she was born.

Suddenly the two worlds she'd been straddling collided, and so many things made sense.

Why her mother had always been so disdainful of her.

Her mother. She wasn't even sure she could give that name to Lady Wilmont any longer.

Some things are the same, the important ones, Quince

had said. *But time is like a garden, touched by winter one year, kissed by a gentle spring the next. You never know what will take root and bloom.*

In one life, William's plan had worked. And in this one, obviously Lady Wilmont had scorned her cousin and given her the cut direct, as had the rest of their Uppington-Higgins relations.

Leaving Finella and her child to find their own way in the world.

No wonder Finny had reacted with such venom over Aurora's letter that morning and why the former Lady Wilmont had all but left her box rather than sit so close to Charlotte, a living embodiment of a family disgrace.

Ever so quietly, Charlotte gathered all the letters together and tied them up into a single bundle, which she laid atop Finella's writing desk.

She tidied up the rest of the room, pulled the curtains closed, then tiptoed out.

Charlotte made it no further than the steps and sunk down on them, her legs giving way, as if she'd consumed a bottle of Kimpton's brandy.

Loss, deep and unfathomable, overcame her and she gave way to tears, mourning the loss of everything she'd known, of her proper sensibilities, of her name. For truly, she wasn't Charlotte Wilmont.

Nor even Lottie Townsend.

And now what?

Charlotte couldn't help wondering if she was going to end her days like Finella, in a drunken stupor with nothing but yellowed and tattered memories of a past best left forgotten.

Chapter 12

Sebastian didn't visit Charlotte that night. Or the next. By the third night, she thought she'd go mad. Whatever was she to do?

Almost as bad as Sebastian's desertion was the knowledge that Finella was her mother. Charlotte had so many questions: Had William married Lady Portia? How and when had Finella entered the trade? And why had she allowed her daughter to do the same?

Yet every time she opened her mouth to ask, she stopped herself. Finella had been on edge since Kimpton's marriage, and the last thing Charlotte wanted to do was pry into old wounds and set the lady off on another bender.

Even now, as they stood together in the foyer, an awkward uneasiness rose up between the two of them. Finella, she suspected, felt some guilt over Sebastian's disappearance.

"You needn't pace about all evening," Finella told her as she rummaged about her purse. Dressed to the nines, right down to nearly every piece of jewelry she owned and a few bits borrowed from Lottie's collection, she still had a worn, tired look about her that no amount of finery could hide. "He won't be here for hours . . ." Her voice trailed off and Charlotte could well imagine the rest of the lady's speculation. . . . *if he comes at all . . .*

"He'll be here," Charlotte assured her.

Finella looked up. "Tonight is Lady Routledge's debutante soirée . He'll be *there*. Besides, there's to be an announcement, if the gossip is to be believed."

"What gossip?" Charlotte asked.

"About Miss Burke." Finella tugged the strings on her reticule tight. "Lottie, you can't ignore the truth. He is going to marry that girl. I'm surprised the engagement hasn't been announced, considering he hasn't been here since—"

Since Finella's drunken display. Since he'd accused her of chasing after Rockhurst. Since everything had gone so very wrong.

"Well, in days," Finella concluded, unknotting her purse strings and making another furtive search of the insides.

"Where are you off to?" Charlotte asked, not ready to face another night alone.

Finella's nose wrinkled. "'Tis Wednesday."

"Wednesday?"

"Goodness, Lottie, this affair with Trent has turned you as absentminded as Mrs. Dimbleton cross the way. 'Tis Wednesday." She waited for a moment, then heaved another sigh. "The night I play whist. We'll be at Mrs. Campbell's tonight, for Mrs. Van Horne hasn't been well of late."

Charlotte nodded. Oh, yes. Finella had mentioned it

before. Her weekly whist game with the other aging courtesans of Little Titchfield Street. Some of the most formidable Incognitos of their time, they now spent their nights playing whist and making up outrageous lies about the generosity and virility of their former lovers, flaunting their jewels as if they still had front row boxes at the Opera. They met at Mrs. Van Horne's house because she could claim the highest-ranking former lover, a royal duke, who had left her a tidy annuity payable until her death. That she had outlived the old Lothario by more than forty years was a thorn in the side of his descendants, but it gave the lady a measure of distinction amongst her peers.

"And you?" Finella asked. "What are you to do tonight?" She glanced over at the giant vase filled with hothouse roses that had arrived earlier in the day. From Rockhurst. "Is the earl the reason for your finery?"

"No," Charlotte told her. "Sebastian is going to call tonight."

"He sent a note?" she asked, knowing full well he hadn't. Finella missed nothing that happened in the house.

"No, but he said he would call and I suspect tonight is the night he is going to make his apologies."

"Oh, Lottie," Finella moaned. "You can't do this to yourself or you'll end up in the Thames with your pockets full of rocks like Sarah Whitting last year."

Charlotte straightened her shoulders, not willing to believe anything other than that Sebastian loved her and he was going to call. "Finella, he will call tonight, and if not, he most likely has a very good reason—"

Even before Finella could make a good snort, the bell over the door jangled and both women froze.

"Sebastian," Charlotte whispered like a prayer and

rushed forward. She would have flung the door open if Finella hadn't caught her by the arm.

"Don't be in such a hurry or he'll know he has the upper hand." With a huffy sigh of experience, she towed Charlotte behind her and counted softly to twenty—each number a painful nudge to Charlotte's hammering heart—then slowly opened the door.

Charlotte rose up on her tiptoes to see over Finella's plumes, but to her disappointment it wasn't Sebastian standing in the doorway but a short little man in a dark, plain coat.

"Mrs. Townsend?" he inquired.

"Who's calling?" Finella's fists went to rest on her hips, blocking his path.

"Mr. Bridge. Of Rundell and Bridge, ma'am. I have a package for Mrs. Townsend."

Charlotte's mouth fell open. The jeweler? "I'm Mrs. Townsend."

"Yes, yes, there you are. I have a gift for you." He opened his coat and pulled out a long narrow box. "If I may?" he asked, nodding toward the entry.

Finella, ever the sharp-eyed opportunist, pulled the poor jeweler inside as if she were reeling in a lost cask of well-aged brandy. "There now," she said. "I am so sorry, Mr. Bridge. I didn't recognize you."

"Mrs. Birley," he said, paying her scant heed, his attention fixed on Charlotte. "I was instructed to give this to you directly." He placed the box in her trembling hands. "And tell you it is with his lordship's most sincere apologies."

Finella hustled her way to Charlotte's side and nudged her. "Well?"

Despite the way her fingers trembled, Charlotte managed to get the box open, and what she spied inside left her breathless.

The diamond necklace from the window. The very one that had caused the terrible rift between them.

"Is it to your liking, ma'am?" Mr. Bridge asked.

"I would think so," Finella shot back.

Charlotte, meanwhile, was reading the small note tucked into the satin lining. "'For you. For our future.'" Tears welled up in her eyes. He'd spent a fortune—money he didn't have—to tell her he was so sorry. "Oh, Lord Trent shouldn't have."

"Of course he should," Finella muttered. "And about damn time."

"Lord Trent, ma'am?" Mr. Bridge said from the doorway, where he was making his discreet exit. "Lord Trent didn't purchase those."

"He didn't?" Charlotte said. "Of course he did!"

The man shook his head. "No, ma'am. It was Lord Rockhurst who sent those to you. With his compliments."

The evening, as Finella had predicted, was leaving Charlotte ready to consider a lonely swim in the Thames.

Tired of pacing about the salon and dashing to the window every time she thought she heard a carriage, she'd retrieved a deck of cards from the sideboard and decided to try a simple game of Patience.

She found it nearly as provoking as waiting. Absently, she flipped over the next card and found herself staring at the mocking face of the Queen of Hearts—which bore a startling resemblance to Lavinia Burke.

"Steady, Charlotte," she told herself, getting up from

the table and resuming her pacing about the room. "If Finella finds out you spent the night chatting up the walls and playing Patience, she'll have you committed."

Then again, she could argue that this entire wish nonsense should have been enough to gain her a corner suite at Bedlam.

Sebastian Marlowe . . . in love with her. She'd been a fool to believe in Quince's assertions that it was possible. That his heart had always belonged to her.

Even Tromler had deserted her, for the talented German hadn't struck a single note all night, leaving her in silence and misery.

She looked over at the mocking face of the Queen of Hearts and in an angry, frustrated moment, she swept her hand across the table, sending the cards scattering. Along with the deck went the box from Rundell and Bridge, and the diamond necklace spilled to the carpet as well.

The cold icy stones stared up at her, making her simple wish for love seem such a travesty.

Damn Rockhurst! Damn him and his diamonds.

This was all his fault.

She bent over to pick them up and went to put them back in the box, but for a moment she found herself transfixed by the way they sparkled and glittered, by the sheer weight of them in her hands. Never in her life had she held something so expensive, so utterly beautiful.

Try them on. What harm is it to just try them on?

Charlotte shook her head. *No. Never.* She wanted nothing to do with the earl, with his offerings. Yet when she glanced down at the necklace in her hand, the lure of such perfect stones got the better of her.

Until her dying day, she knew not what she was thinking—mayhap it was Sebastian's apparent desertion—

but she closed her eyes and put them on, her fingers fumbling with the clasp until it clicked into place.

At first the diamonds and gold settings lay cold against her skin, but even as her fingers traced the stones and she turned ever-so-slowly around to see herself in the mirror, they warmed, giving her a sense of power and beauty she'd never realized could be gained by mere gems.

No wonder such tokens are so sought after, she mused, thinking of Finella and her bejeweled cronies. Rising up on her toes to get a better look at herself in the mirror over the mantel, she marveled at the way it fit.

Rockhurst had been right. The necklace seemed made for her, the diamonds accenting the lines of her neck, the large stone in the center pendant falling at the very top of her bosom, calling attention to the bounty bound beneath her satin gown.

"Retirement jewels," Finella would call them, but Charlotte shook her head at the very notion of keeping them—they came at too high a price. For to keep them meant forsaking Sebastian, and she couldn't do that. Not as long as there was even a whisper of hope, the slightest chance of them finding a future together.

Glancing about the room, her wild gaze fell on the bouquet from Rockhurst and she was halfway across the room and about to send it crashing down as well when the bell jangled over the door.

Sebastian.

Until another thought struck her. *Rockhurst.*

"Botheration." Heaving a sigh, she went to answer the door as the bell jangled again, this time with more feeling. Well, perhaps there was a third explanation.

"Finella," she muttered. The lady was probably too tipsy to find her key. "Really, Finella, if you can't keep yourself—" she was saying as she tugged the door open.

She'd been right the first time. *Sebastian.*

"May I come in?" he asked, stiffly, formally.

She pulled the door open for him and bit her lips together for fear she'd say something incoherent or ridiculous.

He swept past her and continued into the salon, his massive black cloak swirling after him. The scent of bay rum drifted past her, and she inhaled in that crazy drunken manner, rather like Finella when she walked past the now-locked liquor cabinet.

Be calm, Charlotte, she told herself. *Don't let him see how distressed you've been.*

What was it Finella always said? Oh, yes. A good courtesan is cool and indifferent.

Instead, she rushed after him and nearly ran into his back.

And when he turned around she could see something had changed.

No, make that everything.

They stared at each other, Charlotte drinking in the sight of him dressed for the evening yet looking tired and haggard. How had it come to this? They should be upstairs by now—half dressed and delirious with desire. Not eyeing each other like strangers.

"I left Lady Routledge's early because we have a matter that needs discussing."

This took her aback. *A matter?* Charlotte felt that unused temper of Lottie's stir, but before she could manage to say anything, Sebastian spoke again. "My mother told me about your scene in the ribbon shop."

"*My* scene?"

"Yes, I heard all about it." His arms crossed over his chest.

Her scene, indeed! She'd had nothing to do with that terrible encounter. Well, nearly nothing. "You weren't there. I merely—"

"You shouldn't have offered," he said, his voice rising sharply. "Why, it's . . . it's outrageous!"

"Sebastian, you weren't there! That shopkeeper was being perfectly odious. And poor Hermione—" She came to a blundering stop when his brow cocked upward at her familiar use of his sister's name.

Demmit, Lady Hermione was her best friend. Well, had been. Would be still, if . . . if only . . .

Oh, however could she explain it to him?

Instead, she tried another tack. "It was nothing but a length of ribbon, and your sister seems to be very nice. 'Tis a shame, when I have money enough—"

"My family's finances are none of your affair." He made this statement with such a stubborn defiance, with such finality, that her long-simmering temper refused to be restrained any longer.

"What is wrong with my money?" she shot back. "'Tis gold like any other's. And I might point out that I haven't any problem with creditors."

He flinched and turned a dark, stormy gaze on her. "Your money? You want me to take *your* money?" His lips curled with disdain.

Charlotte stepped back. Why was he looking at her like this? "If that is how you feel," she said icily, "perhaps you need to return to Lady Routledge's. I would hate to be the reason you are tardy for Miss Burke's performance. I hear it is worth its weight in gold. Ten thousand a year, I'd venture." She watched his jaw work back and forth, saw the frustration in his eyes. "What is the difference, Sebastian, if you marry Miss Burke for her money or you take mine? The fortunes will have been gained in much the same manner."

Suddenly his gaze narrowed, and she felt the weight of it land on her neck. On Rockhurst's diamonds.

Oh, demmit, the diamonds! In her haste to answer the door, she'd forgotten to take them off.

He stared at the necklace, his face a mixture of emotions. "I see I've come too late." He laughed, the bitter sound tearing at her heart. "The irony of all this is that if I had used my winnings from the races at Saunderton's and bought Battersby's ridiculous shares, I'd be a rich man now."

A chill ran down her spine. "What?"

"The *Agatha Skye*," he said, pacing across the room and leaning his head against the mirror, "arrived at the docks this morning. Seven months overdue. Which matters little when the hold is overflowing with Eastern spices and coffee. Battersby's shares are worth a bloody fortune. If I had but spent my winnings on those shares, gambled once more, I would be standing before you a wealthy and independent man."

Charlotte felt the floor shift beneath her.

"Gads, I'm a wretched fool," he said, raking his hand through his dark hair. "I squandered the money on you instead of—"

What did he mean? "Squandered it?"

"Oh, aye, squandered it. Getting you into the museum." He shook his head. "I used to be so sensible—at least that's what everyone says. And I suppose they are right. Then I met you and lost my heart, lost my mind. Why did you do this to me, Lottie? Was it a game to you?"

"No, never!" she shot back, frightened by the desperate light in his eyes. The hurt and pain she saw behind his wild accusations.

"The gambling, the races, all those nights—was it just another lark to you?"

"How can you say such a thing? I thought you—" Heavens, she didn't know what to think. To know where she started and Lottie began, who was the real Sebastian—the man she'd known or the one before her now.

"I thought I did as well—" His words trailed off and he nodded at the diamonds at her throat. "But I see it was all for naught. You've made your choice."

"No!" she shot out, her fingers tugging at the necklace, trying to remove it. "It's not like that. I only want you."

"You only want me?" He spat out the words as if they were poison on his tongue. "Whatever for? To make a mockery of? To turn me into the latest *on dit*? Because that is what you've done. I'm broke, Lottie. Up the River Tick. If I had been sensible, like my parents begged me, I'd be married to Miss Burke by now and I wouldn't be here. But now, because of you, because I loved you, I've jeopardized even that. And for what? So I could see you standing there in another man's offering."

Charlotte snapped. Not Lottie, not even a bit of Lottie, but Charlotte Wilmont. The hypocrisy behind his words, Finella's circumstances, the razor-thin line that cut a good woman out of society for the least infraction.

"How dare you," she said in a low, dangerous voice. "How dare you speak to me like that. You claim to love me, and yet you call me a whore. Who am I, Sebastian? The woman you love or just merely another man's leavings?"

He turned his back to her, and she knew she'd struck a chord, but she dug deeper, angry beyond reason. "You won't take my money, fine. But explain to me how taking my ill-gained fortune is so different from you taking Miss Burke's dowry? How hard is it to see that if you marry that whey-faced chit, you'll be the one picking up the reticule of money from the dresser in the morning?" she said, throwing his mother's words at him.

He spun around and stared at her, and she felt both the heat of his anger and a long-simmering frustration over their tenuous situation boil over.

Charlotte sucked in a deep breath. She'd never been so furious in her life. So enflamed. And then, just as suddenly, so full of desire. Her breasts ached, her body pulsed with need at the sight of his fury. Oh, heavens, she wanted him now more than she had ever before. Three days away from him, away from his kiss, his touch, his claiming, made her burn with hunger.

She didn't care that they were fighting, that this was all but the end of their affair—for there was no denying that there was only one solution: Sebastian must marry Miss Burke.

But that didn't stop Charlotte from wanting him.

One more time.

"How dare you," he sputtered. "I'll show you the difference." With that, he closed the distance between them and his mouth crashed down on hers.

Charlotte's anger turned into a passionate fury. Her hands balled up in fists and beat against his chest, in a rage over his presumption, in anger over her own overwhelming desire for him.

He acknowledged her protest by catching hold of her hands and pinning them behind her back, much as he had the first morning she'd awakened in his bed. But this time, there was none of his good humor, no jests over her ill humor. Just his fury holding her in place so he could take out his frustrations in this endless kiss.

And what a kiss it was. His tongue swept over hers, demanding his share, opening her and exploring her, taking what was his with little regard for her needs.

But it was enough for Charlotte. This pirate-like raid on her lips was making her toes curl, her body come alive with a dangerous, unyielding passion. This fire he ignited, set to blaze within her, called for one thing, and one thing only.

Retribution.

Yet how could she turn this tide with her hands behind her back?

He pushed her up against the wall, the solid plaster behind her one prison, his hard, muscled body another. His body. Up against hers. He had her there, at his whim, at his mercy, as now, with one hand freed, he began to stroke her, raid the treasure beneath her gown as if it were gold to be stolen.

Her gown came up, over her thighs, over her hips, his hand tugging at the sateen, seeking the silk of her skin beneath. His fingers ran a hot trail up the front of her thigh, lingering over the apex, teasing her, testing her, enough so to send her rebellious hips arching to meet his touch.

With one finger, he dipped beneath her shift and explored her, opened her up. Her thighs parted, quickly and willingly. He had his cache—and he knew it—swirling his finger around the nub hidden beneath, teasing her into a breathy moan.

Wet and trembling, she almost hated herself for wanting him so utterly, for being so susceptible to his touch.

"Do you want me, Lottie? Do you want me inside you?"

"No," she lied. She was still mad at him, still despised the way he'd mocked her.

His finger went deeper, slipping inside her, into the heated moist slit that belied her emphatic denial. He stroked, tempted her further. "Tell me that you want me."

"Never," she managed, shifting closer to him, feeling the beginnings of her release start to build. She'd greedily steal this orgasm and leave him wanting. That would serve him right.

More so, she wanted him to beg, wanted him to be in this same dangerous, trembling state.

But how could she do that when he had her thusly, pinned against the wall, her hands trapped?

Her hips arched again, and this time they came in contact with the hard evidence of his desire. Of his obvious needs.

That place where he could be brought to heel. *Every man's Achilles' heel.*

Without a second thought, she pushed herself off the wall and up against him, her breasts flattened against his chest, her hips riding up and down, letting her stroke him. Tease him.

How she loved the feel of him, of knowing what that steely length could do to her once it was freed, once it stood noble and erect. She rode up against him, letting it press against her, ease some of her own frustrations, fuel her already rampant imagination.

She hadn't spent a fortnight in his arms not to know what made this man come alive. The power she yielded over his desires.

Sebastian's mouth came back over hers, his kiss full of frustration and need. He released her wrists and she im-

mediately put her hands to good use—letting her fingers
do what her hips had been—stroking him. She put her
palms on either side of him and ran her thumbs up and
down his hardened length.

"Demmit, Lottie," he moaned. "What are you doing
to me?"

"Much the same as you are doing to me," she said, letting her fingers tease him again.

He pulled her gown higher, tugging it over her head
and tossing it aside, so she stood before him in her shift.
Immediately he pulled her breasts free, and his head
dipped to take one of her nipples in his mouth.

Oh, he would have to do that, she thought, feeling her
advantage slip away in this game of wills. Her hands fell
away from him, dropping to her sides, impotent against
his assault. His tongue swirled over her, teasing her into a
tight void of desire. He continued to lap and suckle, while
his other hand dove back between her thighs and began
to stroke her again.

Why did he have to know her so well? For he knew just
how to stroke her, just how to bring her to that dizzy
brink, leave her panting and moaning, and then stop and
leave her on that abyss, aching for completion.

And that is just what he did, and he looked down at
her, his dark gaze glittering with victory.

Oh, this battle isn't over, she vowed. And she knew
exactly how to turn the tables, sliding down the front of
him until she knelt before him. She might look like she
was submitting, but with his pants open and his manhood
freed, she truly held the better hand. And then she looked
up at him, one hand cupping his balls, the other holding
his erection, the tides of war shifted.

Starting slowly, she ran her tongue over the tip, tasting him. Her fingers made a slow, lazy trail up the length of him.

Sebastian groaned, his hands fisting into her hair.

She took him slowly into her mouth, letting her tongue run over him, and then bringing it back out. Back and forth, she went, slowly taking him in her mouth, then quickly drawing him out, teasing him, as he had her, until his body started to shake and she knew his release was so very close.

Charlotte smiled, and stopped, rising up, letting her hands claim his body, letting him feel her.

"That is how I dare," she whispered, answering his earlier question. "Because I can."

He didn't say a word; he merely growled something unintelligible, and finished it by catching her mouth in a demanding kiss. Then, just as suddenly, she was up in his arms and he was storming from the salon, headed for the stairs.

Her arms wound around his neck, clinging to him, her gaze running ahead, up into the darkness above, up to her bedroom, where they would most surely finish this dangerous game.

With one hand she went to take off the diamonds, but he stopped and said, "Leave them on so I don't forget who and what you are."

His savage words were like a blow and only served to renew her anger, her frustration, her passions.

Fine, if that was how he wanted to remember her, then she'd let him have this fantasy. Let him take it with him for the rest of his life. Into his cold marriage . . .

She'd give him a night that would be forever burned into his memory. And worse yet, into hers . . .

"Then take me now, demmit," she said as he stood still, poised halfway up the stairs. "Take me now, and be done with it, if you dare."

He stopped and looked at her, saw the challenge burning in her eyes, and without a word, he put her down on the steps. The carpeted tread was no more comfortable than the wall had been, but she wasn't interested in a downy mattress or satin sheets—she wanted him, and she wanted him now. His fingers closed over the top of her shift and tore it in half, exposing her to him.

Charlotte shivered, trembled. He towered above her, and she suddenly wondered at the sense of her own brazen invitation. He didn't even bother to disrobe, just came down on top of her, catching hold of her hips and driving himself into her in one quick stroke.

"Oooh," she gasped, as much at this hot, rough invasion as at how her already thrumming body reacted to it—arching up to meet his eager, hard thrust.

Sebastian drove into her again, and Charlotte heard herself calling to him, "Yes, Sebastian. Oh, now, please."

Her heels dug into the steps, pushing her body up, while one hand caught hold of the baluster. She met him, thrust for thrust, ragged breath for passionate moan.

Over her, Sebastian's body tightened, his thrusts hard and fast, seeking the same thing she sought—release.

He groaned, and his body stilled for only a second before he shuddered, and then climaxed, pushing himself inside her completely, filling her with his hot release. That was enough to tip Charlotte over the edge and into that trembling bliss of completion.

The tumultuous waves that crashed within her pulled the last vestiges of his release from him, and he heaved one final, deep, breathy sigh.

For a few moments they lay there, on the steps, a tangle of limbs and spent passions, not quite holding each other, but still joined. The anger and frustration that had fueled this tempestuous display had gone the way of their passion, into the ethers.

Charlotte continued to quake and tremble around him, and she thought her release would never end—not that she wanted it to. And when it finally did, she looked up and found Sebastian watching her, one brow cocked arrogantly.

Oh, yes, he was quite pleased with himself.

"Gads, Trent, what have you done to me?" she said, giving her words a bit of Lottie's flair by adding a saucy toss of her head.

"What I intend to do to you until morning comes," he replied, and with that gauntlet, he rose, hauling her with him.

And then he carried her up the remaining stairs to her room and made good his vow.

Charlotte was still trying to catch her breath hours later when they both finally gave in to exhaustion.

"Gads, Lottie, I don't know what came over me," Sebastian said, laying beside her, propped up on one elbow, his fingers tracing lazy circles around her nipples. "My behavior was inexcusable."

"Maybe the first time," she told him. "But not the second or third."

He grinned and leaned over and kissed her, softly and gently and full of the love that was their fate, their destiny.

There is a way for us to be together, she told herself. *There must be.*

But how?

"I came over here last night with every intention of . . . well, we'll get to that in a moment . . . and then when I saw you in those diamonds, I—"

"Sshh." She shook her head at him. "Don't say another word. I was foolish to try them on. 'T'was all I was doing—trying them on, but I had no intentions of ever—"

"I know that now. Still, I was an utter ass last night. Between my parents and the Burkes, I felt trapped. I came here because you make me feel so alive, so free. I swear, you are the only person who understands me. Who doesn't look at me and see only a title." Then he took a deep breath and stared down at her, his features utterly serious. "Hear me out, Lottie. I've got something to ask you."

"Ask me?" Her mouth went dry.

He held up one hand. "Please don't refuse me this time until you've heard my reasoning as to why we should wed."

Wed? He was going to ask her to marry him? If that wasn't shocking enough, there was the other part of his plea.

Please don't refuse me this time . . .

He'd asked her before? And Lottie had said no?

Charlotte moved her lips to say an emphatic "yes" before he changed his mind, before she made a cake of herself and let Lottie's unpredictable nature do something unthinkable.

Like deny her heart. Let go of her wish.

Meanwhile, he'd turned from her and was leaning over the bed, fishing through his discarded clothes. Catching hold of his waistcoat, he slipped his hand into the pocket and retrieved something.

Dear heavens. He'd bought a ring for her. No wonder the sight of her in Rockhurst's diamonds had sent him over the edge.

Charlotte took another deep breath. If they were to marry, there would never be any need to disavow her wish. They'd be together always. Yet a plaguing doubt nudged at her willful heart.

Whatever is wrong with marrying Sebastian? she argued to herself.

And then to her horror, he told her.

"We won't live with my family. My mother has made it clear that she will remove herself and my sisters to the Abbey if I choose this course."

"She'd leave London?" Charlotte whispered. The Lady Walbrook she knew loved London, adored everything about town life. That she would cede her place in her home rather than live with Charlotte said much about her opposition to the match.

"Oh, aye," he said. "She made a great cake of herself about it yesterday. Said that I was driving her from her home."

Charlotte tried to breathe, tried to tell herself that eventually it would all work out.

Lady Walbrook would come around. She'd learn to love Charlotte as she had before in her other life. And eventually, she'd forgive the pair once she saw how happy Sebastian was, married to the woman he loved.

"Then she went on and on as to how I was ruining the girls' chances at decent matches." He heaved a sigh and shook his head. "What utter nonsense," he said as he rolled over on his back, his hands tucked beneath his head.

Charlotte closed her eyes and tried to blot out the vision of Cordelia, Hermione, and Viola, growing old together at Walbrook Abbey. The Marlowe sisters had nothing but their sterling reputation and their looks to recommend them to a good match. There was no significant dowry for any of them to attract a lofty catch—that is, unless . . .

"Sebastian," she began, unwilling to give up, even as an image of the trio—unwed and unloved in their exile—danced about her mind. "You can have my money. It would provide the girls ample dowries. Perhaps it would go some way toward mending fences with your mother."

He snorted. "She already told me she won't take a farthing from you. 'Tis why she is leaving Town. She thinks the entire family will be tainted by your money." He rolled again. "I told her that I didn't plan on taking any of your ill-gained fortune."

Ill-gained fortune. So they were back to that again. Lottie's temper roused and Charlotte did her best to tamp it back down. Besides, she'd thought that after the tender way they'd finally made up, perhaps Sebastian had changed his mind about her money.

Apparently not.

And as much as she wanted to marry him, spend every moment of her life with him, she now knew for certain that Lottie Townsend's past was a wall between them that could never be razed.

The former lovers . . . the gold, jewels, and property Lottie had accumulated . . . the reputation that came with being London's most coveted courtesan.

Everyone was right. She couldn't just get married to Sebastian. There was no escaping her past. And it wasn't just Finella and Lady Walbrook who had the right of it—Rockhurst had pointed out the futility of such a match as well.

Sebastian rolled toward her, reaching out to toy with a strand of her hair. "Mother doesn't see why I just don't marry Miss Burke and keep things between us as they are now." He heaved another impossible sigh and gazed down at her with an innocence that surprised her.

How could this rakish, intelligent man not see the truth that was so evident to his mother?

To Charlotte.

"Your mother is right," she heard herself saying.

"Oh, not you as well," he groaned. "Lottie, I'm not going to listen to any more dire female prattle. I am going out today and secure a Special License and then you and I are going to be wed." He bounded out of bed, as if that was the end of the matter, and began to get dressed.

"No!" The emphatic reply startled even her. But she knew one thing for certain: His proposal wasn't the right thing to do. That he couldn't see it told Charlotte that he loved her too deeply to look beyond his own heart. "Your mother is right. You should marry Miss Burke."

Sebastian had already tugged on his smallclothes and had his breeches in hand. "You'd have me marry *her*?"

She pulled the sheet up over herself and nodded. "Yes." Then she added, rather forced out, "Why not?"

"Why not?" He flung his breeches aside. "How can you even suggest such a thing?"

"I don't see that there's anything wrong with her."

"Nothing wrong? Everything's wrong about her. She's never made me feel like this—"

He returned to the bed and caught hold of Charlotte, tugging her into his arms. His lips covered hers in a hungry, angry kiss. Immediately, that burning passion between them sparked to life, blazing quickly to a hot and needy bonfire.

His hand found first her bare breast, the nipple already tight and expectant. He spent little time, his fingers trailing downward until they reached their prize hidden beneath her nether curls, her reward—for he stroked her, teased her until she swayed against him, her body pleading with him to make love to her.

And even as an unbidden moan of pleasure escaped her lips, he released her and held her at arm's length.

"Can you imagine me doing that to her?"

No, she couldn't.

Charlotte struggled to catch her breath, gather her wits about her. She'd gotten her wish. For one marvelous, perfect fortnight.

Now it was time to let it go.

Slowly and deliberately, she chose her words. "Have you ever tried that with Miss Burke?"

His nostrils flared, and he dropped her back on the bed. "Of course not! She's a . . ." His outrage sputtered to an impotent halt, realizing only too late the condemnation of his words.

Charlotte sat up. "She's a what, Sebastian? A lady?"

"Demmit, Lottie, you know what I mean."

"I know exactly what you mean," she told him with the cool, icy tones of a woman insulted. "Now leave." She pointed at the door.

He shook his head and tried to smile at her, that dazzling one capable of melting her heart. "Come now, Lottie my love, 'twas said in anger and you misunderstood me. I meant it not." He leaned forward to catch her anew, but she slipped from his grasp and got out of bed. Tugging on her wrapper, she pointed again at the door. "It is time you left, Lord Trent. You were right before. I don't love you. I don't want this any longer."

This life. This wish.

She didn't know what she expected, that suddenly she would be Charlotte Wilmont again. Now she wished she'd listened to Quince the other day, but something told her it wasn't any harder to undo her wish than it had been to make it. That all she had to do was disavow it and everything would go back to the way it was. Yet she'd done that and nothing had changed; the ring remained stuck to her hand and she still stood in Lottie's house, in Lottie's life.

All of it the same but for Sebastian's regard.

His eyes held a flinty anger, his jaw set in a hard line. "And this is your response? I ask you to marry me. I offer you a respectable life and you refuse me?"

She didn't dare open her mouth, for the lure of it all still held her heart. *Marry you? Yes, Sebastian. Yes, please.*

Instead she nodded, her rebellious lips pressed together tight.

"Damn you to hell, Lottie Townsend," he said, donning his clothes with all due haste. "See if you don't regret this. See if you don't."

She already did.

He started to rush from the room, but he stopped and leaned over to retrieve something she couldn't see. Then he held it up.

Rockhurst's diamonds.

They glittered still, even in the poor light of the nearly guttered candles.

Without a word, he tossed them down atop the satin sheets, amidst the tangled wreckage of her bed that still held the warmth of their once entwined bodies. Then he stormed out.

Charlotte stood rooted in place, her body racked with

sobs that she didn't dare give voice to until she knew he wouldn't hear.

And when the front door slammed shut, she collapsed atop the bed, her hand unwittingly curling around the cold, wretched diamonds, and she began to cry. Sobbed until she could barely breathe.

It wasn't until a few hours later, as the sun started to peek over the rooftops of London, that Charlotte sobbed her last and fell into a deep, exhausted sleep.

The sort that held no thoughts of wishes. No dreams of love.

Or what that tenuous, fragile notion cost one's heart.

Chapter 13

May 10, 1810
What Should Have Been an Ordinary Thursday

Sebastian Marlowe, Viscount Trent, woke up oddly disconcerted, as if he'd been out all night on a bender. Or had gotten into a row. Maybe even gambled away the family fortunes.

Which was quite simply impossible for a sensible man like Sebastian.

Still, he couldn't help but feel that something was just not quite right with his world.

"Good morning, my lord," his valet, Wilks, called out from the dressing room. "'Tis good to see you finally up."

There was a pinched set to the man's words that gave Sebastian pause. "What time is it, Wilks?"

"Two, my lord."

"Two?" Sebastian flung back the covers and got up. "Two? How can that be?"

"You were sleeping rather soundly, my lord," the man said, as he chose a coat and cravat for the viscount. "But your bath is ready and your mother is holding breakfast for you."

"My mother?" That didn't bode well. Sebastian ran a hand through his hair and took a deep breath. How could it be two in the afternoon? Why, he'd missed his morning ride and a quiet breakfast without his madcap family about.

They were the ones who slept the day away, not him.

He hustled toward the tub and got in, soaping himself and making haste with his usually leisurely morning ablutions.

"Remind me, Wilks, what is on my schedule for today?" he called out, worried he'd forgotten something else other than getting up.

Wilks was busy examining a perfectly pressed cravat. "You are attending the opera tonight with Lord and Lady Burke and Miss Burke."

Sebastian shook his head. "Are you sure there isn't something else I'm supposed to be doing today?"

"I can check with her ladyship," he offered.

"No! The last thing I need is my mother's interference with my life."

"Yes, my lord."

Bathed and dressed, Sebastian went downstairs half an hour later and took his place at the head of the table. His paper held no interest to him, for how could one read over his sisters' chatter?

"Sebastian?" his mother asked from her end of the table. "Whatever is wrong with you today? You look positively distracted."

For that matter, he was, for he was digging around in

his waistcoat pocket, for what he knew not, but it seemed there was supposed to be something in there.

Something quite valuable.

He looked up and found all four pairs of eyes watching him.

Heavens, he was becoming as odd as the rest of his family.

Lady Walbrook, who apparently wasn't expecting an answer, launched into her next subject. "Sebastian, Viola tells me you picked my orange blossoms for Miss Burke."

He shot his little sister a dark glance, but she was too busy buttering a roll to notice. "And I forgot to thank you for them, Mother. Lavinia quite adored them."

"Lavinia! Harrumph! I was going to use those for Hermione and Viola's costumes. You've quite ruined their performance now. You and your Miss Burke." She further sniffed her disapproval. "You mustn't spend so much time with her, people are beginning to talk. Why, Lady Routledge is quite convinced you are on the verge of proposing. She positively intimated the other day that there would be a betrothal announcement at her soirée."

Sebastian's gaze snapped up. "Oh, demmit! The Burkes!"

"Yes, the Burkes. Presumptuous mushrooms!" his mother said. "Why, I don't know—"

"Their Venetian breakfast. It was this morning!"

His mother blinked. "Oh, yes, I do believe you're right."

He rose immediately. He needed to get over there. He needed to apologize. This was disastrous. "Perhaps if we hurry—" he began, glancing at the clock, which betrayed the real truth.

"Why, it is well and done by now," his mother said,

giving voice to what he already knew. "There's no point in rushing over there—you'll look the fool."

He groaned and sat back down only to find his sister Hermione gloating like a cat over her plate. "You needn't look so pleased," he told her.

"As it is, I am quite pleased. Now perhaps Miss Burke will refuse your suit."

"That would be a godsend," his mother muttered.

Sebastian chose not to reply, which was odd in itself. Of course he was going to marry Miss Burke, but for some reason arguing the matter with his mother didn't hold any appeal today.

Unfortunately, his silence only gave the lady another opportunity to add to her lecture. "Your father would not approve of such a match. He never liked Lord Burke, and I don't think he'd hold a very high opinion of the man's daughter."

"Since my father is not here to give his opinion, madame, you will have to trust my judgment."

She waved her hands about. "I think I can speak for your father. After all, we have been married for lo these last thirty years." She frowned. "You are only marrying that girl for her money."

"And the adjoining lands in Kent and the title she'll be giving her firstborn," Griffin pointed out.

"No," Viola said, holding out her cup for Fenwick to refill with chocolate. "He is marrying her because she is as dull as he is."

Sebastian straightened. "Miss Burke is not dull. And neither am I."

His family, for once, diplomatically said nothing—for almost a minute, which, he reasoned, had to be some sort of record.

"You would do well to heed this," Lady Walbrook announced with great flourish: "So wise so young, they say do never live long."

Shakespeare. Whenever a crisis arrived, his mother lobbed quotations from Shakespeare at her enemies like the French might fire cannonballs. And often with equally disastrous results. "Mother, I am of no mind to take advice from a dead playwright."

"You would do well to heed the man, Sebastian. He knew a thing or two about love."

"That would be well and good, Mother," Hermione interjected, "but that quote is from *Richard the Third.*" She glanced over at her brother. "A tragedy, all the same."

Again an uncomfortable silence reigned at the breakfast table.

Why couldn't his family understand the very essential need for him to make an advantageous marriage?

"I have some good news," Griffin announced. "I've been granted a presentation to the Royal Science Society. Sir Joshua arranged for my paper on time travel and future societies to be presented at the next meeting. A fortnight isn't much time to perfect my theory on—"

"The twenty-fourth?" Lady Walbrook interrupted.

"Yes," he replied. "The Thursday after—"

"Oh, no, that will never do," she declared.

"Why not?" Griffin asked.

The countess heaved an aggrieved sigh. "That's the night of Lady Routledge's soirée. I need you for the girls' tableaux. Cordelia has outright refused to come up from Bath, and I need a third to play—"

Everyone at the table groaned.

Viola slunk so far down in her seat that all that could be seen was the top of her dark head.

"What?" his mother asked, always oblivious to her family's despair over her theatrical leanings.

"Mother, please don't," Sebastian asked. "Can't the girls do something a little . . . a little less . . ."

"Embarrassing?" Viola muttered from beneath the tablecloth.

"Humiliating?" Hermione offered.

"Wretched?" Griffin finished.

"I'll have you know my tableaux are highly anticipated," their mother said. She shook out her napkin and shot a haughty gaze at all of them.

"By every gossip and old cat looking for a good laugh," Griffin muttered under his breath.

His mother turned her attention back in Sebastian's direction, an effort worthy of Nelson. "My dear boy, promise you won't marry that dull girl. She will be the death of your spirit. Your delightful *joie de vivre*."

Hermione choked on her toast. "Him?" she asked, jerking her thumb at Sebastian. "Mother, aren't you putting on the brown a bit?"

The lady ignored her daughter, even if she had the right of it. No one would have ever called Sebastian the life and soul of a party.

The clock on the mantel chimed, and Sebastian knew that his first order of business, and the honorable thing to do, was to make his apologies to the Burkes for his, and his family's, absence at their breakfast fête. And as relieved as he was to have an excuse to get away from his family, he found he wasn't all that anxious to call on the baron and his wife, or even the lovely Miss Burke.

How could it be that overnight his conquest for the heiress's affections no longer seemed as important as it once had, for there was some truth to his mother's dire warnings—Lavinia Burke was a bit dull.

He shook his head. This is what came of sitting down for a meal with his family. *Joie de vivre,* indeed! Lavinia, dull? What utter nonsense! If he sat here much longer he'd start quoting Shakespeare and take to wearing a turban like his mother's elderly cousin, Merlin.

"I must be away," he said, rising abruptly.

"Oh, yes," Hermione said. "Viola, Griffin, you promised to come with me to the park. We must hurry!" The three of them dashed out of the dining room ahead of him like a stampede.

His mother sent one last sally after him. "Oh, Sebastian, how I wish you would come to your senses on this matter and find someone to love. A Titania to ignite your passions."

Sebastian paused at the doorway. "Mother, I will not make you any such promise. Besides, everyone knows wishes never come true."

The morning dawned much the same for Charlotte. She found herself back in her old narrow bed in the house on Queen Street.

Apparently she'd found the way to dissolve her wish without Quince's help, for nothing of it remained but the odd little ring still stubbornly affixed to her finger.

She pulled her pillow over her face and stifled the terrible wrenching sob that rose up from her broken heart. "Sebastian. Oh, Sebastian, what will I do without you?"

"You'll go get him, that's what you'll do," a familiar voice said.

She plucked the pillow off her face and looked around the room.

"Quince!" Charlotte cried out, starting to get out of bed, until she realized she was still stark naked from the night before.

The old lady smiled and tossed over an old nightrail.

Charlotte pulled on the prim and proper muslin gown and sighed at the high neck and lack of anything feminine—not even a single bit of ribbon or embroidery to make it more appealing.

"Now, now," Quince told her. "All is not lost."

"But it is. I let him go." Charlotte closed her eyes. "I had to," she managed to choke out before she started to cry.

"I know, my dear, I know," Quince murmured soothingly as she came over to the edge of the bed and sat down beside her. "But all is not lost."

"How can you say that?" Charlotte asked between sniffles. "I'm not *her* anymore."

"Not who?" Quince asked, passing over the same worn handkerchief as before.

"Lottie," she said, heaving another sigh and sniffling into the bit of linen. "I'm just Charlotte now."

Quince laughed, the merry sound sparkling with sunshine. "You foolish girl, of course you are still her. Who else would you be?"

Charlotte waved her hands over her dull nightrail, her tangled curls. "Look at me, do I look like a courtesan?"

Quince's nose wrinkled. "Not in that wretched gown. But it is what is underneath the muslin that matters. You have all the same curves, the same grace that made Mrs. Townsend the talk of London."

Charlotte snorted, much as Finny had when Charlotte had protested that one of Lottie's gowns was unseemly.

"Aha!" Quince said, pointing at her. "I see your time as Lottie wasn't wasted entirely."

Charlotte paused for a second, grasping at a bit of hope, but a second more fateful matter came into her thoughts. "But it is too late. Sebastian is most likely set to wed Miss Burke by now."

The lady shook her head. "No more than he was when you left this life. 'Tis . . . oh, bother calendars," she muttered as she counted on her fingers. "The tenth."

"The day after I made my wish," Charlotte said.

"Yes," Quince replied. "Everything is as it was. Nothing has changed." She paused for a moment. "Except you, and perhaps a few lingering memories in others, here and there."

An odd thrill ran down Charlotte's spine. She did remember—all of it. "Do you think he remembers?"

"With some help, he might," Quince said softly. "But not as you do. His memories will be more like vague thoughts, odd recollections."

Charlotte nodded. If he could fall in love with her once, then perhaps . . .

"But I must caution you," Quince said. "You haven't much time. After a fortnight, all of this, your memories, his feelings, all of it will be gone. You must hurry if you are to recapture his heart."

Two weeks? Charlotte shook her head. "What good will a courtesan's manners and knowledge do for me?" she asked. "Sebastian is set to propose to Miss Burke. What chance do I have against her?" She flung herself backward on the bed and covered her face with her hands as a sob slipped from her lips.

There was a loud sigh from Quince who sat patiently waiting for Charlotte to come to her senses.

She peeked through her fingers. "And what would you have me do?"

"What would Lottie do?"

Charlotte blew out a breath. "Put on her blue velvet gown, go to the opera, and flirt outrageously with Rockhurst in the plain view of one and all."

"Then that is what you will do," Quince said, gliding over to the wardrobe and throwing open the doors. She peered inside, then glanced back over her shoulder, her brows furrowed. "There isn't much to work with here."

"Exactly my point," Charlotte said. "What you suggest is impossible. Why, I don't own a single gown worthy of such a feat, never mind the fact that I have never even been introduced to the earl." Charlotte paused. "At least not here. Not as Miss Wilmont." She buried her face in her hands again and groaned. "Oh, Quince, it is impossible. I cannot compete with Miss Burke, not with my limited means and lack of social connections. Not in a fortnight's time."

"Then you have to stop thinking like Charlotte and use every wile Lottie possessed. They are still there—right inside you," Quince told her, crossing the room and poking a bony finger into Charlotte's forehead. "You know everything you need to know to win Sebastian's heart— which is yours by right if only you will claim it."

"Truly?" she whispered.

Quince nodded. "Aye. Make your wish come true, Charlotte. Miss Burke has many advantages, but you hold something far more valuable."

"And what is that?"

"The knowledge of how to make love to him."

Charlotte sat back. "I can't just throw myself at him! I would be ruined."

But even as she protested, she recalled a thousand and one ways she and Sebastian had made love—and not just inside her bedroom.

In stolen glances across the Opera House.

With the brush of her hand over the top of his sleeve while riding in the park.

With a single stolen kiss.

She knew how he loved that French vintage Rockhurst bought from a smuggler in Hastings. That he found Townley's collection breathtaking, could quote Coleridge's poetry, and loved to count the freckles on her back.

Yet she hadn't considered one other problem.

"The Sebastian I knew as Lottie was a rakish, devil-may-care sort," Charlotte said. "And my Sebastian is rather . . . well, as his sisters like to say, dull and overly sensible. I don't know if he'll be enticed with the things Lottie offered."

The lady smiled. "He still loves all those things, he just doesn't realize it. *Yet.* And I doubt Miss Burke is the woman to show him . . . that is, unless you let her."

Charlotte's gaze flew up, a sharp stab of jealousy dividing her doubts. Miss Burke kissing Sebastian? Waking up beside him?

No! Never!

But even in her momentary bravado, those aching doubts moved back in. "But how will I ever—"

Quince threw up her hands. "Have you not learned anything? He is no more different than you are. You must help him discover the rakish side he's been hiding all these years."

Help Sebastian discover his inner Corinthian? The man who loved reading Coleridge in bed, driving through the country at haphazard speeds, taking a wager at the blink of an eye, a man who let his passions rule? The idea of awakening that man brought a sly smile to Charlotte's lips. "Do you really think—"

"Yes," Quince rushed to tell her. "I do!"

Charlotte faltered to a stop. How could she have forgotten?

"He must marry Miss Burke," she said, defeat filling her words. She turned her back to Quince to hide her disappointment.

"Whyever for?"

"The money. The Marlowes are up the River Tick."

"Then you'll have to change that as well, I imagine," Quince said matter-of-factly, as if finding a fortune in a fortnight was as easily conjured as a blue velvet gown.

"This will never work," Charlotte said, pacing toward her closet. "My life as Lottie was one thing, but I'm only Charlotte now. My mother will never . . ."

Yet when she turned around, she found the room empty. Quince had vanished.

Then into the sudden stillness of the room, Charlotte heard a tiny whisper. "You have everything you need, my dear. I promise you."

"How can that be?" Charlotte asked. This time, there were no answers. Frustrated, she plopped back down on her bed, only to find herself perched atop something hard and unforgiving beneath her sheets.

What the devil, she thought as she absently poked her fingers around under the coverlet. And as she dug deeper, an image rose up the back of her mind.

No, it couldn't be. She flew up, yanked the coverlet back and gasped.

For there in the sheets lay the diamonds from Rock-hurst.

Slowly she reached out and took up the hard, cool stones, still not quite sure whether or not to believe that this boon had followed her home.

Yet they were so very real, sparkling and twinkling in the morning light. And if they were real, then that meant anything was possible.

"I told you so," came another whisper and a little laugh. "Put them to good use, my dear. Put it all to good use."

Sebastian collected his hat, gloves, and walking stick from Fenwick, and went striding out the front door flee-ing his mother's advice before, for some unlikely reason, it took root and made sense.

Yet his escape came to an abrupt halt the moment his foot came off the last step and hit the sidewalk, for he found himself colliding with a blinding flash of muslin.

His walking stick clattered to the ground as his arms wound around the lady to catch her before she ended up in a heap.

For a startling moment, like a flash of recognition, the curves beneath his grasp seemed as familiar as his own two hands. The way the lady fit against him, the faint hint of violets tickling his nose—shot him out of his reverie like a cannon blast.

And suddenly his all-too-important errand, his orderly schedule was all but forgotten.

"My deepest apologies, madame," he murmured, look-ing down at the ugliest, plainest bonnet he'd ever seen. He didn't know what he'd expected to find in his arms—a creature capable of beguiling his senses utterly and completely—but certainly not this plain little wren.

And then she glanced up from beneath the bare brim of her poor hat and the pair of eyes that gazed up at him pierced his heart.

Blue. So clear and blue, they took his breath away. So familiar he didn't know what to make of it—for they belonged to none other than that little spinster friend of Hermione's. He took another look—certain he'd been mistaken—and found himself further captivated by a tendril of hair that had escaped her bonnet. When had her hair changed to that shade of brown, no longer like a sparrow's wing but rich and full of fire?

And how would it look freed from its pins and spread out over silk sheets, those eyes looking up at him with desire and passion, the curves beneath his hands naked and trembling at his touch?

"Are you well, my lord?" she was asking, looking up with a knowing little glance that left Sebastian with the jolting impression that she could read his thoughts.

He let her go so suddenly that she nearly tumbled backward, but he didn't catch her again. Didn't risk the chance of holding her and coming up with any more rakish thoughts about his sister's best friend.

Gads, how frightfully embarrassing. He'd all but made a cake of himself, holding her so . . . so infamously . . . so very rakishly, and now he suspected he needed to apologize to her for his untoward behavior.

Oh, the devil take him, what was her name?

And then it came to him. "My regrets, Lottie. I fear I didn't see you there." Then he realized he had taken hold of her again, her arm that was, quite shamelessly, right out in the middle of plain view of everyone on Berkeley Square. He released her again (more reluctantly than he cared to admit) and was at a loss to say anything further.

"There is nothing to apologize for, my lord," she said, sliding past him and making her way up the front steps like a graceful, beguiling cat.

Like Titania entering her court.

For a moment all he could do was gape after her, until she shot another sly glance at him from over her shoulder, as if she had known he would still be standing there, staring at her in this ruttish manner.

And to make matters worse, she looked quite pleased with herself, basking under his rakish attentions.

Sebastian shuddered, then snatched up his walking stick and made a hasty bow before he took off down the street at a good clip, taking flight toward the Burkes' fashionable house in Grosvenor Square as if the French were hot on his heels.

It wasn't until he'd pulled the bell at their door that he realized what he had called the lady.

Lottie?

The name was all too familiar, too intimate for such a greeting.

Intimate. Now there was a word he didn't want to use in the same sentence as . . . oh, demmit, what was her name? Wilcox? Wilson? Wilmont! Miss Wilmont. Not Lottie, not even Charlotte. But plain and ordinary Miss Wilmont.

He took a deep breath and let it out, as his mother often suggested to remedy the dark recesses of one's mind.

It didn't work. With his eyes closed, he found himself imagining Miss Wilmont in her altogether reclining on a chaise with a knowing little look on her pert face—her lips tilted with satisfaction and her bright blue eyes sparkling with delight.

His eyes sprang open and he found the Burkes' butler, Prouse, standing there staring at him.

Gaping, more like it.

"Yes, hello, Prouse. Good day," he muttered as he was shown in. Whatever was wrong with him? He made a Herculean effort to shake off these unsettling notions as the Burkes' butler led him down the hall to the salon, where Lavinia was awaiting him and he would be swept back into the familiar routine of his life.

His suddenly dull existence.

Charlotte gaped as she watched Sebastian flee down the street. What had he called her?

Lottie.

No, she'd heard him wrong. He couldn't have.

Yet there it was, his strong, deep voice still resonating in her ears. *Lottie.*

She started to laugh, the possibilities unfolding before her.

"Miss Wilmont?" Fenwick called down from the doorway. "Is that you?"

"Good morning, Mr. Fenwick!" she replied, bounding up the last of the steps.

"You seem quite improved from yesterday, miss, if you don't mind me saying."

"I feel like an entirely new person," she confided.

He nodded. "Lady Hermione is not in. She and Lady Viola have gone for a walk in the park with the young Mr. Marlowe. However, she thought you might call and asked me to direct you to join her in her usual spot."

"Perfect!" Charlotte told him, spinning on one heel and bounding back down the steps. She hurried across the square and was at the park in a thrice.

For the first time in her life, she stood at the threshold of the throng parading about the park and didn't feel in the least bit overwhelmed by London's finest.

How different everything and everyone looked, she mused from her new perspective as she made her way toward the rhododendron grove that Hermione favored.

Sebastian's sister always liked to take up her position near the grand bushes, especially now that they were in a riot of blooms, as she waited for the Earl of Rockhurst to ride by. She claimed the setting gave her a dramatic backdrop, and in true Hermione fashion, she was dressed in a rainbow of colors, from her bright orange pelisse to her wide-brimmed purple hat with its explosion of dyed ostrich plumes.

Viola stood beside her sister, quite ordinary in her relatively normal muslin, and spent her time watching the carriages and handsome rakes on horses parading past, as if she were making notes for when her time came and she was finally out in society.

Griffin, who was supposed to be escorting his sisters, was nowhere to be seen.

"Hermione!" Charlotte called out. "Oh, there you are!" She hugged her friend to her and held her close, so very thrilled to see her again. Oh, it felt like ages since she'd seen her bosom bow.

"Oh, Charlotte!" Hermione enthused. "You are out and come to the park! Tell me you have good news, for you look quite recovered. No! No! Let me guess—the solicitor found an annuity or some rich property that he missed yesterday? Oh, say it is true."

Charlotte took a step back and smiled. Hermione had just unwittingly solved her first problem. How to explain the diamonds. "You are right. He discovered a necklace that was supposed to come with the ring."

Hermione puffed up. "I knew it. What is the bother of an inheritance if it isn't worthwhile?" She paused. "It is worthwhile, isn't it?"

"Very," Charlotte told her. "But it is a secret, and you must be very discreet about it." She glanced over at Viola. "Both of you!"

For heavens knew what her mother and Finella would say if they discovered she'd had a diamond necklace in her possession.

The younger girl shrugged. "'T'isn't like anyone listens to me."

"Oh, a necklace! That's perfect," Hermione mused. "First you must sell it!"

"That is what I intend to do—with Griffin's help," Charlotte confided.

Hermione nodded in agreement. "He's forever selling the things he wins at cards to fund his experiments. He'll know just how to do it, for Lord knows we wouldn't want to ask Sebastian to help us."

Viola added a breathy snort and rolled her gaze upward.

"Oh, Charlotte, I am utterly relieved at your news," Hermione said, continuing blithely on. "For Sebastian is determined to marry Miss Burke and we haven't much time to change his mind."

Viola tipped up on her toes and looked over her sister's shoulder. "And worse yet, here they come."

Hermione and Charlotte turned in unison to see Sebastian strolling up the walkway with the infamous Miss Burke on his arm.

Hermione groaned as dramatically as if she were Banquo's ghost. "A pox on that girl. And worse yet, she's got those dreadful Dewmont sisters trailing after her."

Viola sniffed and turned her back to the entire assembly, as if that were enough to vanquish them.

Charlotte didn't really see Miss Burke or her friends—her gaze was fixed on Sebastian. It was all she could do not to rush to his arms, to demand a kiss, offer him so much more.

She barely even heard Hermione as she began to complain, "Oh, heavens, this is a disaster. Now here comes the earl with his aunt, Lady Routledge. My afternoon is positively ruined," she declared, pushing back the flurry of plumes in her hat, which persisted in falling in her face.

Rockhurst? Charlotte's gaze rose, and she found herself looking up at the devilish earl. And to her shock, he was staring at her, and right there and then he pulled his carriage to a quick stop.

Hermione gasped. "He's stopping."

"Don't toss up your breakfast," Viola offered. "Though that might not be a bad idea. Maybe with your kippers all over his boots he'd finally notice you, Minny."

Charlotte shot the younger girl a quelling glance, which to her amazement, actually worked on the usually irrepressible little Marlowe.

"Look, Lord Trent, there are your sisters," Miss Burke declared, steering the viscount in their direction, the Dewmont sisters following like ducklings in her imperial wake.

Miss Lavinia Burke was in every sense of the word a perfect Original. Her taste in clothes elegant and stylish, her manners kindly bestowed (if it hadn't been for the haughty manner in which she held herself, Charlotte might have even thought the girl meant every word of her smooth greeting).

"Lady Hermione! And Lady Viola! How delightful to find you here!" She glanced around. "And unescorted."

That censorious bit prodded Sebastian into action. "Yes, what are you two doing out here alone?"

Charlotte noticed that he kept his gaze fixed on his sisters and didn't spare her a moment's glance.

Hermione straightened. "Griffin is just over that way a bit, with Sir Joshua and Miss Kendell. He promised quite faithfully to return forthwith, so there is nothing amiss, Sebastian. Besides, we have Charlotte with us as well."

"Miss Wilmont," he said, bowing slightly to her.

"Lord Trent, how nice to see you . . . again." She let the word purr off her tongue like Lottie might, full of innuendo that she had no right to claim.

"Again?" Hermione and Miss Burke asked at the same time, the former with surprise and the latter with feminine suspicion.

"I bumped into Miss Wilmont as I was leaving the house," he explained.

"Yes, and I have the bruises to prove it," she teased back.

Miss Burke's pert, pink lips worked into a firm line as she eyed Charlotte. But once she'd taken in the outmoded bonnet, the plain gown, and the lack of anything fashionable, she dismissed her without a moment's hesitation, turning slightly from Charlotte and saying to Hermione and Viola, "I was just telling your dear brother that I haven't spent enough time with the two of you, and how I wished we had gone to school together, Lady Hermione, so I would have the advantage of those kindred years."

Viola made a gagging noise, which she quickly turned

into a cough when Sebastian shot a dark glance in her wayward direction.

Miss Burke didn't wait for any response, because perhaps she hadn't expected one, for she was now intent on striking the perfect pose for the benefit of her patroness, Lady Routledge.

And of course, the venerable matron spied her nearly immediately, for hadn't she been the one to declare Lavinia Burke the Season's first and foremost Original and urge (more to the point, bully) the other hostesses and society denizens follow suit?

"Yes, Rockhurst, you were right, it is Miss Burke," the lady was saying as she strolled forward with her nephew on her arm.

To Charlotte's dismay, Rowan trotted along at the earl's side. The dog stopped immediately when he spotted her, then he let out a low, menacing growl.

"Rowan!" Rockhurst snapped at the beast, tugging at a leash that barely restrained the enormous creature. "Where are your manners? Sit!"

The dog did as he was ordered, but his uneasy eyes never left Charlotte.

"That animal is a menace, Rockhurst!" Lady Routledge declared. She heaved a great sigh and turned toward the assembled company. "Well, who have we here?"

"As always it is a great honor to see you, my lady," Miss Burke was saying in that false gay voice of hers. "Such a fine party we make now."

The old dowager eyed the Marlowes like a terrier looking for something to chew. "Ah, Trent, there you are. And your sisters as well. I just received your mother's note this morning, along with her submission for my program.

A scene from *A Midsummer's Night Dream,* I see. Should be quite the dramatic moment of the evening."

The Dewmont twins snickered, for everyone knew that Lady Walbrook's renditions of the Bard were infamous for going horribly awry. Lavinia simply put her gloved hand over her mouth to cover a malicious smile.

Hermione blushed to her roots, and Charlotte did her best to quell a growing sense of indignation for her friend.

"Will Lady Cordelia be taking part?" Miss Burke inquired once she'd recovered.

"No," Hermione said in clipped tones. "She's in Bath for the rest of the Season."

"More of her Roman studies with your aunt, Lady Davy. They are the eccentric pair, I would guess."

Charlotte's gaze flew to Sebastian. Why wasn't he doing anything? Like putting a muzzle on this smug little chit instead of allowing her to continue to degrade his family?

But from what she could see, he appeared lost in thought, as if he hadn't heard a thing. Well, the devil take him. If he wasn't going to do anything, then she would.

"What are you doing, Miss Burke?" Charlotte asked. "For the soirée, that is."

Silence stopped the party cold as everyone looked in her direction, for she knew no one had given much consideration to her participation until this moment.

Miss Burke looked down her pert nose at Charlotte. "I am reciting an ode on the sanctity of marriage, which I composed myself." The girl preened a bit. "I fear I have a bit of bluestocking in me."

"Never, Lavinia!" one of the Dewmont sisters enthused, the other one joining in like a witless robin. "Not you!"

Miss Burke demurred, as expected, then to Charlotte's horror turned back toward Hermione and looked about to pounce again.

So Charlotte waded back into the fray with every bit of Lottie's sharp tongue. "That sounds rather dull to me, if I do say so. I mean, truly, Miss Burke, what do you know of marriage, let alone men?"

Chapter 14

Sebastian had, since the first moment he'd approached his sisters, found himself watching Lottie.

Demmit, Miss Wilmont.

Whatever was the matter with him today that he couldn't remember her deuced name?

More to the point, what had happened to his sister's mousy spinster of a friend?

She didn't look any different, with her dull gown and plain bonnet, but there was something altogether changed about her.

Beside him, Miss Burke drew in a deep breath. "Well, I suppose I know quite a bit about men, Miss . . . Miss—"

"Wilmont," Sebastian supplied. Much to his chagrin, he realized he'd been woolgathering and had missed whatever Hermione's friend had said that now had Lavinia at points.

"Miss Wilmont," his soon-to-be betrothed was saying, baring her teeth behind a gracious smile. "Perhaps when you've engaged the affections of a man"—her hand came up and twined around his forearm—"you'll be able to provide us your opinions on the subject."

Sebastian glanced down at the feminine glove atop his sleeve and wondered when her touch had started to feel like leg irons.

"I'd say she's engaged mine," the Earl of Rockhurst interjected, shooting Miss Wilmont a wicked smile that brought a pretty pink blush to the lady's fair cheeks.

Sebastian's gut tightened immediately. What the devil was the earl about? First and foremost, he'd never liked Rockhurst—his reputation alone put the man beyond the pale, but to see him casting his roaming gaze in Miss Wilmont's direction, well, it was enough to make any decent man concerned.

Yes, that was it. He was just concerned for the lady's reputation . . . her virtue . . .

Once again visions of a Miss Wilmont unclad and lying beneath him danced before his eyes.

Sebastian shuttered his eyes and began to rub his temple. Perhaps he needed to see a surgeon . . . or, at the very least, an oculist.

"Oh, do be quiet, Rockhurst," Lady Routledge was saying, sounding more than a bit peeved over seeing her social choice for the Season being bested. "I don't believe you were asked."

The earl looked about to argue the point, but his aunt stifled him with a hearty "thwack" of her fan into his chest.

The rakish devil had the audacity to wink at Miss Wilmont before he stepped back and out of his aunt's reach.

"Then I must ask, Miss Wilmont," Lavinia said, "what are you performing for Lady Routledge's soirée?" The girl paused as she shot a triumphant smile toward her friends.

Sebastian could never remember which Dewmont sister was which, only that their chatter nearly drove him mad. And more to the point, he'd never imagined either of them in their shifts . . . let alone their altogether. So why did this Miss Wilmont have him in this perplexing State?

"I wasn't invited," Miss Wilmont replied without any shame.

"Oh, how embarrassing," Lavinia said demurely. "I didn't know."

"Not invited?" Lady Routledge exclaimed. "You're Sir Nestor's daughter, are you not?"

Miss Wilmont nodded.

"An oversight, my dear," the old matron said with an air of insincerity that sent her nephew into a coughing fit. "Of course you must come! But do say, what is your talent? A concerto on the pianoforte perhaps? Singing, I'd guess. I remember your mother's cousin, Finella Uppington-Higgins, now she had a memorable voice."

"None of those, I fear," Charlotte replied.

"No talent!" Lady Routledge bristled. "Impossible. Every true lady of the *ton* possesses a talent. It is the mark of breeding, of education . . . why, of respectability."

Miss Burke opened her mouth to add her opinion on the matter, but Miss Wilmont spoke up quickly, cutting the younger girl off. "I think, my lady, that sometimes it is better for one to know their limitations than subject a hapless audience to those shortcomings."

"Harrumph! Every young lady should have some trait that endears her to good company."

"Then I suppose with my limitations, I would have to

provide the entertainment," she countered. "Find someone of exceptional skill to make up for my lack in singing, or playing, or elocution."

"And you think you can recognize true talent, Miss Wilmont?" Lady Routledge said, her eyes narrowing. "Without the benefits of schooling and lessons and the time in Society that has obviously not been given you?"

"Yes," Miss Wilmont replied. "It is the duty of every hostess to see her guests well entertained. And I would think that is the finest talent of all."

"Harrumph!" Lady Routledge drove her cane into the ground and looked completely vexed at being bested by this slip of a spinster.

Meanwhile, their rapid-fire repartee had left the rest of the company standing on the sidelines—mute and a bit shell-shocked.

"I think she has you there, Aunt," the earl interjected, only adding to the lady's irritation. "I daresay that after all the screeching last year, you'd welcome a decent bit of music or oration."

Lady Routledge shot her nephew a look that suggested she wished him in Surrey, if not further, say like the darkest reaches of India. "Then Miss Wilmont, I ask you to come to my soirée and prove your point. If you have no talent, as you profess, then provide someone to stand in your stead."

"But my lady," Miss Burke protested, "the point of the evening is to show the talents of well-bred ladies." Her hot glance in Miss Wilmont's direction suggested she found the other girl most likely lacking both in talent and breeding.

"Yes, it is," Lady Routledge declared. "But I think

such presumption demands examination. Therefore, Miss Wilmont, prove your superiority over the rest of the ladies this Season and provide a talent for the evening that surpasses anything seen before in our elevated circle."

A stunned silence surrounded the party. For what was there to say to such a challenge? It was patently unfair and only proffered to embarrass Miss Wilmont.

Sebastian didn't like it, not one bit, and neither did Rockhurst, it seemed, given the dark scowl on the other man's face. But this time, Sebastian wasn't about to let him rise to Miss Wilmont's defense. The man had no connection to the lady and therefore no right to it.

He ignored the fact that he had little claim either, other than a tenuous one through his sister. "Lady Routledge, I think you are demanding too much of Miss Wilmont. How is she to engage someone to your exacting standards in such a short time period?"

Lavinia's fingers tightened over his sleeve, and he felt much like the earl's wolfhound, being tugged back on a short leash.

A notion that set as well with him as it did with Rowan.

But it was all worth it when Miss Wilmont turned a smile in his direction. "My lord, you needn't worry for my sake. I am quite certain I can produce a substitute that will awe and astound Lady Routledge's guests."

Her utter confidence set him aback. How could this be? As far as he knew, Miss Wilmont never went out, and now she was challenging one of London's most exacting hostesses? She was either mad or, as his old Irish nanny would have held, a changeling.

"Lord Trent? Lord Trent!" Lavinia was saying. She tugged at his arm. "My lord, are you listening to me?"

Sebastian sighed and looked down at the girl. "Yes, Miss Burke?"

Lavinia tossed her head slightly. "I would like to return home. Now. I am starting to feel the sun."

He shook his head. "We'll have to see my sisters home first, and Miss Wilmont as well, since my miscreant brother has now disappeared." He nodded toward the empty space where Griffin and the Kendells had been standing.

"That will never do," she complained.

"Then come along with me, Miss Burke," Lady Routledge declared. "You and your friends can accompany me in Rockhurst's barouche." She turned to her nephew. "I suppose you and that beast of yours can fend for yourselves."

"We always do," the earl replied, making an elegant bow toward his aunt.

"Harrumph! Much to my never-ending despair, I'd add." She turned, cane in hand, nose in the air. "Miss Burke, you and your friends will attend me. I want to hear more on this ode to marriage."

No one dared gainsay Lady Routledge when she made up her mind, and Miss Burke, ever the conscientious (and grateful) debutante, smiled. "It would be our honor, my lady," she said, though the hot glance she shot at Sebastian was a portent of an argument to come.

Oh, he'd made quite a muddle of things today. First, he'd missed the Venetian breakfast, then he'd failed to notice her new hat when he'd arrived to apologize. In his defense, she always had a new hat, so what was there to notice?

It would most likely take the rest of his mother's orange

blossoms and a promise to escort her and the Dewmont sisters shopping every day for a week to get him back into her good graces.

And like Rowan on his leash, Sebastian was starting to chafe under his nearly-intended's demands. He'd only won her hand thus far because her father wanted to see their adjoining properties joined and, further, have the baron's newly gained title (which would pass to Lavinia's firstborn son) united with an ancient one such as the earldom of Walbrook.

Oh, there might have been other, more illustrious, suitors for Lavinia's hand, but Lord Burke had settled on Sebastian for one other important reason: The Marlowe debts that the baron would settle upon their marriage would give him an upper hand for the rest of his life over his more noble son-in-law.

And it seemed his daughter understood that arrangement as well.

As Rockhurst's carriage rolled away, Sebastian turned his annoyance on his sisters. And Miss Wilmont.

"We are going home," he announced. "Rockhurst," he said, nodding curtly toward the earl, hoping the fellow would take a hint and leave.

"I fear I can't go with you," Miss Wilmont declared. "I have an errand to complete." She glanced over his shoulder at the park beyond. "I had hoped your brother could be of assistance. If you don't mind, I'll wait here for him to return."

Wait? Alone? Or worse, with Rockhurst and his Shetland-pony-sized dog attracting more attention than a gypsy caravan?

And there was one other part of her refusal that stung

his pride: What was wrong with *him* that she couldn't ask for his assistance?

Sebastian straightened and did his best to ignore his trampled pride. "Perhaps I can be of assistance." If anything to speed along this scene and get them all out of the park and away from all the speculative glances being sent in their direction.

"If you could, that would be most kind," she said, glancing up at him from beneath that horrid bonnet of hers and letting the sparkle in her clear blue eyes undo his heart.

Gads, when had spinsters started flirting like Cyprians?

Miss Wilmont shot him one more sly, deliberate smile before she opened her reticule and fished around inside it a bit, then pulled from her bag the most astounding sight.

A diamond necklace of remarkable worth.

"Oh my!" Hermione gasped. "Oh, my Charlotte! They are incredible."

There was no doubt the gems were real given the way they sparkled even in the meager sunshine. But instead of being dazzled by their brilliance, as it appeared the others were, Sebastian took a step back.

For all of a sudden he was assailed with a feeling of hot, angry jealousy that had no explanation. No reason. Like everything else about this oddly disconcerting day, seeing Miss Wilmont with those diamonds had him up in arms.

"Good God!" Rockhurst exclaimed. "Wherever did you get that?"

"Her aunt," Hermione informed them. "Charlotte received them as part of her inheritance." She turned a smug smile toward Sebastian. "So as I told you yesterday, Charlotte is now someone of consequence."

"I don't think—" she started to say.

"You cannot sell those," he blurted out, even when the last thing he wanted to see was their tempting beauty entwined around her neck.

The lady paused, one regal brow rising slightly. "Whyever not?"

Ruffled at being crossed, Sebastian rose to her bait. "Well, it is improper for a lady to sell her jewels. Highly irregular." She'd asked for his advice and he had given it. He crossed his arms over his chest and considered the matter closed.

He should have known better by now.

The lady tucked them back in her purse. "They are mine and mine to sell, Lord Trent. And if you won't help me, then I will—"

"Have you consulted your mother on this matter?" he interjected. From the quick, stubborn set of her jaw, he had his answer. "At the very least, your family solicitor should be the one to—"

"Lord Trent," she shot back. "Do you consult your mother on every one of your business transactions?"

Viola let out a low whistle and stepped back. Hermione followed suit and looked to be bracing herself for the impending explosion.

He ignored them both, as well as a grinning Rockhurst. The earl held his ground with a jaunty pose and a look of admiration for Miss Wilmont that was starting to border on worship.

"Consult my mother? Utter madness, madame."

The lady smiled at him. "My point, sir, is that I am six

and twenty and know my mind on the subject. I think it is ridiculous that just because I am gently bred, I am not credited with having the capacity to manage my own affairs. Do you think me feeble-minded?"

At the moment, he was quite sure the lady didn't want his opinion of her.

Rockhurst nudged him with his walking stick. "She bested my aunt and your Miss Burke, so I'd suggest taking cover before she decides to run for Parliament and makes a mockery of all we hold dear."

Sebastian wasn't about to back down. This presumptuous chit was taking delight in provoking him, and he wasn't going to tolerate it. "Miss Wilmont, do you have any idea how much those are worth?"

"Fifteen hundred pounds," she declared, pulling her reticule strings tight and looking up at him as if it were perfectly normal for a twenty-six-year-old spinster to be running about Hyde Park with a queen's ransom in jewels.

Sebastian nearly choked. "Do I dare ask, whatever do you need with such a sum?"

She shot him a level glance. "First, I want to buy a dress."

Oh, that did it. The lady was mad. He was going to speak to his mother about Hermione and Viola's continued association with this Miss Wilmont.

"A blue one," she added, as if only to pique him further.

"The one at Madame Claudius's shop!" Hermione said, sounding all too enthused. "I do believe it will fit you perfectly, Charlotte."

"She is not going to sell those gems," Sebastian said. "It isn't sensible."

Miss Wilmont set her shoulders and faced him, and for

a moment Sebastian had to wonder if the earl didn't have the right of it. This woman was about to be his undoing.

Luckily for him, Rockhurst stepped between them, almost like an able second.

But for which side, Sebastian was unsure.

"Miss Wilmont," the earl said, "I do think what Lord Trent is saying is that they would look better on you than in the window of a pawnshop."

"I meant no such thing!" Sebastian declared.

"Then you prefer the blue dress?" Hermione posed, a vexing little smile perched on her lips.

Sebastian ground his teeth. He didn't know what was worse . . . the notion of Miss Wilmont selling her family gems like some common lightskirt or the possibility that she might look quite fetching in a blue gown.

"Perhaps," Rockhurst began, "there is a better solution to this dilemma. I'll buy your diamonds, Miss Wilmont."

"You-u-u?" Sebastian sputtered. This was going from scandalous to outright ruinous. And demmit if Miss Wilmont didn't look the least bit surprised by Rockhurst's generosity. "If this were to get out, why, the scandal—"

"You are too kind, my lord," she said, stepping around Sebastian as if he were now but a minor impediment to her ridiculous plans.

"I think it for the best," the rakish earl was telling her. "If I buy them, then your sale can be kept between ourselves and there will be no need for the unseemly gossip that Lord Trent fears might impugn your reputation."

As the two struck their bargain, Sebastian alternated between vexation and disgust. Vexation at Rockhurst for riding in like the proverbial knight-errant and disgust at his sisters and Miss Wilmont for their dewy-eyed infatuation of the man.

After Charlotte handed over her inheritance to Rockhurst, Hermione declared them ready to go home, if only to fetch their mother so she could assist them in shopping for Charlotte.

"A new dress demands an occasion," Rockhurst said. "And I have the perfect idea. Miss Wilmont, will you . . . and your friend, of course," he added, bowing slightly to Hermione, "accompany me to the opera tonight? Why, just this morning, I had a note from Lord and Lady Gwynn that they would be unable to join my party tonight."

Sebastian coughed. A likely story, indeed! "I don't think—"

"She'd be delighted," Hermione said, cutting him off. "As would I."

"Well, we shall see," Sebastian told her. "Mother may have a different opinion on this matter." An invitation from Rockhurst? The earl's black reputation bordered constantly on scandal, and no matron in her right mind would want her daughter connected to such a man.

He paused for a moment. *No matron in her right mind.* Oh, demmit, that ruled out his mother, for the countess could never be counted on to follow Society's dictates.

"Bring your delightful mother as well," Rockhurst said. "Unfortunately there won't be room for you and Miss Burke, Trent. But you'll have a grand view of us from their box."

Something about the entire scenario seemed overly familiar to Sebastian.

And another niggling suspicion told him he wasn't going to like it in the least.

* * *

From the moment Charlotte entered the Opera House on Lord Rockhurst's arm, the *ton*'s fascination with Miss Burke ended.

Especially given the scandalous cut of Miss Wilmont's blue velvet gown.

To Charlotte's amazement, the dress at Madame Claudius's shop was the same one Lottie had ordered. And the relieved modiste had been only too happy to sell the gown to her, confessing that the lady who'd consigned it had disappeared, her house on Little Titchfield street now empty.

Now only one question remained. Would the dress that had so inflamed her rakish lover conquer this Sebastian's proper armor?

"You are causing quite a stir," Rockhurst murmured after he had introduced Charlotte to Lord Pilsley in the next box and escorted her to her seat in the very front of his cozy box.

The very spot where she could be seen by all. Meanwhile, Hermione and her mother took their seats behind the earl, Lady Walbrook extolling his choice box and the fine view, while Hermione sat uncharacteristically mute.

"Why, no one will miss us," Lady Walbrook declared.

"Oh, heavens, this will never do," Charlotte said, realizing that eventually the gossip would arrive at Queen Street and Lady Wilmont would be less than pleased that Charlotte had gone out with Rockhurst without telling her.

"Mother isn't going to like this," she said under her breath.

"Your mother won't approve of your newfound popularity?" Rockhurst said.

"She won't be pleased when she finds out my invitation to the opera came from you."

"You didn't tell her I invited you?"

"Heavens no," Charlotte shot back, once again her Lottie nature getting the better of her.

Rockhurst laughed loud and thoroughly, drawing even more attention to the box. "Miss Wilmont, you astound me."

"I doubt that," Charlotte said, glancing across the way to the Burkes' box.

The earl shook his head. "No, there is something altogether unique about you. One moment you make me feel as if I've known you for years, and I have to remind myself that we've just met."

Charlotte glanced at him, more than a little bit alarmed. Not the earl as well! He wasn't supposed to remember! The last thing she needed was to be fending off his advances while trying to regain Sebastian's heart.

Shooting another furtive glance toward the Burkes' box, she did her best to quell her disappointment that it remained empty.

Demmit, she thought, borrowing one of Lottie's favorite curses, *when are they going to arrive?*

"Miss Wilmont?" Rockhurst said softly.

"Um, yes," she said, not really listening to him.

"Is there something, or rather someone, on the other side there who is of interest to you?"

Charlotte bit her lip and turned toward her host. "Oh, dear, was it that obvious?"

"Only to me," he confided. "Let me guess—since the only box over there that is still empty belongs to Lord Burke, I have to guess that the subject of your sighs and looks of despair might be Lord Trent."

"I'm sorry . . . it is just that—"

"No, don't worry about it," he said with an easy laugh. "I have a talent for not seeing what is right before my eyes." He leaned toward her and whispered, "And I think your quarry has finally arrived." He nodded ever-so-slightly toward the Burkes' box, where Lord and Lady Burke were taking their seats, followed by their daughter and her escort, Lord Trent.

Charlotte drew a deep breath even as Sebastian's gaze swept the room and locked with hers. She felt, rather than saw, his reaction—how his body tensed, his gaze devoured her.

Instantly she was Lottie again and Sebastian her eager lover, chomping at the bit for the entertainment to end so they could come together in a tangle of passion, of illicit love.

As the music played and the singers gave their plaintive performance, Charlotte spent more time watching Sebastian than the opera.

Remember, she wished. *Remember what we were to each other.*

And when the intermission arrived, she nearly leaped from her seat, in all eagerness to join the crowds in the hallway. To chance an encounter with Sebastian.

"Miss Wilmont," Rockhurst said, a look of mock innocence on his handsome face. "Shall we take a turn?"

"Oh, yes, of course," Charlotte said as she spied Sebastian escorting Miss Burke out into the hallway.

"Come along then and let us bedevil your adversary," he said.

"My wha-a-a-t?"

"Miss Burke."

"Oh, I have nothing—" Charlotte began to protest, but

then she caught the mischievous light in Rockhurst's eyes. "Well, perhaps a little."

He laughed. "Poor Miss Burke," he declared. "But then again I do so love seeing my aunt's protégées getting a bit of a comeuppance. Let us see what we can do to further your cause." They rose and turned, only to find Hermione standing at the ready, her eager face glowing up at the earl.

The earl paused and leaned over. "What is Sebastian's sister's name?" he whispered even as he shot the lady in question a dazzling smile.

"Lady Hermione," Charlotte returned.

"Ah, yes," the man said. "Lady Hermione, a turn about the hallway? Your mother appears quite engaged."

And so she was, Lady Walbrook giving a theatrical critique to a poor, beleaguered Lord Pilsley.

"Yes, oh, absolutely," Hermione replied. "Let's go find that vexsome brother of mine and show him Charlotte's new dress."

Rockhurst laughed. "The poor man hasn't a chance."

At first, Charlotte could barely breathe in the crush of the hallway, but then as the crowd noticed first Rockhurst, and then the mysterious lady on his arm, they parted.

If she hadn't spent a fortnight as Lottie Townsend, Charlotte would never have been able to endure such a gauntlet of curious glances and speculative whispers. Ladies and matrons, courtesans and debutantes, rakes and lords alike stared at her. Taking a cue from one of Finny's lectures, she held her gaze straight and aloof and walked at the earl's side as if she'd been out in society all her life.

"Dear heavens, Charlotte," Hermione whispered, quite in her element with all the attention they were drawing. "I can't wait to see Sebastian's face."

"Ah yes, and here he is," Rockhurst said. "Let's see how he approves of your new gown, Miss Wilmont."

And just as quickly as their promenade had begun, it came to a hasty halt, like two lines drawn across a field for battle.

Rockhurst, Hermione, and Charlotte on one side, and Miss Burke and Sebastian on the other. Lord and Lady Burke brought up the rear like a pair of reinforcements.

"Rather like the field at Hastings, I have to imagine," Rockhurst murmured.

Charlotte tipped back her shoulders and made good use of her bodice. "Yes, I can almost hear Miss Burke firing the first sally."

"I wager we take them in the end." He leaned over and whispered in her ear, "Blue is your color, Miss Wilmont."

Whatever Rockhurst said to Miss Wilmont to make her blush so prettily, Sebastian decided he didn't like it.

Not in the least.

"Oh bother," Miss Burke sighed. "There is that vulgar Miss Wilmont with Rockhurst. I suppose we must greet them, since your sister is with them."

Sebastian hadn't the least idea why Miss Burke sounded so put out, but her sentiment echoed his own.

He had no desire to be anywhere near Miss Wilmont.

This evening was a complete disaster as it was. Since the first moment he'd entered the Burkes' box, he hadn't been able to keep his gaze off the vexsome spinster, now transformed into an astounding beauty.

How could a gown do such a thing? But it wasn't just the blue velvet, for it seemed the lady had been lit within by a fiery light. And to his utter frustration, the rest of the *ton* had noticed as well.

In truth, the better question was, how had he not seen her before?

Greetings went all around, and Miss Burke stepped forward. "Miss Wilmont, such a lovely gown."

"Thank you," Charlotte replied.

Lavinia looked ready to open her mouth and make some further comment when there was a rustle of panic in the crowd around them, and suddenly everyone started rushing toward their boxes.

Rockhurst spied the trouble almost immediately. "The devil take him, here comes Battersby."

Everyone groaned. Except, Sebastian noted, Miss Wilmont. He watched a calculating light rise in her eyes, and as it did, he couldn't help but feel a niggle of trepidation, of impending disaster.

"Come Lavinia, Trent," Lord Burke said. "Quickly. Before we spend the rest of the evening cornered by him."

"Is it truly Lord Battersby?" Charlotte said, spinning around and rising up on her toes. "He's still got his shares to sell?"

"Yes, yes," Rockhurst said, trying to steer her and Hermione away. "He and those wretched shares are ruining the Season."

To everyone's horror, Charlotte freed herself from Rockhurst and spun around. "Lord Battersby! A moment, sir, if you can."

"No, Charlotte," Hermione said, catching her by the arm. "Everyone knows he's desperate."

"So am I," she shot back, crossing the empty space. Before anyone could stop her, she was off. "Lord Battersby, if you please, a moment of your time."

Sebastian, Rockhurst, and Lord Burke used a different turn of phrase—they all three swore. "Demmit."

"I've got to stop her," Sebastian said.

"I think it will take both of us," Rockhurst replied, and they were hot on her heels.

"Lord Battersby," Charlotte continued, "I must speak with you."

The tall, thin man spun around, an expression of shock on his face. Most likely, this was the first time anyone had actually invited his company all Season.

"Excuse my forward nature," she was saying, "but do you still have shares left in the *Agatha Skye*?"

"Shares? My shares?" Lord Battersby said, pulling off his spectacles and cleaning them quickly before hastily shoving them back on and blinking his owlish eyes at Miss Wilmont. "Is your father interested, Miss . . . Miss . . ."

"Wilmont," she supplied. "No, my lord. I am."

Battersby frowned, then caught sight of the earl and Sebastian. "Very funny, Rockhurst. Putting this poor girl up to me, getting my hopes up." He glanced over at the viscount. "'Spect better of you, Trent. Always seemed an honorable sort."

"It isn't their doing, my lord," Miss Wilmont told him. "I want to buy your shares."

Sebastian groaned. First she'd sold her diamonds to Rockhurst and now she was making a complete scene by haranguing Battersby to sell his worthless shares to her, and right in the middle of intermission with a more eager audience than the players could hope for.

"Yes, 'tis only a jest," Rockhurst said, trying to pull her back. "Good laugh, eh, Battersby?"

"Not at all," the man said, smoothing out his ill-cut jacket.

"I'm not joking," she insisted, tugging herself free of the earl again and setting herself front and center before Battersby. "I want to buy your shares."

The poor man blinked and stared, having probably never seen so much female attributes right in his face. "Well, I . . . that is to say . . ."

Sebastian leaned over her shoulder. "Miss Wilmont, you are making a scene," he advised her. "Those shares are worthless."

"Not to me," she whispered back. "I have fourteen hundred pounds." She paused for a moment. "Oh, dear, make that thirteen hundred. I must keep back a hundred pounds for Herr Tromler."

Sebastian knew better than to ask. "Herr Tromler?"

"Yes, the violinist for Lady Routledge's soirée. He'll need money for clothes, I have to imagine."

Both Sebastian and Rockhurst groaned.

Battersby glanced up from Charlotte's bodice to shake his head. "Thirteen hundred? Oh, no, that will buy only a third of them, miss, and I can only sell them in their entirety."

Charlotte heaved a sigh. "But that is all I have."

"Sorry, miss," the man replied.

"Too bad," Sebastian told her, "but I assure you there will be a better investment for your money than those shares."

She glanced over her shoulder at the departing

Battersby, and then back at Sebastian. Her blue eyes held a wild, desperate light that tugged at his heart.

"I must buy those shares. Please, help me convince him to sell them to me."

"But they are worthless," he argued. "It is wishful thinking to believe that ship will come to port now, not after so many months."

She paused and looked at him. "Sometimes, wishes are all we have." Her hand came to rest on his sleeve. "Please, help me make this one come true."

Sebastian would never understand what it was that made his sensible world turn completely upside down at that moment—the desolate, plaintive light in her eyes or the touch of her hand, which sent a rare shiver down his spine.

"Battersby, hold up there for a moment," he heard himself saying.

The man turned around. "What, you as well, Trent? Making sport of me like Rockhurst?"

"No, nothing like that." Sebastian swallowed and took another breath. This was madness, insanity, and yet for a wild moment he could only hear her plea.

Sometimes, wishes are all we have.

"I'll take the other third," he said, calculating it would take every bit of ready cash he had to buy them. " 'Tis all I can do, but you're better off with two-thirds sold than none, I'd imagine."

Battersby eyed Sebastian and then Miss Wilmont, his narrow lips pursed into a thin, wary line. Then he shook his head. "No. The contract for the shares stipulates that I can only sell the lot of them. All or nothing."

Sebastian looked down at Miss Wilmont. "I can't do anything more."

Expecting to find disappointment on her face, instead

she smiled up at him. "You've done more than you can imagine."

"Trent, are you out of your mind?" To Sebastian's horror, Miss Burke and her father had come up behind them. The baron spoke again, his voice rising with each word. "Tossing good money after bad. No wonder your family is in such dire straits."

It wasn't the first time the newly elevated merchant had thrown that fact into Sebastian's face—and up until now he'd done his best to ignore it. After all, it was the situation shared by many an impoverished noble family—enduring the slights of the newly rich.

"It is none of your concern, sir," Sebastian told him.

"Good money tossed in the gutter is always my concern. I hope you aren't expecting me to pay this debt."

Sebastian pulled himself up to his full height and faced his future father-in-law. "My finances are none of your concern."

"Rightly so," Rockhurst chimed in. "Won't let you horde in on the opportunity, Burke, you sly fellow, you. Think you can talk us out of Battersby's shares when you want them for yourself?"

Burke turned a brilliant shade of red. "Why, I never—"

"Good," Rockhurst said, turning to Battersby. "I'll take the other third, my good man. There you have it, the entire lot sold."

Battersby's owlish eyes blinked and quivered. "All of them?"

"Yes," Sebastian said. "A partnership of sorts. That ought to satisfy the shareholder's contract." He shuddered to think of such a thing—in business with a headstrong and most likely mad spinster and the worst gambler and rake in London.

In truth, he agreed more with Mr. Burke than he did his own judgment.

"Certainly," Battersby said, recovering from his shock and then grinning from ear to ear. "A partnership can be arranged. Yes, indeed. They are yours."

With the deal struck, Rockhurst volunteered his solicitor to handle the papers—on the morrow, at Miss Wilmont's insistence.

"Oh, madness! Utter madness, I say," Lord Burke declared. "I'm rethinking my opinion of you, Trent. Indeed I am!"

And before Sebastian knew it, the bell was ringing for everyone to return to their seats, and he did so in a daze, with a glowering Lavinia at his side. The second act proved a poor substitute for the drama that had played out in the hallway, and Sebastian found himself the subject of curious glances and speculative looks.

Worse yet, all too soon he found himself inside the Burkes' carriage, where a stony silence reigned. When they got to the fashionable mansion, the baron and his wife hurried inside, while Lavinia uncharacteristically lingered behind. "Well, isn't that Miss Wilmont remarkable!" she announced.

"Yes, indeed," Sebastian replied a little too enthusiastically.

His almost betrothed sniffed. Clearly, Lavinia wasn't about to let this upstart spinster take her spotlight. And certainly not Sebastian's affections. "How entirely vulgar of her to purchase those shares. And at the opera! Why, she looked like a fishmonger's wife chasing poor Lord Battersby down like that."

"I don't think it was as bad as all that," Sebastian replied.

Her perfect brows rose. "Did you notice her gown? Really, at her age, it was shameful. I am sure you and I are of the same mind on that point. I daresay, you wouldn't want a lady who held your esteem to dress in such a showy fashion."

Sebastian wasn't about to reveal his opinion of Miss Wilmont's display—the blue of her gown against her hair and sparkling eyes, her proud carriage and secret glances. Oh, he'd noticed those. How could he not have, when every time she'd looked at him his body had reacted like that of an untried lad?

The only shame of it was that every man in the Opera House had noticed her as well.

Miss Burke, completely unaware of the direction of his thoughts, continued unabashedly. "I think it is mortifying when ladies who have certainly passed any matrimonial hope come out in Society. They are such depressing creatures. I daresay Miss Wilmont—"

"Don't!" Sebastian shot out.

"Don't what?" Miss Burke replied, looking up at him with a bit of angry disdain so at odds with her usually perfect composure.

"Don't say another word about her. I won't hear it."

"Lord Trent, you might as well get used to hearing about her. After tonight, everyone in the *ton* is going to be talking about her."

"Then I expect you to refrain from joining such poor company."

"Whyever not?" she asked, sounding as askance as if he'd asked her to go out in public in her chemise. "We just witnessed the finest *on dit* of the Season, and everyone will want to hear about it. Of course I will do my best to lessen your role in it." She paused for a moment. "You should know that I entirely forgive you for your moment of weakness in all this."

Sebastian stepped back from her. "You forgive me?"

She seemed utterly unaware of the anger behind his words. "Of course, you dear man! You were only helping that odd Miss Wilmont because of her close association to your sisters. I will make sure people understand that you felt it your duty to—"

"Miss Burke, I will repeat my earlier order. You will say nothing ill about Miss Wilmont. Is that understood?"

The mutinous light in her eyes surprised him, and he suddenly saw his well-made and fought for match begin to sputter.

And with it, his family's future. He thought of the long-owed mountain of debts on his father's desk, of the merchants who were at the end of their patience and willing credit. His family was in dire straits, and it was up to him to save them with this bride-to-be.

Swallowing a bitter pill, Sebastian demurred, at least for the moment. "Come now, Miss Burke, you had the right of it earlier, I am only thinking of my sisters' welfare. I would hate to see any hint of scandal touch them, and you in turn, if you were ever to call them by that name as well."

Miss Burke smiled up at him so sweetly that Sebastian swore he must have imagined that flash of anger before.

Hadn't he been wrong about so many things today?

Miss Burke turned and went up the remaining steps to her door. "Is that the only reason, Lord Trent?"

"Only reason for what?"

"Why you do not want me to say anything about Miss Wilmont's scandalous conduct tonight—for your sisters' sake, that is?"

He straightened up. "Yes, of course. What other reason could there be?"

"What other reason, indeed," she replied.

Chapter 15

"There you are!" rose the deep, menacing greeting from behind Quince as she stood in a moonlit corner of Hyde Park.

After fourteen hundred and forty-three years, she had become quite adept at avoiding Milton. Amongst the brick walls, cobbled streets, and smoky confines of London it was even easier to escape detection, but Quince now knew just how determined Milton was to retrieve his ring.

This time, she mused, as she came to a twirling stop on the grassy knoll atop which she was dancing. "Where are your manners, Milton? Sneaking up on a lady like that." She eyed him warily, stepping slowly and cautiously out of his reach.

Dressed like a gentleman, he conveyed the very commanding and elegant presence of a duke. No matter that he couldn't be seen by anyone but her, Milton's vanity wouldn't allow him to turn up as anything less than a grand lord.

"I knew if I waited, you'd eventually come to the park," he mused, circling around her, moving like a menacing cat.

Quince muttered an ancient curse. Of course she'd come to the park. After what had seemed like an eternity in this dirty, wretched city, she'd needed to wiggle her toes in a bed of moss, feel the bark of a tree beneath her touch, let the soft murmur of the wind as it danced through the leaves whisper its secrets into her ears.

It had been a risk, but she'd only meant to come bask in the moonlight for a wee bit before she fled back to her hiding spot.

Apparently, she'd danced in the silvery light a moment too long.

"Come join me, Milton," she said, holding out her hand. "Wouldn't you like to dance with me again?"

"No."

Undeterred, she stretched her hand out further. "Come, Milton, the moonlight is magical tonight. Don't you remember that night in Wales when we—"

"Quince, my ring," he said, his arms crossing over his chest, leaving nothing but icy disdain between them. "I want only my ring."

"Churlish scullion," she muttered, bringing her hand back and making one more absentminded twirl before she came to a stop. "As for your ring, if I had it, do you think I would be out here dancing?"

"The only place you should be is retrieving it."

"It's still on her hand," Quince said, smoothing out her skirt as she awaited the explosion.

It came.

"How can that be?!" Milton's usually cool features mottled with rage.

"How should I know?" she told him, considering how she was going to escape his wrath this time. Perhaps she could brazen it out and hope he'd just depart. "But it is still there and there is nothing I can do about it."

"But she disavowed her wish." His eyes narrowed. "Therefore the ring should have fallen free."

Quince didn't even bother to ask how he knew about the change in Charlotte's wish. It only meant he was paying close attention to the ring and more determined than ever to regain it. "Not necessarily . . ."

"Not unless you meddled," he said. "You interfered with the wish, didn't you?"

"What a terrible thing to suggest when I have—"

"Terrible? Hardly," he shot back. "Lo, you've gone too far this time, Quince. Shifting the timelines back and forth. Don't think it hasn't gone unnoticed."

Quince tipped her nose up in the air, even while her toes curled inward. *Be brave, lass,* she told herself. *Don't let him see your fear.* Still, she couldn't resist prodding him just a little. "It will all come to rights once he falls in love with her again."

Milton circled her. "You're betting my ring on human love? Have you gone mad?"

Quince felt that odd magic of his start to ensnare her. "She loves him so, and if he could just see past—"

This was no longer about Charlotte and Sebastian, and they both knew it.

He threw up his hands. "I am not listening to this." He started to storm away, then stopped and turned around, wagging a finger at her. "I am going to do what I should have done to begin with."

"Milton!" she called out, hurrying after him. "Whatever do you mean?"

"You know exactly what I mean. What I should have done in the first place. End this wish."

And before Quince could stop him, he disappeared into the night and into places not even she dared tread.

Charlotte stood in the Marlowe library, her finger tracing the titles on the spines as she searched for a specific volume of poetry.

"Just in case you can't find someone for Lady Routledge's soirée," Hermione had said, "you must have a piece memorized to perform."

Stretching up on her tiptoes, Charlotte continued her search. French novels. Shelley. Blake. Shakespeare. More Shakespeare. Oh, where was the volume she sought?

Behind her, she heard a door open and close. "Blessed saints, Hermione, I can't find Coleridge." She rose up a little higher. "You'd think it would be front and center, considering how much your—" she said as she turned around.

In the doorway stood a stunned-looking Sebastian. Suddenly Charlotte forgot entirely what she was saying, what she was searching for, feeling as tongue-tied as she'd always been around him.

That is until he said—well, demanded really—"What are you doing here?"

It was enough to dislodge the lump in her throat. "'Tis nice to see you too, Lord Trent," she replied, doing her best to keep the elation she felt out of her greeting.

Whatever was he doing home so soon? Obviously he hadn't lingered overly long with Miss Burke.

Unfortunately, she couldn't help but smile at that.

"I said, what are you doing here?"

"Spending the night with Hermione," she replied.

His jaw set with a firm line.

Must have been some ride home with the Burkes, she mused.

Sebastian came a little further into the library, looking to his left and right. "Where is she?"

"Upstairs," Charlotte told him. She nodded toward the shelves. "You wouldn't happen to know where the volume of Coleridge is, would you?"

"Top shelf, third row over," he said. "Whatever do you want with him?"

"Hermione wants me to learn a poem for Lady Routledge's in case I can't find Herr Tromler." She glanced over her shoulder at him. "I thought Coleridge would be so . . . so . . . edifying."

Sebastian's eyes widened. "You don't mean to tell me that you intend to read *Coleridge* at Lady Routledge's soirée?"

"Whyever not?"

"Well, for one thing, it's not done. He's hardly proper, if not outright—"

"But you like his work," Charlotte interjected, recalling the afternoon they'd spent in the countryside, taking turns reading from that very same book of verse . . . and making love in turn.

"I-I-I—" He paused and stared at her. "That is beside the point."

She glanced up at the lofty reaches. "You wouldn't mind reaching it for me, would you?"

"Yes, I would."

Charlotte thought of another strategy. "I wager I could guess your favorite verse. If I'm right, you must get it down for me."

"Oh, so should I add soothsayer to your list of charms?"

"You think I'm charming?" she said, turning from the shelves and crossing the room toward him. For a moment she thought he was going to meet her halfway, catch her in his arms and ravage her.

At least that's what she wished for, so fervently that it was almost possible to believe it could happen.

But at the last possible second, he took a deep breath, sidestepped her, and went to the bookshelf and reached up for the volume.

Even as he passed her by, she inhaled deeply, filling her senses with the very scent of him—bay rum and that dangerous, masculine air of a rake.

She teetered atop her shoes for a second, lost in the memories that seemed both so close and yet so very far away.

"Which poem?" he asked.

"Wha-a-at?" she managed, returning to the world where she was simply Charlotte.

"You said you could guess my favorite poem, so I want to know which one you think is my favorite."

Charlotte's eyes closed. "Page twenty-seven." She listened as he thumbed through the pages. When it seemed he'd found it, she finished, " 'Recollections of Love.' " She turned around and opened her eyes to find him gaping down at the open book in his hands and then up at her.

"How did you know that?"

There isn't anything I don't know about you, she wanted to tell him. *You like coffee not tea in the morning, but with three lumps of sugar and lots of cream. You hate green waistcoats, and you love playing whist but only when I let you win. When we make love, you get this certain look on your face when you are about to find your—*

"How did you know that?" he repeated.

"A lucky guess," she said, wondering just how mad he would think her if she told him the truth.

I was your mistress, Sebastian. And we loved each other, so deeply, so thoroughly that if you would but try to remember, try to recall, we could be in that delirious place yet again. . . .

"Luck, indeed," he said, shoving the book out toward her.

She took it, and for a moment they stood there, connected by these pages that had one afternoon inflamed their passions.

He glanced down at her, and for a moment she swore he remembered, felt every bit of the desire coursing through her body.

"I should go," he stammered, turning and heading toward the door. But once there he stopped, muttering something she couldn't quite make out.

She watched him, his hands fisted at his sides, his shoulders taut and set. "Is something wrong?" she asked, not daring to step closer for fear he'd flee all the way to Scotland.

"Yes," he ground out. "I mean, no."

"Oh," she whispered. "Did you quarrel with Miss Burke? Is that why you are home so early?"

He turned around. "No, certainly not. She isn't the type to—"

"No, I suppose she isn't," Charlotte conceded. What if Quince was wrong? What if she had just gone mad and all of her memories of Sebastian were merely dreams and fancies?

Walk away now, Charlotte, her sensible side warned her. *Before you make an utter fool of yourself. Before your heart breaks completely in two.*

For it was tearing her apart right now to stand here and not to be in his arms. Not to be kissing him. With her clothes still right and proper and perfectly in order . . .

Charlotte trembled. Oh, this was pure torture.

Then she looked at him and remembered the times he'd been so passionate, so fiery, so close to her—when he'd been piqued and jealous and angry with her.

Yes, that was it! Why hadn't she thought of that before? She needed to rouse him.

"Truly, I can't see Miss Burke ever saying naught," she added quickly. "You've most likely chosen very wisely."

His brows furrowed. "What does that mean?"

"Oh, nothing," Charlotte said, ignoring his suspicious tone and strolling to the large chair near the fireplace. She draped herself in a most unladylike fashion on the arm. "She seems so amiable."

If one could consider a viper in muslin amiable.

"Exactly," he said. "Miss Burke is a lady, and she would never contradict—"

"Of course not," Charlotte interrupted yet again, though she was paying him little heed, instead taking her time by examining her nails. She heaved a bored sigh. "She's entirely proper, quite staid in her affections, I have to imagine. Some might call such a paragon terribly dull, but I suppose you'd find her lack of passion perfectly satisfactory." She let her words settle down into his imagination and then looked up at him and shifted ever so slightly, like Lottie might have, subtly lifting her bosom so it strained at the top of her bodice. She let her lips tip in a sly, secret smile. "But is that what you really want, Lord Trent? A man who secretly reads Coleridge?"

She sent him the exact same look that Arbuckle had claimed gave her portrait as Helen of Troy the perfect expression—the kind of come-hither glance that could entice a man to leave hearth and kin, to launch a thousand ships, to breach a hundred defenses to claim her heart.

Claim her as his own.

She must have captured it perfectly, because Sebastian's mouth fell open in an expression of shock and amazement. "Lottie, I—"

Lottie. Charlotte sat up. Hearing her name on his lips was a heady lure. She rose and took a few tentative steps toward him.

But this wasn't the same rakish man who'd opened her eyes to love . . . at least not yet, she reasoned as she mused how best to awaken him.

Rouse him.

Memories assailed her—of him sweeping into the house on Little Titchfield Street hungry for her kiss, of him naked—gloriously so, of all those nights he'd claimed her. She let that passion bubble up inside her, and she shot him a hooded glance that promised passion and danger.

Sebastian reeled back, bumping into the door, closing it and making it so they were all alone and secluded in the cozy room. "Forgive me," he stammered. "I don't know why I keep calling you that. Highly improper."

And while he might appear flustered and ready to take flight, Charlotte knew this man well enough to know that he was tempted. Despite his honor, despite the complete impropriety of this scene, Sebastian Marlowe found her tempting.

And that was all she needed.

As his hand went to the latch, she took a few more steps. "I suppose so. But is it wrong if I don't mind?" She smiled again and moved closer still, feeling with each passing second like her Cyprian twin.

"*Lottie,*" he managed again. "I don't know why, but it fits you." He stood stock still, poised and taut. The tension between them, those ethereal memories, leaving them both transfixed . . .

"We shouldn't be down here alone," he finally said, as if he was warning her. "It isn't proper. It isn't done. Why, someone might think I was . . . well, that I was . . ."

"Trying to ruin me?" Charlotte smiled. "Would you ruin me, Lord Trent?"

Sebastian repeated Miss Wilmont's question over in his mind.

Would you ruin me, Lord Trent?

His gaze moved quickly from the swell of her bodice to the curve of her neck to the full line of her lips, pursed and ready to be devoured.

Where the devil had this minx come from? Whatever had happened to Hermione's mousy friend, who had seemed more akin to the draperies than to his father's lush and very ripe fertility statues?

Would you ruin me, Lord Trent? Her question continued to rattle about in his mind until something else, something even more unsettling, hit him.

What if her query wasn't a question but a request?

Ruin me . . .

"Wha-a-at?" he finally managed to stammer, sounding like the worst sort of country greenling.

"You heard me," she said, moving closer, sliding across the room like a sultry cat. "Would you ruin me?"

Since he couldn't manage the words, he forced himself to shake his head.

Never, he thought as he tried to recall the dull spinster whose name he could never remember. *Well, not intentionally ruin,* he amended as she moved closer, his fingers itching to trace the line of her bodice, the curve of her breasts.

What the devil was he thinking? This was Miss Charlotte Wilmont. A respectable lady. "Miss Wilmont," he managed to say.

"Lottie," she corrected. *"Lottie."* The name rolled off her lips in a slow purr, echoing again through his wayward thoughts.

Lottie, my love, come to me.

His gaze flew to hers, unsure if he'd thought those words or actually said them aloud.

The sparkle in her eyes suggested he had said them aloud—or that she knew his every thought. For the last time a woman had looked at him like that she'd been his . . . mistress.

He shook his head. "Miss Wilmont, I think you should . . . I mean, we must . . ."

She quirked a single brow at him and sauntered closer, slowly and seductively, all hips and curves and dangerous wiles, her head tipped slightly, a knowing smile on her lips.

Where the hell had a spinster learned to move like that?

And that light . . . oh, to hell with that light in her eyes . . . it beckoned like a wrecker's lamp across a storm-tossed sea—promising no sanctuary, no safety.

Demmit, he *was* going mad.

She took another tempting step toward him, and now he could smell her. Violets. Soft and enticing.

Ruin me.

Oh, there was no doubt now, hers hadn't been a question.

"Miss Wilmont, you are a respectable woman." Even to his ears, his statement sounded like it was more for his benefit than hers.

"Not a lady?" she asked.

"Yes, well, of course, but . . ." Thank God every lady in London didn't possess Miss Wilmont's sudden charm. The entire country would be lost.

"But what?" She'd eased herself right up in front of him, and she'd done it so seamlessly that one second he'd been holding his own against her, and then she was before him, his defenses breached, his desire finding the voice he'd been struggling to rein in.

"I'm a gentleman," he told her.

"I've always found you a bit rakish." She glanced up from beneath her lashes and her eyes twinkled as if they held some secret knowledge that not even he was privy to.

Him? Rakish? Why, of all the foolish . . .

Yet even as much as he would like to tell her that her suggestion was utter nonsense, for everyone knew he was the sensible Marlowe, his shoulders straightened, he found himself rising up to his full height, and he had the nearly uncontrollable desire to take her in his arms and show her just how rakish he could be.

Ply her gown from her body, undo her garters, pull the pins from her tangle of brown hair, and make love to her on this very carpet.

His gaze met hers and he had the distinct feeling she wouldn't be opposed to such a scandalous notion. That she desired him as much as he . . .

Sebastian tried to breathe even as she rose up on her slippers, on her very tiptoes, and caught his coat lapels to steady herself.

Then she tugged him closer. "Sebastian," she whispered, her intimate use of his name sending a thunderbolt of desire through his already throbbing senses. "Kiss me."

And instead of waiting for his reply, she did just that, pressed her lips to his, without any coyness, without any pretense, without even waiting.

In one swift kiss, Miss Wilmont ruined him.

For a moment, he stood there, stunned and in denial. This wasn't happening.

Not to him, of all people.

He wasn't rakish. He was sensible. And sensible gentlemen didn't . . .

But Miss Wilmont did. Her tongue swept over his lips and he groaned, a sound that seemed to rumble from his very soul, full of need and desire and a passion that he didn't know he possessed.

But she did. Her fingers twisted tighter into his jacket, claiming him, gathering him closer yet.

His manhood, already stiff, went rock hard as she came up against him, his entire length throbbing to life.

"Lottie," he growled into her ear. "Lottie, you minx, what are you doing to me?"

To his delight, she shivered in his arms. "I thought it

was obvious." Her body moved again, against him, with him, molding to him, exploring him.

Ruin me.

Images assailed his imagination. *This brazen chit, gloriously naked, her bare legs twined with his, her body arching to meet his. And he was inside her, stroking her, her passionate cries urging him on.*

Sebastian! Oh, now, Sebastian!

His body tightened anew, and he jolted back to the moment at hand. To the woman in his arms. He sought her lips eagerly, with a newfound passion, kissing her, tasting her, devouring every bit of the desire she offered.

Overcome with need, he swung her around and pinned her up against the door so he could press himself into her. Instead of protesting, she responded with a deep moan of desire, pulling up her skirt so she could wind a leg around him, so she could ride against him.

He lost any sense of reason, any bit of sensibility. Instead, he freed a breast from her gown, his thumb rolling over the nipple until it hardened. And now it was her turn to tremble in submission, in unanswered desire.

He pressed against her harder, rougher, letting his other hand roam beneath her upraised skirt, to run over her soft, trembling thigh, to that very hot and wet place that was so very ready for him.

Their mouths, once fused in a heady kiss, wrenched apart, even as his fingers found her, as her hand closed brazenly over the front of his trousers, as her fingers traced the length of him.

Gone was the spinster. Lost was Miss Wilmont. The respectable lady fled in the wake of this dangerous, passionate awakening.

In her stead stood a vixen who seemed to understand his every desire, aroused his every need . . .

And she'd awakened this rakish side of him that he'd never known he possessed. Unleashed this dark stranger inside him, this reckless, dangerous man who seemed to know exactly what she wanted . . . and just how to give it to her.

He leaned over and captured her bare nipple in his mouth and sucked, long and hard, pulling it into his mouth and letting his tongue tease the taut peak. She arched toward him, opening herself to him, and he continued while his fingers did much the same dance over another tight, hard spot.

She was wet and slick, and he flicked his finger over her until she was rocking against him, murmuring something unintelligible but perfectly understood.

Ruin me . . . Ruin me now . . .

Somehow, she'd gotten his breeches open and freed him, running her hand up and down him, her fingers tracing a dangerous, teasing line over the wet tip.

Testing him, begging him.

Her hips arched again against his hand, seeking out what she held.

In a flash, he saw her, naked and resplendent in satin sheets, her brown hair shimmering in the candlelight, her body hazy in a sheen of need, writhing and calling to him.

Oh, Sebastian! Now, Sebastian!

And there he was. *Throwing himself atop her, reckless and rakish. Thrusting into her, hard. Claiming her body as his, filling her, stroking the waves of her need with sure, long thrusts.*

"Demmit," he swore as he caught her hips and raised her up, ready to fill her right there and then, even as he tried to fathom how he'd come to this.

This rakish, dangerous desire. This uncontrollable need.

"I'm going to ruin you like this," he told her.

"I wouldn't call it ruin," she said breathlessly, as her body moved all-too-willingly against his.

Then into his hazy, desire-clouded thoughts came a voice that jolted Sebastian back to sensibility.

"Charlotte? Charlotte, are you still down there?"

Hermione!

It didn't take Sebastian but a moment to take in the sight before him and consider what his sister would discover if she ventured into the library.

Miss Wilmont all topsy-turvy and tousled. Her eyes smoky with desire, her lips swollen from the force of his kisses. All but ruined, utterly and so completely.

Then he took another glance at this disheveled, gloriously aroused woman. He'd done this?

"Charlotte?! Where are you?" Hermione's insistent voice clamored yet again.

Sebastian glanced once more at Charlotte, then shoved her into the middle of the room.

"Do something," he whispered, waving his hands at her rumpled, half-on gown.

"Like this," she teased back, pulling her bodice down lower and coming toward him.

Gads, this was going to be a disaster, he thought, even as his gaze went hungrily back to the site of her perfect breasts.

She looked like a veritable Helen of Troy, one of

Townley's Grecian beauties, one of Arbuckle's seductive oil-bound belles.

Hermione's determined step trod down the staircase. "Charlotte? Whatever is wrong with you? Are you in there reading one of Mother's French novels? She keeps those on the top shelf for a reason."

Now that Sebastian had wrenched himself out of Miss Wilmont's arms, his sensible nature roared back into some semblance of control. "Get dressed," he ordered softly, straightening his own clothes as fast as he could.

She did so, slowly and seductively, and it was all he could do not to bolt the library door shut and claim her once again.

No! No! No! he told himself.

Remember Miss Bird. No, that wasn't it. Miss Burton. Oh, demmit, what was her name?

Burke! Miss Lavinia Burke and her ten thousand a year.

Then he looked at Lottie, and the comparison sent a chill of dread through his impassioned limbs as he watched her pull her tumbled curls up through her fingers and pin them back into some semblance of order.

If you could call anything about Charlotte Wilmont ordered.

Just as she finished, the door swung open and Sebastian found himself hidden behind it.

"There you are!" Hermione said, a bit of annoyance to her words. Then again, his sister was easily annoyed. "I was calling you from the second landing. Didn't you hear me?"

"No, I fear I'd succumbed to the charms of . . ."

Sebastian held his breath.

". . . a delightful bit of poetry. It was quite stirring."

His body quaked and stirred, responding to her softly seductive words like a hound to the horn.

"You look flushed," Hermione said. "Are you feeling well?"

Quite well, he would have told his sister if she'd been talking to him. Why, he'd never felt so alive, as if he'd been awakened from a long sleep, restless and ready for something unexpected, something one only found in dreams.

"Really, Charlotte, are you listening to me?" Hermione asked. "You don't look well. Should I call for my mother?"

His mother? Why not just invite in Lady Parwich from across the square and the rest of Mayfair, for that matter?

Meanwhile, Charlotte had picked up the volume of Coleridge and moved to the door. Her hand reached behind it and out of Hermione's sight. "Oh, heavens, don't bother your mother. Truly, I feel glorious," she said, her fingers tracing a line along his lips.

Sebastian nearly moaned, his body hardening anew.

"It was a wonderful evening," Hermione enthused. "I just wish Rockhurst had noticed me. If you weren't my best friend, I'd be quite jealous over the attentions he paid you."

Sebastian froze immediately. How had he forgotten Rockhurst? The earl had been more than attentive to Lottie tonight.

Miss Wilmont, he corrected himself. Better to think of her as Miss Wilmont, proper spinster, than Lottie-the-vixen-meant-to-tempt-his-soul.

"I have no interest in him," Charlotte demurred, her hand stroking Sebastian's stubbled chin, his lips, the line of his jaw. "Besides, Rockhurst doesn't like poetry. I could never be interested in a man who didn't adore Coleridge."

Hermione sniffed. "You and Sebastian. He loves that fellow as well. Though its hard to believe, considering how stuffy and proper my brother is and how scandalous those verses are. That's why Mother keeps them up on the top shelf—so Viola won't read them."

Her touch became too much for Sebastian, and his newly awakened rakish side demanded revenge. He caught her hand and kissed the palm, then drew one of her fingers into his mouth and suckled it.

When he heard her stifle a gasp, he smiled. Served the teasing little minx right.

Hermione's gown rustled. "Are you sure you're well, Charlotte? You look odd."

"I was just thinking of which poem I was going to memorize in the event I can't find Herr Tromler."

"You're not thinking of reciting one of Coleridge's verses, are you?"

"Actually, I was," Charlotte said.

Sebastian's mouth opened in shock, and she was able to free her hand.

"But Charlotte," Hermione protested. "You'll cause a scandal if you recite one of those verses!"

"Yes, I know," she said, leaning quickly behind the door and winking saucily at Sebastian before she ducked away, following Hermione toward the stairs.

"Sebastian will never fall in love with you if you find yourself embroiled in a scandal," his sister advised.

"I wouldn't worry about your brother. I think you will find him quite changed."

Sebastian would have liked to argue with her, but that

would have required him to reveal his position. Cause the scandal that Miss Wilmont seemed all too determined to create.

He wasn't changed, he would have told them both. Told *her*. He wasn't.

Oh, but he was.

Their voices grew fainter, and he found himself straining to hear Charlotte's dulcet tones just once more.

But it was his sister's final statement that left him staggering.

"I suppose you know best," Hermione conceded. "You're the one in love with him, after all."

Chapter 16

You're the one in love with him, after all.

That simple revelation sent Sebastian hightailing it into the night.

Miss Wilmont, in love with him?

A ridiculous notion, he told himself as he strode through the cold, dark streets of London.

The bracing air had a way of clearing his thoughts, and by the time he looked up to gain his bearings, he found himself in front of White's. Seeking the sanctuary of his club, he vowed that first thing in the morning he'd make his apologies to the lady and then forget the entire interlude as nothing more than a momentary lapse in judgment.

Love, indeed! He would just put Miss Wilmont and her silken tresses and perfect curves out of his mind.

But escaping the divine little spinster proved to be all but impossible.

Arbuckle's portrait of Diana hung in the billiard room, and while he'd never paid it any attention before, the goddess of the hunt now taunted Sebastian from her oaken frame. Gads, it was as if Miss Wilmont had modeled for the artist—the same tresses, the same lines, the same wild, seductive tip of her lips.

He deliberately put his back to the taunting minx.

Then there was the general furor in the room around the betting book. Though he'd never been a man to wager recklessly, if at all, tonight he approached the knot of rakes and Corinthians, suddenly feeling an odd sort of a kindred spirit to their wild and lively bravado and boasting.

"I've wagered five hundred pounds that Miss Wilmont will marry before the end of the Season."

"But to whom?" came another. "Now *that* will make the wager interesting."

"I'll marry her," a fellow called out from a card table. "If you have to be leg-shackled, I say find a bonny bit to take to your bed, and she's quite the fetching little chit."

A handful of jests and comments about Miss Wilmont's attributes, seen and unseen, were bantered about, and suddenly Sebastian's momentary jovialness turned quite foul.

How could this be? He hadn't a quick temper. He was a sensible, rational fellow.

"Devil take Rockhurst!" called out the Earl of Lyman. The man waved for his glass to be refilled, though he appeared already well into his cups. "I don't know how he does it. Discovers the jewels of society buried right beneath our noses."

There was a general murmur of agreement.

Lyman continued. "I'll take your bet, Kingston. And I'll add to it."

Everyone waited, eager to hear this next challenge.

"I'll wager I can best Rockhurst and steal the lady's

affections from him. I'll taste her lips before Rockhurst can ply her heart with diamonds and other trinkets."

Laughter and rowdy jests filled the room, while Sebastian felt his mood grow even blacker. *Diamonds and trinkets.*

"Isn't her mother an Uppington-Higgins?" one of the older fellows was asking.

"Yes, yes, indeed," another of the aged, bleary-eyed rakes declared. "Blithe spirits those Uppington-Higgins ladies. Flirtatious bits, if you know what I mean."

"Then my job shouldn't be all that difficult," Lyman joked, and a round of rough, masculine laughter followed.

Sebastian never knew what hit him, but just the very thought of Lyman going anywhere near Lottie, least of all this very public denouncement of her virtue, drove him past reason, past sensible.

Never mind that he'd nearly ruined her but an hour earlier, he wasn't about to listen to this. Not from such a despicable, loathsome lout as Lyman.

Sebastian bolted through the throng and caught the earl by the throat. He continued until he had him up against the wall and dangling in the air.

"Hear me well, Lyman," he told the man. "You go near the lady and I will personally put a bullet through your heart."

White's had never known such a stunned moment of silence.

Lyman gurgled and choked a reply.

Sebastian tightened his grasp. "You will apologize for besmirching Miss Wilmont's character and then you will leave London."

Again, Lyman could only choke out an unintelligible answer.

In his blind rage, Sebastian hadn't realized that some-one had come to stand beside him.

Rockhurst.

"I believe you will need to let go of him," the earl said in his usual cultured and sardonic tones, "if you want him to reply."

Sebastian's rage cooled as he glanced from Rockhurst's smooth demeanor to Lyman's blue face. He released the man at once.

Lyman sucked in a deep breath, and when he found enough air, his face went from pasty to crimson. "How dare you, Trent."

Sebastian, who had never been in a fight in his life, let alone a scuffle, wasn't quite sure what to do next. But one thing was for certain—he didn't want Lyman anywhere near Lottie.

Oh, demmit, he needed to think of her as Miss Wil-mont or he'd be in a worse fix than the one currently star-ing him in the eye.

"I demand satisfaction for this affront," Lyman sput-tered. "My second will call in the morning."

"If you can find one," Rockhurst said, taking a com-manding stand at Sebastian's elbow. "Because when you face Trent here, know that I will be beside him." The earl turned to Sebastian. "If you don't mind."

"Glad to have you," Sebastian said, surprised by the earl's offer. Perhaps he'd been wrong about Rockhurst.

Lyman shoved past the two of them and stormed out of White's in a blind rage. With the man gone, Sebastian found himself the center of attention.

"Damn fine thing, Trent. Defending a lady."

"Needed to be done, I thought."

"Steady, good man, as always," another claimed.

He was clapped on the back, handed one drink, then another, and before he knew it, he and Rockhurst were the heroes of the night.

Rockhurst for his discovery of Miss Wilmont, and Sebastian for the defense of her honor.

And by the next day, the story had grown to epic proportions, and Miss Charlotte Wilmont not only outshone Miss Lavinia Burke as the *ton*'s leading Original; she'd eclipsed her.

When the first bouquet of flowers arrived at Queen Street, Lady Wilmont barely took notice. After all, she was still in a pique over Aunt Ursula's inheritance betrayal.

After the bell rang for the thirty-third time, and the front hall, morning room, and dining room were filled with flowers, and their once poor and empty salver overflowed with calling cards and invitations, she roused herself from her cloud of outrage and demanded that Charlotte attend her.

Finella stood hovering in the corner.

"What have you done?" Lady Wilmont demanded.

"Nothing," Charlotte said.

"Nothing indeed!" the lady shot back. "Lady Burke was just here and said you went to the opera last night with the Earl of Rockhurst. Rockhurst, Charlotte! What am I to think?"

"He invited me and Lady Hermione. It wasn't anything extraordinary. Besides, Lady Walbrook chaperoned us."

"Nothing extraordinary, she says," Lady Wilmont shot at Finella. "And did you know that she was going with *him?*"

Finella shook her head, casting an alarmed glance at Charlotte as well.

Lady Wilmont groaned. "And if this deception isn't bad enough, Lady Burke also said that there is to be a duel fought over your *reputation*." The way she said the last word implied that Charlotte's honor was already in question.

"A duel," Charlotte whispered. Oh, heavens no.

"Yes, pistols, I hear. This is unbelievable, so I will ask again, what have you done?"

"I didn't—" Charlotte tried to tell her.

"There is nothing more to be done," Lady Wilmont declared, "but to turn down all the invitations and remain in seclusion until the scandal dies down."

"What?" both Charlotte and Finella said.

Charlotte cast a glance at her newfound ally and saw a look of despair in her eyes that she knew only too well. It was the same miserable light that had been in her own eyes until she'd put Aunt Ursula's ring on her finger and made her fateful wish.

"Aurora," Finella was saying, "I think you are being unreasonable. Perhaps this is Charlotte's opportunity for a Season."

"A Season? At her age?" Lady Wilmont snorted, then shook her head. "She has no dowry, nothing to attract a man. Look at her! She hasn't a bit of Uppington-Higgins to her."

That last part made Finella color, and Charlotte glanced from the woman she'd always called mother to the woman who had borne her.

For as Quince had said, some things couldn't be changed. Like her parents. Her true origins.

Meanwhile, Lady Wilmont was taking a closer inspection of Charlotte.

"When did you start doing your hair like that?"

Charlotte's hand went to the curls and ribbons. "I just thought—"

"And where did you get that gown?"

Charlotte certainly couldn't explain the boon she'd gained from selling Lottie's diamonds. "Lady Walbrook gave it to me," she said quickly. "She had it made for Lady Cordelia but decided the colors didn't suit her."

"Harrumph!" Lady Wilmont's nose wrinkled. "No wonder we've a florist shop in here, if you've been going about town with your bosom showing like that." She drew her handkerchief to her nose. "You will send that dress back to Lady Walbrook. I'll not take such tawdry charity from those Marlowes."

"But—" Charlotte protested.

"And we will refuse these invitations. I am not going out with you and find myself the subject of every wagging tongue."

"But I—" Charlotte could see her dream falling to the wayside. She must see Sebastian again. They'd been so close in the library, he'd been ever so rakish, and his eyes, why, he'd looked at her as he had before.

Oh, Lottie . . .

"Not another word, Charlotte," Lady Wilmont said, pointing toward the door. "Now go change your gown and keep to your room. Finella, fetch me that salver so I can start sending out suitable replies."

Charlotte thought of brooking another protest, of telling Lady Wilmont that she had no right to order her about, not at her age, not when she wasn't even her mother, and she would have if it hadn't been for a pleading glance from Finella, who was returning with the pile of invitations.

Please don't, her eyes begged Charlotte.

But Mother, I must, Charlotte wanted to tell her, until she spied in Finella's apron pocket one notable envelope.

Just like the one she'd seen the other day at the Marlowes.

An invitation to Lady Routledge's soirée.

Charlotte's eyes widened. Finella had held it back. And when her gaze rose to meet the lady's, she found a very Finny-esque sparkle there.

A light of defiance and understanding that gave Charlotte hope.

It was nearly a week before Charlotte was able, with Finella's help, to sneak out for the afternoon. She went straight to Hermione's, for she had very little time left to locate Herr Tromler before the soirée. She'd sent a note ahead to her friend asking her to hire a hackney and finagle her brother Griffin's services as an escort.

"I don't know where he is," Hermione declared as Charlotte met her on the front steps precisely at two o'clock. "Fenwick says Grif left an hour ago to fetch a book from Hatchards, and that he promised quite faithfully to be back by now, but he is nowhere to be seen."

Charlotte pressed her lips together. If she were still Lottie, she wouldn't have thought twice about venturing about without a proper escort, but now she had Hermione's reputation, as well as her own, to consider.

"Griffin and his theories!" the girl was saying, now more than annoyed with her brother. "He'll be there until the store closes and not remember in the least that he was supposed to help us." She heaved an aggrieved sigh. "And Sebastian is nowhere to be found. He's been at his club or off with Rockhurst every day. What with the duel and all, he's become as popular as you."

Charlotte was still in horror over the now notorious duel. Heavens, her rakish Lord Trent might have been a crack shot, but what about this Sebastian?

"Mother is in alt," Hermione confided. "She's sure the Burkes will never allow his suit now."

"But what if Lyman were to . . ." Charlotte couldn't even finish it.

Hermione waved aside such concerns. "You haven't heard, have you? Of course not, you've been locked up. Lyman's mother called him home. Apparently, she's dying." Hermione laughed. "She's always on her deathbed when the earl's disgraceful tendencies and hot temper get him into trouble. It will all blow over."

Charlotte wasn't so sure.

"Oh, bother," Hermione said, her neck craning to look up the street. "Speak of the devil."

"Lyman?" Charlotte said, her gaze turning in the same direction. She didn't possess Hermione's height, so she hadn't the other girl's advantage.

" 'Tis Sebastian. We're in a coil now! He'll never let us go to Little Titchfield Street. Not that he's ever been there, but I can't believe he doesn't know of it."

Sebastian? Charlotte rose up on her toes. Oh, dear, he would ruin everything.

Or would he?

"He'll help us," Charlotte averred. *He must.*

Hermione shook her head. "I wouldn't be so sure."

Her brother's great stride came to a faltering stop when he looked up the steps and his unsuspecting gaze met Charlotte's.

"Miss Wilmont!" he said, not even sparing his sister a greeting.

Not that Hermione noticed. "Where have you been?" she asked, even as the carriage came around and stopped before them.

Sebastian looked from the conveyance to Charlotte. "Are you leaving?"

Hermione wove her arm around Charlotte's and towed her friend down the steps. "We are off on an errand. Good afternoon to you."

His eyes narrowed, and he stepped into their path. "What sort of errand? And without your maid?"

Hermione shot him an aggrieved look. "What does it matter to you? You've been gone for days now." She paused and took in his attire. "Have you even changed your clothes?"

Charlotte looked at the man who was usually so perfectly dressed and shaved and wondered at his transformation. Not that she minded his rumpled state. Why, he looked as if he'd spent those missing days in her bed, all tousled and scraggly and stubbly.

Except he lacked one thing.

He didn't look very sated. No, Sebastian Marlowe had the look of a man haunted and bedeviled.

And Charlotte thought to toss another log onto the pyre. "We are off to hire my musician."

"Hmm, seems well enough," he said, scratching his chin and casting another hooded glance in her direction.

Hermione took this as their cue to escape, and she

dragged Charlotte around him and toward the waiting carriage.

"Yes, the fellow lives on Little Titchfield Street," Charlotte said offhandedly as Hermione climbed into the hackney and she was about to follow suit.

"Now you've done it," Hermione muttered.

"Little Titchfield Street!" came the passionate explosion. "Madame, have you gone mad?!"

Charlotte smiled, then turned and asked ever so innocently, "Is something amiss?"

"Why, why, that's where . . . I mean to say, there are certain . . . Good God, Miss Wilmont! Hermione! What are you thinking? Going to such a street?" He glanced around. "Does Mother know about this?"

Hermione grinned, then lied. "Oh, yes. She asked Griffin to come with us, but he's disappeared again, and now we must go alone." She shrugged and settled back into her seat.

Charlotte smiled sweetly at Sebastian and closed the carriage door. In his face.

It didn't remain so for long.

He yanked it open and climbed in. "You two can't go there unescorted. Are you mad?"

"But we must go," Hermione protested. "If we don't, Charlotte will never be able to hire her violinist in time for Lady Routledge's soirée."

"'Tis that, or I recite a series of verses by Coleridge," Charlotte told him sweetly and watched with delight as a vein in his forehead looked ready to explode.

Hermione, taking a cue from her friend, continued the innocent performance. "Oh, dear, Sebastian. This is such a muddle! Wherever are we to find someone to help us now?"

Charlotte would have felt sorry for him if she hadn't wanted so desperately for him to go with them to Little Titchfield Street.

How would he react when he stood beside No. 4? Would he remember?

Please, Sebastian, come with us, she silently pleaded.

Then Hermione played the perfect card. "I suppose the Earl of Rockhurst might be willing to go with us. Don't you think we could implore upon him for his service as a proper escort, Charlotte? He has such a wicked tendre for you, I daresay he'd brave the wilds of Africa to gain your favor."

Her brother sucked in a deep breath at this suggestion and threw himself into the seat opposite them. "To Little Titchfield Street," he ordered the driver, and the carriage set out.

While he hardly looked thrilled at the prospect, or even vaguely pleased to be in her company, when they turned the corner he finally said, "Let us be done with this as quickly as possible before anyone else discovers what we are about. And no more of this nonsense about Rockhurst. Do you hear me, Hermione?"

Hermione grinned from ear to ear, while Charlotte tucked Arbuckle's favorite smile on her lips and gazed happily out the window.

Sebastian glowered and stewed the entire ride.

Little Titchfield Street! He was going to make a point of speaking to his mother about Hermione's continued friendship with this scandalous Miss Wilmont.

No, he'd better not do that. Knowing his mother, she'd consider Miss Wilmont's blithe spirit a delightful influence.

He shot a furtive glance across the carriage at her and felt vexed to find her looking out the window, as tranquil and serene as if they were off to Bond Street for an afternoon of shopping rather than Little Titchfield Street.

Truly, how could a respectable young lady be acquainted with anyone who inhabited that notorious avenue? A most excellent question, indeed.

"Miss Wilmont, how do you know this musician?" For a second, he swore she flinched.

"My mother's cousin, Finella. She heard him play once."

He had a feeling this wasn't quite the truth, but he didn't see how he could argue the point without looking more foolish than he already felt in her presence.

Unlike the other day, when she'd been decked in her evening finery, today she wore a dull, wretched gown. Despite it, he certainly hadn't mistaken her for the curtains. No, he'd never do that again.

He inhaled ever so subtly and caught a hint of her perfume, a blend that teased his body awake, back into that state of arousal that had led to their dangerous interlude in the library.

It had been a blunder, he now knew. Look at what kissing Miss Wilmont had cost him. He'd caused a scandal in his club, been challenged to a duel, and obtained a newfound notoriety that didn't let him go anywhere in Town without arousing speculation and unwanted attentions.

But despite all that, he found himself taking another tentative sniff of the air. This time all he caught was a hint of Cook's scones. A moment later, he noticed the basket sitting beside Hermione.

"What is that?"

"Provisions," Hermione told him. "For Herr Tromler."

"You intend to entice the man with scones?"

Hermione tipped open the basket. "And salt pork and apples, cheeses, a bottle of father's sherry, a pot of jam and butter, and a small ham."

"You've emptied our larder?" Sebastian crossed his arms over his chest.

"The ham was from Charlotte," Hermione said defensively.

"I haven't any money left to pay the man," Charlotte told him. "But I suspect this might entice him to perform."

"You had a hundred pounds left from buying those ridiculous shares," he argued.

"You bought them as well," Hermione interjected.

"Don't remind me," Sebastian shot back. "That still doesn't explain where your other hundred pounds went."

Miss Wilmont glanced up at him and smiled. Demmit, he hated it when she looked like that. It was a harbinger of something he knew he wasn't going to like.

"I had to buy another dress," she said. "One befitting Lady Routledge's soirée."

Oh, heavens, not another of *her* evening gowns, he silently groaned. That last one had nearly been his undoing, what with its bodice down to . . . *there,* and the way it curved around . . . her . . . well, *curves.*

"Don't be such a cross-patch, Sebastian," Hermione was saying. "Charlotte will have money enough when the *Agatha Skye* returns. I daresay, we all will."

Charlotte nodded, and Sebastian nearly ordered the driver to take them to the nearest convent. He'd deposit these two with the good sisters and save England—well,

the good men of London at the very least—from their
madcap schemes.

Might even find himself with a marquisate for his
troubles.

Sebastian had to wonder what his sister would say if
she knew their family was on the brink of ruin? With his
father's continued absence and drain on the family coffers to finance his explorations, along with his mother's
and sisters' unrestrained spending, they would soon find
themselves in debtor's prison.

Then again, hadn't he caught himself once or twice in
the last week wondering what his life would be like if the
ill-fated ship did return with its holds full of spice and
riches?

No, dreams and wishes wouldn't save them now. The
Agatha Skye, indeed! Pure folly. The only course of action was for him to hurry up and secure Miss Burke's
hand in marriage.

And where once the thought that he would be able to
save his family name from the disgrace of ruin had given
him a measure of satisfaction, it no longer held the same
sense of accomplishment.

Not since he'd kissed Lottie and tasted the passion of
something he'd never imagined.

But before this conundrum could confound him further, the carriage came to a stop and the driver opened
the door.

Hermione went to scramble down, but Sebastian
stopped her. "You and Miss Wilmont will stay in the carriage and out of sight until I ascertain if this . . . this—"

"Herr Tromler," Charlotte supplied.

"Yes, Herr Tromler lives here." He got down and

closed the door. "Stay put," he ordered both of them, then marched toward the door.

He stopped halfway up, his gaze fixed on a sign in the window of the house next door.

To Let.

For some unfathomable reason, the little empty residence at No. 4, Little Titchfield Street, stopped him. He looked up into the shuttered windows and empty flower boxes and frowned.

Suddenly a different version of the house filled his mind. Lace curtains. A welcome light in the front window. Winsome feminine laughter spilling out. And music. Haunting, elegant strains that could fill a soul with longing. And the door was all wrong. Green, when it should have been blue.

The same hue as Lottie's eyes.

"What a charming little house," came a winsome voice at his side.

He turned to find Miss Wilmont, basket in hand, gazing up at the address with a look of longing and regret.

But for what? he wondered, especially when he had the very same feelings.

"Wouldn't that be a wonderful little house to live in?" she asked.

"Here?" he sputtered. "I daresay the neighborhood—"

"I don't see anything wrong with it, besides, it's the house I like," she said, tipping her head and studying it. "But something isn't right."

"The door," he replied absently.

"Yes!" she said. "It should be—"

"Blue," they both said at the same time.

Sebastian gazed down at her, her blue eyes beseeching him for something, something he couldn't give her. For to surrender to his desire for this woman would put his entire family in dire straits. He looked back at the empty little house and realized he had only one, lonely choice.

Yet when he looked down at her again, it was only to discover Charlotte was gone. In those few seconds, she'd gone up the next set of steps and rung the bell at Herr Tromler's boardinghouse.

"Really, Miss Wilmont," he protested, "you should allow me to make the inquiries."

She stepped aside and allowed him to ring the bell again.

The door opened only partially, and a pinched-faced woman with a shock of dirty gray hair stared out. "Off with ye! I don't rent rooms for just the afternoon."

"Madame, we are most certainly not looking for such a thing," he told her in his most lofty of tones.

The woman appeared unimpressed. "Then what do ye want?"

"We wish to see Herr Tromler."

The landlady's eyes narrowed to flinty slits. "What business do you got with 'im?"

"None of yours, madame. Now summon him immediately."

The lady snorted and crossed her arms over her skinny chest. "Why should I do that?"

Much to Sebastian's chagrin, Charlotte edged past him. "If you please, ma'am, we'd like to hire him to play his violin at a party. In Mayfair."

Two words lit the landlady's greedy eyes. "Hire" and "Mayfair."

"You'll pay 'im?" she asked suspiciously.

"Yes, ma'am," Charlotte told her. "In gold."

"Wait here," she said before she went scurrying up the

stairs. Halfway up, she stopped and came back down. Catching Charlotte and Sebastian by the arms, she pulled them inside the foyer and closed the door. "Better you wait inside." Then she raced back up the stairs, screeching at the top of her lungs, "Tromler! Mr. Tromler! You've got guests. The paying type!"

"I would have got to the reason for our visit without your help," he muttered.

"Yes, my lord," she replied most contritely. And it would have been sincere if it hadn't been for the mischievous sparkle in her eyes.

He leaned over. "I thought you didn't have any gold left."

"I don't."

"Then how do you propose to pay the man, like you promised his landlady?"

"I was sort of hoping you might make a small donation to the arts."

Before he could tell her that under no circumstances was he going to invest in any more of her harebrained schemes, a shabby-looking fellow came down, his nose twitching almost immediately as Charlotte very wisely pulled the cloth from the basket and let the scent of warm scones waft up toward him.

"Herr Tromler," she said, holding out her hand and letting the fellow raise it to his lips. "It is a great honor to meet you."

The landlady, who was watching the proceedings like a hawk (most likely for any sign of the promised gold) snorted.

Charlotte ignored her. "Can I implore upon you to come and play Thursday night at Lady Routledge's soirée?"

For a second the man's eyes lit up, but then his small

chest fell, as did his gaze. "I fear I can't, Fräulein. I sold my only coat last week."

"And you'll be selling your trousers and that instrument of yours if you don't pay what ye still owe me," the landlady added.

Leaning forward, Charlotte pressed the basket into his hands. "I think you will find a replacement for your lost jacket beneath the ham."

"A jacket?" Sebastian said.

"A ham?" the landlady echoed with the same astonished tone. She poked her thin nose over Herr Tromler's shoulder and eyed the bounty.

Charlotte smiled at the poor musician. "I thought you might like something befitting such a special evening— and I believe you'll find it fits quite admirably."

Sebastian stared at her, then at Herr Tromler. Where the devil had she gotten a man's coat when she professed to have no money?

As she struck the final arrangements with Tromler, Sebastian took another look at the fellow, who, though thin, was about his own height.

His height?

No, she wouldn't have! She couldn't have!

With their business concluded, Sebastian escorted her out the door, but before they got down the steps he had to ask, "Miss Wilmont?"

"Yes, Lord Trent?"

"Should I be surprised Thursday night when that man appears at Lady Routledge's soirée in a jacket that looks vaguely familiar?"

She smiled up at him. "Well, it won't be much of a surprise now, will it?"

Well, of all the cheek!

They continued down the next two steps.

"Lord Trent?"

"Yes, Miss Wilmont?"

"Try not to be too surprised if Herr Tromler's shirt, cravat, and waistcoat also look oddly familiar."

He closed his eyes. It seemed that "oddly familiar" was becoming the order of the day. Heavens, he only hoped that Lavinia didn't notice. The girl had an eye for clothes that was second only to her father's ability to compound interest.

"Miss Wilmont?"

"Yes, my lord?"

"Are you done meddling in my life?"

The smile she shot him this time came straight from Arbuckle's portrait of Diana. "Not in the least, Sebastian."

Why had he bothered to ask?

Sebastian's worries about their reputations hadn't been for naught. For Little Titchfield Street had a steady stream of visitors, day and night, and there was one pair of eyes that spied the smiling Charlotte and a rumpled-looking Lord Trent coming down the steps of No. 5.

Miss Wilmont and Lord Trent together on Little Titchfield Street?

Why, it was scandalous!

One might even say *ruinous*.

Chapter 17

May 24, 1810
A Fateful Thursday If Ever There Was One

Charlotte woke up the morning of Lady Routledge's soirée feeling more confident than she had all week.

Sebastian had remembered something about the house on Little Titchfield Street. He'd remembered the door. It might not seem like much, but to Charlotte it was a bit of hope.

Now all that was left was for her to attend the soirée (for Finella had promised to help her sneak out) and when Herr Tromler played, his sonatas would entice Sebastian to seduce her again.

And if . . . just if, she thought, hugging herself to contain her joy, she could gain another kiss, she doubted he would be able to set her aside.

Ever.

Only adding to that good fortune was the fact that this

was the morning that the *Agatha Skye* would arrive at the London docks and their shares would be worth a fortune!

He wouldn't be forced to marry Miss Burke, and then he would be free to . . .

Charlotte stopped herself. She didn't even want to think it lest something happen to curse her good fortune.

She needn't have held her tongue. For Charlotte's luck had indeed run out that morning.

For when she went to open her bedroom door, she found it locked.

Sebastian had done his best to regain Miss Burke's good graces, as well as those of her parents.

He'd banished any thoughts of Lottie . . . *Miss Wilmont* . . . from his thoughts. And tonight, after Lavinia's reading, they'd announce their betrothal and it would be for the best.

Yes, he told himself for the hundredth time, marriage to Miss Burke was for the best.

But much to his chagrin, their arrival at the Routledge town house coincided with his family's. He had hoped to keep the Burkes and Marlowes at opposite corners until everything was sorted out.

He didn't trust his mother or sisters not to come up with some outlandish scheme to stop him. Especially since they would most likely have Miss Wilmont's capable assistance.

"Lady Hermione! How delightful!" Lavinia called out as his sister climbed down from their hired hackney. "Your costume! So very noteworthy . . . I almost wish I was doing a theatrical reading, but alas my ode to marriage requires a more modest and somber gown."

She opened her cloak to reveal an expensive white gown trimmed with gold thread and sparkling crystal beads.

"An ode to marriage?" Griffin quipped. "Perhaps you should have just brought a pair of leg shackles, swung 'em about a bit."

"Harrumph!" Lady Burke glared at the Marlowes, then pressed her daughter and Sebastian forward. That is until a commotion at the door stopped them all.

"I'm sorry, sir, but you are not on the invitation list."

"But zee Miss Wilmont invited me."

Sebastian recognized Herr Tromler's voice immediately.

The formidable majordomo remained stalwart. "Without Miss Wilmont, I am afraid I am unable to allow you inside."

"Oh, dear!" Hermione gasped. "Charlotte hasn't arrived yet."

Since they were the last of the guests, and the street was already empty, it didn't appear she was going to arrive in time.

Hermione reached up and tugged on her brother's coat. "Sebastian, you must go fetch Charlotte!"

Before he could answer, Miss Burke turned around. "Why would he do that?"

Her icy tones didn't stop Hermione. "Because if Charlotte doesn't arrive, Herr Tromler won't be able to perform."

Lady Burke added her opinion to the discussion. "Miss Wilmont has most likely come to her senses and returned to her rightful place on the shelf." The lady shot a pointed glance at Sebastian, then back at Hermione. "She has no talents, no money, and nothing to recommend her." She glanced over at Tromler. "'Tis no wonder she decided not to make herself ridiculous by passing off that shabby fellow as a talented musician. Why, just look at that awful coat!"

Lady Walbrook, who up until this moment had been busy chatting with another matron, turned around. "Lady Burke," she said in her most patronizing tone, the one Sebastian knew she used only when she was close to making a scene, "whatever is this about dear Charlotte?"

"She hasn't arrived yet, and Sebastian won't fetch her," Viola reported, looking only too pleased to be part of the growing fray.

"And Herr Tromler will not be able to play," Hermione added quickly. "Charlotte avers he is a virtuoso, Mother. And we shall miss his London premiere!"

This scene began to spin dangerously out of control, and Sebastian found himself in the eye of the storm, torn and tossed in all directions.

As indeed he was.

Miss Burke wound her arm around Sebastian's and tugged him closer, pulling him from his family. "Sebastian, we must go inside now. All the best seats will be taken."

But he stood fast. And when she looked up at him, furious and cold in her disdain, he found himself transfixed.

It became, as his mother might say, a most defining moment.

When Lavinia Burke tipped up her nose in a snooty sort of pose that perfectly mirrored her mother's contempt, right there and then he saw what his future would be if he married her.

Married to her money and bound forever to her family in obligation and association.

He couldn't ever see her feeding a hungry musician with a basket of goodies she'd scavenged together. Or bartering the price of worthless shares in a lost ship. Or looking with longing at an empty little house on Little Titchfield Street and wishing she could live at such an address.

And then he saw what would be so utterly lacking in his life.

Passion. The life-changing, unending, dangerous desire that had the ability to rob a man of his good sense.

Good sense, he decided, didn't necessarily equate a good life.

Oh, and then he knew only one thing.

Lottie. He wanted his Lottie. He wanted a life of poetry and struggle. Of passion and endless kisses.

"Where can I find her?" he asked Hermione.

His sister's eyes brimmed over with tears. "No. 11, Queen Street."

"You don't mean you are going to leave and bring her here?" Miss Burke asked. "If you do this, Lord Trent, I will never forgive you."

He removed her hand from his sleeve, suddenly tired of feeling shackled. "If I don't do this, I will never forgive myself."

"Harrumph!" sputtered Lady Burke, catching hold of her daughter and marching up and into the Routledge town house.

Lady Walbrook stepped in front of him. And he saw something in her eyes that he rarely found there. A beaming light that glowed with pride.

"Bless you, Sebastian. Your father would be so proud."

"I've ruined my chances with the Burkes," he told her.

"We Marlowes have always made our own luck, my dear boy. Our fortunes come from the heart."

And all Sebastian could do was hope and wish she was right.

Charlotte sat on her narrow bed without a tear left to be shed. Her mother had been adamant; she was not going to Lady Routledge's soirée.

Not after Lady Burke had called and told a mortified Lady Wilmont that Charlotte had been seen house hunting on Little Titchfield Street with a gentleman.

"And that," Lady Burke had declared, "could mean only *one* thing."

Lady Wilmont's reaction had been swift and vehement. No daughter of hers was going to disgrace the name of Wilmont, and therefore Charlotte was going to remain locked in her room until she was too old to be a lure to any man's scandalous intentions.

Charlotte had pleaded and cried, pounded and begged to be released, but so far Lady Wilmont would not hear a word of it.

And now here she was, hours later, ready for an evening she couldn't attend. She'd held out a whisper of hope that Quince's magic would restore her dreams, and so she'd donned the gown she'd bought for the night and had kept hidden beneath her bed. Between sniffles and bouts of self-pity, she'd fixed her hair and made a thousand different wishes.

Each and every one having to do with Sebastian.

Charlotte twisted the ring on her finger and cursed the day it had arrived in her life.

"'T'would have been better to never have known his love than to lose it all over again," she whispered.

And what of the *Agatha Skye*? Hadn't it arrived this morning in triumph? Surely someone would have come to the house to tell her the good news, and then certainly her mother would have relented.

Yet as she glanced over at the clock, she bit back another spate of tears. Ten o'clock. Lady Routledge's soirée had probably already begun. Hermione and Viola had survived another of their mother's theatrical ordeals, Miss Burke had wowed her audience with her edifying and perfectly recited ode.

And Sebastian? Most likely he was announcing his betrothal to Lavinia as Lady Burke had told her mother.

Her only joy was that Herr Tromler would make up for her absence and tonight he would triumph.

It was, however, a small comfort.

She heaved a sigh and rose from the bed, ready to put away her finery and consign her life to one of ashes and her mother's petty complaints, when she heard the distant and distinct jangle of the bell over the front door.

And a few moments later, a second discordant ring echoed through the house.

By the time the bell rang a third time, Charlotte had her ear pressed to the door.

Downstairs, she heard the creak of the front door and the low rumble of voices. But before long, the words rose hot and clear up to the far reaches of her room.

"Get out of my house!" Lady Wilmont shouted.

Charlotte's heart hammered. Though she hadn't any wishes left, she closed her eyes and made the only one that mattered.

Then there was the patter of feet coming up the steps, and she backed away from the door.

Finella unlocked it and entered in a flutter and a rush. "Do you love Lord Trent?" she asked breathlessly.

"What?" Charlotte couldn't believe it.

Finella stood for a moment, most likely transfixed by the sight of Charlotte in her velvet finery, but she recovered quickly, catching her by the hand and smiling at her. "Do you love Lord Trent?"

"Yes," Charlotte whispered.

"Does he love you?"

"I could only wish for something so wonderful," she told her.

"Wish no more," Finella said. "The viscount is downstairs trying to breach Aurora's defenses. Claims he'll have you tonight, and no one is going to stop him."

Charlotte's eyes welled with newfound tears. "He's here? For me?"

"Yes, yes. So don't just stand there. You have a debut to make."

Charlotte followed Finella down the stairs still not entirely willing to believe this change of fortunes—that is, until they turned the last landing and she spied him in the entry hall arguing with Lady Wilmont.

"—I don't care what you were told, my intentions toward your daughter are—"

Then he saw her.

Lady Wilmont forgotten, he swept past the angry matron and stood at the bottom of the steps with his hand outstretched for Charlotte.

"You look breathtaking," he said as her fingers closed around his.

"You came for me?" she whispered back.

"Yes, who else?"

"But I thought—" Her gaze met his. She couldn't say it. Couldn't risk asking it. Her heart teetered on the brink of breaking or rejoicing.

"Don't ever think that again. You are the only woman for me."

"But I have no fortune. No dowry," she told him, trying to free her fingers. But he held onto her, and as much as she wanted to send him back to Miss Burke and her ten thousand a year, her heart was close to bursting with joy.

"We Marlowes make our fortunes, or so I've been told," he replied. "And I've decided to make mine with you."

"Not without my blessing, you scoundrel!" Lady Wilmont protested. "I know exactly what your intentions are!" She turned toward Finella. "Blood will tell! And now it has."

"Aurora!" Finella protested. "Let her go to the soirée. It is Charlotte's chance to have a place in society."

"Not if she is going to go out and run afoul. She'll bring shame and ruin on this house just like—"

"As I said before, madame," Sebastian interjected, "I am only taking her to Lady Routledge's. There is nothing improper in that."

Lady Wilmont's jaw worked back and forth until a malevolent light blazed in her gaze. "She has no escort. She cannot go with you without a chaperone. I forbid it."

Charlotte took a deep breath. There was nothing left to do but one thing. It was time to use everything she'd learned as Lottie.

"Mother," she said. "Will you go with me?"

"I certainly will not appear in public with you, you reckless jade!" Lady Wilmont declared.

Charlotte shook her head. "I wasn't speaking to you."

She turned to Finella. "Will you go with me . . . Mother?"

Even as she made her request, she realized what she was doing. Declaring herself a bastard to the world, to Sebastian.

She didn't dare look at him right now, as her gaze locked with Finella's tear-filled eyes.

"How did you know?" the lady asked.

"Does it matter?" Charlotte replied even as she turned to Sebastian. "I suppose you have the right to know. I'm not really a Wilmont. Finella bore me out of wedlock—"

"No!" protested Lady Wilmont.

Charlotte continued, now with no fear of what her *faux* parent could do. "She made a bargain with Lady Wilmont to claim me as her own to save her reputation—and possibly save herself—for if I'd been a boy, I would have been able to inherit Lord Wilmont's titles and lands instead of his cousin."

"And she promised you would be a boy," Aurora wailed, pointing at Finella. "And so I agreed to her idiotic plan, only because Nestor's titles were to pass to his spendthrift and wretched cousin, and I needed a child to inherit. A son. And then she had you and then there was nothing left to do but raise you as my own daughter. I lost my home, my place in society, and what did my foolish charity gain me?"

"A fine young woman," Sebastian said, reaching over and taking Charlotte's hand.

The three ladies stared at him.

"It doesn't matter to you?" Charlotte asked.

He shook his head and grinned, quite rakishly. "It might have mattered once, but not now."

She smiled back.

"It will matter when all society knows the truth of her birth," Lady Wilmont spat, still furious.

"Aurora, you will hold your tongue," Finella said, sounding to Charlotte like her beloved, calculating, no-nonsense Finny. "Or I will cast you out of this house tonight. It is still *my* house."

Aurora drew herself up. "You wouldn't dare!"

"I would and I will!" Finella told her. "You leave Charlotte be. She is well and safe with Lord Trent."

"She was seen on Little Titchfield Street with this man," Aurora shot back. "He has no intention of marrying her. Lady Burke told me so."

"Lady Burke?" Sebastian said.

Aurora's nose rose in the air. "Yes. She and I are old school friends. She came by yesterday and told me everything—she told me you were all but betrothed to her daughter—not that your Marlowe tendencies aren't keeping you from luring Charlotte into a life of sin. She heard from a very reliable source that you were offering Charlotte a house on Little Titchfield Street! We all know what *that* means."

"Yes," Charlotte said. "I can imagine who that reliable source might be. Lord Burke. Most likely visiting his mistress at Number 15. Poor woman."

Lady Wilmont's eyes widened.

Charlotte and Sebastian looked at each other and laughed.

"Now I know why you want to buy that house!" he teased. "To watch the comings and goings."

"Oh, this is scandalous!" Lady Wilmont declared. "Finella, you needn't throw me out, I'm leaving."

But no one seemed to notice, for Sebastian had taken

his Lottie into his arms and was kissing her, and Finella, well, she was busy crying tears of joy for her dear daughter, for somehow, for someway, all her wishes for Charlotte had suddenly come true.

They arrived at Lady Routledge's just as Miss Burke was finishing her recitation.

> *"A flower spent, a life of repent,*
> *My will is but my master's, my heart his."*

She paused for a moment, an imperial tip to her nose.

Then the polite applause rose in the room, led by Lady Routledge, who nudged those closest to her to clap their hands with a little more enthusiasm.

The lady came up to the stage, beaming in joy at her ingénue. "Oh, yes, Miss Burke! So edifying, so stirring! Dear me, it almost makes me want to seek another husband." She sighed and then continued on as Miss Burke sought her seat in the front row between her beaming parents, "I had thought there was to be one more performance, Miss Charlotte Wilmont, but unfortunately, Lady Burke informed me that the lady will be unable to attend and will have to forfeit her wager with me."

"Oh, that isn't so, Lady Routledge! I am here," Charlotte called out from the back of the room.

All eyes turned, for most everyone had heard of the challenge and was there for the evening just to see if Miss Wilmont might actually best the imperious old matron.

"Oh, my, so you are!" the lady said, sounding none too pleased.

Charlotte pushed her way to the front of the crowd, towing a disgruntled Herr Tromler along. "I fear I am going to make a dreadful hostess if I can't even arrive on time," she said in a loud aside to Lady Routledge's guests.

There was a genial round of laughter to her announcement, which buoyed her spirits.

"Yes, but you must perform," Miss Burke pointed out. "You were to share a talent."

Charlotte laughed. "Miss Burke, your memory is amiss. I have no talents. Save a good enough ear to know that I should never force anyone outside the church walls to listen to me sing." She climbed atop the tiny stage that had been set up at the head of the room and paused.

What a difference a fortnight made. Why, before her wish she would never have dreamt of getting up before all these people, and now . . .

All she had to do was look at the light of love in Sebastian's eyes, remember the power of his kiss, and she could have borne being presented at court.

"I hope I will make up for my rare lack of talent and my late appearance by introducing you to Herr Tromler." She waved him forward. "I ask only your indulgence for a few minutes, for I think you will find your patience well-spent."

The man shuffled forward in his borrowed coat and frightening thatch of hair that appeared to defy any comb. When he got to the stage, he glared at his audience.

Murmurs of dismay whispered through the room, and most of the front row pushed their chairs back.

"Herr Tromler," Charlotte whispered to him. "Play something that speaks of love." Then she turned a radiant smile toward him.

His sharp brows and hawkish gaze softened. "For you, Fräulein Wilmont, I would play anything. Even something as complicated as love."

She stepped off the stage, and Tromler tucked his violin under his chin. For a moment he closed his eyes, and everyone in the room held their breath.

Not a moment after he touched his bow to the strings, the sweet strains of music filled the room and another refrain echoed forth—sighs of rapture as the jaded hearts of the *ton* melted amidst the sweet and wanton music that came from Tromler's violin.

Charlotte made her way to Sebastian's side. He too was as awestruck as the rest of Lady Routledge's guests.

But not for long. Charlotte slid her hand into his, and when the warmth of their fingers twined together, Sebastian awoke as if from a dream and stared down at her.

He said not a word but pulled her swiftly and quickly from the salon into an adjoining room, where he immediately kissed her.

Kissed her until a soft moan of desire escaped her, until her legs wavered beneath her.

"I'll be ruined by tomorrow if we continue," she whispered to him, even as a thunderous roar of applause erupted from the salon.

"We'll be married tomorrow, so it will matter not," he told her quite sensibly.

Chapter 18

May 29, 1810
A Perfect Tuesday for a Wedding and a Few Surprises

While Sebastian had promised Charlotte the night of Lady Routledge's soirée that they would be married the next day, their delighted but horrified mothers had insisted on a little more respectable waiting period, say three months.

Sebastian, nearly as impatient as his bride to be wed, had conceded and agreed to five days, but only under protest.

So with a Special License procured, the entire *ton* abuzz over this startling turn of events, Lord Trent's wedding to Miss Charlotte Wilmont became the event of the Season, with the Marlowe house overflowing with guests. Invited and uninvited.

Lady Walbrook didn't mind the crush in the least, for as she liked to declare (to anyone who would listen), "I am just so delighted that Sebastian has finally shown some sensibility about marriage and chosen such a perfect bride."

Perfect was one of the words that came to Sebastian's mind as he stood at the bottom of the stairs awaiting Charlotte to make her way down. His jaw dropped when she appeared in a low-cut Grecian-styled gown that made every other male in the room curse Trent for his "bloody good luck."

At the sight of Charlotte, Herr Tromler struck up a flurry of winsome and romantic notes that added the perfect backdrop to their wedding. There wasn't a dry eye in the house as Miss Charlotte Wilmont gently lay her hand onto Lord Trent's sleeve and they made their way down the aisle to the vicar.

Almost immediately, Charlotte turned to Sebastian and said, "Why are we starting so late?"

"Rockhurst," Sebastian whispered back, smiling apologetically at the beaming guests on either side of them.

Charlotte glanced up toward the best man and scowled. No shy bridal nerves for her.

"I'd forgive him if I were you," Sebastian whispered over to her, a wry grin on his lips.

"Whatever for? We'll be stuck here for a good three hours listening to toasts and other nonsense. And now he's added another hour to that!"

She sputtered something else that sounded most like a curse and Sebastian had to cover his mouth to keep from laughing aloud. Yes, life with his Lottie would never be dull.

They had arrived before the vicar, and the man stood with one brow arched, shooting them the most baneful look. The good man wasn't fond of the notion of hasty weddings, and he had his own suspicions about this licentious pair, but since the archbishop had signed the license, what was he to do? "Dearly beloved—" he began.

Sebastian leaned over and whispered to Charlotte, "The earl was late because he was bringing good news."

"I see no good news in coming late—"

"The *Agatha Skye* docked this morning."

This stopped her tirade. But if Sebastian thought she would be as shocked as he had been when the earl had told him of the unexpected arrival, he was wrong.

"About demmed time," the bride huffed.

"We're rich, Charlotte," he whispered back. "You've saved me and my family from ruin. I don't know how I'll ever thank you."

Charlotte tipped her head toward him and sent a sly, slanted glance up at him. "Well, if Rockhurst hadn't been late, we'd be that much closer to you getting a start on that."

"Ahem," the vicar coughed.

Sebastian and Charlotte nodded in unison at the man to get on with the vows.

"Whatever is taking so long?" she whispered to her groom.

"I haven't the vaguest notion," he replied.

"And so," the vicar intoned, "with this ring—"

And in no time, Sebastian slipped a new ring on Charlotte's hand. One filled not with wishes but with the promise of a future marked with passion and, most importantly, love.

"Go up to her and wish her many happy returns and then get my ring," Milton was saying as yet another toast was raised to the happy bride and groom.

"Yes, Milton," Quince said. "I know what to do."

"Harrumph," he snorted. "If that were true—"

Quince ignored him and made her way through the crowd, her gaze fixed on the happy bride.

"Charlotte, my dear girl, there you are! And so beautiful!" Quince reached out to catch Charlotte's hands. "I am so very happy for you."

"Oh, Quince," Charlotte said, hugging the woman close. "How can I ever thank you?"

"Don't you think of such a thing. Does my heart good to see you so happy." Quince smiled, then felt an odd nudge in the middle of her back. *Yes, yes. I'll get on with this.* "But since you mention it, there is one small favor," she said, glancing over her shoulder to where Milton stood pressed uncomfortably into a corner. "I need the ring back." She paused, then leaned forward and said, "If it were ever to fall into the wrong hands—"

"Oh, yes!" Charlotte exclaimed. "How right you are. I never thought of that." She handed Quince the bouquet of violets she'd been carrying, then glanced down at her hand. "Oh, dear! Oh, my! It's gone! I had it before the ceremony, but now it's gone."

Quince didn't know whether to be elated or panicked. "Never mind, dear, you enjoy your wedding. And enjoy your life. 'Tis what you wished for."

"But the ring—"

"Don't fret another moment about it," Quince assured her. "I'll find it."

I'd better and be quick about it before someone else does, she thought as she worked her way back to Milton.

He greeted her with an extended hand and exactly four tersely issued words. "Give it to me." Make that six words. "Now, Quince."

"Can't," Quince told him as she settled against the wall beside him.

"And why not?"

"'Tis gone," she said.

"How can that be?" Milton blustered. "It was on her hand when she came in for the ceremony."

"Well, it isn't on it now. It must have fallen from her finger in the last hour or so."

"Well, go find it," he ordered.

Now it was Quince's turn to snort. "If you want it so badly, you go find it," she said, waving her hand toward the crowded room. Given Milton's distaste for mortals, she found it shocking when he actually took a deep breath and waded into their midst to start searching.

She cursed under her breath, for he really meant to gain his ring back this time. And she wasn't quite ready to let him have it back. Not yet. So she joined him in the search.

"Have you found it?" he asked when they bumped into each other near the punch table. Milton was down on his hands and knees searching the floor, doing his best to remain unseen and unstepped upon.

"No," she told him. "Have you?"

"Would I still be here if I had?"

Much to her amazement, Viola Marlowe happened by and turned a quizzical eye on them. "Excuse me, sir, have you lost something?" she said directly to Milton.

Quince looked up at the girl in shock. *She could see him?*

"Yes," he said, "but I do believe I found it." He held up a watch fob, which was enough to satisfy the youngest Marlowe, who smiled, then tripped away into the crowd.

"She can see you," Quince said, still a bit stunned.

"Yes, and can you imagine if *she* found my ring what might happen?"

Quince shuddered and continued her search, now with a little more urgency. "If you weren't so bound and determined to have it back—"

Milton froze as a soft humming filled the room. Quince heard it as well and got to her feet.

"Goodness," she whispered. "Someone has found it." She looked frantically about the throng of guests to determine who had it, but it was impossible to tell. There were just too many people in the room.

"Be calm," Milton said as he rose from the floor, though he looked anything but. "It isn't too late, as long as they don't—"

And then it was.

"Oh, if only . . ." came a soft whisper.

"No!" gasped Milton. "Not again."

"Oh, how I wish—"

Then it was cast, a new wish, and the room thrummed and spun around them.

"Quince!" he cried out in his anger. "This is all your doing!"

But when he looked around to find her, she was already gone. Bid by the ring, bound by the promise by which it had been wrought.

"This is the last one, Quince," he whispered into the ethers. "The very last one."

And before he slipped into shadows, he could have sworn he heard her soft, delighted laughter teasing him, just as it had on their wedding night.

Charlotte leaned over and laid her head on Sebastian's shoulder as they rode away from the Marlowes' town house off on their honeymoon. It was nearly ten, and they probably wouldn't get much further than an inn outside of town, but Charlotte didn't care. Now and forever, she and Sebastian would be together, and she couldn't think of a better future.

Rockhurst had loaned them his curricle, and Sebastian sat grinning beside her, positively in alt over the opportunity of driving such a reckless vehicle.

"I thought we would never get out of there," she said as they pulled out of Berkeley Square.

"If you hadn't invited half of London, we might have been able to leave hours ago," he said, casting a bemused glance at her.

"I didn't invite all those people. Why, I didn't even know most of them," she shot back.

"Oh, but they seemed to know you," he teased back. "My very own Original. Did you hear Lady Routledge claiming that she'd introduced us as a favor to your mother?"

Charlotte laughed. "Yes. But I don't mind in the least—she's taken in Herr Tromler and means to see that all the world hears him play. She's quite determined."

He snorted. "Speaking of determined, whatever were you thinking introducing Finella to Lord Boxley? Why, he's twenty years her junior!"

She smiled to herself. Finella, now her dearest mother in truth. If anything, she deserved a chance at happiness. The one she missed all those years ago. Now that the truth had finally been revealed, Finella's sharp lines had softened, and mother and daughter had found a camaraderie that freed them both from the conventions that had kept them apart all these years. "She's not that much older than him. Besides, they looked quite smitten, don't you think?"

"Quite," he said, still shaking his head over the unlikely pairing. "And Lady Wilmont? Were you matchmaking yet again when you seated her next to Lord Pilsley?"

"Oh, absolutely," she said without any reserve. "Did you see her smiling and flirting with him? Apparently they shared a bit of *tendrè* years ago, and now that he's widowed, well . . ."

"Are you going to make a career of this penchant for matchmaking?" he asked.

"Well, you do have four unmarried siblings." Charlotte tipped her head back and smiled seductively at him. "Or do you like the idea of setting up our house with your entire family underfoot?"

He replied without hesitation, "How can I help?"

They both laughed, then fell into a companionable silence, Charlotte wishing they were well and out of London and at the inn where Sebastian had taken rooms for the night. Their wedding night. She sighed impatiently and wished them ten miles further ahead—that is, until they turned onto Great Russell Street and a large building came into view.

Charlotte sat up. "Sebastian?"

"Yes, Lady Trent?"

She smiled. *Lady Trent*. Now she finally had a name she could truly call her own. "Do you have thirty quid?"

"Married just a few hours and already you want my money?" He made a low, teasing whistle.

"Do you have it?" she asked impatiently as they drew closer to the massive structure on their left.

"Yes. But why do you want thirty quid?"

Charlotte didn't answer, but leaned over and fished around beneath the curricle's seat. There it was, the stash of bottles Rockhurst kept beneath. She grinned. "Pull over," she told him, pointing to the curb.

"Whatever for?" Sebastian asked.

"Because I want to go see Townley's statues," she said, pointing at the British Museum, which they were about to pass.

"Charlotte, 'tis late at night.The museum isn't open. Besides, even if it were, we haven't the necessary tickets."

"We've got everything we need," she told him, plucking out one of Rockhurst's bottles of French wine. "Besides, I want you to sketch me tonight."

"Sketch you?" He glanced over at her. "How did you know that I—"

She grinned. "Please, Sebastian?"

He pulled the carriage to a stop. "Am I to understand you correctly that you want to enter the British Museum at night, using means, that I have to assume, are highly irregular if not outright illegal, and then have me sketch you?"

She nodded. "In the nude. The sketching part, that is."

Sebastian nodded. "You're quite possibly mad."

"But you love me," she whispered back.

"So I do," he said before he gathered her into his arms and kissed her, thoroughly and soundly. And by the time he was done, she watched him take a nonchalant glance up at the museum, his eyes alight with a dangerous, calculating gleam.

But before she could ask him again, he answered her, kissing her again, this time more rakishly than the last, his hands claiming her body and tugging her up against him.

Charlotte sighed with delight.

She'd gotten her wish. She was now and forever the woman Sebastian loved. And when his hand slid so daringly, so very rakishly beneath her gown, she realized something else.

She'd gotten her wish and so very much more. . . .

Author's Note

Let me get a few historical notes cleared up first. In the early years of the British Museum, anyone who wished to see the collections was required to apply for permission, and only those deemed worthy were extended the much-coveted tickets. Even then, they were hustled through the rooms with only a few minutes to take in the treasures. By the time the Townley Gallery was built in 1808, the rules were relaxing, and by the year of this story, 1810, those rules were no longer in place. Since I wanted my story specifically set in 1810, I fudged the time line a little. But why was I so set on having Charlotte's story take place in 1810? Well, the fashions, of course! I gathered Charlotte's, Finny's, and even Sebastian's wardrobe from the extensive fashion plate collection of fellow author Candice Hern, and you can see the exact gowns and clothes these characters wore in the book on her website, candicehern.com/collections/elizabethboyle/mistress.htm.

Now on to very important matters. You might have noticed that there is another wish to be granted. Poor Milton! At this rate (and with so many Marlowes to choose from), he may never get his ring back. Make sure to visit my website, elizabethboyle.com, for all the latest news and hints as to who will be Quince's next victim, I mean, er, beneficiary of her romantic encouragement.

Until then, best wishes and all my love,

Elizabeth Boyle

*Next month, don't miss these exciting
new love stories only from
Avon Books*

How to Seduce a Duke by Kathryn Caskie

An Avon Romantic Treasure

Mary Royle may—or may not—be the "secret" daughter of a prince, but what she lacks in pedigree she makes up for in determination. When Mary sets her cap for Viscount Wetherly, she is foiled by her "intended's" older brother, the Duke of Blackstone, who will do anything to stop the marriage—even wed the chit himself!

Secrets of the Highwayman by Sara Mackenzie

An Avon Contemporary Romance

Nathaniel Raven was a notorious highwayman until his betrayal and murder. Now, awake in present-day England and determined to avenge his death, Nathaniel turns to Melanie Jones, a beautiful solicitor from London, for aid. But can they overcome the odds and find the peace that true love can bring?

Deliciously Wicked by Robyn DeHart

An Avon Romance

When Meg Piddington stumbles into the Viscount Mandeville's arms, neither expects it to become the perfect alibi. Wrongfully accused of a crime, Gareth tries to focus on clearing his name, but Meg is more of a distraction than he anticipated, tempting him to claim something he has no right to want.

Taken By Storm by Donna Fletcher

An Avon Romance

Imprisoned while trying to track down his brother, Burke Longton is stunned to meet his rescuer, the beautiful and courageous Storm. But there is something mysterious behind those deep blue eyes of hers, and Burke is determined to uncover the truth about the woman he has come to love.

Avon Romances

the best in
exceptional authors and unforgettable novels!

AVON T̶ bag

deserves a great book!

0-06-082388-7
$12.95 ($16.95 Can.)

0-06-113423-6
$12.95 ($16.95 Can.)

0-06-075592-X
$12.95 ($16.95 Can.)

0-06-08993
$12.95 ($16.

78668-X
19.50 Can.)

Visit www.AuthorTracker.com for exclusive
information on your favorite HarperCollins authors.

Available wherever books are sold, or call 1-800-331-3761 to order.

ATP 0906